COAST-TO-COAST RAVES FOR
GERALD A. BROWNE'S
BESTSELLING
19 PURCHASE STREET

"Superb . . . a console of our contemporary night-
mares at which the author fingers every sinister
key . . . Gerald Browne proceeds with perfect
confidence!"

—*New York Times*

"Thriller of a tale . . . hardly for the squeamish!"
—*ALA Booklist*

"Recommended reading!"

—*Chicago Sun-Times*

"Filled with the ingredients of a bestseller!"
—*Library Journal*

"Breathless, mind-boggling, never lets up!"
—*John Barkham Reviews*

"Will keep your eyebails bulging!"
—*Los Angeles Times*

GREEN ICE

GERALD A. BROWNE

BERKLEY BOOKS, NEW YORK

This Berkley book contains the complete
text of the original hardcover edition.
It has been completely reset in a typeface
designed for easy reading, and was printed
from new film.

GREEN ICE

A Berkley Book/published by arrangement with
Delacorte Press

PRINTING HISTORY
Delacorte edition published 1978
Dell edition/April 1979
Berkley edition/August 1984

ISBN:0-425-07261-4

A BERKLEY BOOK ® TM 757,375
Berkley Books are published by The Berkley Publishing Group,
200 Madison Avenue, New York, New York 10016.
The name ''BERKLEY'' and the stylized ''B'' with design
are trademarks belonging to Berkley Publishing Corporation.
PRINTED IN THE UNITED STATES OF AMERICA

For Bunky

1 >>>

Hikers.

Nothing more than that from the looks of them. They had bedrolls and backpacks, with canteens and cooking pans dangling behind, clunking. One had on a bright blue sweater. Another wore a yellow, orange, green patterned poncho, known as a *ruana*. They certainly were not trying to go unnoticed.

Five hikers in a line, picking the easiest way down. The slope was so steep they had to traverse back and forth, and it was covered entirely with long grass in neat overlapping layers that seemed to resent being disturbed, retaliated by causing the hikers to slip.

From where they were, the town of Chiquinquirá should have been in sight. Only three miles away. However, an early morning mist lay like a silvery lid over the mountain basin the town occupied. The surrounding Andean peaks and snowfields were decapitated by a high haze. In the clear between the sky mist and the ground haze the hikers felt caught, pressed. There was the urge to give in to the pitch of the slope, to hurry by sliding straight down. Instead, they kept their nerve, patiently zigzagged, and finally, after nearly half an hour, they reached bottom, where the sharp angle of the slope met another similar, forming a wedgelike trough. Easier going then, much less of an incline. The hikers made better time, were encouraged, nearly sure. Chiquinquirá soon. When they got there they would have time to spare. The train to Bogotá wasn't scheduled until two. They planned to split up, go sightseeing, shop around for religious mementos, relax in a park or at a table at a cantina. Do ordinary things. They wouldn't be with one another again until Bogotá.

By now the sun had won out over the haze and was burning away the mist. The hikers made shadows which preceded them, evaded their steps, led them on down the mountain

1

trough to a road. Raw dirt, rain-holed and rutted, it just barely qualified as a road, was not even acknowledged on local maps. Created merely by use, it had perhaps once been a route for the Spaniards to and from the mines.

The hikers didn't intend to take the road. They would cross over and continue more directly down to the town.

They didn't see the jeep until they were crossing, out in the open. It was parked off to the side, less than a hundred feet away, nearly concealed by bushes. Four soldiers were standing near the jeep, casually, as though waiting. Three of them carried automatic rifles; the other was a Lieutenant.

There was the shout to halt.

The hikers obeyed.

Three of the soldiers walked over to them, took separate positions around. Then the Lieutenant came over. He was taller than any of his men. His uniform was wrinkled and there were wine spots on his shirt, but his Lieutenant bars were polished.

Lieutenant Costas. He appeared indifferent while actually scrutinizing the hikers with experienced eyes.

Three young men, a young woman and an older man. He decided they probably weren't carrying weapons, although he wasn't sure about the one wearing the *ruana*.

"What were you doing up there?" Lieutenant Costas asked the older hiker.

"Studying formations."

"Birds?"

"Soil."

"For how many days?"

"Ten."

"You were reported seen up there two weeks ago."

"Perhaps it really has been that long. It is healthy to lose track of time."

The Lieutenant agreed. "Show me your identity."

Papers were handed over. The Lieutenant glanced at a photograph of the man he was facing. He read the accompanying name aloud: "Professor Julio Santos."

"Yes."

"Are you related to Senator Santos?"

"He is a cousin."

"Then, no doubt you had official permission."

"Yes."

"In writing."

"You have my word, Lieutenant, we are an expedition from the university. These are students." Professor Santos spoke evenly, in a tone that conveyed understanding for a man performing his duty.

The Lieutenant appraised the students. The girl was pretty. They all appeared frightened. From being at gunpoint. That was natural.

"I will be spending some time with my cousin next Sunday," the Professor said.

Lieutenant Costas yawned without bothering to cover his mouth. He'd gotten up at dawn for this. If it hadn't been for that imposition, perhaps . . .

"We must search you," he said.

Professor Santos continued to be mild-mannered.

"Surely you do not want to cause us to miss the twelve o'clock train to Bogotá."

"Two o'clock," the Lieutenant corrected.

Professor Santos removed his backpack. So did the others. They placed the packs together on the ground and moved aside.

Two of the soldiers went through the packs. A dutiful, rather than methodical search, although they did feel into the toes of shoes and unroll pairs of socks. They found that most of what the packs contained was food. Soon they had everything strewn about.

The Lieutenant reprimanded them for their carelessness, but possibly that was not really why he was angry.

His temper distracted the men, made them nervous, so they were not as thorough with their search as they could have been. They gathered the hikers' belongings into a pile and began stuffing them back into the packs.

The Lieutenant told them to forget that, to search the hikers.

Pockets were emptied. Legs were frisked all the way up, also arms, waists, backs and fronts. The girl, too, was searched in that manner. The soldiers took longer with her. Ignoring the protests of Professor Santos and the other hikers, they felt and handled her all over.

At first she just stood there, eyes set, body rigid, allowing it. But then, she reacted, pulled away, and when the soldiers tried to get their hands on her again, she clawed at them.

The Lieutenant wondered why the girl hadn't struggled at

the start. Could it be she'd had a second thought, decided it would be more convincing if she put up a fight?

No matter. Suspicions were worthless. Nothing had been found.

Let them go catch their train.

At that moment a canteen slipped from where it had been precariously placed atop the piled contents of the packs. As it landed on the road it rattled in an unusual way.

The hikers made a move toward their belongings.

Lieutenant Costas snapped at them to stay as they were. He picked up the canteen, shook it.

Something inside.

He unscrewed the cap, inverted the canteen. Water flowed out and through his fingers. Eight green stones dropped into the cup of his hand.

Uncut emeralds. Each about the size of his index finger from first knuckle to tip.

Lieutenant Costas held one up to his right eye, up to the sun, sighted through it, saw a hint of the clear, brilliant green that lay within the rough stone. He approved with a sort of high-pitched humming grunt.

The soldiers were more alert now, rifles up.

The Lieutenant himself searched through everything again. He tore apart a partial loaf of corn bread to find twelve emeralds. A bag of dried prunes—fifteen prunes. Each contained an emerald instead of a pit. Four bars of homemade soap were broken open to reveal emeralds stuck inside. And there were more of the precious stones hidden in the other canteens.

Finally, Lieutenant Costas was satisfied that there were no more emeralds in any of the packs. He ordered the hikers—poachers now—to remove their clothes. They did as told. Their clothes were piled in the middle of the road. The Lieutenant set fire to them. He used rocks to knock the heels from their boots and made sure the boots didn't have false toe compartments. When the clothes were reduced to ashes, the Lieutenant got a forked stick, which he used to scratch and rake. Flakes of burned fabric were stirred to float up and then down upon him, flecking his back and shoulders. He didn't notice. He was preoccupied with the pleasure of finding eighteen more uncut emeralds among the ashes. They were hot. He poked them out of the ashes and poured water on them, causing a puff

and a sizzle but no steam. He picked them up, placed them
with the others he'd collected in his officer's cap.

The poachers, while they were being more and more exposed, had to stand there naked. They didn't seem to mind
that. Rather than allowing it to humiliate them, they used their
nakedness to communicate defiance. They stood straight and
still, arms at sides, eyes level. It was more difficult for the girl,
of course. She felt shame. But she knew it was better for her to
keep still, that any movement, even as slight and innocent as
shifting her weight, would only increase the attention the soldiers were already paying her. She covered herself with
thoughts of times past in safe, pleasant places. A young man
named Miguel.

The poachers thought next they would be questioned. They
readied their minds for that. However, Lieutenant Costas
walked by them without a word, went and sat alone in the jeep.

He had kept count of the emeralds, believed he knew how
many there were: eighty-two. He counted again and was
pleased to find he'd been wrong. Eighty-seven. He placed the
cap containing the emeralds on the seat next to him. Chewed at
his thumbnail to help him think.

These people he'd caught, they were not *esmeralderos*—the
sort who spent full time after emeralds, stealing, killing for
them. They didn't have that in their eyes or ways. These
people weren't carrying weapons, not even knives. The moment he'd found the emeralds in the canteen, an *esmeraldero*
would have begun bargaining, offering to split with him, then
offering all, then trying to bluff his way out of it by claiming
there were many more emeralds where these had come from,
promising unlimited wealth. No, these people were *novicios*,
inexperienced, but not without cleverness. Concealing the
stones in the prunes, for example. An *esmeraldero* would
never have thought of such a thing. Neither would an
esmeraldero have hidden stones in a canteen. Such an obvious
place he had almost overlooked it today. What were these three
young men, and the older man, and the girl? Five together.
Esmeralderos worked alone or at most in pairs. Because it was
difficult enough for one man to trust just one other man when it
came to emeralds.

Lieutenant Costas noticed the sooty particles on the shoulders of his shirt. He tried to brush them off, but that smudged

them into the fabric, looked dirtier. He was scheduled for a
four-day leave starting tomorrow. He would have some shirts
made.

As for that older man, the one who claimed he was a professor, no need to worry about him. He was no more a cousin
of Senator Santos than he was a mere hiker, Lieutenant Costas
thought.

Thought of his choices.

He could place the poachers under arrest, take them in for
prosecution. He'd have to turn the evidence, all the emeralds,
over to his commanding officer, who, if in a rare honest mood,
might see that they were passed on to their legal owner: The
Concession.

Or he could release the poachers, keep the emeralds for
himself. Not even report the incident. Perhaps the poachers
would be so grateful they would forget it happened, especially
forget what he looked like. But would his men never mention it
to anyone?

There was the other way to deal with it.

He called the soldiers over to the jeep one at a time. Gave
them instructions and two emeralds each, two of the smallest
ones. He had thought of giving them three but changed his
mind at the last moment.

The men were glad to get anything. Their service pay was
only a hundred pesos a month, about four dollars. The emeralds would bring ten times that from the local undercover
dealer, who specialized in buying stones from enlisted men.
He paid very little but never questioned.

The Lieutenant would turn in forty stones when he made his
report. That would leave him forty-one to sell to a connection
in Bogotá. Someone he did such business with regularly, could
trust. God help him, though, if The Concession ever found him
out. The mere thought made his stomach contract. Anyway,
his men were now conspirators. And they also knew the
penalty.

For a better view the Lieutenant stood up in the jeep, leaned
forward against the top of the windshield, at ease.

One of the soldiers used the barrel of his rifle to force the girl
aside. Then, facing the others, the soldiers took solid stances
and pulled.

They fired in bursts, spraying point-blank. The poachers

absorbed many bullets after they were already dead. They lay in contorted positions, extremities twitching.

The girl couldn't scream. She doubled over and vomited.

The soldiers waited until she was no longer retching. The Lieutenant had suggested she might have more emeralds hidden. If so, the men could have them.

They didn't feel any.

When they had each taken a turn with her, the first who'd had her wanted her again.

She never struggled. They demanded that she move, but she might as well have been dead.

Within minutes, she was.

2 ⋙

     In New York City that December morning, Joseph A. Wiley sat at his practically impervious desk.

It wasn't his desk, really, and he took care never to refer to it as his. He always called it *the* desk. "I left the marketing recommendations on *the* desk." He had the same attitude toward that portion of space where he was now, on the thirty-second floor. It was *the* office rather than his. No matter that the plastic nameplate outside, just to the left of the door, permanently said Joseph Wiley. It was in a metal bracket that would allow it to be removed at any second.

In *the* office there was also *the* swivel chair, upholstered in one kind of plastic and situated so it rolled about on a clear sheet of a harder kind to save *the* wall-to-wall carpet. *The* lithograph of a landscape that couldn't possibly offend or delight, *the* inevitable dying split-leaf rhododendron, and *the* ashtray stolen from Lutèce.

Wiley often ignored the ashtray, placed his lighted cigarettes on the edge of the desk. When a forgotten cigarette burned all the way down and out, it caused only a tarry residue that aggravated Wiley's smoker's guilt until wiped away. The desk's defiant veneer, Wiley knew, was also unaffected by coffee, vodka, and anger.

It was employee-proof.

Wiley had known more than his share of such desks. He'd had nine jobs in the past twelve years. Nine, not counting those he'd moonlighted. He'd worked at: two advertising, one real estate, two public relations, one insurance, two networks and a talent. All on the semimanagement level in the $20,000- to $40,000-a-year range.

Not once had Wiley been fired. Each employer had wanted him to stay on. Every time he'd gone after a new job, he'd landed it.

It helped that he doctored up his résumé, made up for any

blank spots, amputated a job here, a job there. Stretched dates so his employment past appeared to have flowed nicely without too much jumping around, so they wouldn't say right off that something had to be wrong with him. If that was lying, Wiley reasoned it was for their benefit as much as his. He was merely shaping and presenting his history as they would want it. To match the way he looked.

That was it. His looks. He looked good. Doing business depended more on that than anyone wanted to admit. First impression was often first consideration. It was more pleasant to have confidence in a good-looking man; he was easier for a client to like. And if that man just happened to have ability, he was practically unbeatable.

Early enough, Wiley came to realize this value was the soft underbelly of the hard business world. And that was where he chose to cut it.

He wasn't too handsome. Strong, slightly imperfect features. There were those who said he reminded them of Paul Newman, though he didn't have Newman's blue eyes. Wiley's eyes were a variegated green, close to a deep forest shade. He still had all his hair, and it was still dark except at the temples. Looked his age. Forty-two. Squint lines. He was six feet exactly, with shoes on, and his weight was never more than a few pounds above or below one seventy-five.

Being that slim, he wore clothes well. He was smart about clothes, strategic. Went for quality rather than more of a less-expensive assortment. Instead of two suits from Saks, one from Dunhill or DeNoyer. Not so many shirts, but those he had were Turnbull and Asser, bought when Bonwit's had a sale. Actually he had two kinds of wardrobe. Like everything else, split. One for them, one for him. His consisted mainly of jeans, sweaters and penny loafers.

If Wiley had stuck with any of his jobs, more than likely he would by now have been on top of one of those heaps, or at least close to it. He was intelligent, imaginative and a hard worker—when he was working. However, sticking was literally how he thought of it. Getting stuck. He was too ambitious for that. It wasn't quick enough for him.

There had been a time when he believed it would be. In high school, many of his good, young times, most of his best, were sacrificed to studying. He was accepted at MIT, worked any spare hours to pay his way and in his second year got a scholarship for winning the middleweight boxing championship in the National Collegiate Athletic Association regional finals. He had a frustrating, accurate left jab, backed up by a right that could stun, especially in close. His opponents were usually overconfident because he didn't have the look of a fighter.

He graduated twenty-third in a class of seven hundred, went on to get his Master of Science degree in electrical engineering.

America was promises.

Recruiters from several important electronics firms went after him, the way the pros went after a two-hundred-thirty-pound sure-handed tight-end. A prime prospect.

Humes Electronics in Houston got him. For twenty thousand a year, which wasn't bad for a start then, in 1958. Humes threw in a new car as an added inducement, on the condition that he not reveal that to anyone. Special treatment? He found out later the car bonus was almost routine.

He was assigned to a phase of Humes' responsibility in the space program and enjoyed being a part of that, did well at it, made some new friends at Humes and at NASA. On his annual review he was told management was pleased with him. Bright future if he kept up the good work. Praise and a raise of two thousand a year, which was no more than average.

Foot on the first rung, he thought. To share being pleased with himself, he called home. Father and Mother pressed their ears to the same phone to hear him, their only. They were happy he was happy. There would be more money, he promised, there would be plenty of money. Someday soon, they'd never have to worry about money. His father, off the subject, said he'd heard Houston was having a hot spell.

Wiley had been sending money home each month. A couple hundred. They hadn't asked for it, told him he shouldn't. But being able to help them gave him a good feeling, and he kept sending it. Besides, it left him with more than enough to spend.

The better life he wanted for them: It was nearly always in his letters, mentioned when he phoned. At first, respecting his father's pride, he hadn't hit directly upon it, merely sown the idea of how their circumstances might be changed. His father had been a spinner at a woolen mill for twenty years. His mother had worked regularly as a stitcher at another mill. He would remove them from the grind that was wearing out their lives in that shitty little New England town.

His parents accepted his wanting to provide for them as his way of conveying care for them. They expected nothing and went on working in the mills.

Three years with Humes took a lot out of Wiley. He saw ahead more clearly and further, and realized the track there was too slow for him. They gave him pre-computed raises, on schedule. Advancement was held out in front to keep him going. No matter that he already excelled at his work, contributed more than most of the men who had been with Humes longer and were rungs above him. It seemed prerequisite that he put the time in, keep in place, wait.

He couldn't.

He went for another job. Got it. At Special Dynamics in Los Angeles. More money than he'd been making at Humes—however, not much more. Actually, not much of a change in any way. Wiley detected humdrum in the personnel director's welcoming spiel, was escorted into the president's office for an immediate dose of top-level interest. A smile that was merely a mouth being pulled upward at the corners, a handshake too vigorous to be true, a couple of stock phrases.

Wiley felt processed, rather than important.

He was assigned to a phase of the lunar vehicle project.

At Special Dynamics he tried a different approach. On his own time he came up with an improved system of electronic circuitry. It took six months of his nights and weekends to develop it: a much smaller, lighter, equally efficient circuitry that was perfect for the lunar vehicle project. It also had many other possible commercial applications.

Wiley knew better than to show it to his phase manager or even the project supervisor, though he would have welcomed their suggestions and support. The idea was too stealable. Wiley took it right to the top. Laid it like an apple on the desk of the president, who considered this meeting with Wiley a matter of employee relations, a dutiful hesitation in the sentence of his busy morning. He looked over Wiley's diagrams. No show of reaction from the president, who removed his glasses, cleaned them and took another, longer look at each page. "Seems good," he said, a bit indecisively. But Wiley

translated the man's eyes, saw the dollar signs in them and was
sure he would get his share.

Two days later the president's secretary delivered a sealed
envelope to Wiley. It contained a check for three thousand
dollars, which, an accompanying personal letter explained,
was a bonus. Wiley should keep up the fine work.

Hey, wait a minute, this was like something out of Dickens.
He was no fucking Bob Cratchit.

He wanted to see the president, but the president had left for
a four-day Palm Springs weekend and from there would be
going to Washington, D.C., for ten days.

An executive vice-president sat Wiley down, tried to calm
him. Wasn't the three-thousand bonus enough?

Hell, no.

What did Wiley want?

No lousy bonus. He wanted what was fair, and if he didn't
get it, he'd take his idea elsewhere.

Couldn't do that.

Try to stop him.

Wiley's file was brought from personnel. The executive
vice-president marked a check in the margin of the application
form Wiley had signed the day he'd come to work for Special
Dynamics. One paragraph among many pertaining to company
rules and policies. Nothing anyone starting a job would bother
to read. In so many words it said all inventions or original
designs an employee created while working for Special Dynamics belonged exclusively to Special Dynamics.

Was there anything else the executive vice-president could
do for Wiley?

Wiley bit his tongue, asked for a recommendation, went
home and did some shadowboxing.

Wiser, more bitter, Wiley changed to a job with Litting
Industries. For about the same salary he'd been making. No
special reason for his choosing Litting. Just a job. He put in his
hours. Got his paychecks. At credible intervals he phoned in
that he had the flu and went to the beach.

Three years of that.

Wiley was thirty.

About then was when he met Harry Galanoy. A florid-faced,
overweight man who wore wash-and-wear shirts and suits with
a synthetic shine. Galanoy was thirty-five. He lived two apartments down from Wiley, overlooking the pool, at a typical

medium-priced place in Van Nuys. Wiley had seen Galanoy numerous times coming and going but had never said more than a neighborly hello. One afternoon Wiley took his drink and cigarette out on the balcony. Below at poolside were a pair of sometime actresses who shared a ground-floor apartment. They had only the bottoms of bikinis on, were lying fronts up, slicked.

Galanoy came from his apartment.

He and Wiley shared the view for a while.

Galanoy shrugged. "Seen two, seen them all."

Wiley smiled, nodded.

One of the girls rolled over to get done on the other side, her breasts squashed beneath her. It appeared painful.

"Buy you a drink?" Galanoy offered.

Wiley accepted, followed Galanoy inside.

Galanoy talked freely, especially about himself. He'd worked off and on at various things, mainly as a salesman. All it took to get rich was a gimmick, he said. Like the Hula Hoop. Nothing but a goddamn plastic ring. Made millions. Same thing with that stuff called Silly Putty. Who knew what might catch on next. The injector razor, the ballpoint pen. Sweet Jesus, how he wished he'd thought up the ballpoint.

So did Wiley.

Their conversation went on for five Scotches, kept on the topic of getting rich quick. Wiley did most of the listening, but at one point he related his experience with Special Dynamics. Galanoy was only slightly sympathetic, said Wiley shouldn't have counted on anything so complicated. The simpler the gimmick, the better. The Hula Hoop, he reminded.

Wiley spent quite a lot of time with Galanoy after that. At first he suspected the man might be trying to con him into something. Then he told himself he was only amused by the way Galanoy carried on about making millions easy. Galanoy hardly ever spoke of anything else—except his ulcer. He had a peptic ulcer, which he complained about with a kind of pride.

Harry Galanoy.

He didn't convert Wiley. The proselytizing had been done long before—in the public school system, where it was said that as undoubtedly as George Washington was the father of our country, anyone could make it from nothing all the way to the top in this land.

God bless.

During the 1940's, Wiley had sat in elementary classrooms where "No talking" was a commandment and talking back an offense, and had his thinking saturated with the need to achieve. Had ambition tied in a knot to his future manhood. There were names to keep in mind, such as Frick and Carnegie, Ford, Mellon and John D. himself, during the course in U.S. History—compulsory. John D. appeared cadaverous in photographs. Skin and bones and millions of dollars. Wiley always thought there was something incongruous and repulsive in that, but it would be irreverent to mention it. A Miss Pearson and a Miss Selkirk and a Mr. Mosely taught and tested and passed Wiley on in the general direction of opportunity.

Anyone who didn't make it was a lamebrain.

It was a free-for-all.

The red, white, and blue grindstone.

"A guy can burn his nose and his ass down to the bone on it," Galanoy said.

Wiley had already come to that conclusion.

Galanoy had a stockpile of gimmicks in mind.

The one he and Wiley went partners on was a mail-order idea. The investment was $15,000.

Galanoy sold his car for $1500 and scraped up another $1000. Wiley had $2000 in checking. He called home, and before he could finish explaining the deal, his father said he'd send the money right off. *Your money*, his father called it. His parents had been putting into a separate account whatever Wiley had sent over the years. Saving it for when he might want it. Ten thousand and some.

He lost it all.

Galanoy moved somewhere and never called.

Wiley tried not to remember him.

He tried to concentrate on his job at Litting. His imagination kept veering toward ways to make a financial killing. After about six months of paydays, he quit, gave in to it and, ever since, had been on the cycle:

Think of a gimmick.

Hold down a job long enough to get a stake.

Try the gimmick.

Go back to a job.

Think of another gimmick.

Often it was just a matter of timing. He tried selling organic food before the big demand. The same with hanging plants for city apartments. He was a little late getting into posters, water-beds, backgammon sets. He missed out entirely on an indoor tennis complex in Westchester, American Indian jewelry, musk oil, mood rings, pet rocks, Art Deco furniture, imprinted T-shirts, and frozen yogurt.

He had bad luck with a tropical fish venture when the heating system failed on a January night, froze the entire stock in blocks of ice that shattered the glass of all the aquariums.

Korean ginseng. He was right on time with that, when its libidinal benefits were only in the rumor stage. He'd heard about it from a pretty Korean model who chomped on those phallic-shaped roots as though they were carrots—and demonstrated excellent results. She claimed she had a cheap and plentiful source of ginseng roots, tea, and extract—a man in Namchiang, Korea, which happened to be her hometown. Wiley put up the money. She flew. The only excuse he could find to forgive her was she must have been extremely home-sick.

Wiley had another business adventure with an Oriental. A man named Chun Ta Ha, who hoped his constant smile compensated for his inability to speak English. Ta Ha had jumped ship in Boston, made his way to New York City and was working in the Hop Tee Hand Laundry on West Seventy-second Street when Wiley met him. He was the son of a farmer in Canton and was astonished at the prices being paid here for Chinese vegetables. Wiley saw the possibilities. Ta Ha would grow, they both would reap.

They rented an abandoned warehouse downtown, in the Bowery area. A large, dark, awfully damp place. Perfect. They bought forty-three field-kitchen kettles from an army surplus dealer in New Jersey. The kettles were four feet in diameter, had drain holes in their bottoms. They also bought five hundred pounds of mung beans, a portion of which they washed and soaked and put into the kettles. Ta Ha hosed the beans down three or four times a day, kept them damp.

They were in business.

Within five days they had their first harvest. Two tons of bean sprouts they could wholesale for twenty-five cents a pound.

A thousand dollars, just like that.

What was great about it was the beans did practically all the work. With more kettles and more beans, there could be a harvest every day. All they had to do was pack them. A thousand dollars a day, every day. A take of over a quarter million dollars a year.

Ta Ha giggled, and Wiley's voice echoed in that place as he joyfully shouted, "Sprout, you little moneymaking bastards!"

On the seventh day of production Wiley received a frantic telephone call in Chinese from Ta Ha. Wiley didn't know what was wrong until he saw it.

Rats had eaten all the bean sprouts.

Rats. There was no way to stop them. It seemed as though the word had been passed to every rodent in the city. Despite traps, poisons, and wire mesh covers, the rats kept on coming—to eat Wiley and Ta Ha out of a fortune.

In such ways success eluded Wiley. However, each near-miss only made him all the more determined. His schemes weren't really quixotic, he told himself; his time would come.

Now there he was at *the* office, thirty-two New York City floors above the ordinary level of life. His hopes this day were higher than ever. He was close to pulling off a deal that would net him millions. A simple little gimmick: clear plastic disks about the size of a quarter that could be worn as medallions or charms or carried in the pocket. Sealed within each disk would be a pinch of dirt, certified to be a pinch of the old homeland. From Ireland or Italy, Poland, Greece, Puerto Rico, Israel, or wherever. Millions of people were latter-day Americans. Most families had been here only two or three generations. Practically the entire country retained pride in some foreign land.

Wiley had gotten the idea one Sunday when trying to get crosstown in a cab while there was a parade on Fifth Avenue. The cab driver was bitching: "Every fucking Saturday and Sunday and every fucking holiday somebody's jamming up traffic with a parade. If it ain't the wops, it's the Polacks or somebody."

The very next day Wiley found a manufacturer in Brooklyn who specialized in molding the sort of cheap little plastic toys that came in bubble-gum machines. The manufacturer would deliver the disks complete with dirt sealed inside for two cents a unit in million-unit lots. It took considerable time and effort to arrange for dirt to be shipped from the various countries, but finally Wiley had it lined up.

He took his gimmick to the largest cereal company. Positive reaction. A fantastic premium, they thought. An actual pinch of the homeland for a boxtop and only fifty cents. The cereal people gave Wiley an initial order for twenty million units. If the premiums were moderately successful they'd reorder, and projected they should be able to sell at least another twenty to thirty million.

Wiley stood to make a nickel a unit—a million dollars right off.

The cereal people had one condition. They didn't want any part of a fraud. The soil had to be absolutely certified as to its foreign origin.

Absolutely, Wiley agreed.

And today was the day.

There were 17 fifty-gallon drums of foreign soil sitting in the customs depot on the dock in Hoboken. Wiley couldn't think of much else. He wasn't even aware of Miss Kerby, the secretary standing in the doorway.

"I was wondering if it was all right with you if I didn't get back from lunch on time," she said. "I want to go Christmas shopping at Bloomies."

Wiley glanced at her quizzically. All he'd heard was Bloomies.

"Mr. Farley and Mr. Carlino said it was all right with them," Miss Kerby said.

Wiley shared Miss Kerby with Farley and Carlino. She had a huge behind, a tiny voice, and a habit of blaming others for her mistakes. "Said *what* was all right?"

Miss Kerby repeated her request.

Wiley didn't care if she went to Macy's in Nairobi—as a matter of fact, he'd prefer she did.

"Don't forget your lunch with Mr. Codd," Miss Kerby said.

"I thought Farley was taking him."

"It's your turn." She smiled for punishment.

Wiley decided not to let it spoil his day. Nothing could spoil this day.

He lighted another cigarette from the still-burning stub of his last, transferred a thick sheaf of papers from incoming to outgoing. He'd take care of those next time around—but doubted he'd still be there.

The phone rang.

Miss Kerby didn't get it, just for spite.

It was the divorce lawyer: "I have news for you. I met with her lawyer this morning. She was there."

Wiley and Jennifer had been married for three years come January, separated for the last six months. His first marriage, her second.

"She's asking for too much, but that's normal." the divorce lawyer said.

"What more does she want?" It seemed every week the ante had gone up.

"I didn't realize she was so unstable."

"She cried."

"No."

"She turned her back to you."

"What a ball-breaker!"

Wiley resented anyone else saying that.

"Tell you one thing, I'd like to get this woman on the stand. I'd tear her to pieces."

"I don't really want to give her a hard time," Wiley said.

"You haven't been seeing her, have you?"

"No."

"I mean it now, it's important. Have you been going to bed with her?"

Wiley was sure someone else had been doing that.

"From what I made of her this morning, if she ever got in court under heavy fire she'd fold," the divorce lawyer said.

"Drop her case?"

"No, pull a collapse."

"What do you mean?"

"What I said. Literally. She'd collapse."

"She's not that fragile."

"Soon as she started getting the worst of it she'd have a mental breakdown, blame you, put herself into one of those rest-home mansions up in Scarsdale or someplace. No divorce. You couldn't divorce her for seven years, and you'd be stuck for a hundred a day plus psychiatric expenses."

"That ever happen?"

"Some guys have been paying for years. Poor bastards."

"Jennifer wouldn't go that far."

"Want to bet seven years on it? Hold a second . . . I've got to take this other call."

The silence made Wiley aware he was clenching the receiver. Before the call he'd been only normally tense. He sat forward, flexed his back, let his head go dead weight, and rotated it one way and then the other. A deep breath. Closed eyes.

Recall.

Her with him, wading through dry fall grass on Nantucket. To a tree set apart as though estranged. Leafless, black, networked branches. The nearest house, a new one that looked unoccupied, a hundred yards away. The ocean only a silver line on the afternoon horizon because the land was so level. Sitting, lying, the grass all around tall enough to hide them. It took a while for them to become confident enough of the place. Their sex-making was no swifter than it would have been if they had been surely secluded—and better than any of the several times before, with a sort of intensifying thievery to it.

And afterward . . . her thinking aloud: "We go well together."

They laughed at the word *go*.

She had also said at other times: "You're spoiling me for any other man, which, of course, would be fine if there never had to be anyone else." And: "I'm vulnerable again. My telling you I am proves it." And: "I promise I'll never expect more of you than I do now."

She had helped him fight the rats, stayed up all night two nights in a row with him in that horrible damp warehouse, trying to protect the bean sprouts. The rats didn't frighten her. The first one she saw, she attacked with a piece of pipe, broke its back.

Right after the rats they had gone to Arlington, Virginia, where no waiting period was required. Bought a nosegay at one of the flower shops around the corner from the courthouse and were serviced by the same judge who had married the Kissingers. She gave her age as twenty-nine on the license application. A two-year lie.

Jennifer looked married the moment she was. Her eyes and mouth seemed relieved.

As it turned out—she had a thin voice that became whinier. Insisted on calling him Joseph.

When she was nude, her walk changed, shorter steps, a sort of awkward ballerina waddle with toes pointed out.

Yellow to purplish bruises on her thighs from everyday slight collisions, because her body was almost depleted of potassium from years of taking extremely strong diuretics. She was compulsive about keeping underweight, feared gaining like death.

She had every possible thing monogrammed.

She sent away for a dwarf banana tree to grow at home. And a hanging strawberry garden that didn't have a chance above the radiator.

Soiled or not, whatever she wore she sent to the cleaners after only one wearing.

She had a nightly bowel habit that was the most unromantic thing he could have possibly heard just before bedtime.

As it turned out . . .

"I'm fed up with your bigshot ideas. I want security. I want to own a house and be like everyone else. You're a compulsive neurotic. You and your fucking financial roller coaster," she said. "If you quit this job, I'm going to quit you. I mean it."

Her and him in the dark in their king-size bed. A space like a firebreak between them.

"Hello . . . you still there?" The divorce lawyer.

"Yeah."

"Sorry about the interruption. I didn't think it would take that long. Anyway, now she's accusing you of trying to influence her to commit sodomy."

"That's ridiculous."

"It's in her sworn statement."

"Sodomy?"

"In this state sodomy includes every sex act except straight old-fashioned. She claims you wanted her to indulge orally."

How twisted around, Wiley thought. "What does she want?"

She wanted the apartment on Central Park West, which was a five-room, $60,000 cooperative with $20,000 equity. He was to continue making the mortgage payments and paying the monthly maintenance charges for five years. She wanted all the furnishings. She wanted the car, which was only five months from being paid for. She wanted $25,000 cash. She wanted him to pay for any charges she had made as his wife up through October 1, rather than only to August 1, the date when he had notified the stores. She had hurried out to a grudgeful, greedy shopping binge an hour after he'd left. At Bendel's, Bergdorf's, Altman's, all over. She also wanted him to pay for the weekly visit to her $60-per-session psychiatrist, for a year.

Wiley could have the dog.

He was short of breath, that angry.

"Settle," the divorce lawyer advised. "It'll be cheaper in the long run."

One thing Wiley had never been impetuous about was women. A number of times over the years he'd been close to marriage, and often he looked back on a couple of those times with regret. Now what he'd been afraid would happen had happened. Nevertheless, as much as he had grown to despise Jennifer, he didn't blame her as much as he blamed himself. His age had had something to do with it. And that good sex out in the open on Nantucket, combined almost immediately with the confederate battle of the rats.

"Okay," he told the lawyer, "I agree to all but one thing—she keeps the dog." Wiley had always disliked the dog, and she knew it. A slobbering Kerry Blue with a miserable disposition that was continually curling up at his feet and farting.

"I have the papers ready for you to sign. I'll send them over." Before clicking off, the lawyer remembered one more thing: Jennifer wanted Wiley to take care of all legal fees.

Within a half hour a messenger arrived with the papers, and Wiley thought about signing them "Nelson Rockefeller." But then he reasoned that in another way he might actually be getting off easy, just in time, before he cashed in on his pinch-of-the-old-homeland gimmick and she wanted a million.

Good-bye, Jennifer.

Eleven o'clock.

The coffee wagon came around. Wiley bought a black in a styrofoam cup. And a French cruller that was sweet and greasy. He stood at the window blowing on the coffee. His view was west across Third Avenue. It had snowed two inches the night before, and the cloud ceiling was still low, gray. The fifty- and sixty-story office buildings over on Madison and Fifth were out of sight. There was mist being blown around the Waldorf Towers a few blocks away.

At that moment it seemed as if something passed before Wiley's eyes, no more than a single flicker that interrupted his gaze for a fraction of a second. A reflection on the window glass, he decided. What else could it have been?

A few minutes later, Miss Kerby came in and told him, "Mr. Endicott jumped off the roof."

Endicott. Chairman of the Board, the man that chauffeur and limousine waited for double-parked out front every afternoon.

The man who made the important pitches, the crucial presentations, who pacified the restless clients. The man who made the most, who gave the Christmas bonuses. He couldn't have been more than sixty-five, must have had everything to live for. How could he do it? Forty-seven floors. Jesus.

That was what Wiley had seen at the window. Endicott on his way down.

Sirens.

Why the rush?

Wiley heard someone out in the corridor say: "He didn't leave a note or anything." And someone else said, with some spite: "Maybe he was pushed."

Wiley kept picturing Endicott going off the edge.

He closed the door. Tried to think of anything else. He even took back some of that work from the outgoing tray. He was supposed to meet Codd at The Four Seasons at twelve-thirty. He now had the suicide as a legitimate excuse. But he might as well go. Codd was a bore, one of the clients' brand managers who could ruin a good marketing program with his improvements. Every day someone took Codd to a $50 lunch. A waste of $13,000 a year. Codd liked going to The Four Seasons. Last time Wiley had done the duty Codd had drunk so much before, during, and after, that on the way back to the office he'd thrown up all over some flowers on the sidewalk in front of a small florist shop on Lexington. It had cost an extra $50 that Wiley had difficulty explaining on his expense sheet.

Five minutes to twelve.

The mailroom boy knocked and came in. It was his second run for the day. His first had been interoffice correspondence; this was regular mail. He dropped several letters into Wiley's incoming tray. Among the normal junk mail, one letter stood out. From the United States Treasury Department Customs Service.

Dear Sir:

In reference to your shipments via TransOceanic Service, bills of lading nos. 19753 through 19769. Please be advised that you are in violation of Section 76, Title 8, U.S. Code.

By order of the Imports Compliance Division you are hereby notified that this office has confiscated and dis-

posed of the above-mentioned shipments. A penalty of
$25.00 per container is due immediately. You may pay by
certified check or money order. Personal checks are not
acceptable. Unless the amount due, $425.00, is received
by this office within 30 days of receipt of this letter,
further penalties will be assessed.

                              Respectfully,
                              John W. Gallwise
                              Director
                              New York Seaport Area

Wiley couldn't phone fast enough. He finally got someone at
the Imports Compliance Division who knew what Section 76,
Title 8, was. It had to do with preventing possibly con-
taminated material or substances from entering this country.
The trouble with foreign soil was it might contain anthrax
spores, among other things.

Wiley was so stunned he even said thank you before hanging
up. He got up, and before he even realized he was standing, he
had his topcoat on. He went out, down the corridor to the
elevator, where he said hello in return to someone's hello,
although everyone, everything now seemed unfamiliar to him.

The elevator was packed. His toe got stepped on and his back
got poked. When the doors parted, he didn't react with typical
city urgency, was pressed from behind, then shoved roughly out
into the lobby. He stood there, got bumped like an obstacle, and
then almost carried along by the stream of hurry to and through
the doors to the outside. A crowd out there was spending part of
their lunchtime getting a look at the spot on the sidewalk where
Endicott had hit. The body had been taken away, but as yet no
one had bothered to clean up the blood. After a couple hours of
being walked on, it wouldn't show. One woman was relating
how Endicott had just missed her, by no more than a foot.
Proved it with reddish splatters on her panty hose.

All this brought Wiley partially back to reality. At least, he
thought, he wasn't dead. He went south to the corner of Third
and Fifty-fourth, stepped off the curb without looking, and
went ankle-deep in slush with one foot and to the same depth
with the other in slush mixed with dog turds. He crossed over.
A fast taxi went by close behind, splashing slush up the back of
his trouser legs and coat. Wiley just took it. He read store signs
as he walked.

10,000 ORIGINAL OIL PAINTINGS
from $5.00 EACH

The *from* was so small it wasn't readable more than a yard away.

LEASE EXPIRED—
EVERYTHING MUST GO!

That clothing store had been expiring for two years.

Wiley continued walking south to Fifty-third. His head was clearing now, but everything around seemed accelerated.

What a morning. He'd been blackmailed by a crazy, greedy wife, witnessed the middle of a suicide, had millions taken practically right out of his hands by some tight-assed customs official, and had stepped in cold wet shit.

At the corner of Third and Fifty-second he was supposed to cross over. The Four Seasons was only a block and a half away, between Park and Lexington. But, at that point, his legs refused to cooperate. His mind said he should go have lunch with Codd, drink a lot of good wine and order Strasbourg *foie gras* at fifteen dollars for a starter. However, there he was, walking away in the opposite direction, headed for Second Avenue.

He let himself believe he didn't really know where his legs were taking him. Up Second to Fifty-fifth, to where he'd been temporarily living for six months. Overpriced apartment 10-G, next door to the 10-F overpriced call girl.

Wiley unlocked the three different locks on his door and went in. The place hadn't been cleaned or even straightened in four days. His maid's back was bothering her, which probably really meant she'd hit the numbers.

He undressed, took everything off. Turned on the lamp, drew the drapes, pushed a table and a chair aside, removed the lampshade. The bare two-hundred-watt bulb produced a shadow of the bare him on the wall. He went right into some footwork, sidestepping, shuffling, skipping, mixing it up. He added some weaving and bobbing, feints with his head and shoulders and hands. Then he started throwing lefts and rights. Jab with the left, jab, jab setting up the right hook. Combinations, left hook, right hook, left cross, uppercuts. He went full out for fifteen minutes, was sweating, gasping for breath. For nearly another fifteen he went on hitting at nothing.

It didn't work. Not this time.

While he was cooling off with a beer and having two con-secutive cigarettes, he thought about what he might do. While in the shower, he decided definitely.

He packed quickly, but had more clothes than he had lug-gage for. Left out all the business suits, ties, and shoes. He felt lighter when he closed the closet door on them.

By the time he was dressed it was two-forty.

He went out and hailed a cab to the bank, got there just before three. He withdrew everything from both his checking and savings. Twelve thousand four hundred and some he'd intended to use as a cushion while he was getting his dirt-in-a-disk gimmick under way.

Now it was his fuck-you money.

Fuck you, Jennifer.

He took it in brand-new hundreds. Didn't have the patience to buy traveler's checks. For precaution he noted the serial number of the first bill was F20011812E. Easy to remember— 2001, the Kubrick film; 1812, War of; and the F and the E for Fuck Everything. He riffled the bills, saw they were in a series; the last bill was F20011936E.

Another cab.

"What time's your flight?"

He told the cabby five o'clock.

"What airline?"

He had no idea.

"Overseas or domestic?"

"What difference does it make?"

"You have to check in an hour ahead when you're going overseas."

"Just get me there."

Thirty minutes later he was nearing Kennedy. There were the cargo areas and the service hangars and the signs in se-quence over the parkway that gave the turnoffs to various airlines designated by color and number. Green 1, Blue 2, Red 3, Orange 4.

"What airline you want?" The cabby was irritated.

Wiley almost said he didn't know, but told him, "Keep going."

He let Green 1 and its list of airlines go by.

Blue 2 coming up, offering Japan Air Lines, Iberia, Alitàlia, Air India, Lufthansa, Aeromexico.

"Turn here!" Wiley shouted.

The cabby just made it.

Wiley had taken two years of Spanish to get into college and two years of it to get out. Besides, although he didn't believe anyone could live anywhere on five dollars a day, maybe he could on ten dollars a day in Mexico. At that rate he'd have nearly four years coming.

3 ⟩⟩⟩

Wiley was in First Class.

It wasn't worth fifty dollars more, but there were no seats available in Economy. The next flight wasn't till the next morning. He didn't want to wait, retreat, even for that long.

So First Class it was. Champagne and plenty of leg room. Since takeoff he'd been trying to get used to the idea of his new direction. He was displaced, but also liberated. Perhaps it was the champagne on a lunchless stomach, but every once in a while he felt somewhat giddy, close to laughing.

Another long sip of Piper-Heidseick. He held it in his mouth, swished it, and let it fizzle and burn his gums. He was being offered an assortment of canapés. He chose the caviar, several. Might as well get his money's worth. He remembered an article he'd read a while back in *The New York Times*—an interview with a man celebrating his hundredth birthday, who attributed his longevity to sloth. The oldster claimed ambition was a killer; he had never done more than just enough to get by. One hundred years.

For once in your life you're really going to enjoy life, Wiley promised himself.

He was being asked about dinner by the stewardess: broiled squab or filet mignon or double lamb chops *noisette*?

"Some of each," Wiley said.

Fine with her, she kept right on smiling.

Just before dinner the woman seated next to Wiley struck up a conversation. They had exchanged perfunctory fellow-passenger smiles on first sight, but since then Wiley had taken little notice of her.

She was a time-fighter, losing the battle, of course, but prolonging it at any price. There was that sort of self-pampered expensiveness about her. Ten years ago she had been thirty-eight trying to appear twenty-nine. Now she would settle for thirty-eight.

27

"Do you spend much time in Mexico?" was her opener.

"Acapulco," Wiley said. He'd been there once.

"We used to like it there. My husband calls it Alcohol-puka." She laughed, showing perfect caps and gold crowns. "That's my husband." She indicated with her chin a man across the aisle two seats forward, having a Scotch on the rocks and looking his age.

Wiley thought perhaps the husband had chosen to enjoy sitting apart, or maybe it had been her idea, and then again, very possibly it was a mutual arrangement.

"I'm Doris Gimble," she said.

Wiley said his name.

"In case you're wondering, we're not even related to the department store people," she said. "They spell their name *e-l*, ours is *l-e*."

Wiley was thinking about how much her tan must have cost. He'd be getting one a lot cheaper.

"What do you do, Mr. Wiley?"

"Nothing."

"Really?"

"Honest."

She seemed impressed. She reappraised him, didn't try to be subtle about it, looked him down and up and down, lingered a moment on his shoes. He had on a pair of hundred-dollar loafers from Ferragamo.

"We're in plastics," she said.

Wiley winced inside at the word.

"At least we were until a few years ago," she continued. "Now the business more or less runs itself."

Like a money machine, Wiley thought.

Dinner was brought. Wiley's tray was piled with three entrées. He ate nearly everything on his tray and then chose a napoleon from the dessert cart. Mrs. Gimble, meanwhile, poked at her squab, pushed at her potatoes and had a few grapes and a small wedge of Edam for dessert. As though what had been placed before her was old age. Meticulously, she removed the skins and seeds from the grapes. Before the meal, she had taken two green capsules and a tiny white pill, which Wiley had assumed were vitamins. Now he wasn't sure.

"Are you, by any chance, on the junket?" she asked.

Wiley thought she'd said "junk." She repeated her question.

"No."

"What a shame."

Wiley agreed politely.

"It's a fabulous resort. Two or three planeloads are being flown down from New York, and there'll be others. Just about everyone who is anyone, from all over. We could have taken the charter yesterday, and that would have been fun, but Allen had this long-standing date with his cardiologist." She paused, changed tone. "Maybe it was for the best."

Her eyes locked with Wiley's for a moment. It seemed she had hands in her eyes.

Wiley looked away, out of reach. "Where is this place?"

"Near Manzanillo, on the west coast. Do you know where Manzanillo is?"

"Yes," Wiley fibbed.

"The place is called Las Hadas, which means 'the fairies' or perhaps 'fairyland,' I think. All I know in Spanish is hello, good-bye, thanks and a few naughty words." She laughed for punctuation. "Anyway," she went on, "to promote the place a lot of the right people have been invited. You know, those who make news or at least will talk it up in the right circles."

"Right."

"It's going to cost Argenti a fortune, putting all of us up for a week. But Argenti can afford it."

Evidently Wiley should have known who this Argenti person was, so he didn't ask.

The movie screen was being lowered, sterilized ear-sets were being distributed.

Did Wiley want a brandy or some other after-dinner drink before the movie began? He ordered a B&B. Strega for Mrs. Gimble.

"Where, exactly, are you headed?" she asked.

"Nowhere."

"Just wandering?"

"Just wandering."

"Then, heavens, why don't you consider coming to the party? I can arrange it with Argenti. And I'm sure you'll fit right in."

4 >>>

The flight was on time until it reached Mexico City, where it was ordered into a holding pattern for an hour. Air traffic was a chronic problem there because so many national flights went in and out of Benito Juárez International Airport.

At Immigration Wiley was asked how long he intended to stay in Mexico.

Maybe a lifetime, he thought. "Maybe a month," he said.

He got through customs quickly and was fought over by three porters who must have sensed he would overtip in U.S. money. He did. Almost twice too much per bag, but it seemed cheap enough to him, and he was glad to be led straight out of the terminal to a street-level taxi stand.

On the way into town a change came over him. He stopped looking out, slouched down, the tip of his spine on the edge of the seat, chin to chest. Why was he so suddenly depressed, feeling out of place? Because he was alone now, with no fellow passengers or anything to distract him? Whatever, it had caught up with him all at once.

He'd told the driver the Hotel del Paseo. Other than the Hilton and the El Presidente, the del Paseo was the only hotel he knew in the city. A girl he'd dated in '72 and '73 had praised the place after staying there a week while doing fashion photos. It would be too expensive for him to stay there permanently. First thing tomorrow he'd go looking for an apartment. He'd keep to his allowance of ten dollars a day. That First Class fare had cost him five days' allowance, and this taxi . . . he should have taken a bus, but what the hell.

They were coming into the city on Avenida Santa Teresa de Mier and, after a couple of sharp rights, reached the Paseo de la Reforma. Wide straight street, tall new buildings, reflections patterning across steel and glass, slick storefronts, bars, restaurants, neon signs contending for attention, the competitive traffic and its fumes.

The taxi pulled up at the entrance of the Hotel del Paseo. Wiley and his three pieces of luggage were deposited on the sidewalk.

The cab driver was waiting to be paid.

The doorman was expecting his tip.

The porter was ready to take the bags in.

Wiley hesitated. He glanced around and upward. He closed his eyes for a moment, listened, and knew he could just as well have been in New York. He'd only traded city for city, one milieu for another.

But he wasn't in the trap yet, not all the way.

He slapped dollar tips into the hands of the doorman and the porter, had his luggage put back in the cab, got in, and when the cab was under way, he let out a deep breath, as though he'd just experienced a very close call.

There was an 11:40 plane to Guadalajara. According to the map of Mexico Wiley had bought at the airport, that was as close as he could get.

The intercity flight was a test of nerves and plane. Immediately upon takeoff, the DC-9 was put into as steep a climb as it could tolerate. The cabin pressure had to catch up with the altitude. At twenty-five thousand feet the jet leveled off so abruptly that stomachs lurched upward against hearts and throats.

Wiley glanced around at the other passengers. They all appeared to be Mexicans, and completely unconcerned. This was a normal flight. After about a half hour the plane began its descent. It did not go into a nice long, comfortable glide pattern but, as though it had only this one chance to land, nosed down into what was practically a dive. Again the pressure and the altitude didn't match. Wiley's ears were full. Sharp pains needled his eye sockets as his sinuses reacted. The DC-9 pulled out of it abruptly, causing everyone to feel for a few moments as though their bowels were loaded with lead. But the landing was smooth, perfect.

In Guadalajara, Wiley got a room with bath for twelve dollars. By then it was close to two. He ordered up three bottles of *cerveza* Carta Blanca, uncapped one and gulped it while, with jacket and shoes off, he lay on the bed in the near-dark. He didn't think he was sleepy, his mind was racing; possibly it would be a sleepless night. The beer tasted especially good. Great beer in Mexico. Maybe he should call for a couple more before the bar closed. That was his last thought before his eyes closed for the night.

He slept, despite his trousers binding his crotch and his shirt cutting him at the underarms, for six hours. He got up feeling weary, heavy-headed, and knew himself well enough to know it wasn't really tiredness. Yesterday had been so bad.

He dragged himself through a shower and shave, put on a change of clothes. As an afterthought he shoved the two unopened bottles of beer into one of his bags, making a point, albeit small, of his resolve to be frugal.

Instead of breakfasting at the hotel, he checked out, asked directions and walked. On the way, still in a sort of funk, he stopped in at a bank to exchange 100 dollars for 1249 pesos. Then, at an ordinary restaurant, a narrow but clean place, he sat at a counter for tortillas and eggs over easy. He had difficulty explaining "over easy" to the waiter, and the eggs arrived mauled and overdone. He pumped some runny ketchup-looking sauce on them and ate quickly. At once he realized the sauce was hot, but not until after he'd cleaned his plate did he really start to radiate inside. Each breath he took only seemed to fan that inner flame. No amount of water would extinguish it.

One good thing—it had lifted him out of that funk.

At a brisker pace now, he walked to Avenida Niños Héroes, found number 942-A, the Avis office. A choice of a Ford Galaxy at 260 pesos a day, 162 centavos per kilometer, or a Volkswagen at 150 pesos a day, 125 centavos per kilometer. He preferred cars with power (had once temporarily owned a Porsche Carrera), but signed up for the Volks, using his Bank-Americard and wondering how long it would take before the bill caught up with him. And where.

He drove back to the hotel, picked up his bags, and was on his way. A five-hour drive ahead. It felt better to be going somewhere.

Route 80 was straight enough so he didn't have to keep his mind entirely on it. He thought of his immediate prospects. At the least he was in for a week of plenty with the rest of the freeloaders. Then there was the chance that, while mingling, a business opportunity of some sort would present itself. Maybe

someone such as Mr. Gimble would like his style and make
him an offer. More likely, though, it would be someone like
Mrs. Gimble. What the hell was the difference? Big business
had been buying his looks for years. He ought to be used to
being used.

Fortune hunter.

Sure, why not?

He'd charm the pants off her, whoever she was. She'd be
divorced, probably, or wealthy in her own right. He wouldn't
go for anyone married; trouble enough without that. She'd be
forty maybe, no more than fifty. Attractive, once a great
beauty and still attractive. An intelligent, generous person. He
wouldn't try to fool her. After the preliminaries, but before
getting into anything too much, he'd lay it on the line to her,
make a deal. It probably happened all the time. And, actually,
his being new at it was an advantage.

The other side of his thoughts wanted to know if he'd come
to *that*.

Evasively, he took interest in the scenery, noticed he was
passing close by Lake Chapala, the place D. H. Lawrence
wrote about. Along the way, towns such as Cocula, Tecalitlán,
and others so small he didn't get their names. The countryside
was tropical but in its dry season. Still green, however, always
green. He must have passed a thousand people on burros. And,
it seemed, just as many churches. He was impatient with the
Volks. He started humming and then singing. Often he did that
when he was driving alone, sang right out full, trying for
perfection as though he were a performer.

For once in my life . . .

He didn't remember all the words, dah-dee-dahed some of the
lines:

> *For once I can say*
> *This is mine, you can't take it.*
> *Long as I know I got love,*
> *I can make it.*
> *For once in my life,*
> *I have someone who needs me.*

A sign pointing off to the left said Purificación—15 Km.

Maybe that was where he should go. Get purified. He'd bet it
was really a scroungy little town. The worst.

A few miles farther on, the air got heavier and cooler and
smelled of the sea. He let up on the gas pedal, only to stomp
back down on it, and the Volks kept running as though it were
scared. Route 80 ended when it reached the Pacific, joined
Route 200 that ran down the coast from Puerto Vallarta. Wiley
turned left, headed south, had only about forty more miles to
go, with the ocean now on the right to keep him company. He
was thirsty and hungry, but he'd wait.

There was a hitchhiker at the roadside, wearing a cardboard
sign in front: LAS HADAS, in handprinted red letters. A lean
young fellow, Wiley thought as he went by, a gringo, probably
a migrant American dope smoker from the looks of him: Cas-
tro-type field cap with a wide beak, huge dark glasses, navy
surplus blue chambray shirt, baggy cotton twill trousers tied at
the ankles, green-striped tennis shoes, and a khaki duffel bag.

Wiley had no qualms, really, about picking up someone like
that. He'd done plenty of thumbing around in his day. They'd
called it "bumming" then. It was just that he wasn't in the
mood for talk. Or maybe he was.

He slammed on the brakes, began backing up. The hitchhiker ran for the car. In the rearview mirror Wiley saw that
there was something not quite right about the hitchhiker's way
of running, sort of mincy. Oh, well, too late now.

The duffel bag was being thrown in back.

The hitchhiker was getting in, smiling, saying "Thanks."

Wiley tried to hide his surprise with activity, got the Volks
in gear, and lighted a cigarette.

The hitchhiker took off the sign. Her chambray shirt was
unbuttoned three down.

She took off the Fidel cap and shook down her hair. It was
healthy thick, to her shoulders, a rich brown shade with cop-
pery glints.

She took off the sunglasses, used index finger and thumb to
massage where they had made pressure marks on the bridge of
her nose. Her eyes were an unusual blue, deep and at the same
time bright and textured like lapis lazuli.

For a mile, two, three she didn't say anything, kept her eyes
straight ahead, and although she was in profile to Wiley, he
believed she knew he was sizing her up.

She was in her late twenties, could look younger if she

wanted. Very pretty, fine-featured, with a well-defined chin
and cheekbones and a nearly perfect nose. Her mouth had just
a trace of a natural moue to it, so it was never slack or without
expression. No makeup. An immaculate, well-sunned complexion. At first Wiley thought her eyelashes, upper and lower,
were too long and thick to be true; on second glance he believed them. He also stole a glance at her neck, the long line of
her throat, the leanness of her wrists and bare ankles. Beneath
those floppy trousers would be excellent legs.

Wiley mentally pinched himself.

Incredible. There she'd been, this lovely creature, standing
on the roadside, miles from anywhere, halfway down the coast
of Mexico. Asking for a ride. And he'd almost passed her by.
Almost. Maybe his luck was changing. He wished she'd say
something. He waited a while longer before asking, "Where
you coming from?"

"Puerto Vallarta."

"What's up there?"

"It's just a place."

"Aren't you afraid to be hitching around alone?"

"No." Definitely.

"I thought you were a guy."

"You can still think so."

A cold one, Wiley thought. That was all right. He wasn't
feeling any too warm toward the opposite sex either. He
lighted another cigarette from the stub of the one he'd been
smoking. She glanced at the cigarette, disapproving.

He took a deep drag.

She sighed tolerance.

He noticed she had a small drawstring leather pouch tied to
her belt. For safekeeping pesos or possibly a stash. It appeared
fat, heavy.

"Your car?" she asked.

"A rental."

"I thought so."

"Why?"

"People usually match their cars. You and this one don't go
together."

"Right now we do."

If she asked what he meant by that, he was ready to tell her
some about himself and his circumstances. He needed ventilation.

She closed her eyes, lowered her head, chin to chest.

Taking a nap? No one could just drop off like that, Wiley thought. She was shutting him out. He could feel it. She was probably the sort who never got beyond herself. To hell with her. He watched the countryside, hummed fragments of another song. But several times he had to hold himself in check from saying such things as "Hey, look at those burros" or "That cloud formation over there looks like a man with a hat on" or "You have lovely hands." Her hands in her lap lay lightly one upon the other, palms up.

Wiley wished he had something special to place in her hand, to surprise her with a tribute, from stranger to stranger, something of exceptional value that would awaken her, and from then on she would be whatever he ever wanted a woman to be, even if only for the next thirty miles.

He hummed louder.

She licked her lips.

He kept on humming.

She kept her eyes closed but smiled.

Next thing she was kneeling on the seat, reaching back for her duffel bag and saying, "I'm Lillian Holbrook."

He told her his name. For some reason it sounded a little better to him.

"What do you like to be called?" she asked.

"Anything but Joseph."

"I hate Lil, always reminds me of a Hong Kong hooker." She removed a canteen from the duffel bag. "Want some water?"

She unscrewed the cap, and he took a swig. Then she took a swig, and it occurred to Wiley that her lips were touching where his had touched. It wasn't like him to have such a thought. He was probably suffering some kind of shock from yesterday.

"In case you're wondering about this water, it's bottled, Evian. Guaranteed not to contain any little Mexican trotting bugs. Are you hungry?"

He wasn't sure. He related his breakfast experience, the hot sauce.

She told him: "In Mexico I make it a rule never to eat anything red, not even if it looks like cherry ice cream. I still get fooled, but it's about ninety percent insurance."

He decided he was hungry.

She took a papaya from her duffel bag. And a knife. She pressed on its handle to make a six-inch blade snap out. "Switchblades are illegal in the United States," she said.

"I know."

"Down here you can buy them anywhere. With a regular kind of knife I always break my nails trying to pull the blade open."

There was an incongruity to seeing her with the knife in hand. It was a weapon, not a utensil.

She sliced the papaya in half.

"Look." She held up half for him to see its inner perfection. Black seeds like shiny buckshot in a precise arrangement against the vivid yellow flesh of the fruit.

"A shame to disturb it," she said. "Want to just look at it a while?"

"Sure."

She studied the papaya halves, apparently fascinated by how beautiful and exactly alike they were. When she held them up for him to appreciate, it seemed she was being generous.

Wiley's stomach growled.

She suggested they eat one half and admire the other. She scraped the seeds out and cut a chunk that she offered to Wiley on the point of the knife. He had to be careful. Hit a pothole he'd lose his tongue.

The papaya was bland, disappointing. No temptation to eat the other half. She placed it on the dashboard, propped against the windshield on its side like an exhibit.

"What will you do in Las Hadas?" he asked.

"I'll find something."

"Does that mean you'll be hunting?"

"I suppose. How about you?"

"I've been invited."

"Really?"

"In a roundabout way."

She nodded as though she knew exactly what that meant.

Wiley decided it would be best if he told her the truth, no matter what. A good clean start, he'd keep it that way. He told her about Mrs. Gimble. He didn't mention the new ambitions that lady and Las Hadas had brought out in him. Didn't have to.

"There'll be a lot of money there," Lillian said.

"Probably."

"For sure. A wonderful unhappy hunting ground." She beamed.

"Are you hoping to hit it rich?"

"Aren't you?"

"It never occurred to me," he said.

"Bullshit."

"Why bullshit?"

"You're attractive . . . no, that's a self-conscious understatement. You're extremely attractive and even without trying you have a sort of charm about you. That's exactly it, you're charming. And here you are on your way to the gold mine in a rented VW."

"You were hitchhiking."

She thought about that. "I'm not denying anything."

"Neither am I."

"So, as it turns out, we're both going to Las Hadas to take care of business."

"Okay, Lil."

"Not that kind of business."

"That's what it gets to eventually, doesn't it?"

She shrugged. "No less for you."

He was suddenly depressed again, further down than before, but now for an altogether different reason. Lillian. He had an impetuous notion to tell her to hell with Las Hadas, they could turn off before there or go on by. Together.

She seemed to sense his change in mood. "Don't worry about it," she said brightly. "It's a nice dishonorable profession."

They remained silent for a while. He lighted another cigarette, and she returned to looking straight ahead. The road was just barely wide enough, had narrow soft shoulders that dropped off into ditches on each side. A line of palms grew along there, and many of another kind of tree.

"Those are cork trees," Lillian said.

"Most people think cork comes from the ocean."

"And jellyfish come in flavors. . . ."

He didn't even smile.

"You're a mopish son of a bitch," she said.

She was right, he thought, laugh it up.

He told an off-color joke, his all-time best.

She laughed so hard she got a side pain. Contagious laughter. He could hardly steer. They both ended up weak and teary-eyed.

They passed through a town. No sign of its name. It was merely a couple of small houses, a *cantina*, and, of course, a church. Not a person in sight, nothing moving until the speed of the VW caused some chickens to flutter up.

A half mile farther down the road a black car, a six-year-old Dodge, overtook the VW, came alongside. It was so caked with dust that the insignia and the word *Policia* were hardly visible on its door.

Wiley pulled over. The police car pulled up in front.

"Now we'll find out who you really are," Lillian quipped.

Wiley had lost his humor. He got a flash of himself in a small-town Mexican jail, eating *cucaracha* sandwiches. He'd heard they locked you up for hardly any reason and forgot which key. He hoped to Christ it wasn't a stash of grass Lillian had in that drawstring pouch.

Two policemen were coming toward the car. They looked very much alike, narrow-shouldered and fat-waisted. Both were out of shape, but they were wearing revolvers. In the States, as a measure of caution, one would have remained in the police car, Wiley thought. Why not here?

"*Buenos días, señor.*"

"*Buenos días.*"

One of the policemen had collar burn, the skin of his neck inflamed, a pimply rash. The other had hair growing out of his ears.

Sore Neck asked to see Wiley's driver's license.

Wiley handed it out along with his passport.

Lillian was amused.

Wiley hoped the policemen didn't notice.

"*La velocidad máxima es cincuenta kilómetros,*" Sore Neck said.

Wiley gave the excuse that he hadn't seen any road signs saying fifty was the limit.

"The wind blows them down," Sore Neck said.

Wiley doubted that.

Hairy Ears went around the VW, thumping on it with the heel of his fist as though searching for a secret compartment. Meanwhile Sore Neck took another look at Wiley's license and passport. And another.

Lillian began clicking her teeth.

Hairy Ears got down and examined the VW underneath.

"*Muy malo, señor*," Sore Neck said, his lower lip over his upper.

It seemed to Wiley that Sore Neck was trying to appear grim. Trying.

Lillian was still clicking her teeth. Better that than an offending laugh, Wiley thought.

The two policemen stood side by side, their heads cocked a little, looking at Wiley with what he translated as a trace of expectancy.

Lillian clicked some more and nudged Wiley.

He thought he heard her whisper: "Hundred pesos."

Did he dare? For trying to bribe an official, they might give him four life sentences to be served consecutively. He smiled weakly at the policemen.

They didn't smile back.

He took out 100 pesos.

"Each," Lillian whispered.

He held his breath as he extended the two 100-peso notes out the window.

Sore Neck took his. Hairy Ears took his. All smiles now.

Hairy Ears said the VW was leaking a little brake fluid underneath but—thumping on the fender—it was a good car.

Everyone said *gracias* five or six times.

Afterward, when they were under way again, Wiley asked Lillian why all that clattering of teeth?

"I thought you'd get it."

"Get what?"

"*La mordida.*"

"The bite?"

"They were only putting the bite on you. They count on it as though it were part of their salary. Now they'll go back to the cantina, stand drinks for everybody and probably won't stop anyone else for at least three or four hours."

"For a while there I thought maybe that's how you got when you got nervous, or you'd suddenly developed an awful chill."

"You're not as sharp as I thought."

"How come you know so much about Mexico?"

"I've been here," she said ambiguously. "Besides, didn't it give you a sense of power—not a big one, but at least a taste—buying those policemen off like that?"

"No," Wiley replied too quickly.

Lillian's glance told him she knew better.

"About ten miles to go," he said.

It was midafternoon. The hottest part of the day was over, but the temperature was still hanging near ninety.

"We're practically there," he said.

They passed a man on a burro, slouched, hat down over his eyes, arms limp as though riding asleep. A woman, walking behind, had hold of the burro's tail.

Lillian grunted.

"Only fifteen minutes more," Wiley said.

"We might stop for a swim," she said, matter of fact.

It was like a reprieve, but he said, "Maybe you want to wait until we get there. I mean, it'll be more convenient and everything, won't it?" Say no, he said inside, say absolutely not.

"Probably," she said.

"Yeah."

"But then there'll be all that bother with getting settled in first . . . and everything."

At that point the highway didn't run right along the ocean because the coastline jutted out. Wiley slowed the Volks, found a side road. It was overgrown and rutted, but it took them within a few feet of the beach. Fine white sand, not a mark on it except tiny starlike tracks of birds. The Pacific licked up, slicked and darkened, then slid back into itself. On the shoulder of the beach was the deposit line, where shells and other little sea things had been washed up.

Lillian found a driftwood stick.

She removed her shoes, trousers, and shirt. All she had on then was a pair of white bikini underpants. She was neither shy nor shameless. Her attitude was one of unconforming independence, a confidence in herself that included her body. Hers was hers. Provocation wasn't her intention, or at least it wasn't uppermost in her mind.

Wiley managed not to look at her as she undressed, told himself he'd see her soon enough. He kept his undershorts on. He looked up to see her, faced away, walking toward the water. She had the stick in hand. She used it to scratch a line in the sand from the shoulder of the beach all the way to the reach of the surf.

She turned, told him, "That side of the line is your beach. This side is mine."

Wiley nodded.

This was the first time he'd stood beside her. She was taller than he'd thought. About five-eight barefoot.

"And, remember, the line goes out for a long ways," as she indicated the sea.

Wiley tried not to look directly at her breasts. Her skin was equally suntanned there. Pink nipples. He'd never known a brunette with such pink nipples. It made them look innocent, like the tips of a baby's fingers.

She strode to the water. It came to meet her. She went right in, swam straight out until she was over her head, had to tread. She looked back to the beach. Wiley was still standing there.

"Can't you swim?" she shouted.

He didn't reply. He'd been caught up by the sight of her.

"At least you can wade."

He ran into the surf, dove in and swam to within twenty feet of her. They treaded and swam and floated, keeping their distance.

"You're a good swimmer," she said.

"I guess."

They swam to shore, dropped onto the sand, respecting the line she had drawn between them. She lay prone, her position like an embrace, one leg straight, the other angled up. Her arms and hands seemed to be hugging the warm sand, while one cheek rested upon it. She was looking at Wiley.

He lay face up, his forearm shading his eyes. He got a Jennifer thought—but only a tiny one. Surprising how much she was reduced now, to practically nothing, when just yesterday she had been so magnified. He blinked. Jennifer had become that easy to erase.

This woman, Lillian, Wiley thought, he had known her little more than an hour and the effect she was having on him was way out of honest proportion. He was just lonely, raw lonely, and badly in need of a refill of self-assurance. He wanted to cross the line, hold her, press full length against her, arouse her with his arousal, be mouth to mouth with her. . . . Perhaps not take it all the way, just to know the willingness was there. . . . It meant nothing really. By tomorrow he would see her differently. Timing was everything. She had just happened into his rawest moment.

He probably wouldn't be seeing much of her once they got to Las Hadas. So, he might as well see as much as he could of her now. He stopped stealing, looked directly at her, wherever he wanted. Her, rolling over onto her back now, with her hipbones sharply defined and her stomach concave. Sand on her skin. It seemed cruel on her breasts, the sand. Through her soaked panties he could see the dark triangle.

"How long have you been a mercenary?" she asked.

Mercenary? It took him a moment to get it.

"Since yesterday."

She thought he was being facetious.

She told him: "I might be able to help you in Las Hadas. Listen around, talk you up, steer some likely ones your way."

"You'd expect me to return the favor, of course."

He took her silence to mean yes. He detested the idea.

She sat up. "I suppose you know women are going for much younger men these days. Not even men, as a matter of fact. Boys. Seventeen-, eighteen-year-olds." She shrugged, looked off down the beach, so he couldn't see her grin. "I understand it's a matter of stamina."

"Nothing beats experience."

"Still, there's a lot to be said for naîveté." She swished her hair back and forth so it could dry faster. "It's refreshing, ego-nourishing. It's . . ."

"Too fast and fumbly."

She grinned right at him, a crooked grin, slightly higher on the left. The unevenness didn't show when she laughed, only when she grinned. It gave her left cheek a commalike dimple, but it also conveyed the impression that she was a bit of a wiseass.

"You'll do all right," she told him. "You have a good body."

5 ⤳⤳⤳

Las Hadas.

Wiley had expected it to be the sort of resort hotel that qualified for its *deluxe* designation by being only slightly cleaner, roomier, better furnished and more dependably staffed than ordinary.

Not so.

It was six hundred acres. A paradisaical village in itself, built from the ground up at a cost of 35 million. Dollars, not pesos. Situated on an easy slope at the merest indentation of coastline, it was protected by its own newly constructed breakwater. The quality of the original beach there would have been outstanding almost anywhere else in the world, but shiploads of even finer-grained, whiter sand had been brought in from Hawaii.

Two hundred white bungalows were placed modularly on and along the slope. Although they were clustered, they did not seem to be pushing one another for space. There was privacy and, at the same time, an intimacy created by connecting walls, terraces, and little secret walkways.

The architectural style was difficult to define, simply because, as pure and clean as it appeared, it was such a concoction. Part Monte Carlo, part Alexandria, some Mexican pueblo, of course, but mainly Moorish—like a mazy section of Marrakesh minus the babble and beggars. Minarets, onion-shaped spires, winding-staired towers, cupolas, gazebos, lattices, all sorts of twists and turns and surprising curlicues. As though the designer, given freedom to express any caprice, had put whimsy to service.

There were five restaurants, six bars, three nightclubs, eight tennis courts, numerous shops, a golf course, a cinema, and, for sudden pangs of piety or emergency expiations, a chapel.

A deep-water marina accommodated those who preferred to arrive privately by sea.

Three swimming pools. One was the largest in Mexico, perhaps in the world. Surely the most impressive. Right at beach-side, a free-form, lagoonlike pool holding two million liters of water that was purified twice and softened three times daily. So large a pool it was an obstacle. A bridge of woven rope was suspended across its middle to avoid the long walk around.

Cars were not permitted beyond the main entrance.

That rule was actually a convenience for Wiley, who felt self-conscious about the VW. Just ahead, a dark gray Daimler limousine was cruising in to unload, and ahead of that on the circular drive was a black Mercedes 600. All sorts of large, costly cars idled near the entrance and were parked around, their substantial composure hyphenated here and there by the incorrigible colors and lines of the smaller expensive cars such as Ferrari Dinos, Lotus Elites, Excaliburs and Maserati Boras. Off to the right of the entrance, parked in precise order like a fleet, were seven Bentley sedans, seven exactly alike, white with a family crest intricately handpainted on the left front door panel. The crest of Argenti.

Wiley drove past, around the drive and back out. No need to start with such a handicap. Lillian agreed. He parked the car well out of notice on the side road. They had to walk nearly a quarter mile. Lillian helped by carrying the smallest, lightest piece of Wiley's luggage.

As they neared the entrance Wiley hesitated to study the situation. New arrivals were getting all the attention. He spotted a this-year's Rolls Royce Corniche convertible, a deep-blue seventy-thousand-dollar beauty, parked in perfect position almost opposite the entrance.

He went to it, approaching from the blind side. Lillian followed. The car wasn't locked. Wiley tossed the baggage in the back, got in and climbed over into the driver's seat. Lillian got in and, following Wiley's instructions, quietly closed the door.

The key was in the ignition.

Wiley started the car up, opened the window and pressed the horn. Three brief imperative honks, a shout, then three more honks that even the busiest porters could not disregard.

Wiley got out of the Corniche. Stood there beside it. He didn't have to resort to words. His air conveyed impatience, and three porters hurried toward the car to look after the baggage as Wiley and Lillian strolled on in.

The reception area was crowded. About a hundred people. Many greats had arrived at once, and evidently not everything had been well enough planned in advance. There was confusion about where to put who. The manager was trying to please and placate just about everyone, because just about everyone was important and used to being treated accordingly. Adding to the disorder, the guests were greeting and gushing all over one another, with a lot of double cheek-kissing and insincere but enthusiastic embracing.

There they were, the powerful and the spoiled, the ones who enjoyed making news. Flaunting, narcissistic, they were already forming new erotic alliances with their eyes, with no more than a flick of a glance, agreeing.

There was a delicate intensity about most of the men, like tightrope walkers who out of habit were unable to take a solid stance. The women wore their assertiveness as though it were an accessory. They were quite blunt, flourishing their mental competence and physical advantages. Thus, an atmosphere of bisexuality prevailed. Their clothes, gestures, the quick-change artistry of their facial expressions and manner of speaking all contributed. Sexual chameleons. But not altogether evil. It was more a social way. *Au courant* to look in both directions for pleasure, if only for appearance—to keep in, not to be left out. Worst of all was to have a reputation for being dull.

Present also were the usual camp followers. A few leading players from the movies, strangers with familiar faces, some overused, passé. Along with other types of entertainers—sharp wits, sharp tongues, atrocious characters, bizarre personalities, needed for perverse amusement, suffering by comparison, making the powerful and beautiful appreciate themselves all the more.

Wiley felt out of place. If he fit in, as Mrs. Gimble had predicted, he had to do some serious self-reappraising, he thought. He turned to speak to Lillian.

She wasn't there.

She'd slipped away, nowhere in sight. Probably, Wiley decided, she didn't want to be seen with him because that would cramp her ambitions. Couldn't blame her. But at least she could have said good-bye, thanks for the lift, or anything.

What now? Wiley wondered. Ask for Mrs. Gimble? She was his only in, had offered to arrange things with what's-his-

name . . . Argenti. However, that would mean getting into the
battle going on at the reception desk. He was there on such a
flimsy invitation.

He spotted a porter.

He remembered *la mordida*, grabbed the porter's arm, said
"Por favor" and slipped him 600 pesos. Fifty dollars. Extravagant, but worth it if it worked.

The porter understood the money. He took Wiley's luggage
and provided interference through the crowd, across the reception area and outside to a courtyard, where there was an electric cart with a white awning top. Luggage and Wiley aboard,
the porter started the cart and steered it down the cobblestone
street.

"What number is your bungalow, *señor*?"

First to Wiley's mind came eleven. He skipped from it to
thirty, then to seventy-five, and told the porter, "Seventy-
eight."

The porter nodded and said, as though he'd heard, "One-
fourteen."

Wiley confirmed that and sat back to enjoy the ride. Along
the way they passed people. Several said hello because he
appeared to be someone they should know, or wanted to. Two
Mrs. Gimble types gave him just enough of an eye, and a little
farther on, so did a man and a woman together.

No sign of Lillian.

Wiley thought perhaps she'd been ejected. If so, what was
he doing there? His concern was canceled by recalling how
efficient she'd been.

The cart turned left, climbed up a narrower street, then right
for a short distance. It stopped at the foot of a flight of wide
white stairs that led to a landing. A heavy white door was
discreetly numbered *114*. The porter used his passkey. He
placed the luggage inside, said *"Muchas gracias"* twice and
departed.

It was a large square room, about twenty by twenty, with a
high, domed ceiling. White splashed sparingly with yellow,
green, blue. The floor was white marble, strategically softened
with thick curly-wool rugs, also white. Two facing sofas and a
matching chair were covered in a natural muslin-like linen that
incorporated an almost indiscernible blue stripe. On a table of
inch-thick milk glass was a silver salver of fruit, next to the
latest issues of *Vogue* and *Réalités*, next to a cut-crystal con-

tainer of Dunhill cigarettes, next to a humidor containing a dozen Havanas.

Off to one side was a small, wet bar, already well stocked, including two bottles of Tattinger '62.

Three oil paintings and two pen sketches on the walls. Well done, certainly of value. Wiley went up close to one, a small boldly stroked landscape. It was just ordinarily hung with wire. He remembered his hotel in Acapulco had horrible lithographs screwed to the walls. Didn't rich people steal? Or perhaps when they did, it was never mentioned, merely added to the bill. Smart way to sell paintings, Wiley thought.

It occurred to him there was no bed. Were the sofas convertible? That didn't seem in keeping.

Two doors on the interior wall. One was a closet. The other would surely be the bath. However, Wiley discovered it opened into another room, the bedroom, nearly as large a room as the first and just as tastefully appointed. The bed was king-size. Fresh-cut flowers were on the side table by a window. And there was the bath, all marble and chrome, with a tub large enough for two or even three, depending.

Sweet Jesus, he'd appropriated a suite. He would have settled for a reasonably comfortable room. According to law, the price tag had to be somewhere. Wiley found it, practically hidden on the inside frame of a closet door.

Three thousand seven hundred fifty pesos per day.

Three hundred dollars a day.

His next thought was to run, get out.

But he didn't want to, really. Besides, 114 had been the porter's choice. The porter had to know something. Yes, he definitely should trust the porter.

He unpacked, undressed, took a shower to wash away the sand and seawater film left from that swim with Lillian. Washing her away, he thought, and when he was rubbing dry with a huge yellow-striped towel, his mind was free of her. Next moment, however, she jumped back in full force. Time would help. By tomorrow, maybe even by later that night, she'd be vague, in proper perspective.

As for now, he was hungry. That half of a half of a papaya hadn't been much to go on. Should he push his luck as far as room service?

He called and asked what they had to offer. It was only six o'clock. Did he want an early dinner or only something to tide him over? They would send him a menu. No, he'd tell them what he wanted, and they could tell him what they didn't have. He'd start with some smoked Scottish salmon. Make that a double order. Then some soup, say, cream of avocado. Steamed mussels with butter sauce. Roast rack of lamb, charred outside, pink in the middle; cottage-fried potatoes, and arugola and endive salad. He'd do his own oil-and-vinegar dressing. Chocolate mousse for dessert and, as an afterthought, an assortment of cheeses, especially Brie. Coffee, of course. And a carton of Camels.

"*Sí, señor*."

Maybe the guy hadn't understood a word, Wiley thought. Anyway, he'd already clicked off.

Wearing only a towel, Wiley poured a vodka on the rocks and lighted a cigarette. He took it out onto the walled terrace that went with the suite. He looked down on the tops of other bungalows and out to sea. The water was calming. The sun was becoming yellower, headed toward sinking. Jasmine contributed to the air.

A fragment of laughter, a heart-shaped sound, came from somewhere nearby.

Wiley pulled hard on his drink, felt it hit inside and spread, like an injection. He went back to the living room, sat on the couch. He was paging through *Réalités*—detesting the fact that a pair of Jacob chairs that no one would ever sit on had sold for eighteen thousand dollars at the Hôtel Drouot auction on October 3, 1976—when he heard someone at the front door.

Room service?

Couldn't be. Too soon.

Keys in the lock.

A porter, a different one, entered carrying luggage. Followed in by a man of about forty. A lean man in a gray business suit, white shirt, gray silk tie. Evidently from somewhere north because he had a topcoat over his arm, a gray homburg and a black Hermès attaché case in hand.

Wiley, literally caught with his pants down, peered over the back of the sofa. He'd better take the offensive, could always retreat. "What's this?" he asked, acting rankled.

"I'm terribly sorry. I thought this was my suite," the man in gray said. He was as reticent and his voice as colorless as his appearance. He introduced himself: Arnold Prentiss, an American.

"There must be some mistake," Wiley told him.

"My mistake," Prentiss said. "I've never seen such organized confusion."

The porter examined the key that was stamped *114*.

Wiley told the porter, "Find Mr. Prentiss another suite."

"*Sí señor.*"

"That's the best solution, don't you think?"

Prentiss agreed. He apologized for the disturbance.

When they were gone, Wiley went in the bathroom, sprayed on some underarm antiperspirant, gazed into the mirror.

Look at me looking at me, he thought solemnly, living on the edge, getting by on pure nerve. It certainly was no ballroom dance. He grinned a sardonic sorry-for-himself sort of grin. It changed, grew into an I-don't-give-a-shit smile. Looking on the brighter side, he *was* having a hell of a lot of fun.

One thing, though, he wished he'd thought to get the 114 key from the porter. He didn't want to risk asking for one at the front desk.

Dinner arrived. He had it served on the terrace. He'd forgotten to order wine, sent the waiter back for a bottle of Mouton-Rothschild '67. In the dimming light he ate slowly, enjoying every mouthful, treating himself. He noticed the orange and red bougainvillea against the white wall, then saw it lose color. The waiter had lighted candles. It was almost pleasant to eat alone.

The phone rang. Like an alarm.

He let it ring, and finally it stopped.

It rang again.

On impulse he went in and answered it. No response. Someone was on the other end; he could hear breathing. Then whoever it was clicked off.

Wrong number, Wiley decided. It gave him an idea, a long shot. He got the hotel operator on the phone. Was there a Miss Holbrook registered, Miss Lillian Holbrook? Without hesitation, the operator said Miss Holbrook was in bungalow 11.

He'd certainly been right about her being able to take care of herself. Should he give her a call? Better yet, he'd make it face to face.

He dressed, put on a pair of straight-legged jeans, French-made, and a cream-colored pure-silk shirt. The jeans fit so snugly that their pockets were practically useless. Nowhere for him to carry his money. One hundred and twenty brand-new hundred-dollar bills. He'd have to hide it somewhere in the suite. He recalled those American Express commercials against carrying cash. Every hiding place seemed obvious, because suddenly Mexican hotel maids were ingenious thieves.

The lamp. Big, fat, original ceramic lamp. He turned it over on its side, used the round end of a nail file to undo the screws that held its base. Because the money was new, it didn't make too thick a wad. It fit into the hollow of the base with room to spare. He replaced the base, straightened the lamp, and felt fairly secure about it.

Bungalow 11, Wiley found, was quite a ways over and higher up the slope. A choice location it shared with only one other bungalow. Those two bungalows were twice as large as any of the others. Wiley walked by it. The front was solid, no way of seeing in. He decided against going right up and ringing the bell. There was the distasteful but real possibility he'd be intruding upon a very personal moment.

Should he just leave be?

Along one side of the house was a narrow walkway, nearly concealed by bougainvillea. Wiley went down along the side. A high wall there went around the entire rear of the place, like a compound. The roof of the adjacent bungalow would help. He climbed a latticed inset to the roof. Now, just below him was the private terrace of bungalow 11, and across the way the bungalow itself, all the windows and doors wide open, lights on.

His eyes were like binoculars. His view of the living room featured a sweating silver champagne bucket with the cloth-wrapped neck of a bottle protruding. Layers of lazy smoke in the air. He heard a Janis Ian on the hi-fi. The window to the far left showed him the bedroom. The closet was open. An array of colors, clothes, dresses. Were those all hers?

Pale green in motion.

It was Lillian in an ankle-length strapless dress, with the skirt slit nearly to the hip on one side. A flowing, defining fabric. Wiley caught only a glimpse of her, but it was enough to cause him to clutch inside, a sensation that wasn't fright but similar. She was incredibly beautiful, wearing some makeup now, but still not much.

Wiley heard her, out of view, say: "How much did you lose?"

"Twenty thousand." A man's voice.

"Why don't you pay your bets?"

"Sometimes I forget, I have so much on my mind. You know how it is."

"But you're always right there when you win."

"A few thousand more or less matters to me?" He had an accent. "Anyway, instead of money, Lucio wanted me to settle in ponies for polo. I gave him four."

"The worst of your string, no doubt."

"I let him choose."

"Really?"

"I had faith in his poor judgment. Of course, he cheated himself miserably." He spoke with iambic exaggeration, up and down scale several times in one sentence. Obviously an Italian.

"That cigar is suffocating," Lillian complained.

The man now came into Wiley's view of the living room. He was about 210 or 220 pounds, four or five inches over six feet. Mixed black and gray hair, a short curly mass of it, and a matching full beard made his head seem abnormally large. A Herculean head. For the same reason his eyes appeared small, set deep in under bushy brows. With the beard it was difficult to see exactly where his mouth was when closed. Altogether, a powerful-looking man. He was wearing a double-breasted white dinner jacket, no tie, at least not at the moment. That bothered Wiley.

Now Lillian came into view.

"Put it out," she said.

"Why begrudge me such a small pleasure?" He tossed the cigar out the window onto the terrace, where it lay smoldering. "I'll do anything for you," he said.

"I'm sorry, Meno. I feel cranky tonight for some reason."

Meno. The name meant nothing to Wiley.

"Perhaps you do not want to be with me?"

"Perhaps."

"Am I not generous enough for you?"

"You're generous."

Meno embraced her from behind. "Be nice, my angel." He was the typical cooing Italian lover. "Be nice to me." One hand caressed her bare shoulder, the other went for her breast. She stepped away from him. He shrugged as though it was her loss.

She was gone from Wiley's sight, then suddenly she reappeared in the double doorway twenty feet away and gazed straight out. Wiley was taken by surprise. He ducked down a little late.

He heard her footsteps on the terra-cotta tiles of the terrace. One, two, three, four, pause.

"You really shouldn't buy me so many expensive things," she said.

"Why not?" Meno came out to her.

"Well, it is rather . . . embarrassing."

She sounded so obviously coy, Wiley thought.

"I want people to talk about us," Meno said. "It is good for my reputation."

"Your reputation is bad enough."

"I am a roué?"

"You are."

"I chase after beautiful women."

"You do."

"They chase after me."

"By the hundreds," she said.

"They are as forgotten as meals. You are the only . . ."

"We are going to dinner, aren't we?"

"I have a more appetizing suggestion."

"You always do." She added a little wicked laugh.

Wiley felt cheap and foolish. He wanted away from there. If he moved, they'd surely hear him. He pressed his fingers to his ears, closed his eyes, tried to think of some excuse for himself. To hell with it. He couldn't, wouldn't stay there another minute.

As noiselessly as possible, he crept across the roof, climbed down and walked away.

6 ⤳⤳⤳

To bed at ten, to sleep at half past three.

At four Wiley got another phone call. Again, no response to his hello and someone breathing on the other end of the line.

Another such call at six. Wiley told whoever it was to fuck off.

He got up at eight feeling as though he'd been on the phone all night. He decided on a walk before breakfast, took an apple from the salver and went out. A cloudless day, the sun so bright it was shining the blue out of most of the sky. He'd forgotten sunglasses. That was truly him, he thought, not programmed for sunglasses in December.

He walked down to the private beach. No one there yet, except hotel beach boys raking the sand and washing down the catamarans resting just above the surf line. No one at the lagoonlike swimming pool either. Cushions were being distributed for the sunners to come. From the bar, a circular thatched structure located in the center of the pool, came the clinking of glasses and bottles being made ready. Incongruous, a sort of sad sound at this hour.

Wiley walked along the quay of the marina. A number of good-sized boats were tied up. Two were especially impressive. The largest, about a 250-footer, had a sleek black hull and polished chrome fittings. On its stern was the name *Oscuro,* and beneath that, *Panama.* Moored next to it was a 200-or-so footer that sat lower in the water, had racier contours and, with its white hull fitted with brass, a more virtuous demeanor. It was called *Sea Cloud.* Its port of registry was also Panama.

As Wiley passed by the yachts, like anyone who'd never owned one, he wondered how it would be. He imagined himself coming topside in the morning, scanning the horizon, arbitrarily pointing out a direction and telling the captain,

"That way." He guessed the price of those largest two yachts. The black, five million easy. The white, perhaps a million less.

Wiley thought of the secondhand boat his father had recently bought, for a couple thousand, a 21-foot Bonanza cruiser he was overhauling, enjoying having that to do. For nearly three years now, Wiley's parents had lived on the Florida Keys just south of the seven-mile bridge near Bahia Honda. They had sent him photos of their mobile home that was really immobilized, with a yard and permanent fence around it. They liked it there, they said, and had made many new friends, also retired. Wiley had put off visiting them. Two months ago he'd sent for an offering brochure on a $300,000 home in Boca Raton.

He walked out on the breakwater, all the way to the tip. Removed his shirt and sat on a slanty rock just above the ocean. The water was deeper there, choppier, but he could still see bottom. Dark triangular shapes moving there, probably shadows. But no, they were darting and skimming slowly along. One came nearly to the surface, and Wiley saw what it was.

Diamond-shaped, about six feet across, with a whipping tail. A manta ray.

Mysterious creature. The way it looked, it had to be unfriendly. There were dozens of them. Interesting to watch. Every once in a while one would turn belly up, causing a flash of white. And also, every once in a while Wiley caught glimpses of sharks. Big ones. They hadn't been there at first. Had they come because they sensed his presence? He removed the apple from his pocket, shined it on the leg of his white duck trousers before taking a bite.

It was mealy. He tossed it into the ocean, half-expecting the mantas and sharks to fight over it. They ignored it. Evidently not vegetarians.

The sun felt beneficial, untightening his back and shoulders. He could see up the coast from there, quite a way. The beach reduced by distance to a white thread. Somewhere along there they'd swum yesterday. Probably Lillian got satisfaction from causing impact, he thought. The hit-and-run type. Lucky for him, it had been only a scrape, no damage suffered. She'd drawn the line, and he'd respected it. Dumb him.

He took his time walking back.

The pool area was getting crowded now. Cushions being plumped, chaises adjusted, towels spread, lotions applied. Waiters were serving coffee and croissants. Wiley sat at a table on the perimeter, in the shade, and faced away from the pool to escape the glare that had given him a headache. He assumed he could have breakfast there.

His name was called.

Mrs. Gimble was sitting up on a chaise about fifteen places from him. Wiley didn't recognize her immediately because she was stripped to a bikini. She beckoned him to her. He waved, smiled, was going to let that suffice but then decided better not alienate her.

"Mr. Wiley. What a delightful surprise."

He took her extended hand, anticipating a shake, but she drew him down to her for face kisses left and right. This transferred some sweet-smelling oil to his cheeks. He glanced around for Mr. Gimble, saw him a dozen places away, soaking up sun and the surrounding scenery.

"So, you decided to wander here," Mrs. Gimble beamed. "I hoped you would."

"A friend from Mexico City dragged me along."

"Oh?" She was visibly disappointed.

"An old school chum."

As soon as he said that, he wondered why. Was he really going to become a social opportunist? It had been merely a self-humoring notion yesterday. In the back of his mind (or was it the front now?) was the idea of using Mrs. Gimble to make some suitable acquaintances. He sat on the adjacent cushioned lounger. A waiter placed a tray on the nearby low table.

"Another cup and more coffee," Mrs. Gimble told the waiter, the tone of her voice altered for the waiter, close to a command.

Wiley thought how he'd hate being ordered around by her. Or by anyone, for that matter. "I was about to have breakfast," he said.

"I'll butter you a croissant."

She did so without waiting for him to say he wanted it. She also spread on a lot of raspberry jam, like an additional reward. He accepted it. For herself she poured coffee and laced it with a tumbler of cognac.

"I enjoy getting *up* in the morning," she said. "Join me?"

Why not? It wasn't his usual behavior, but he would have to go through plenty of changes. "I'll have something cold."

"Fruity?"

"Not this season."

She laughed rather automatically.

If being smartass glib was a prerequisite, it was going to be tough, he thought.

"Have a Coco-loco," she suggested.

"What's that?"

She ordered it.

A young girl passed close by, wearing only a bikini bottom. A slim, haughty creature about eighteen. She had a tiny gold loop hung from just below her left nipple.

Mrs. Gimble saw him notice. "They were doing that in St. Tropez a few summers ago, having their breasts pierced."

It looked painful to Wiley.

"That's the intention," Mrs. Gimble said. "Seems everything's getting more and more flavored with S and M."

His Coco-loco came. Gin, vodka and rum over shaved ice, served in a fresh coconut with a pair of straws sticking up like an antenna. Wiley took a long sip, managed to conceal a grimace.

"Have you ever done any acting?" Mrs. Gimble wanted to know.

"Why do you ask?"

"You have a most attractive squint, as though you were searching for something in the distance or scrutinizing everything, everyone around you. Most film stars have it, that same squinty intensity."

He was about to explain that this morning he'd accidentally broken both his pairs of sunglasses, but at that moment someone opened his eyes.

The man with the Herculean head, the one who had been with Lillian last night, was making his way through the sunbathers, stopping to speak and shake or kiss hands. There was an outgoing, robust quality about him. He seemed to know almost everyone. He had on only a pair of white sharkskin shorts, revealing how extremely hirsute he was, even across his shoulders and back. He came to Mrs. Gimble and Wiley.

"I assume you've met our host?" Mrs. Gimble said.

"Briefly," Wiley said. He shook hands with Meno Argenti.

"I don't recall," Argenti said. "Usually I'm excellent at remembering people, make a point of it."

"I'm Joseph Wiley." Said as though it should mean something.

"Oh, yes," Argenti said, faking it. "I beg your pardon. Enjoy yourselves." He went on a short way to greet a swarthy-complexioned bald man, who was with a pair of shapely young girls. Argenti called the man General. He flattered the girls, and they reacted as though they'd received gifts. They opened a leather case and began setting up a game of some sort. Argenti joined them. The moment he sat, a drink was at hand. The waiter had been following him around with it, just in case.

So that was Lillian's benefactor, Wiley thought. The big man, top man. Well, good for her.

Mrs. Gimble was on the subject of young women, girls, admitting what they offered but emphasizing how importunate they were, unappreciative and eventually, when one got right down to it, disappointing.

Wiley grunted agreeably, while actually paying attention to Argenti, guessing his age was at least fifty. Argenti and the General were talking about going fishing for marlin. Argenti was patronizing the General to some extent. He offered the use of his yacht. The General accepted. The two girls were overjoyed. The General pinched one of the girls on the inside of her thigh as high up as possible. The other one reached across for a cigarette and intentionally elbowed the General's groin. He too had an accent, but not Italian. Spanish was Wiley's guess, confirmed when he heard the man's last name: Botero. Wiley also heard mention of Lillian. He got only a fragment of it, something to do with that evening.

"My husband suffers from angina," Mrs. Gimble was saying. "Whenever things get too active, he gets pains in his chest."

"Looks healthy enough to me."

"He is really. I allow him the excuse." She did a know-what-I-mean glance. "He's playing cards or whatever with someone tonight, and I'm seeing a friend from Dallas. Perhaps you know her. Hendy?"

"Who?"

"Sarah Jean Hendricks. Why not have dinner with us?" As though it had just occurred to her.

"Don't mind if I do."

"I won't," she promised wryly.

At that moment Wiley caught sight of Lillian, on the opposite side of the pool. He watched her cross over via the suspended rope bridge. She had on a pale blue full-length overdress of crepe de chine, unbuttoned three down from the neck and seven up to the crotch. A matching visored scarf bound round and tied at the nape of her neck; a woven net bag slung over her shoulder. She said hellos and distributed some smiles along the way but didn't pause. It seemed to Wiley she was headed straight for him, coming to him. She stopped when she reached Argenti, who stood to greet her, kissed her a bit lingeringly on each cheek, cooed some compliments Italian-style and made sure he attracted attention. Wiley couldn't really blame Argenti for it. She was a beauty to be proud of.

"Oh, you're playing that silly game," she said.

"We've just begun," General Botero said. "You can catch up."

"No, thanks. It's even more boring than backgammon."

They were playing Petropolis, a wealthier version of Monopoly that involved joint ventures, conglomerates and just about every other aspect of international high finance. The Go point was, appropriately, the Geneva airport. The play money was in denominations of one thousand to one million. Instead of houses or hotels, a player tried to accumulate oil wells.

Lillian would settle for some sun. She removed her overdress. Her bathing suit was a white maillot, slick as a second skin, a stretchy material, opaque but so close to nothing it could be bunched up and concealed in a fist. She lay front down on a lounger, hands beneath her chin.

Wiley was right in her line of sight, no more than ten feet from her. She seemed to be gazing at him. She was. She smiled and said, "You're burning."

"I've been out since around nine."

Argenti glanced over to see whom she was talking to. If he was concerned, he didn't show it.

"Don't try for so much the first day," Lillian advised. Her eyes discreetly indicated Mrs. Gimble.

That lady gulped her laced coffee and acted detached.

"Maybe I already have," Wiley said.

"I doubt that." Lillian got up, picked up her overdress and told him, "Anyway, how about a drink in the shade?"

He followed her to a table beneath a nearby thatch-roofed

area. From where they were seated, Wiley could see Argenti in the background. And Mrs. Gimble. He'd been unintentionally rude to her, had forgotten his manners in his susceptibility to Lillian. He couldn't remember saying good-bye, vaguely remembered Mrs. Gimble saying "*A bientôt.*" Oh, well, he'd make it up to her somehow. As for Argenti . . . He was on Argenti's territory.

"He might be jealous," Wiley said.

"So?"

"I don't want to spoil what you've got going."

"You won't."

"Sure?"

"Positive."

A waiter came. Lillian ordered a plain Perrier with a squeeze of lime. Wiley started to order tequila on the rocks, which had just come to mind because it would sound good. Instead he told her, "I really don't want a drink. All I've had to eat so far today is one bite of a bad apple."

"Poor soul. Do you have Montezuma's revenge? Intestinal infection?"

"No."

"Then let's get you something."

She held out her hand for him to take, and they went from the pool area to an open-air restaurant situated on a ledge among the white bungalows. She had a fresh fruit salad topped with *crème fraîche*, while he had grilled lobster and a beer.

"I'm vegetarian," she said.

If that was true, she was certainly a recommendation for it, he thought.

"How's the hunting?" she asked.

"I'm not doing nearly as well as you."

"See that one?" She indicated a severe-looking middle-aged woman with thin lips and a sharp chin. "They say she collects Monets and men."

"And the Monets last."

"You've worked Cap Ferrat, of course, and Nice."

"Neither."

"How about Deauville?"

He evaded the question with: "You've known Argenti before."

"Obviously."

"See him often?"

"Here and there, off and on."

"What does he do besides own this place?"

"Owns other things, a financier. He lives in Bogotá." She looked off and up, wasn't interested in the topic. "Want to play with me this afternoon?"

"Play what?" Not that it mattered.

She didn't tell him. She showed him. In high spirits, she led him up over the hill to the golf course.

He told her, "I don't golf."

"What a sin." She ran ahead and then turned and walked backward. "Do you know what a snooger is?"

"A what?"

"I thought not." She laughed.

Wiley couldn't remember ever having heard a prettier sound. He caught up to her, put an arm around. Side against side they went across a fairway and on through some rough. She stopped them at a level spot where the ground was practically bare, composed of a pale clay packed by weather and baked by sun. Only a few scrubby plants grew there. She pulled them out by their roots, telling Wiley to help. They cleared an area about fifteen feet square. She kneeled, put her face close to the ground, examined the surface, from one angle and then another. Like a golfer studying a green. Then she used her feet to tamp where they'd pulled the plants up, making it level. Wiley did the same without being told. He felt foolish. He asked what the hell they were doing, but she was intent on digging into her net bag for something.

Two nails and some string.

Ordinary three-inch carpentry nails and regular wrapping string.

"Five feet . . . anyway, just about," she said, referring to the length of the string. "I measured it from my toes to my nose."

The nails were knotted to the string, one on each end. In the center of the cleared area she pressed one of the nails into the ground. Wiley was to make sure it stayed in place. She stretched the string taut and, using the other nail, moved with it to make a line on the ground all the way round. A near-perfect circle, ten feet in diameter. At the center she marked a cross. "Now what shall we play for?" she asked.

"Play *what* for?"

"You still don't know?"

GERALD A. BROWNE

62

He had to admit he didn't.

"This is going to be murder." She grinned her lopsided grin. "But when it comes to competition, I'm without conscience."

From her net bag she brought out a leather drawstring pouch, the same one she'd had tied to her belt yesterday. She opened it. He recognized the clicking sound of its contents a split second before she poured them out.

Marbles.

Aggies, alleys, migs, immies and glassies, including just about every color in swirls and patches, veins and ribbons, slivers and bubbles, some milky opaque, others watery clear.

Wiley didn't try to conceal his delight. He got right into it, held several of the marbles in his hand, felt their shape and weight, reexperiencing.

Lillian was anxious to get started. Again she wanted to know what the stakes would be.

Wiley suggested a dollar a marble.

"Not money. Let's play for something important."

"How about for the fun of it?"

"That's okay, but I'd like to make it a little more exciting. For instance, we could play for time."

"Meaning what?"

"Loser has to do whatever the winner wants for a certain length of time."

"Sounds like slavery."

"Just temporary."

"Is that what you normally play for?"

"Not since I was ten."

He believed her.

"Or what we could do," she said, "is play for something more precise."

"Such as?"

"Kisses." She read his eyes and added, "Above-the-waist kisses."

She could have limited it to above the neck, he thought. Better start play before she made any less rewarding suggestions.

She placed thirteen marbles in the center of the ring.

"You can use my best shooter," she said, as though that was a supreme gesture. She tossed him a black-and-white aggie about twice as large as the other marbles. "I paid a kid from the Bronx fifty dollars for it. Chip it, and I'll chip you."

According to the rules, they would shoot from outside the ring to try to knock any of the thirteen marbles ("hoodles") out beyond the perimeter. The first player to knock seven hoodles out was the winner.

"No cunny thumbs," she said.

"No cunny thumbs."

"From you that sounds dirty." It meant, when making a shot, at least one knuckle had to be resting on the ground.

She hunkered down, one knee in the dirt. She placed her shooter against the ball of her first finger, thumb behind, took quick aim, and flicked it.

Excellent form.

Her shooter skimmed fast across the hard clay surface. Collided with a crack, knocking one of the hoodles out of the ring.

"Nice shot."

She took the compliment, shot again. She knocked four out before missing.

Wiley's turn.

She watched him closely, and he felt that in her eyes this might be a test for him. He knocked a hoodle out on his first try. It had looked good, easy, but he knew it was mostly luck. He was about to let go his second shot when she told him, "No hunching."

"I wasn't."

"Just reminding."

Hunching was moving the hand forward over the edge of the ring. Being extra careful not to do it now hurt Wiley's concentration. He shot and missed, way off.

She hunkered down again, both knees in the dirt, and with admirable accuracy proceeded to knock out three more hoodles, winning that game.

She was six ahead.

Did she want to collect now?

She said she could wait.

They played most of the afternoon. After the first four or five games the competition lost some of its edge, at least enough so that they talked of other things.

"What were you originally?" she asked. "Nearly everyone was something else originally."

"I was into electronics."

She seemed interested. "You got out because you weren't good at it."

64 GERALD A. BROWNE

"No."

"Why then?"

He told her about it, briefly, the high and low points of MIT, Humes, Special Dynamics, Litting. For him it was like touching on old scarred-over wounds, didn't hurt.

"What were *you* originally?" he asked.

"No fair asking the same question."

"All right then, tell me, is Argenti really important to you?"

She thought a moment. "In one way yes, in another no."

Wiley decided he'd better not try to corner her.

Three Mexican children watched from the bushes, curious. Two boys and a girl out to earn centavos by searching for lost golf balls. All about the same age, ten. Lillian called them over. They admired the marbles, handling them as though they were precious. Lillian showed them how to play and took pleasure in it. Her patience surprised Wiley. He decided she must have been from a poor family.

The children left.

Lillian lost her touch for the last few games. Wiley won big, closed the gap, ended up five ahead.

"I'll pay off now," she said.

She kissed him once on the forehead, once on the chin, once on each cheek—all brief pecks—saving the one on the mouth for last, good and long.

"I thought the winner was supposed to do the kissing," he said.

"Nope. Otherwise I would have won."

He kissed her anyway, and they held together after the kiss for a long while.

On their way back to the hotel he asked when he might see her again. She promised soon. Considering the circumstances, particularly Argenti, he thought it would be unfair to press her for more of a commitment. He told her he was staying in 114, in case of emergency . . . or anything. At her bungalow they didn't say good-bye. She went up the stairs to the landing, turned for a last look. Both her knees were caked with dirt.

Wiley didn't go directly to 114. He went down to the beach, to walk just above the reach of the water, where the sand was firmer. The sun was going down. Not much day left. Wiley bet himself he was the happiest sad man in the world. It occurred to him that he was still married to Jennifer.

After nearly an hour he returned to his bungalow. He still

didn't have a key and hadn't wanted to leave the front door unlocked, so he'd been coming and going over the terrace wall, in and out through the bathroom window.

First thing he did inside was check to see if his twelve thousand was still in the base of the lamp. It was. He washed up, then lay on the bed. He was sunburned, and his back was slightly stiff from the marble playing. All that bending over. In great shape, he thought. He'd forgotten to smoke all afternoon. He opened the bedside table drawer for a fresh pack of cigarettes.

There was something else in the drawer.

A drawstring pouch. Similar to Lillian's, except black chamois. Immediately, he thought she had put it there while he was out walking on the beach. How had she gotten in? Over the wall? He wouldn't put it past her. No doubt it contained marbles, perhaps her precious black German shooter and maybe even a note.

He opened the pouch and emptied its contents onto the bed.

They were green.

They weren't marbles.

Seven stones of various sizes, averaging about three quarters of an inch by a half inch. Six-sided, rough on the ends as though they were chunks broken from natural hexagonal columns. Not perfectly green, each stone variegated from a deep to a lighter, brighter shade, with traces of a silvery-black substance that seemed to be only on the surface.

Wiley thought he'd never seen anything like them. But then he recalled something: a school class afternoon, a sixth-grade visit to the Museum of Natural History on Central Park West. There had been glass-enclosed cases exhibiting examples of minerals and gems. He'd been most fascinated with the uncut diamonds, rubies, and emeralds.

These stones reminded him of those emeralds, had all the characteristics he vaguely remembered. Of course, they could be something else entirely, something not valuable, only semiprecious. But then, why in a pouch so finely made, soft and expensive? Anyway, emeralds or not, how had they gotten there in the drawer? He doubted Lillian had anything to do with it. Evidently it was meant that he should find them. Why him? Perhaps not him. But if not, then who?

Prentiss came to mind. Prentiss, the man who had been assigned this suite. The mild-mannered American. Now that

Wiley thought of it, Prentiss had looked more as though he was there to do business than to vacation.

Wiley examined the stones more closely. He noticed clear patches on the end of each stone, like little windows. Not natural, but made by polishing away that much of the surface. He switched on the lamp, held one of the stones up and sighted into it. He saw in through one window and out the other.

In between, a blazing green.

He wished he had a magnifying glass or, better, the kind of glass jewelers put to an eye, a loupe, he believed they called it. Not that that would have enabled him to know more. He'd never had anything out of the ordinary to do with gems.

The phone rang.

This time, after he said hello twice, a voice on the other end asked, "Did you receive the samples?"

"Yes," Wiley said without thinking.

"Yes what?"

"I . . . I'm looking at them now."

"Your recommendations are impressive, Prentiss. However, because we have never met you or done business with you before, we prefer to deal on a reasonably modest basis. We offer you six thousand carats at five hundred a carat—the quality, of course, equal to that of the samples."

Wiley thought he'd better set things straight. But he didn't have a chance. The caller clicked off. No matter. Whoever it was would realize the mistake soon enough. The stones were definitely emeralds. He put them in the bag and back into the drawer.

A nap. He rolled over onto his right side and dropped off deep. He slept for nearly an hour. The last forty-five minutes were shallow while he did arithmetic. Simple multiplication but, in semiconsciousness, difficult. Five hundred times six thousand. The zeros were confusing, too many wouldn't stay in place. The sun came to him just before he awoke.

Three million dollars.

His sunburn was worse now. His face felt tight enough to crack. He hoped it wouldn't blister. There was nothing among his toilet articles to do it any good. He poured a drink, Stolichnaya on the rocks. On impulse he dabbed some vodka on his forehead and fanned himself. It was cooling. He opened the double windows of the living room front and back so there was cross ventilation. Gave himself a vodka rub, splashed it on. The breeze delivered blessed relief.

He had dinner alone in his suite.

He managed to resist calling Lillian until ten o'clock. He would hang up if Argenti answered.

She answered. She didn't sound surprised or put off.

Could he see her?

When?

Tonight.

No.

For only a few minutes. One drink.

Perhaps tomorrow.

He hated *perhaps*.

"You're a hell of a shooter," he said.

"Know what a snooger is now?" she asked.

"No."

"A near-miss."

"Would you care for me more if I were rich?" He realized how sophomoric that sounded.

"Who said I cared for you at all?"

"You don't."

"I do, but I didn't say so. Lots of things are left unsaid."

"Well, would you?"

"Rich?"

"Yeah."

"I don't know. I suppose I should say I wouldn't care more if you had money . . . but then again, honestly, neither would I care less."

He was just as ambivalent about how to take that.

"Anyway," she told him, "you're hunching."

He backed off, made sure before he signed off the impression was casual, carefree. Again she didn't say good-bye, and he said, "See you."

Three million dollars.

Three million would change a lot of things.

Could he cut himself in for even a slice of that? Possibly. From what he'd gathered, the cryptic phone calls and all, this was an underhanded deal. They, whoever they were, had mistaken him for Prentiss because he'd taken Prentiss' suite. By their own words, they had never met Prentiss. On the other hand, Wiley had. What would happen if he went on posing as

Prentiss? They'd expect him to hand over three million for the six thousand carats. But it might not be out of line, perhaps even more credible, if he asked to examine all the emeralds before closing the deal. Most likely they'd permit it. All he'd need was three or four hours, time enough to locate Prentiss. Assuming the seller's identity, he could offer the emeralds to Prentiss at, say six hundred instead of five hundred a carat. If Prentiss didn't go for it, Wiley could merely return the emeralds to the sellers, stall on some excuse or other and disappear. But if Prentiss went for it . . . Wiley would pay the sellers their three-million asking price and keep the difference: six hundred thousand.

Tempting thought.

It could work.

There'd be danger all the way. If he got found out, they'd probably do more than just rough him up.

Wasn't it worth the chance? Didn't it suit his reckless new life-style? Lillian was only another reason in favor of it.

An absolute must would be that the sellers and Prentiss remain apart for the time being. Everything would depend on that. Where was Prentiss now? Probably waiting for *the* phone call. Or perhaps Prentiss wasn't as straight-laced as he appeared, had, by now, dived headfirst into the erotic milieu.

Six hundred thousand . . .

7 ⤸⤸⤸

Six o'clock the next morning.

Another phone call. Same voice.

"Are you ready for the goods?"

"Yes." A part of Wiley warned him to stay out of it. He suppressed it.

"We will meet in two hours."

"Where?"

A long pause. Wiley thought the man had rung off.

"Playa de Soledad."

Solitude Beach.

Wiley asked a porter for directions, was told it was about seventeen kilometers to the north, he should watch for a dirt road on the left. Maybe there would be a sign, sometimes there was. Perhaps the *Señor* should take a taxi.

His better judgment told him to go alone. He drove the Volks. Along the way there were numerous dirt roads off to the left, one or two nearly every kilometer. But then, none at all at seventeen kilometers, or eighteen. Either the porter had been wrong, or Wiley had missed it. Fortunately he'd allowed himself some time. He turned around, drove back slowly, and there was a road, easily visible from that direction. That could be it.

It was only a quarter mile to the beach. He was ten minutes early. If this wasn't Solitude Beach, it looked it. Not a sign of anyone, or of anyone's ever having been there. Both ways, up and down the beach about two hundred yards, were rock formations, like craggy ramparts. Pelicans on them.

Wiley lighted a cigarette as he walked to the water's edge. The tide was ebbing. He took a deep drag and, before exhaling half of it, took another. Five minutes went by. Ten. He would wait until eight-fifteen, no later. If he was on the wrong beach, perhaps that was how it was meant to be.

He was still there at eight-twenty.

A man came out of the foliage and stood just beyond the growth line, about fifty feet away. He observed Wiley for a long moment before starting toward him. A chunkily built man, overweight but powerful. He wasn't dressed for there, had on a fresh white flannel suit, collarless white shirt. Pointy-toed white shoes. As he came nearer, Wiley realized from his features and the bluish-brown cast of his skin that he was an East Indian. What hair he had was black and dry, tufted left and right and around, making a bushy horseshoe shape on his skull. He carried a white Panama-type straw hat in his right hand.

"Mr. Prentiss?"

Tell him who you really are, smartass, Wiley thought, but responded with an indefinite nod.

"We wondered where you were."

The same voice, same man as on the phone. He had a small gold bead, like a drop of dew, on the flare of his left nostril. Wiley told him, "I've been waiting."

"In the wrong place."

"These beaches all look alike."

"No matter." He smiled, but not with his eyes. "This is equally suitable."

Another man appeared on the shoulder of the beach. It was Prentiss.

At that same moment the Indian revealed the gun he'd been holding hidden under his hat—a thirty-two automatic.

This was the first time Wiley had ever been up against a gun. He feinted a move left, stepped in and let go a right with all he had. It caught the Indian just in front of his left ear. Heavy-weight that he was, he didn't go down, but it did knock him off balance enough to give Wiley a chance to run.

A run for his life down the beach, darting from side to side to make himself a more difficult target. Two shots. Missed, but so close he heard them sing by. He kept running full out until no more shots. He glanced back. The Indian hadn't pursued, was standing there with his gun lowered because Wiley was now out of range.

Wiley would go for cover.

But another man in white stepped out of the foliage at that point of the beach, raised his gun and fired. The bullet tore into Wiley's right side a couple of inches above the hipbone. It was like someone with red-hot teeth had taken a bite of his flesh.

He didn't know how badly he was wounded. He'd run until he dropped.

A third man in white was farther down the beach at the water's edge. Wiley was cut off. He stopped. They were coming, converging on him. He had only one way to go. Into the sea. A struggling run with the bottom sand, soft and giving, the water of varying depth, handicapping his legs as it flowed in and out. He stumbled in the trench just offshore where the sea fought itself. He fell face down.

Shots, bullets spliffed the water around him.

Not yet deep enough for him to swim. Hands and knees on the bottom, he tried to crawl but got nowhere because of the undertow, had to stand and expose himself to their fire. The water was alternately his enemy and ally, fought him, helped him. Wading was as fast as he could go. Surely a bullet would stop him. Keep going, keep going. Enough depth now. He dove forward, churned his arms and kicked, swam till he was certain he was more than far enough from shore.

Treading water, he looked back.

They were standing in a group on the beach, well above the surf line, as though to avoid getting their shoes wet. The four of them were looking out at him. Prentiss, in his dark suit, stood out. So did the chunky Indian because of his build. They had put their guns away, evidently satisfied to leave him to the sea. No doubt they still intended to keep an eye on him. If he swam up or down the coast, they would be waiting wherever he tried to come ashore.

Unless they lost sight of him. Perhaps, he thought, he could swim far out, a half mile or so. At that distance with only his head above water, he wouldn't be visible from shore. Then he'd swim up the coast a ways and in to land.

He removed his shoes and all his clothes. That helped.

Now that the anesthesia of fright was wearing off, his side began to hurt. The salt water was getting to the wound. He floated on his back to get a look, saw it wasn't serious, little more than a graze. There was a lot of blood, though.

Sweet Jesus! That was why they were standing so complacently onshore. They knew he was bleeding. They'd let the sharks finish him. Of all the ways he didn't want to go. . . .

He kept his arms and legs moving.

He thought he felt something woosh by beneath him. And again. Another. He believed he felt the scaly skin of a shark

brush him as it went by. He thrashed the water, wasted energy.
Don't panic, he told himself. But he had plenty of reason to
panic, out of his element, in the element of those shadowy
lethal swimmers he'd observed from the breakwater yesterday.
And he was no mealy apple.

Something broke the surface no more than twenty feet away.
A huge black slippery thing, a dripping black monster, came
straight up out of the sea. A manta ray. With a wingspan of ten
to twelve feet. At the peak of its leap, it spat out one of Wiley's
shoes, then flopped back into the water with a smack.

Done for now, Wiley thought. He was already exhausted,
yet couldn't float to rest, had to keep in motion. He'd rather
face those bastards on the beach. He would come out of the
water bare-ass, hands up, so they might not kill him right off.
Maybe he'd get the chance to explain, to persuade them to let
him live. He started swimming to shore.

He didn't hear the Riva speedboat until it was practically on
him. It seemed that it meant to run him down. At the last
second it swerved, abruptly reversed its engine, so he swam
right into the varnished side of it.

The boat rolled in the swells, loomed and dipped.

Wiley reached for it.

A hand grabbed his wrist. A strong sailor hauled him out of
the water as though he were a mere catch. Threw him roughly
onto the rear passenger seat.

Next to Lillian, who tossed a towel.

8 ➤➤➤

She had a car waiting on one of the old docks of Manzanillo.

A blue Rolls Royce Corniche convertible with top down. The same seventy-thousand-dollar beauty Wiley had used the day before for an impressive arrival at Las Hadas.

"Argenti's?" Wiley asked

"No." She got into the driver's seat.

"Who let you borrow it?"

"No one."

"You stole it?"

"Cover yourself."

Dockworkers were snickering and shouting appropriate obscenities, because Wiley had on only a white terry-cloth robe, a full-length lady's robe with the words *Sea Cloud* stitched on one of its pockets. It didn't have a belt, so holding it closed made him appear mincy.

Wiley didn't care. He was suffering an adrenergic hangover from having been so high on danger and then so suddenly safe. Emotional bends.

Lillian started the Rolls and drove slowly down the dock. She activated the electric top, snapped it in place. Evidently she was familiar with the car. Wiley sat favoring his right side, not to bloody the fine leather upholstery. His wound had soaked a large splotch through the robe. There would be a doctor at the hotel.

"Perfect timing," he said.

"When?"

"Out there off the beach. Too perfect."

"You might say thanks."

"Thanks, but you didn't just happen along."

"I've been keeping an eye on you."

"Why?"

"At least I don't go peeping over garden walls."

"Who does?"

"You did."

"Never."

"I don't mind if you're a little kinky. Maybe it even makes you more interesting."

"Never did that before in my life."

"A latency. I brought it out."

"It's not and you didn't. Anyway, how come you were right there on cue with the speedboat?"

"I overheard something."

"What?"

"Your name taken in vain."

"By whom?"

"Just heard."

"I don't buy that."

"Okay. I take a speedboat ride every morning."

"Sure you do."

"Wouldn't miss it for the world."

"Even on Sundays and holidays, right?"

"Even when there's no water around."

There was, Wiley thought, a slim possibility she'd overheard Prentiss or someone else as she'd said. There was really no absolute reason to believe she was involved any more than that. *Suspect* maybe, but not believe. He asked her straight, "Do you know a guy named Prentiss?"

Her answer was an emphatically honest no.

They had passed through Manzanillo. She turned right on Route 200, headed south. Las Hadas was north of the town. Wiley told her that.

"I know," she said calmly.

"This is no time for errands, Lillian. I'm bleeding to death."

"You will for sure if you go back to Las Hadas."

"Those guys? They wouldn't try anything there. Too crowded. That's why they wanted me on that beach."

No comment from Lillian.

"Besides, Argenti wouldn't tolerate any trouble. Bad for the image. The last thing they'd want is to annoy such a man."

Lillian kept driving south.

"Well, what the hell am I supposed to do? All my clothes, passport, everything I own is in that suite."

"Poor soul."

He told her about the twelve thousand he had hidden in the lamp base.

"We'll send for everything," she assured him.

"Where are we going?"

"Are you really bleeding much?"

He opened the robe to see, used a clean dry part of it to wipe most of the blood away.

"Not so much now," he said. It occurred to him that if that gun had been fired an eighth of an inch to the left, or if that man in white had pulled the muzzle left to that slight extent, the bullet would have hit him bull's-eye in the navel. An eighth of an inch wasn't much to be alive by.

"Put some pressure on it," she advised.

"To hell."

"That'll help stop the bleeding. Poor soul, is it spurting or oozing?"

"More of an ooze."

"Then let it have air."

"Where'd you get to be such an expert on blood?"

"I was a visiting nurse." She smiled to herself as though it were true. "Wiley, do you believe omission is the same as lying?"

"Depends."

"I don't. Most times, if you leave things out that would be lies, people put them in, so, in a way, they lie to themselves. That happens to me a lot."

"You lie to yourself?"

"No. I omit. It's a sort of habit, I suppose."

"You haven't done that with me."

She reached beneath the seat for a tape cartridge, which she shoved into the player attached below the burled walnut instrument panel. It was The Captain and Tennille:

> I'm a woman who's seen
> How the world can be mean
> And life can abuse.
> But I'm a woman, oh, yeah,
> Who can make you
> Feel like a man . . .

Lillian sang low along with it and the impression Wiley got

was the one he wanted: She was singing to him. He gazed out the window, saw a sign that said Colima—3 Km, and a route marker displaying the number 110. He turned to ask again where they were going, but the breath for his words was stopped by the sight of her in profile. Her lips parting and closing. It was as though he'd never before noticed anyone sing. She kept her eyes on the road ahead. What were her thoughts? Was he in them? He wished she would turn and smile his way, say a lot with a smile. She knew he was observing her, didn't she? Her hands on the polished wood steering wheel, handling the car with easy efficiency. He appreciated her hands, imagined them touching her, envied them. He imagined her hands were his hands.

A swerve to barely miss a pair of overloaded burros.

Brought Wiley out of it.

"Where are we going?" he asked.

"You'll see."

They had passed through Colima. The smaller town of Tamazula would be next, still on Route 110.

No matter where, the important thing, the marvelous thing—even though he'd been slightly shot in his side, was bareass, needed a shave, was hungry, thirsty—he was with her.

With her.

"I need a cigarette," he said.

"No one *needs* a cigarette."

"I do."

"In the glove compartment."

He looked, none there. He suspected she had known.

Lightly and hopefully she told him, "We could take that to mean you're supposed to do without."

"Stop somewhere."

"Quit right now, cold turkey."

"Nope."

"For me?"

"I don't know you that well."

She pulled over at a roadside cantina. Several *hombres* were practicing laziness on the veranda.

"You wouldn't make me go in looking like this, would you, not really?" Wiley said.

"It's your funeral."

"Do me this favor and I'll owe you some."

She thought a moment, sighed her distaste and went into the cantina. She returned with two packs, tossed them to him.

"Didn't they have Camels?"

"Only those."

Wiley had never heard of the brand: Bandidos Supremos. Literally translated: "Supreme Outlaws." There was no cellophane wrapping. On the front of the pack was a crudely drawn man, long mustache, wearing a large sombrero with tasseled brim. The drawing was made worse because the black of the printing was off-register, so the outlaw appeared insanely evil, especially his mouth and eyes.

Lillian got the Rolls under way.

Wiley lighted an Outlaw. As was his habit, he inhaled the very first puff. It was like taking a deep breath over a barrel of smouldering tar. He gasped, just managed to not choke, exhaled loudly. He examined the cigarette. It was loosely rolled, dark tobacco. The smoke that rose from its end was sickly yellowish. It smelled only vaguely like a cigarette, more like a blacktop road being repaired in July. Wiley's empty stomach warned it wouldn't tolerate another puff.

Lillian didn't seem bothered by the smoke. He wished she'd complain, but she didn't, and finally he lowered the window. He didn't throw the Outlaw out until it had burned down to a stub. He took as few puffs as possible, with his head turned so she wouldn't see he wasn't inhaling. He wondered how she'd known which awful brand to get.

"What about this car?"

"What about it?"

"Who does it belong to?"

"When were you born?" she asked.

Not this time, he decided. "The car, where did you get it?"

"Mendoza Brothers."

"Who are they?"

"Dealers in Mexico City."

"Dope?"

"Rolls Royces. God, you're suspicious!"

9

The drive took thirteen hours, including a twenty-minute stop in Quiroga to buy Wiley a pair of *pantalones*, natural woven cotton trousers that tied at the waist like pajamas. And a matching pullover shirt. An extremely uncomfortable outfit, because for some reason, perhaps to exaggerate quality, the manufacturers had starched them heavily. Wiley felt like a stiff version of a peasant extra in the movie *Viva Zapata*.

Nevertheless, the clothes did allow them to stop to eat just outside Morelia. They had to settle for less of a place because they hadn't bought Wiley any shoes. Lillian ordered an avocado and tomato salad; Wiley, against Lillian's advice, a steak. It came so overfried it curled upward around the edges. He ate all of it. No one took notice that he was barefoot, or even that his shirt was bloodstained. He drank two bottles of Carta Blanca beer and took another for along the way.

The check.

For a moment he forgot his pockets were empty. No slipping him money under the table; Lillian just paid up. Wiley asked to borrow twenty-five pesos. She gave it to him without a second thought and then was angry at herself because he bought three packs of Camels. He offered to drive from Morelia on, but she insisted she'd make better time because she knew the road, which was tricky with mountains.

During the long drive Wiley didn't learn much more about Lillian. The way she obviously evaded his questions was frustrating. Why was she so closed about herself? Ashamed of something? How could he convey, convince her, that anything she'd done or been before wasn't important enough to keep secret? So what if she'd been an opportunist? From what he gathered, she lived in Mexico City. That was where they were headed, for her place. He looked forward to it, imagined it: a small, chic apartment, with expressions of her all around. One

78

bedroom. He would probably be put on the couch. No, think positive, he told himself.

It was night, going on eleven o'clock, when they reached Mexico City. They didn't enter the city proper, turned off before that, went down a few outlying commercial streets and then into a district that became purely residential. The Pedregal area. Wide, nicely kept streets, houses set well back. Passing through, Wiley thought.

Lillian turned a sharp right. The headlights of the Rolls raked across a high wall and hit upon a wood-and-iron gate that opened as though it had expected them and closed behind like a trap. A winding drive, single lane. Tall hedges on both sides.

Then, there was the house. Antique brick, pleasantly vined, three stories, twenty rooms. A series of archways along the front making a long covered walk.

A man came out, smiling, nodding, saying, *"Buenas noches, señorita."* A servant. Lillian told him there was no luggage, that he could put the car away.

They went in, to an elegant reception area, two stories high, hung with a crystal chandelier so huge Wiley felt uncomfortable walking beneath it.

Lillian seemed edgy, somewhat embarrassed. She pulled off her driving gloves, tossed them toward a hall table and missed. Wiley picked them up.

"Mi casa es su casa," she said with a smile that almost asked for consolation.

Her house? Surely she couldn't be serious. More likely belonged to one of her affluent "friends." After all, Wiley reasoned, she had been hitchhiking. . . .

Two, three more servants appeared. They greeted her in a respectful manner, genuinely pleased to see her. She introduced Wiley, told the servants he would be staying on. They should do everything to make him comfortable. *"Sí, señorita,"* they chorused.

She certainly sounded like the lady of the house.

"Hungry?" she asked Wiley.

"No." He was stunned.

"Well, I'm going to try to sauna away all that driving." She seemed eager to leave him, said "Good night" and went quickly up the wide stairs and out of sight.

Did Señor Wiley wish to be shown to his room?

He would also like a bottle of beer.

Wiley followed a servant up to a bannistered landing and a wide corridor. Along the way he saw what a spacious and beautiful house this was. Native tile glazed in subtle shades felt cool and clean beneath his feet. To some extent the decor was in keeping with the Spanish architecture. More prevalent, however, were the tasteful contradictions of authentic period French, English and Italian furnishings. A Louis Quinze commode was flanked by a pair of *bergères* that had somehow survived the ravages of revolution. And wasn't that a Cézanne on the hallway wall? Wiley slowed his stride to make sure.

His room was at the extreme end of the corridor. It was L-shaped, a section of it furnished as a sitting room. Everywhere Wiley looked was something that only a lot of money could buy. He didn't belong there. And, damn it, neither did she. He went to the window, looked down on the ideal blue rectangle of the lighted swimming pool. He would have preferred the one-bedroom apartment, he thought.

The beer was brought. Not just one bottle but four, and not just cold but buried neck down in a bucket of shaved ice. Four crystal goblets. Also on the tray were several sterile gauze compresses, some adhesive tape and a bottle of peroxide. The servant hadn't thought of those. She had, and it made him feel slightly better about everything. He took a shower, dressed his wound and drank a beer from the bottle.

The bed was turned down, open like a fresh envelope. He inserted himself between sheets that felt finer than any ever. Three oversize pillows. His head was flashing on all sorts of thoughts. Clicking off the light didn't diminish them.

Some day it had been. The end, as confusing as the start, had been alarming. He refused to accept that this was her house. If all this belonged to her, he had been deceived. He tried to recall her exact words, to pinpoint her lies, and realized now what she'd meant about omission being one of her habits. At the least, he'd been misled. But, then, he was equally guilty, posing as a fortune chaser. How could it all have gotten so complicated in such a short while?

Sleep now.

He dozed off and, after only three hours, came awake. Wide, sharp awake, with Lillian on the front of his mind. The need to see her. At nearly four in the morning? Ridiculous. Go back to sleep. He tried, but he had to see Lillian, just see her.

He put on his *pantalones* and went out. A stillness to the

place now, as though the structure itself and every object in it were also sleeping. He went down the hallway to the opposite wing.

Numerous doors. He only guessed the one on the end would be hers.

Slowly, noiselessly, he turned the knob, opened the door just enough to look in. Lamps were on, bright. The bed hadn't been slept in, still had its spread on it. He went in. No one there. Perhaps it wasn't hers. But the blouse and slacks she'd worn that night were thrown over the back of a chair. Her shoes were on the floor, her handbag open, its contents spilling on the bed.

No doubt this was her room. He found some of her engraved personal stationery on the desk and, on the mantel, several photographs propped up in enamel and silver frames. Snapshots. Her, arms around an older man slightly shorter than she. A young girl who greatly resembled Lillian, Lillian about age ten. And Lillian again, alone, wearing a visored sailing cap and a double-breasted blazer, smiling over the rail of a ship. Examining that one closely, Wiley saw the ship's name across its stern: *Sea Cloud*. One of the big ones he'd admired at Las Hadas. Handprinted across the top of the photo: CAPTAIN HOLBROOK, 1974. Was it possible?

His need to see her was increased now. Where was she? Spending the night with someone else in the house or somewhere nearby? Inconsiderate, the way she'd just left him standing there in the foyer. Seemed she could hardly wait to get away from him. That anxious to be with someone else?

A door off to the right, Wiley noticed. Probably a storage closet. He took a look.

It was another room, much smaller. Lighted by a fat candle stuck in its own melt on top of a wooden crate. There was the odor of marijuana. A peace symbol was painted large in red on one wall. Two planks supported by bricks served as a low shelf, on which there was a record changer and some LPs. A pair of speakers and paperback books. No other furniture in the room. The floor was bare. Except for an ordinary twin-size mattress.

Lillian was asleep on it.

She lay on her side with her legs drawn up and her hands pressed between her knees. She had kicked away the madras coverlet. All she had on was a faded green tank shirt.

10 ⇾⇾

Back in 1966, on Friday, April 8, Lillian Mayo Holbrook was reported missing.

At 3 P.M. that day she boarded Swissair flight 110 at Cointrin Airport, Geneva. For the early part of the flight she was in First Class, along with five other girls from the school in Gstaad. There had been nothing unusual about her behavior. She drank some wine. The girls had brought their own, knowing they'd be refused service because they were underage, but there was no reason for the flight attendant not to supply them with a corkscrew and glasses so the girls could serve themselves. They quickly finished off three bottles of red, one of white.

They held it well for sixteen-year-olds, were used to it. Nearly every afternoon in Gstaad they would wait outside a wine shop until they could persuade or pay some local to buy a few bottles for them. They hid the wine in the snow, then stole out after dark to get it. Came spring, when the snow melted, the area around the dormitory was littered with empties and, here and there, a misplaced full.

Spring vacation. Well in advance the school had sent each girl's parents a reminder, rather like a warning, that the vacation was scheduled. As an alternative to going home, and all the inconvenience that might require, the school offered chaperoned excursions to either Cairo or Rome. At additional cost, of course.

It was up to the parent(s).

Last holiday, Christmas, one of the alternates offered had been Paris. Lillian was among eight girls who stayed at a hotel on the Rue Poincaré that was not much different from the school dormitory. Except that the tip of the Eiffel Tower could be seen from Lillian's window, and wine was easier to buy but more difficult to hide.

If Lillian was homesick, she didn't let it show. However,

she'd been counting the days to this spring vacation, going home.

Two hours out of Geneva, Lillian left First Class and walked back through Tourist. An exceptionally pretty, long-haired girl wearing a white blouse and a loden-green school blazer. Well noticed, particularly by most of the male passengers. She went up and down the aisle twice, casually, as though taking stock. There were a number of vacant seats. One was next to a man of fifty trying not to look it. Hair dyed, eyes worked on, young-cut suit.

Lillian took that seat and immediately struck up a conversation. The man's name was Mitchell—Paul, call him Paul. He made a point of saying he wasn't flying First Class because it had been fully booked and he hadn't wanted to bump anyone. He was in the motion picture business. Not a producer, the next worst thing, he said. He arranged deals with foreign distributors. Had to fly a lot. Had no strings, used to, but none now. Did Lillian want a cigarette? No. A drink? No. Anything?

Playing cards.

The flight attendant brought a fresh deck.

Lillian and Paul played for over two thousand miles. He should have known from the sharp way she shuffled. He thought she might be cheating, but she couldn't be because they were playing losers deal, so she hardly ever got to handle the cards. By the time the approach to Kennedy was announced he was down four hundred and some. Perhaps they hadn't been playing for dollars really, he suggested. Anyway, he didn't have that much cash on him. Would she accept his personal check? How much in cash did he have? Two hundred seventy-five. Paul thanked her when she settled for two-fifty.

She didn't pick up her baggage. The Holbrook chauffeur was waiting, watching for her outside Customs. She had to go out that way. She waited for a crowd, got behind someone tall, ducked down, slipped around the side. The chauffeur never saw her.

She taxied into the city to Broadway and Forty-ninth, where she asked a likely-looking girl directions to an army-navy surplus store. The nearest was on Eighth Avenue. Lillian found it, went in and bought an entire new old outfit: white regulation navy jeans that laced up the back, and overwashed khaki-

colored tank top and a royal-blue satin zip-up jacket with an
outline map of Korea appliquéd on its back.

She changed in a pay toilet booth at the Port Authority Bus
Terminal, flushed all her identification down the toilet, threw
her school clothes in the trash receptacle. From there she
caught another taxi to Lexington and Fifty-ninth, where she
found a second-floor, all-night beauty shop. Not a wince while
she had her hair cut short as a boy's.

By then it was nine-thirty. Her transformation and the taxi
rides had cost $74. Lillian had left Geneva with only $52. She
was grateful to that man, Paul, and the roommate who had
taught her to play gin seven years and three schools ago. She
still had $228 to go on.

For the first time in her life she took a subway. The
Lexington Avenue downtown local. To where the blue letters
inlaid on the white-tiled station wall announced: ASTOR
PLACE.

She came up out of the ground and walked across Cooper
Square to St. Mark's Place.

The East Village. It was wonderfully confusing, impossible
for her to take it all in—all the loud colors and sounds, long-
haired young men with jeans hanging precariously on their
hipbones, girls so apparently with nothing on underneath.
Lillian tried not to stare or appear out of place, sauntering
along imitatively with a nonchalant, self-likable air. No one
seemed to be taking special notice of her, and that was reassuring.

Several young men and girls were sitting on the steps of a
brownstone. Lillian stopped and faced them. They made room
for her. She climbed up and sat among them. They didn't talk
much, were content to just sit and watch the passersby. Lillian
felt included. As easy as that, she'd become one of them.

She told them her name was Penny. Where she was from
wasn't asked.

Seated next to her was a girl whose taken name was Charity,
a fifteen-year-old with a roundish face and figure. Lillian admired the beads Charity was wearing. Striped blue-and-green
glass strung with intermittent tufts of white feathers. Charity
smiled with her entire face, took off the beads, and looped
them over Lillian's head.

Lillian wanted to give something in return.

"Got any bread?" Charity asked.

"Some."

"I'd dig some frozen peas."

Charity grabbed up her blanket roll, led the way to a market on Second Avenue. Lillian bought a package of Birdseye frozen peas and a can of Fresca for Charity. A Three Musketeers bar for herself.

"How long you been around?" Lillian asked as they walked up Second.

"Where?"

"Here."

"Ten days Sunday."

Charity had seemed such a veteran to Lillian. "Where do you stay?"

"Anyplace." Charity popped some cold raw peas into her mouth, let them melt a little before biting down. "They ain't so good if you eat them fast," she said, "but if you don't, they unfreeze and then ain't so good either." Charity stopped beneath a street light. About four inches shorter than Lillian, she looked up into her eyes and asked, "You stoned?"

Lillian was heavy-eyed. The six-hour time difference from Geneva made it five in the morning for her.

She spent that night in St. Mark's Church, stretched out on a hardwood pew, with her head sharing Charity's blanket roll.

The chauffeur waited two hours at Kennedy Airport before reporting that Miss Holbrook had not arrived.

Laurence Holbrook II thought probably his daughter had changed her mind at the last minute, decided the school trip to Cairo or Rome would be more enjoyable. She'd been given that option.

Mr. Holbrook was disappointed. And relieved. Since Lillian's last time home, last summer, he had again built up his resolve to be a better, closer father. Nothing, neither crucial business nor the most promising pleasure, would be allowed to interfere. He would focus all his attention on Lillian, extend himself to her as never before, really stretch out, in the hope that they would take hold and establish a new span between them. There had always been the blood connection, of course, but very little had ever been exchanged across that either way. Less and less for the past six years. Not even *tempers*. Actually, he had never in his life reprimanded Lillian, never once given her so much as a spanking. Such things had been left to someone else, usually to Evelyn, her mother.

Lillian hadn't been planned.

She was a sort of penalty for, anyway a consequence of, an impetuous moment on the way home from a party in Scarsdale. If Evelyn had kept her hands to herself, if she'd had two or three rather than six or seven champagnes. If they'd left the party earlier, or hadn't gone at all. If there hadn't been a place to pull the car over. If, when he was into it, his coming had happened on an out- rather than an in-stroke, he might have been able to withdraw.

It seemed ironic to Laurence Holbrook II that Lillian, as imposing and complicating as she was, should have resulted from such simply avoidable circumstances.

He would never forget doing ninety on icy roads, trying to get Evelyn home in time. A race against sperm.

Only child Lillian.

If Laurence resented her, it was a feeling too unnatural for him to admit, especially to himself. Any such feelings were coated with demonstrations of just the opposite. Inconsistent doting. Overplaying his role. He would take her to see the sea, get his feet wet with her, let her have anything she wanted for dinner, tuck her in and goodnight kiss her forehead as though it were fragile.

Then, practically ignore her for a month.

Evelyn's constant caring made up for that, as much as it could. From the moment Lillian was toddling, Evelyn took her everywhere, time after time, even to places most mothers went to retreat from their children. With her while she had a facial, had her hair done, shopped at Saks, lunched at the Plaza, went to galleries, auctions at Parke-Bernet. Over the years they were together so much that Lillian took on Evelyn's mannerisms, duplicated her gestures and ways, every nuance exactly. There had been considerable resemblance to start, but by the time Lillian was ten she was like a miniature Evelyn. People said it was remarkable.

Lillian was ten that night at the huge summer house in Seal Harbor, Maine, when she overheard the quarrel between Evelyn and Laurence. She had overheard and even witnessed other such quarrels, many. Usually they happened at night. Sometimes Lillian pretended what she was hearing was a television program. That night they were having a long bad one.

The next morning when Lillian went down to breakfast, Evelyn was already up and out, gone sailing.

Why hadn't she taken Lillian along?

Lillian ran down to the dock. The boat with its red sail was not yet too far out. Lillian shouted, but Evelyn didn't seem to hear, didn't look back. It was a heavy sunless day with a slapping breeze. Lillian sat on the dry, slivery wood of the dock, watched Evelyn sail away, headed directly out to sea. The smaller the red sail got, the thicker dark the sky became, and the breeze turned into a wind and blew windier. The sea, a disturbed color, all chopped up and spitting. Evelyn was a mere speck of red on the horizon that Lillian's eyes tried not to let go.

Evelyn's body washed up five miles down coast. Three days later the ashes of her, in a solid silver urn, were placed in a crypt at St. James Cemetery in Greenwich, Connecticut.

She left everything that was hers to Lillian. Though her social credentials had been less than those of Laurence Holbrook II, Evelyn Mayo had been worth more. The base chunk of the Mayo fortune was made in the mid-1800s by an Irish immigrant, Daniel Mayo. A glib, go-lucky gambler who won some Pennsylvania land with three nines. Found coal on it. The coal also got him into steel, which got him into a number of other profitable things. He died in 1908 at the age of fifty-four, bequeathing some twenty millions to his son Arthur. Arthur Mayo multiplied that. He cleaned up during the Depression. Sensed it coming, liquidated, transferred huge amounts to Europe. Thus, when practically everyone else was going under, willing to sell for next to nothing, Arthur Mayo had the capital. He acquired various large businesses that needed merely his financial transfusion to make them healthy. He pressed his cash advantage mercilessly when it came to real estate, especially choice properties in New York City, Boston and Philadelphia. For a while there, even Arthur Mayo lost track of what he owned and how much all of it was worth. And by the time he got everything in order, World War II broke out to offer other money-making opportunities.

Arthur Mayo never stopped expanding. In 1953 he died at his desk in the Mayo Building, just minutes after finalizing the takeover of a major insurance company. He not only knew how to make money; he knew how to keep it. He had organized the Mayo holdings in such a complex way that it was impossible for the government to eat them up with taxes. The government took its bite, but by comparison it was a mere nibble. There were all sorts of generating funds legally structured around other funds. Like giant boxes containing boxes and so on, until it came down to very little. What's more, it was the sort of fortune already set up with excellent management, thereby leaving its principal beneficiary free to enjoy it.

All that went to Lillian—upon her maturity. Laurence Holbrook II wasn't even named executor. He considered that a slap in the face, but for the sake of his social-macho pride, the less made of it the better.

Lillian was enrolled in a nice school located outside Philadelphia. It was said it was good for her to be away, distracted from hurt by having to contend with new surroundings and strangers.

Over the next six years Lillian went to five such schools. In that same time, Laurence was married and divorced twice. He was perpetually involved with women, although never more than one at a time. Each affair was entered into with the same attitude of new, utmost importance. The only difference among them was it took longer for some to dissipate.

That was another reason Laurence was disappointed that Lillian didn't come home from her Swiss school in the spring of 1966. He had wanted to tell her about the young woman he was now serious about, might marry. He hadn't asked for Lillian's approval before, but she was old enough to appreciate such thoughtfulness. Besides, the previous summer Lillian had let him off the hook. Her last day home they had walked together in the woods around the estate.

"Fatherhood isn't natural," she said. "Did you ever consider that?"

He hadn't.

It was something she'd recently read that stuck with her.

"Not long ago there was no such thing," she said.

"Everyone had a father."

"Yeah. But back in those days no one realized the connection between screwing and having a baby. Simply because the two happened nine months apart."

"How did they think the woman got pregnant?"

"Some mysterious, divine way. Screwing was strictly for fun."

"Millions of years ago, perhaps."

"Only twenty thousand."

His impulse had been to say they knew better now, of course, but just then he was in no mood to defend himself. Seeing that he was willing to let it go at that, she put her arm around him, perhaps consolingly, and as they walked on he thought she was starting to understand him.

Anyway, Lillian would not be home for spring vacation. That left him free to be with Patricia, whom he had met two months ago. Patricia with something in her eyes that he refused to believe was dollar signs. She wanted to go with him to his house in Palm Beach, and now that wouldn't have to be sacrificed.

He took up the phone, dialed half of Patricia's New York number, then pressed the cradle down to get a fresh dial tone. It would be an easy enough point in his favor to express his disappointment to Lillian. He called the school in Gstaad. The headmistress told him that, no, Lillian was not there and, no, Lillian was not in Rome or Cairo. She had departed for home, as allowed by Monsieur.

He called Swissair. Flight 110 had landed on time. The airline night supervisor confirmed that Lillian Holbrook had been a passenger.

He called the police. Kidnapping was assumed. The newspapers and television played it up, milked the story. But gradually *Where is Lillian Holbrook?* gave way to more current issues and misfortunes and crimes. The kidnapping was briefly mentioned in the press eight months later when Laurence Holbrook II married twenty-three-year-old fashion model Darlene Casey.

During the first few weeks Lillian often thought of going home. She felt guilty for causing so much commotion, and according to all the accounts she read and saw, her father seemed sincerely concerned. Ambivalent, restless, she took long late-night walks alone, until she was chased for her body and nearly caught by four studded leather types. From then on, she went up and sat on the roof to think things out.

She decided in her own favor.

She was living then with Charity in a one-room sixth-floor walkup on East Eleventh Street, near Avenue B. A pair of bedrolls, three plates, four mayonnaise jars for glasses, a few odd knives and forks. Stapled to the tops of the windows was heavy brown wrapping paper that could be rolled up and let

down. A Swedish ivy plant, overcared for, on the sill. No
refrigerator. For fifty dollars a month. They earned about a
hundred a month stringing beads, sewing headbands and making simple silver wire jewelry that a guy sold to tourists at his
head shop on MacDougal Street.

Lillian stayed home more than half the time, didn't hang
around St. Mark's Place or take up with anyone except
Charity. She was afraid she'd be recognized. And there were
plenty of bounty hunters around, guys and a few girls who
turned in runaways for whatever they could get from parents.
One or two of the free crash pads were actually operated for
such profit.

Lillian, because of her worth, had to be especially careful.
She kept her hair trimmed short and wore plain wire-rimmed
glasses.

By August she was confident enough to march. Up Fifth
Avenue, with ten thousand others. She and Charity carried a
sign they had water-colored the night before. Delicate
curlicues and pretty swirls around the request: PEACE PLEASE.

She felt on display, intimidated by the onlookers, but after
twenty blocks those feelings were stirred away. Never mind
the ridicule from those on the sidewalks, the obscenities, or
even the more active contempt of construction workers who
threw garbage—she was in the stream of love, part of a gentle,
invulnerable defiance.

She practically skipped up the rest of the avenue, and on into
Central Park to the Sheep Meadow, where the energy of the
day was pooled on the grass in the sun. The word *love* was
everywhere. Most beautiful slogan. Hers now.

Lillian really listened to most of the speeches, contributed
her cheers. She mingled, exchanged tender gazes, got kissed
and hugged by strangers, kissed and hugged other strangers,
helped sing a wistful song and had white daisies rained upon
her from a helicopter.

It was, she thought, the most wonderful day of her life. She
felt changed by it, as though she had passed from confinement
to an openness where she joined a happier part of herself that
had been waiting.

From that day on Lillian was in the thick of it.

She fell in young love twice. First with Michael and his
poetry. Hitchhiked across the country with him. She didn't like
Haight-Ashbury. He did. One morning she left him sleeping.

Caught rides to L.A., crashed around there, ran out of money, worked making beds in a big motel on Cahuenga.

Hitched her way back east.

Her second love was for Dennis and his intensity. He left her to join the Hare Krishnas. She saw him one summer Saturday, bald, barefoot, with a white stripe smeared down his forehead and the bridge of his nose, chanting and shaking bells near Rockefeller Center. Too busy with God to say hello.

She concentrated then on being a better revolutionary, liked the designation.

Fuck the Establishment!

Stopped up pay toilets in Grand Central and elsewhere by flushing down tennis balls that lodged in the pipes.

Carried a pocketful of four-inch flat-headed nails that she placed under the tires of any police cars and limousines outside the Waldorf.

Was proud she'd been busted ten times.

Knew how it was to have Mace in her face.

The Chicago convention, fight night in front of the Hilton: She jumped on the back of a cop who was clubbing someone down. Rode, clawed, kicked for his groin. Came to a few hours later at Northwestern Memorial Hospital, stitched thirty-two times in various places on her skull and with a very puffy upper lip. She asked for a mirror, grinned at herself and made sure she still had all her teeth.

She was around a lot of drugs, of course, but never got into them. Early on she gave everything one try for experience. When a joint was being passed, she passed. Relied on her natural highs and persevered her natural downs. Even at the Woodstock festival she stayed straight. Saturday night up on the fringe of People Hill, a mile from the stage, she climbed a large maple tree and sat out on a branch with a jug of Gallo red while Creedence Clearwater performed electronic chaos. Lillian met up with Charity again that day. Seven-and-a-half-months-pregnant Charity. The young man with her was not the father. They were living on a commune in Massachusetts, near Pittsfield. Did "Penny" know where that was?

She told them maybe someday she'd find it.

"Lots of people rap about you," Charity said. "Did you really shove a hardhat down a Con Ed hole?"

"He started it."

"Better not fuck with you, right?"

Lillian shrugged modestly.

"I love you, Penny."

For the next year Lillian drifted with the action. About the only thing she missed out on was the People's Park hassle in Berkeley. She seemed to have a knack for being wherever there was trouble. Sometimes she brought it.

Money was a problem. She didn't need much but had to scuffle for it. Waitressed, washed cars, tie-dyed T-shirts which she sold on the sidewalk outside Bloomingdale's. Also picked apples, did Tarot readings, learned to cut hair, pasted outdoor posters. Nothing steady.

Soon as possible after the Kent State killings she got a guy, a Nam vet sharpshooter, to teach her guns. The noise bothered her, but there was something agreeable about the smell of it. She only flinched the first time she fired. Not even a blink after that. Some people were naturals, the guy said.

She heard about an abandoned farm in Bethel, New York. A small place. She went there, moved in. Cleaned it up, painted it fresh. Put silver cardboard in place of the broken windowpanes. Couldn't stop the roof from leaking but got the wood stove going after she'd figured out the damper. Grew her own vegetables out back. Corn, cucumbers, tomatoes, lima beans. Five days a week, succotash. She'd never felt so self-sufficient. The ground around the house was overgrown. She let it be. Thigh-high grass with tassel tops, dotted with buttery-yellow flowers and anemic black-eyed Susans. Better than any big manicured lawn any day. Out back in dappled shade she put an old iron bed, springs and mattress. It was a marvelous place to lie with nothing on and just feel good. On hot nights she slept out there, tented in gauzy fabric that kept out some mosquitoes.

Friends—a few she actually knew—came and stayed a night or as long as a month. They nearly always left something behind on purpose. A chair, a painting, a dish, depending upon whether they'd come on foot or wheels. Someone left a broken hi-fi that someone else fixed. Records collected: Dylan, Hendrix, The Stones, Moby Grape, The Who.

Penny's.

It became a place for guys on their way to Canada instead of Vietnam. A safe stop for Weathermen on the run. Wanted young men whose photographs, full-face and profile, were displayed in post offices all over the country. They sat, sipped rosehip tea and predicted violence. The thirty million of the right age would rise up together when the day came.

Vietnamization? What a laugh that was.

But then the war was over, and things changed. The movement started going apart, scattering. Even some of the ones who had been most fervently involved mustered themselves out.

Fewer and fewer people came by Lillian's farm in Bethel. Those who did had selfish destinations.

Lillian left the farm, just left it for anyone.

She went back to New York City. Found an extremely radical couple she'd once known running a spice-and-herb store on Ninth Street. Camomile tea for three-fifty a pound. Jesus. A girl who'd once ripped off some dynamite from a construction site had a boutique on Christopher Street and was hoping to do well enough to eventually move uptown. Another girl was overjoyed at having been accepted into a well-known dance group. The way she talked, she'd been deprived till then.

There were no more crash pads. Doors were closed, triple-locked. You could stay only if you could pay.

Not everyone was like that, of course, but too many.

Lillian sat on the steps of St. Mark's Church and tried to cope with her disappointment. What the hell had happened to the revolution? Had the war been the only thing worth bitching about? Nixon was still in the White House. The Pentagon was still feeding the fat cats. The system was still fucking everybody over, every which way.

Remember Flower Power?

It was impossible that the cause had been that shallow. The revolution wasn't, couldn't be over. Shit, she was just getting her dander up.

She hung around the Village for a week. Thought about getting into Women's Lib but knew, no matter how widespread or active it got, it wouldn't provide the stimulation she was used to. She considered going to Boston or San Francisco to see if things were better there.

Instead she took a subway uptown. The Lexington local. Got off at Fifty-first, walked over to Park to the new Mayo Building.

Executive offices, thirty-seventh floor.

The receptionist had reason to be dubious.

Lillian was wearing a black cowboy hat, a floor-length full-skirted cotton dress, a brown velvet jacket she'd bought third-hand last year. Ankle-high, lace-up work shoes. And she was carrying her bedroll.

It took three hours for Lillian to convince them. Her fingerprints were proof. The head of the Mayo legal department said it was fortunate she'd shown up. In another three days she would have been declared legally dead.

They arranged for a suite of rooms at the Regency.

Next day she went shopping for everything, had her hair done at Cinandre. Felt foolish—and beautiful.

She met her father for dinner at "21." He embraced her twice when she arrived at the table. He was a slightly older version of the man in her memory. As they talked she noticed a humility about him that hadn't been there before. Inconsistent, but it seemed sincere. He didn't appear strained, laughed wryly when he informed her he wasn't married "at the moment."

It came out, however, that he was emotionally and financially debilitated. In three days he would have been allowed to dip as deep as he wanted into the Mayo fortune. Her immediate reaction was that it served him right; he had unmade his own bed. She might have stuck with that opinion seven years ago but couldn't now. What the hell, if it made him happy, he should have a different affair or wife every week. As for money, she had more than they could ever spend. She promised straight out to see that he had an ample account to draw from. No need to alter his life-style. His eyes watered. Over coffee he told her about an incredible girl he'd met last month at a disco.

Since that day Lillian had tried to adjust. Having money wasn't difficult, but not having a cause was miserable.

She was quickly bored by most things, places. Cap Ferrat—at her villa there, everything was too predictable. The same applied to Paris, the Algarve, London. There were times when she longed for danger—the enterprising balance it took to live on the edge of it. She had fantasies of causing riots. Couldn't tolerate New York City anymore. From the window of her apartment on Fifth Avenue she could see the Sheep Meadow—but only kites, Frisbees, baby carriages and ball games now. She'd bought the house in Mexico City, hoping to get away from the United States in a less conforming way. For old times and to break the monotony, she frequently hitchhiked anywhere.

However, it had occurred to her that only the rich could be poor when they chose.

Being too much in the company of people such as those in Las Hadas caused her to get what she called "the crazies." To counteract those spells, she had devised the room, adequately reminiscent of that sixth-floor walkup she had shared with Charity.

Wiley hadn't said a word in nearly three hours. Each time Lillian stopped talking, he'd used silence to get her started again.

He was sitting on the foot of the mattress, little more than a reach from her. The madras spread had fallen from her shoulders. Her head was lowered so that her face was hidden by the fall of her hair.

"I've only told bits and pieces of it before," she said.

A privilege, Wiley thought.

"I feel lightheaded." She presented her face to him. "How do I look?"

Pale, he thought, but that could be the light. Dawn was under way outside, coming in around the brown wrapping paper that served as a shade for the only window. "Perhaps you didn't get enough sleep," he said.

"I'm not at all sleepy."

"Neither am I."

She smiled, and he realized what he'd taken for paleness had been strain. She stood suddenly, arched her back to stretch it. The tank top, which was all she had on, barely reached her waist. "Let's get out of this old place," she said and walked by Wiley, who let pass the opportunity to reach out for her. He followed into the bedroom. She paused, glanced at the bed, decided.

"Last one in has to make breakfast," she said.

Childish, but it was certainly a woman who got a head start, ran out of the bedroom and down the hall. Bare feet smacking the tiled floor, long legs churning, her behind tightening left and right. She took the stairs down recklessly four and five at a time.

Wiley noticed her tank top on the bannister below. His sense of direction led him out to the pool area. There she was, about a hundred feet away, standing on the edge, poised to dive. No contest. He might as well just enjoy the sight of her.

But as he went closer, she remained as she was. Purposely,

it seemed. Same attitude she'd displayed when they'd swum practically nude on that divided beach. Remote and, at the same time, offering.

He was close enough now for a chance to beat her into the water. He casually stepped out of his peasant *pantalones*, as though he'd either conceded or forgotten her challenge. She faked a springing motion. He dove past her.

The water was freezing cold.

He came to the surface spewing, making suffering sounds.

"The heater is being fixed," she explained innocently.

Wiley was tempted to get revenge with some splashes.

She sprang and did a neat slicing dive, came up breathing hard but without a complaint. "Think how cold the water is in Iceland," she said. "By comparison this is tropical."

"Bullshit."

"Try thinking about it that way, it helps."

He kept treading for circulation, putting his tongue between his teeth so they wouldn't chatter. "It's practically boiling."

"By comparison," she reminded him.

They swam eight lengths. Then went into the enclosed cabana to dry off with oversized towels. Wiley was surprised his wound hadn't started bleeding again. He caught Lillian's look on him. She didn't take it away, not immediately.

The cabana was equipped to be independent of the main house. There were two couches, double deep, more like giant chaises. Lillian lay back in one, her head and shoulders propped against several pillows, legs up and straight out on the seat, but crossed. Wiley sat on the edge of the couch opposite. He very much wanted a cigarette, but didn't want to risk spoiling the moment. After all, she could have chosen to cover with a towel.

"Okay, loser, what's for breakfast?" he asked.

She invited him with her arms.

He went across to be in them. They held, pressed against each other full length. They didn't kiss immediately, saved the kiss, were cheek against cheek, each hearing the other's breath.

Every movement of his hands was discovery. The finer texture of her skin, the way each part of her made a nice transition to the next, the way her sides became her breasts. He skimmed her surfaces, matching the shapes of her with the flat or curve of his hands. Here and there his fingers kneaded gently, wanting to feel beneath her surface, the definition of her hips, the back wings of her shoulders, collarbones and their sockets, rib-cage symmetry, the ladder of her spine. When he placed his hand on her left breast, the heel of his hand received the beating of her heart, the crisp racing of it. Nothing extraordinary. Everyone had a heart. But hers, like all else about her, was miraculous.

In only minutes he knew more of her body than he ever had of anyone's. And there was so much more to know.

In that same time her hands, not reluctant, did glides and squeezes for herself. It pleased him that she was able to take without pretending it was mainly to please him.

She claimed him.

He parted her.

He wanted it to be unusually good for her, a time mark. He would rely upon technique, he thought. There, just then, she responded with a tightening as he touched a certain way, place. He would return precisely there, to that. He went on, gathering more to go on, becoming increasingly confident he would be able to please her. But he had to contend with himself, the crowding already in him. Her hands on him—could he block out that those were her hands? He had to take her hands away, as much as he didn't want to, the way they insisted.

She pulled him over onto her. Reached down and found herself with him, pushed upward to have it entirely.

She started coming almost at once. An exceptional, drawn-out come. Unaware of the sound like a note that came from her, long held and sort of painful.

He just did manage to keep going. Until stopped by her when that was how she wanted it, all in, not even a suggestion of out.

He remained still, had to.

"Don't hold back," she whispered. But he was now in control enough not to believe that, and in another moment she told him, "More."

They didn't have breakfast until nearly noon. Lillian prepared it, while Wiley sat at a counter in the spacious kitchen. The cook wasn't anywhere about, nor were any of the other servants. Perhaps Lillian had given them the day off, or perhaps they were somewhere in the huge house, knowing that now was one of those times they should keep out of sight.

"Want sausage?" Lillian asked.

Wiley was ravenous.

She told him: "Actually you shouldn't eat meat."

"I don't see how vegetarians exist."

"I look unhealthy?"

Hardly. Wearing a pair of white silk-satin shorts, styled after the sort a serious runner would wear. A matching top with the number 10 on its back. High-heeled sandals that made the most of her legs. Wiley reminded himself that he had to eat.

"The lesbians in Paris keep their lovers half starved," she said, "so they always have an appetite."

"I need meat," he told her.

"Not really."

"For stamina."

She gave that a thought and got sausage from the refrigerator. She fried it along with a four-egg omelette.

Observing her, Wiley thought she was playing house. She wouldn't enjoy such things if she had to do them, despite the picture of domesticity she'd drawn when she'd told him of the way she'd been on that farm in Bethel.

But she agitated the frying pan with authority to have the sausage links brown evenly, folded the omelette at just the right moment and slid it with a flourish onto his plate.

He dug in.

She spread his napkin for him, as though commenting on his table manners. While he ate she set up a large wicker tray. On it she placed a bowl of deep red plums, black African grapes, tiny tangerines, a tin of Carr's water biscuits and various cheeses such as creamy Tilsit, Tybo and Brie. A dish of fresh raspberries, nuts mixed with Mannouka raisins. Sections of lady peppers sprinkled with sea salt, a pair of fine crystal goblets and three bottles of Mouton-Rothschild '65. As an afterthought, a box of Oreo cookies.

"What else do you want to do today?" she asked.

"What's today, Monday?"

"Could be."

"It's up to you."

"Hopefully," she arched. She picked up the heavy tray and wouldn't let him carry it upstairs.

They were in bed or, if not entirely in it, around it all that afternoon and night. Without too much erotic trickery she tapped a reservoir of loving in Wiley he hadn't known was there. It seemed he couldn't get enough of her, nor she of him, although time after time they experienced extreme satisfaction. He would lie there, feeling delightfully depleted, unable to want to move a muscle. All she had to do was kneel up and push her hair back, or walk to the bathroom, or unconsciously wet her lips, to start him again.

Between times, after after-naps, they ate from the tray she'd prepared and talked, about things such as the United States.

Wiley said he was disappointed in his country. It had disappointed him. Land of opportunity, bullshit. He'd never go back.

In a different way it had disappointed her. A whole revolution had deserted her.

It was something else they had in common.

Something else, she agreed.

He told her about his family in Key West, living in a mobile home.

"They probably like it," she commented.

Wiley couldn't believe that.

He also told her about Jennifer, not all the sordid details, just the sordid highlights.

At first he detected a hint of sympathy for Jennifer; that disappeared, however, when he related some of her tactics, her last-minute charge account binge, for one thing.

"Doesn't sound to me as though you had a good enough lawyer. What did you say his name was?"

"Simon and Simon."

"Simon-ese twins."

Wiley laughed but was seriously regretting he hadn't been able to settle with Jennifer. Leaving her empty-handed had backfired quickly. He wasn't free.

"A married man," Lillian said thoughtfully, "is about the only one of my absolutely inflexible rules I never break." She turned onto her side, knees knifed up in a sleeping position, her back to Wiley.

He thought, twenty-five thousand—no, closer to forty counting attorneys' fees and all—was what he needed to dispense with Jennifer. He'd get it. It had become essential that he get it. At the moment he was too tired to consider how.

He clicked off the light, plumped and positioned his pillow and fit himself snug, front to back, against Lillian.

His mind began shutting down for the night, except for one thought that refused to be put away. It insisted on being said.

"I love you, Lillian."

Nothing from her, not even an *uh-huh*.

She was probably asleep.

11 ➤➤➤

Next morning, when Wiley was shaving with Lillian's razor, it occurred to him that he might already have enough to pay off Jennifer. Possibly more than enough, depending on what the emeralds were worth. The emeralds that had gotten him into that Prentiss scrape in Las Hadas. No doubt those men had searched the suite for them. He'd left the chamois pouch on the bedside table but dropped the emeralds into a bottle of green crème de menthe at the bar. Perhaps a clever enough hiding place.

He figured if that emerald transaction was worth three million, those seven sample emeralds in the pouch had to be fairly valuable. Purely guessing, he thought eight thousand each.

Fifty-six thousand. Add on his twelve thousand cash hidden in the lamp base. Subtract forty for Jennifer. Left him a free man with twenty-eight thousand.

The prospect was so appealing he nicked himself shaving, just below his left earlobe. The sight of blood made him think of that he'd already shed. In a way he'd earned those goddamn emeralds.

Lillian was in the shower, which consisted of numerous separate sprays, including three that spouted from the floor. When she turned it off and stepped out, Wiley told her he had to return to Las Hadas.

"For what?" she asked.

"Can't go around in those forever," meaning the raw cotton *pantalones* crumpled like dirty laundry on the floor.

"I've already arranged for your things to be brought here."

"When?"

"By tonight, they'll be flown down."

"What about my money?"

"That too."

"Who's bringing it?"

"Marianna."

101

"A friend?"

"A sort of personal secretary. Actually I don't give her much to do. She welcomed the responsibility."

"Is she someplace we can reach her?"

"This very moment?"

"Yes."

"I suppose we could radiophone the plane, but by now she may have already been there and gone."

"I left something else in the room, something I forgot to mention."

"Forgot?"

"Anyway, didn't."

"What?"

He told her, what and exactly where. The emeralds.

She chided him with a glance, then went into the bedroom to use the phone. Wiley remained in the bathroom and brushed his teeth, stopping every so often to overhear some of what she was saying. Evidently she got through, gave Marianna instructions regarding the emeralds.

Wiley felt good about it. He'd feel better when he had everything there.

"Meanwhile," Lillian told him, "we're going shopping."

"I've nothing to wear."

"That, darling, is the reason we're going."

"Can't I just hang around like this until tonight?"

"I'm in a shopping mood," she said. She was getting dressed, seemed to give little thought to what she chose to put on. Nevertheless, the result was perfectly fashionable. A beige tunic dress of wool crepe with an elongated coat; tied low, slightly blouson, a scarf of the same. She hid all her hair in a cloche and slipped on a pair of light-scaled Charles Jourdan shoes, also beige.

Wiley had never seen anyone become so chic so quickly. There he was, still standing in his altogether.

"Comb your hair," she said. "I've got a coat for you."

They took the limousine, a Daimler, because they would be needing room, Lillian said. The chauffeur's name was Bryan. Good man. He didn't even blink while holding the car door for Wiley, whose bare legs and bare feet were visible below the coat. It was a trenchcoat, much too large around and with not nearly long-enough sleeves. It had been left by someone, Lillian said. She honestly didn't know who.

"No matter what, I'm not getting out of the car," Wiley said.

"Thought you might want to stand around and flash."

"Okay, pick me a corner."

"What size are you?"

"That matters?"

"I mean in a suit, for instance." She had out a pen and pad.

"I don't want you to buy me any clothes."

"I want to."

"No."

"You're going to spoil my entire day."

He didn't want to make her unhappy, not for a second.

"I want to have lunch at Fouquet's," she said, "to show you off and everything."

He could pay her back whatever she spent, he thought, so he told her, "Forty long."

She jotted that down, along with all his other sizes and measurements. "Now we're really getting intimate," she said with a grin.

"One thing you missed."

"What?"

"Which side I dress on."

"I already knew." She gave him a kiss so he wouldn't think she was such a smartass.

Soon they were in the city's Zona Rosa, near the Paseo de la Reforma. They double-parked on Amberes while she went into one of the shops along there.

Wiley felt restive, slouched down, shoved his hands in the coat pockets. In one he found a box of Dunhill cigarettes with three in it. He lighted up. It tasted good, though stale, because it was his first of the day. Usually by that time he'd finished off close to half a pack. It was foolish of her to believe she could get him to stop. Although, come to think of it, since the night before last he'd smoked only five, maybe six. He took two fast drags, deep ones, to make up for it some.

She came out to the car, threw a couple of packages into the rear seat. "No fair peeking," she said and was gone again, down the street.

Bryan cruised after her, double-parked while she went in various places all the way down Amberes and around Londres and Génova to Avenida Chapultepec. Each time she brought back more packages to the car. After two and a half hours, she got in, flopped into the plush seat and let out an exhausted

sigh. So many packages by then, there was hardly any leg
room.

Bryan drove around while Wiley dressed. Lillian indicated
which packages he should open. He assumed the others contained things for herself.

For him she'd chosen a dark-gray vested suit of fine wool
flannel, with a subtle pinstripe. The trousers were pleated and
cuffed. Its label said Nino Cerruti. To go with it, a pure silk
shirt of a creamy shade, hand-detailed, and a wide silk geo-
metric-patterned necktie. Everything, including shoes and
socks, coordinated and fit perfectly. It wasn't easy for him to
dress in the car, particularly to get his shirt tucked in so it felt
neat, and he thought it only luck that he was able, first try, to
knot the tie nicely without a mirror. She put the finishing touch
on him by stuffing a blue silk square into his breast pocket,
fussing with it.

She was pleased with his appearance.

They had a late lunch.

She passed him money for the bill under the table, and he
didn't mind because the circumstances were temporary. He'd
even up with her that night.

It was nearly nightfall when they arrived home. Wiley had in
mind going straight to bed for a while. But someone was
waiting in the study.

Meno Argenti.

The heavyweight himself, looking casually meticulous as
ever, curly hair and beard glistening. He gave Lillian cheek
kisses and cooed a flattering hello.

She seemed glad to see him. For a moment she forgot to
introduce Wiley.

"We met, I believe," Argenti said during their handshake.

Wiley thought the man's huge hand was in keeping with his
power.

"I was here on business and decided I should surprise. I am
not intruding?"

"'Course not," Lillian said.

Why not the truth? Wiley thought. On second thought,
maybe it was the truth.

"You'll stay for dinner?" she asked.

"Better than that, I'm yours until tomorrow morning," Argenti said. "I assumed you would want me in the same room as
before, so I had my bags taken up."

"Only till tomorrow morning?" Lillian seemed disappointed.

Argenti apologized. "As for my dinner, please, a salad of some sort. I am on a regime."

"What a shame. I was going to have cook do up some of your favorite pastries."

Same room as before, favorite pastries—Wiley felt like a second-string rookie.

They sat there in the study, Lillian on the leather-covered sofa, Argenti and Wiley in facing armchairs. There was an energetic blaze in the fireplace.

"You look well, Meno," Lillian said.

"I conceal my pain."

"Oh?"

"My longing for you. Like a clawing animal that runs through me."

"That's a new one," she said, amused.

"It pleases you?"

"Well, your overheated-blood routine was getting passé."

"My congenital disposition."

"If you say."

"My grandfather at ninety-seven was accused of violating the mayor's daughter," Argenti said. "He was acquitted because of his age."

"And because he didn't do it."

"He most certainly did do it. Considered it a personal insult that anyone should believe otherwise."

Argenti beamed. His teeth seemed extremely white and lethal.

Wiley decided it would be unwise to ever take the man lightly. He could probably live up to his boasts, a dangerous rival. And not only because he was worth millions.

Lillian wanted wine. She called a servant, ordered some white, Le Montrachet '70.

Not quite good enough for Argenti. Besides, he was in the mood for a red. Did she have any Latour Pauillac '70?

No.

Then a Margaux '70, perhaps?

Perhaps.

Wiley, observing closely, believed he saw a flash of pique in Lillian's eyes. She covered it quickly with congeniality.

The servant brought the wine. A bottle of Le Montrachet for

Lillian and Wiley, and a bottle of Pommard '69, nowhere near the quality of the reds Argenti had requested.

Argenti didn't try to disguise his annoyance. He took a sip and put his glass down on a table in a manner that conveyed he'd never touch it again.

Lillian smiled, excused herself and left the room.

Argenti glanced around, at everything except Wiley. He asked, "What do you do, Mr. Wiley?"

Various lies came to mind, but Wiley told him, "This and that, here and there."

"If you are looking for something, I can always use a good man."

"How do you know I'm good?"

"You look it."

That again, Wiley thought.

"Besides," Argenti continued, "I am incredibly intuitive when it comes to judging a man. I am never wrong."

"You just met me."

"I am even better at first impressions."

What, Wiley wondered, could be better than perfect?

"Anyway, my insight also tells me these times are bad for you. Am I correct?"

Wiley didn't want to admit it. But he more or less did, by not denying it.

"I have a spot for you," Argenti said.

"Doing what?"

"Traveling. You would be a sort of courier. Do you enjoy traveling?"

"No, thanks."

"Why not?"

"I couldn't be anyone's messenger boy."

"It would hardly be that, certainly not for a hundred thousand a year. Plus bonuses that would bring it up close to two hundred thousand."

Argenti wasn't serious, merely playing rich man, Wiley decided. No one would offer a stranger two hundred thousand a year.

"On top of that," Argenti continued, "would be whatever you could steal from me. As much as double the amount."

"What makes you assume I'd steal?"

"I would expect you to—to that extent." Argenti stood

abruptly. "I must piss," he announced, as though he might honor Wiley by doing so then and there. He left the study.

Wiley went looking for Lillian, found her in her bedroom, lying on a slant board, with only bikini panties on.

"How'd you get along with Al Capone?" she asked.

"Who?"

"Lucky Luciano."

"Oh, okay."

"I'm sorry I deserted you." She did one situp and fell back. "I already did fifty," she claimed. Her stomach was tight as a drumhead, reminding Wiley of the stomachs of girls in television commercials for exercise salons.

He unknotted his tie, slid it off, unbuttoned his shirt and vest. Sat on the edge of the bed.

"By the way," she told him, "your room is now the first one down on the right."

Because Argenti had taken over that room in the other wing, Wiley realized. It bothered him, but he reasoned that having the room right next to hers was better, anyway. He doubted he'd be using it much.

"Did What's-her-name get back?" he asked.

"Who?"

"From Las Hadas."

"Oh, Marianna. Yes."

"She got everything?"

"Bungalow 114 was occupied by a fashion editor and her model friend. Marianna walked in on them. It was rather embarrassing."

"But she did get my things?"

"Your clothes weren't there."

"Maybe someone packed them and was holding them for me. Did Marianna ask at the front desk?"

"As far as Las Hadas is concerned, darling, you were never there. You never registered."

Fucking thieving Mexicans, Wiley thought. Probably the porter.

"My money . . in the lamp base . . ."

"Gone."

"The emeralds?"

"Not a trace."

Wiley sagged. Now all he had were the clothes he had on, and he couldn't even repay Lillian for those.

"It's my fault," she said.

"No."

"We should have gone back when you wanted to. But I was afraid something might happen . . .to you."

That was a lot better than nothing, he thought.

"I'll make it up to you." She smiled, toothy, and beckoned. He kneeled beside the slant board. She put her hand on the back of his neck to pull his face down for a kiss.

He was numb. It took a short while for the kiss to reach him.

"Poor soul," she murmured.

Dumb fuck, was what he thought of himself. Crème de menthe hadn't been the place to hide those emeralds. But the lamp base. . .it seemed incredible that anyone would think of looking there, take the trouble of unscrewing the base purely on speculation. *His* twelve thousand. . . .

"Why don't you go try to take a nap?" she said.

"You want to get rid of me now that I'm broke?" A tinge of self-pity.

"For an hour or two."

She gave him another, shorter kiss.

Kneeling and bent way over as he was, the blood rushed to his head. Homage to an upside-down woman. He needed to see her eyes, but was too close. He pulled away slightly, told her, "I love you."

"Sounds true." She might as well have soothed his brow.

He was embarrassed. He stood up quickly and brushed at the knees of his trousers.

"These shoes pinch," he said.

"They didn't have them in your width, but I like that style. Don't you?"

He said he did.

"Sometimes you have to sacrifice fit."

"Yeah."

"Have a nice nap and don't worry," she said before he'd even started to leave.

"In case of emergency, knock on the wall," he said.

His new room was almost half the size of the other. Even then, it was much too much for his mood. He removed his clothes, started to throw them over a chair, but decided, being all he had, he'd best treat them better. He opened the closet to get a hanger.

There was practically an entire wardrobe inside.

Everything brand-new and expensive. Everything his size.

He remembered her saying she'd make it up to him. Her shopping spree. All those packages had been for him, and she must have had others sent. But, wait a minute, hadn't that been before Marianna reported his total loss at Las Hadas? So why had Lillian bought all these things? The only possible explanation was that she'd gotten carried away—with wanting to give to him, to please him.

In that spirit, he had to accept. Besides, he told himself, he still intended somehow to repay her.

That night at dinner Wiley felt invisible most of the time. Lillian directed nearly all her attention to Argenti, who soaked it up and reciprocated with scores of flatteries and overtures. Twice Argenti asked Wiley's opinion, then didn't wait for it.

After dinner they had espresso and Amaretto in the game room. Lillian and Argenti played gin rummy for a dollar a point while Wiley watched.

"No kibitzing," Lillian told him.

Wiley had difficulty keeping silent, especially when he saw Lillian make mistakes, such as discarding what Argenti obviously needed. Either she wasn't as good a gin player as she'd claimed or, for some reason, she was letting Argenti win. They set midnight as the time limit for their play. By then Argenti was ahead eleven thousand and very pleased with himself.

She started to write him a check.

"How about shooting for double or nothing?" he asked.

Wiley thought Argenti meant dice, or possibly marbles. He resented the idea of Lillian playing marbles with anyone else. She had before, of course, but from now on. . . .

They went downstairs to a large basement area. There was a shooting range. Off to one side a glass-enclosed cabinet contained numerous rifles and pistols.

They decided on pistols. Lillian got out two Browning nine-millimeter automatics. And several spare clips.

Wiley, leaning against a cement wall and keeping out of the way, thought how incongruous it was to see her with that weapon. It changed her. As though it radiated lethalness up her arm and through her entire person. It was fascinating and frightening. He had the urge to take it from her, pry it from her grip.

She inserted a clip, rammed it home.

"Hearts?" she asked.

"The most out of thirteen," Argenti said.

She flipped a wall switch that illuminated the target range and activated a pair of targets fifty feet away. They were human shapes, average size, made of metal, painted white. Located at left center chest, precisely where the heart would be, was a hole five inches in diameter. Two other, smaller oval-shaped holes were like eye sockets in the head. The targets, on an electric track, moved to the left at changing speeds, erratically up and down, and then to the right. Difficult to predict what the next motion would be.

Argenti offered Lillian first try.

She told him to go ahead.

He stepped to the line confidently, fired off the entire clip.

The explosions of the shots, greater than Wiley had expected, numbed his hearing. The smell of gunpowder seemed to cloud most of the life out of the air.

An electronic scorekeeper, a black glass-faced box on the left wall, flashed the numeral 8.

Easy as that, apparently without even trying, Argenti had put eight bullets into the heart. Out of thirteen.

Wiley was impressed.

Argenti glanced at him. No mistaking the self-assurance in Argenti's eyes.

Perhaps that was the true purpose of this shooting contest, Wiley thought, to warn him off. Was that why Argenti had suggested it?

Lillian was now on the firing line. She raised the pistol, took careful aim and let go at the target. She was unable to control the recoil of the Browning. The muzzle jerked upward. Her shots went high and higher. The last few into the far ceiling.

No hits, not even one.

Wiley remembered her telling him how she'd learned years ago from that sharpshooter. It made him wonder how much truth there was in the rest of her story.

She said to Argenti, "Now I owe you twenty-two thousand." As though it was nothing.

"Try again?" Argenti asked.

Taking unfair advantage, Wiley thought, the son of a bitch.

His impulse was to challenge Argenti, but he didn't have a dime to bet. What's more, he knew zero about shooting. The last and only time he'd held a gun had been over twenty years ago in Texas. An air gun that shot pellets. He hadn't been able to hit an empty beer can at thirty feet.

Lillian released the used clip from her pistol, told Argenti, "I thought I might beat you without your glasses."

"I am wearing contacts," he replied.

"You're a tricker, Meno, that's what."

Argenti raised his hands palms up and pouted to profess his innocence.

Lillian led the way upstairs, back to the game room. She turned on the stereo for disco music while Argenti went behind the bar. Rather as an afterthought, Argenti asked Wiley what he wanted to drink.

"Boilermaker," Wiley said, hoping to confuse the foreigner.

The Italian filled a double shot glass with Old Grand-Dad and opened a Heineken for a chaser. He mixed a concoction of brandy, tequila, bitters and champagne for Lillian and himself. With the dexterity of a professional bartender, even spinning ice in the glasses to frost them. He hadn't asked Lillian what she wanted, evidently knew.

Wiley told himself that noticing such little things was being absurdly sensitive. Sitting at the bar, he took a gulp of the straight whiskey. The way it burned was a suitable minor punishment. He drank some beer from the bottle.

Argenti carried the drinks over to Lillian.

Watch out, honey, yours is drugged, Wiley's imagination said.

Argenti made a toast, personal enough to be nearly whispered, so Wiley wouldn't hear.

Lillian smiled provocatively and clicked her glass against Argenti's.

They sipped and kept their eyes locked. Then they placed their glasses down, and she turned the music up loud and they danced. Argenti hardly moved. He was like a center post, or perhaps an edifice, around which Lillian demonstrated. She pranced, snapped her head, made hip circles and center thrusts, as though to show various sexual proficiencies.

Wiley was reminded of all the love he'd made with her since yesterday morning. Their first time was already nebulous, obscured by so many subsequent sensations. And now, there

she was, at the least mimicking erotically for Argenti. As far as
they were concerned he wasn't there, Wiley felt. He lighted a
cigarette, held the match up, closed an eye and positioned the
flame so it appeared to be about to ignite Argenti's beard.
Wiley imagined Argenti with his whole head afire. And to hell
with her, too. He downed the rest of his whiskey, poured
another, took it and his beer with him and left the room.

He wandered around the house some, eventually was drawn
downstairs to the shooting range.

He got out one of the Browning automatics. It was indeed
heavier than it looked, maybe two pounds, and felt even dead-
lier in his hand. The human-shaped targets were just standing
there. Wiley took aim, pulled the trigger. The pistol nearly
leaped from his hand. Lucky, he thought, that he hadn't shot
himself.

He got a firmer grip, took more careful aim, but still didn't
hit the metal figure. How the hell could he miss? He had it
right in his sights. The fucking gun was off. He pulled the
trigger again and again until he'd emptied the clip without a
hit.

Argenti, he remembered, had put eight out of thirteen in the
heart. And on the move.

He couldn't even put one anyplace, standing still.

He kept at it. Became more familiar with the weapon, figured out how to reload it, found a carton of bullets in a cabinet
drawer. He steadied his right wrist with his left hand, the way
he'd seen police heroes do in films. He decided the trigger was
crucial, had to be teased so it sort of surprised the mechanism
that exploded the bullet. He took up the slack in the trigger,
squeezed it gently, and that was when he registered his first hit
in the heart.

He got so caught up in it that he didn't think nearly so much
about Lillian upstairs with Argenti. He wouldn't be satisfied
until he hit nine out of thirteen. Moving.

He had just hit six, his best score, when he noticed Lillian.
She was seated on the stairs. From her relaxed position, Wiley
assumed she'd been there awhile. She appeared a bit tousled.
From dancing?

"Where's Albert Anastasia?"

"He got sleepy," she said.

After what? Wiley wondered.

"It's almost four," she said. She came over and touched the barrel of the gun. It was hot.

"You've really been blasting away."

"Wasting time." He shrugged.

"Six out of thirteen hearts is much better than average."

Better than she could do, Wiley thought. She couldn't hit the wall.

She smiled softly, and her eyes were soft on him.

He began loving her again.

She picked up the other Browning, checked to see that it was loaded, cocked a bullet into the chamber and stepped to the firing line. She hesitated, faced away from the moving targets, then spun around into a perfect shooting crouch, and, it seemed, didn't even aim. She fired the entire clip, rapidly. Alternate shots at the heart of one target and then another, and then at the eye sockets to make it more difficult.

Thirteen hits.

She put the pistol down. "Let's go to bed," she said, definitely not meaning sleep.

12 ➤➤➤

First thing Wiley said when he awoke that day was, "I love you."

Lillian reached to press a signal button on her bedside table. She got up, drew open the drapes and went back to bed.

Wiley said it again. It was easy to say because it was true.

She said, "I doubt it."

"Why?"

"You're a fortune hunter."

"That's ridiculous."

"You yourself told me."

"I was only bullshitting."

"See, you even admit to lying."

"About that, yes."

"You really love me?"

"Very much."

"I'll bet I could count the ways. Actually, you know, I don't mind that you're an opportunist, as long as you're straight about it."

"I'm not an . . ."

"I think you are. I mean for other reasons."

"Such as?"

"The way you make love."

"It makes itself."

"Certainly nothing amateurish about it."

"You've got to believe me."

"That's how it'd be?" she asked.

"What do you mean?"

"You'd have to let me know when and when not to believe you."

"Don't you want to believe me?"

"Let's brush our teeth," she said.

They went and foamed at the mouth at each other in the long bathroom mirror.

In bed again, pillows plumped and rearranged, she told him, "Say it again."

"I love you."

"It still *sounds* true enough."

"It is."

"But I thought I detected a tinge of deception in the word *you*."

"*You* was the truest part."

"We'll see."

"How can I convince you?"

"We'll think of something," she promised.

Breakfast trays were brought. Hers had a yellow rose on it with a slip of note paper around its stem. She ignored it while she ate, but Wiley couldn't.

Finally, she dabbed at the corners of her mouth, laid her napkin aside and unrolled the note.

Wiley watched her closely while she read it.

"Meno," she said, "thanks me and sends me his heart and says good-bye to you."

"And good riddance."

"And he invites us to Bogotá." She seemed pleased. "Ever been to Bogotá?"

"Colombia?"

"There's another?"

She picked up the rose. Something dropped from its blossom onto the sheet. A green something so blazing it appeared capable of burning. Lillian nudged it with her finger, causing it to disperse several flares. It was a finished emerald of about ten carats. By comparison, the rough emeralds in the pouch at Las Hadas had been paltry pebbles.

"What do you think it's worth?" he asked.

"A quarter-million or so. When it comes to me, Meno has a generous streak."

She held it up to the light for a long moment. Seemed to be seeing something through it. She brought it close to her right eye, held it in place by squinting, no hands, like a monocle. "We're going to Bogotá," she said.

"Not me."

"I knew you didn't love me. First thing I ask, you won't do."

"Try something else."

"Anything?"

"Anything."

"It has to be Bogotá."

"Where would we stay there?"

"Meno's."

Wiley shook his head, definitely not.

"Part of the time," she added.

He thought it over.

She let the emerald drop from her eye, just before she kissed him a good one. "It could be a way of proving you really do love me."

"You'd believe me then?"

"To some extent."

Why was she so set on Bogotá? Maybe, Wiley thought, she needed to experience Argenti on his home ground to get him out of her system. The man did seem to have a hold over her. But then, why so insistent that Wiley go along? Needed him to fall back on? That could be it. However, the way she was maneuvering was emotional blackmail. No matter, if he went along with her, at least he had a chance. He'd keep nicking away at her resistance. He'd be consistent, always there for her for sure, and gradually he'd dissolve her doubts—that fortune-hunter bullshit.

He glanced at the emerald, now nearly lost in the folds of the bedclothes.

Him compete with someone able to give away such a bauble? He didn't have penny one.

Lillian rectified that a bit on the way to the airport. She tucked some bills into his jacket pocket, making as little of it as possible.

"Walking-around money," she said.

"Gigolo."

"Lover," she corrected.

An hour later, Wiley was twenty thousand feet over the Mayan jungle in her Grumman Gulfstream II. She was napping, curled up in a deep-cushioned chair, all but the top of her head under a blanket. Wiley was slouched, his stockinged feet up on the table. He had given himself a tour of the private jet, from tail to cockpit. It was difficult to accept that this six-million-dollar plane belonged to the hitchhiking marble player he loved.

Was he positively certain he'd loved her so much before he knew she was rich?

Honestly, it was difficult to place all that had happened these past few days in proper relation to what he'd felt at any given moment.

He took his passport from his inside jacket pocket. An official temporary passport issued within two hours after she'd merely phoned the American consulate. Another example of what money could buy without changing hands.

He put away the passport.

His mouth told him he wanted a cigarette. He could go aft into one of the staterooms or, more satisfactory, would sneak a smoke right there while she napped. If she caught him, he'd contend the No Smoking sign wasn't on. He had been cut down to less than half a pack a day because she was so adamantly against it. Rather than carry a pack and risk having her notice and confiscate it, he had, before leaving, put a couple of cigarettes in each pocket, except those where they would surely get crushed.

He reached into his left jacket pocket for one. His fingers touched the so-called walking-around money. He took it out.

Benjamin Franklins.

He counted them. Thirty brand-new hundreds.

It wasn't conscious suspicion that told him to notice the serial numbers starting with:

2001 . . . the Kubrick film.

1812 . . . the War of.

FE . . . Fuck Everything.

13 ⟶⟶

The Las Brisas section of Bogotá was a most unlikely place for a modern skyscraper.

The area, for eight to ten blocks in any direction, was a *campesino barrio*, inhabited by the poorest of the poor. Starting with the earth for a floor, a newcomer joined to the walls of neighbors whatever sort of structural material could be found or stolen. Several pieces of old lineoleum overlapped made a roof, odds and ends of planks, sheets of rusted tin, even layers of cardboard formed the walls. Windows and doors were merely holes curtained by any piece of cloth.

On the average, there were five occupants in each of these one-room shanties. If a cousin arrived from the country to make it six, along with his wife and son to make it eight, they were welcome. With so little to share, all the easier to share it.

The *barrio* was an eyesore that no one tried to heal.

In 1973 the skyscraper was proposed. The people who happened to be living on that particular block of Calle 1 in the Las Brisas section were not told or asked about it. One morning the trucks and bulldozers and power shovels came. The shacks were barely standing as they were. The bulldozers plowed through them. Three old people did not get out in time.

Within a week the entire block was razed and cleared.

Those who had lived there grumbled, but they had no legal claim to the land. Nowhere to take their grievance except to confession. The priests advised them not to be angry, for it was against God's will. Accepting that, they put up shacks elsewhere, such as the adjacent Buenos Aires district, where the *barrio* had spread to the foot of the mountains.

As construction of the skyscraper got under way, it did seem the priests had been right. It was a godsend. Discarded bits and pieces of building materials were to be had, and there was such an abundance of planks, steel mesh, plastic, tools and things of that sort, surely some wouldn't be missed. The high fence around the construction site was no more of a problem than the night and weekend watchmen, who slept more than watched.

Thus, the *barrio* benefited from the skyscraper. Only three men were caught stealing and were sent to La Picota Penitenciaría. People agreed, the *barrio* was coming out ahead.

The skyscraper was designed by an architect from Milan, Italy, who had done buildings for Fiat and Olivetti, among others. The supervising contractor was also from Milan, and most of the workers, all the specialists, were brought over from Italy. It was much more expensive, but money was no problem. Actually that additional expense counterbalanced the fact that the builder of the skyscraper had paid only twenty-five pesos—about a dollar—for the land. Through personal arrangement with certain city officials.

Up it went. Thirty-five floors. A sheer tower of glass and matte-black steel, a display of wealth and power sprouted from the midst of poverty, as though fertilized by it. The space around the base of the building was landscaped, and the street was widened and paved.

The *barrio* children were not allowed to use the street for football play. The building was no longer a blessing. There was nothing more to be gotten from it except resentment. Long expensive cars brought generals and other rich men regularly to Número 1.

That was the address it took, etched over its entranceway: Calle 1, Número 1.

Headquarters of La Concesión de Gemas—or as those in and around the business called it, with no less veneration, "The Concession."

It was there that The Concession maintained control of approximately ninety-five percent of the world supply of emeralds. The mines at Muzo and Chivor, Peñas Blancas, Coscuez and Gachala, all within two hundred miles of Bogotá, conveniently provided the monopoly. Mainly the same mines worked in the old days by the Chibcha Indians and then the Spanish *conquistadores*. The mine locations were forgotten during the eighteenth century, rediscovered in the nineteenth. From then till recently, they had been operated by the Colombian government.

There had always been some trouble with poachers and thieves and illegal mining. However, starting in 1969, problems increased drastically. Shipments from the mines were

120 GERALD A. BROWNE

hijacked, and numerous mine officials were killed. Not a day
went by without violence of some sort. The roads, even the
main highways from the departments of Boyacá and San-
tander, were punctuated with the cross-marked graves of pros-
pectors, dealers and smugglers who failed to get their precious
goods to market. The *esmeralderos* preyed on anyone who
might have a stone in his shoe.

The *esmeralderos* were gangs who made a no-man's-land
out of the mountains. They were well armed, well enough to
fight running battles with even the government police or make
a direct raid on an emerald convoy.

Word was that the gangs were becoming rich. Many mine
guards deserted to the other side to get their share. The gangs
grew stronger, the mine forces weakened. When they weren't
fighting government police, the *esmeralderos* went at one another. In 1970 the violence reached its peak. An estimated nine
hundred persons in one way or another connected with emeralds were killed that year. A true figure would have been closer
to two thousand.

The mines had been producing about a million carats of
gem-quality stones each year. Worth about $250 million on the
wholesale market.

By 1971, after two years of strife, the legal yield of the
mines had dropped to ten thousand carats, grossing only $3
million.

And it was costing the government $12 million a year to
operate and protect the mines.

The Colombian Senate was outraged.

Senator Robayo of Boyacá was most vehement. The Minister of Mines was responsible, he said.

The Minister of Defense, Rufino Vega, obliged and sent the
entire Third Infantry Division to the mine areas. In command
was Colonel Fabio Vicente, one of the army's best, a forceful,
straightforward man, honest to the marrow.

After only two weeks it appeared that Colonel Vicente
would clear up the emerald situation. He had the *esmeralderos*
on the run, it was said. They were scattering, hiding, being
captured. On the front page of the newspaper *El Espectador* a
photograph showed eight blindfolded *esmeralderos* a moment
prior to death before an army firing squad. Colonel Vicente
deserved a promotion, at least a special commendation, it was
said.

At the end of the third week, on a Friday morning, a cardboard carton was found on the steps of the Ministry of Defense.

It contained Colonel Vicente's head and feet.

Minister of Defense Vega was furious. He wanted to send additional troops and another highly respected colonel into the mountains.

The situation in the mining areas quickly grew worse than ever, with more incidents than before and fewer legal emeralds coming out. Official figures for the past six months were incredible. Gross profit: $6,225.

Not even a handful of emeralds.

Street dealers on Calle 14 were handling more than that every week.

Senator Robayo came up with an answer. Lease the mines to a private concern, he proposed. Let someone else, a foreigner perhaps, have the worries.

How long a lease?

Ten years.

What would the government make out of it?

Ten million dollars a year, plus twenty percent royalty on all gems sold.

A far cry from the $250 million return it had been making from emeralds only two years ago.

Better than a deficit, Senator Robayo said. At the minimum, $10 million a year. The concessionaire, whoever that might be, would have to guarantee it.

The Minister of Mines, Javier Arias, opposed the Senator's plan. He considered it a personal criticism of his official abilities. He issued a statement to that effect. The newspapers made much of it, and the public was temporarily entertained by the political combat. In that manner the emerald question was removed from the wider arena of the Senate. Yes or no narrowed down to who came out on top, Senator Robayo or Minister Arias.

Did the Senator propose to lease all the mines?

Yes.

To the same concessionaire?

In one deal, yes.

Why not lease the mines individually?

If someone was willing to take the huge financial risk, better to make an overall deal while possible.

Ten million was needed to modernize the Campín football stadium, the Senator reminded. Everyone loved football. Even more people went to watch football than bullfights.

Minister Arias capitulated. He would supervise the leasing of the mines, bidding and negotiations.

Shortly thereafter it was announced that the lease had been awarded to a group of private investors, foreigners incorporated under the name La Concesión de Gemas.

Twelve million dollars a year for twenty years and twenty-two percent royalty were the final terms.

Minister Arias was praised for making a better deal than expected.

The Concession took over.

In 1968 the foremost diamond dealer in Italy was Meno Argenti.

He was one of those few men privileged to travel to London ten times a year for the purpose of purchasing a packet of diamonds at 11 Harrowhouse.

Argenti did business according to the codes set up by the Consolidated Selling System, the organization that held such tight and hardfisted control over the world of diamonds. According to The System's ledger of deportment, Argenti was consistently cooperative. He kept his appointments at Harrowhouse on time; he always accepted his packet, large or small, without comment; he was polite, well-mannered, of proper appearance; and in all his financial transactions with The System, he never came up even a lira short.

For those reasons The System gradually increased Argenti's packet to the half-million-dollar level. Still nowhere near the top worldwide. The System's important favorites, Barry Whitman of New York, for example, were allowed to purchase packets valued at six, seven million. Nevertheless, half a million a packet brought Argenti five million a year—profit.

Hardly a bad living. Especially since he had the usual upper-class Italian indifference toward income taxes.

About that time, Argenti was presented with a proposition that would net him four times what he'd been making in a year. Twenty million, maybe more. All he had to do was side-deal thirty thousand carats of first-quality rough. The diamonds were half of a shipment stolen from Her Majesty's mails two years earlier. The parcel of diamonds, registered, wax-sealed, securely bound and insured, had been posted by The System's branch in Johannesburg. Routine procedure. Normally the mails were safer, more reliable than personal courier. The parcel arrived and was signed for at The System's London headquarters at 11 Harrowhouse. Outwardly it appeared that it hadn't been tampered with; all the wax seals were intact.

Its contents, however, were ordinary gravel.

Somewhere along the way someone had switched parcels, substituting an exact duplicate. A clever someone, resourceful, a stickler for detail. The System's private seal had been convincingly counterfeited, and the postal cancellation seemed authentic—date, ink color and all.

The System had a squabble with the insurance company, with the postal service in the middle. Exactly how many diamonds had been sent? Had they ever actually been sent? Perhaps they had been delivered . . .and The System was, to put it politely, "mistaken." The postal service claimed it had performed its job, had made delivery. According to signed receipt, The System had accepted the parcel and contents.

The insurance claim was settled for ten million. The System ceased complaining about its thirty-million loss and proceeded to try to learn the whereabouts of those sixty thousand carats. No need to involve the police. Publicity of any sort was to be avoided. The System put its own security section to work. Its network of informants and enforcers was alerted. Such was the control of The System, so sensitive was its feel of the entire world diamond market, that any attempt to sell those sixty thousand carats would surely be noticed.

Two years passed.

It was assumed by then that the diamonds had changed hands and The System had given up, chalked it up as a piece of dirty business best forgotten.

Otherwise Argenti, knowing the extreme penalty The System imposed for such duplicity, would never have considered getting involved. He figured he could safely side-deal the diamonds a little at a time along with his regular sales, by a descreet amount added to each of his legal packets. No one would be the wiser. He had a number of clients, never sold all his packet at once.

He made the buy. The hand-over took place in a pharmacy on Rue d'Antibes in Cannes. He asked the pharmacist to recommend something for his allergy. He placed his ordinary paper shopping bag down, purchased some green-and-yellow antihistamine capsules, then picked up his shopping bag. It was, of course, an identical but different bag. He never actually saw the other person, had sensed a presence but followed the instructions not to look.

It had gone smoothly.

At home in Milan, he examined the diamonds. They were indeed fine-quality goods, averaging three to five carats, just the size the market was demanding. No exceptionally large stones which might be noticed or which he'd have to have cleaved.

He placed the diamonds in a safe-deposit box in the Banca Nazionale dell'Agricoltura on the Piazza Fontana.

The next six packets he got from The System he increased with the stolen goods by as much as he thought he could get away with.

Being not so honest was marvelously profitable. He celebrated by buying a chalet in Cortina d'Ampezzo, a large place he had noticed and wanted.

He went to 11 Harrowhouse for his next packet, the seventh since his side-dealing had begun.

He returned to Milan and went to the bank for some additional diamonds. He had come out of the bank and was on his way to his car when a man dressed in black began walking alongside him, on his right. Then another, an ominous twin, appeared on his left. He thought at first they were local thugs, that it was a holdup. That was how complacent he had become. Not until he was at home, seated at eye level with the little black hole of death that was the muzzle of a revolver, did Argenti allow himself to realize he had been caught. By The System.

He never knew how they'd found out. Didn't matter.

The penalty would be his disappearance. Or he'd be found in his car or someplace, having evidently been killed by a robber. Errant diamond dealers were usually dealt with in that manner. No one ever suspected any other motive.

One of the men was talking long-distance with London.

Could Argenti speak to The System? Plead his case?

The question was relayed.

The answer was no.

Would The System grant just one request?

What was the request?

Please get in touch with Count Alessio de Paula and explain.

A very long shot. De Paula was Argenti's second cousin, married to the niece of a member of the board of directors of The System. Argenti hadn't seen or talked to De Paula in five years; the last time was at a chance meeting in Paris at Longchamps racetrack. In all their lives, altogether they hadn't spent more than thirty minutes with each other. But blood was blood, Argenti hoped.

Two hours of looking into the little black hole of death.

The System called back.

Fortunately, De Paula had *not* been out bird shooting or off somewhere with a girl or two from Madame Claude's.

The System passed sentence:

Instead of death Argenti was banned from dealing in diamonds. For the rest of his days he was not to lay hands on a diamond, not even to wear one on his pinkie.

He was to leave Milan on the next plane bound for anywhere except Europe, Asia, Australia, Africa, the United States or Canada. He was never to set foot in any of those places. That left him South America, Central America, Mexico and the polar regions.

He was not to take anything with him except whatever clothes and money he had on him at that moment.

If he violated these terms at any future time, the original penalty would be imposed.

They were so sure of themselves they didn't bother to see Argenti to the airport.

He took an Alitalia flight to Rio de Janeiro.

It was like a vacation, he told himself. A nice change. He strolled along the Avenida Copacabana, kept a high-up month-by-month apartment overlooking the famous curve of beach.

Money wasn't a problem.

The Banco do Londres arranged a transfer of his funds from his bank in Geneva. Over the years he had taken plenty over the Alps. Five million a year for the past ten years. Even after what those thirty thousand stolen carats had cost him, he was left with around twenty-five million. He could do nothing, tastefully, for the rest of his life.

But he was soon restless. Sick of seeing that giant Christ every time he turned around, it seemed. Even bored with all the careless, cooperative girls to be had already practically naked along the beach at Ipanema. And horse racing at the

Jockey Club was impossible to handicap when there were as many as six fixed horses in the same race.

He had the impulse to take a short trip to New York but, remembering how thorough and pervasive The System was, thought better of it. Loathed being restricted. Compromised and took a trip throughout his allowed territory. Just from here to there. Buenos Aires to Lima to Caracas to Santiago to Mexico City to Bogotá.

He thought Bogotá, with its equally dull weather and people, was the worst. Till one Tuesday at midafternoon, only a few hours before he was scheduled to leave, when he happened to be walking along Calle 14.

Prosperous as he appeared, he was set upon with intent to sell by numerous street dealers who flashed uncut emeralds at him as though they were precious secrets.

Then it struck Argenti. The System was inflexible. It would expect no more than the penalty it had imposed and would stick to its side of the bargain no matter what.

Diamonds were one thing . . .

Emeralds another. . . .

He remained in Bogotá. For six months he kept a low profile, lived modestly, avoided the international set and its social scramblers. He took numerous trips into the back country, up around the mine regions of Muzo and Chivor. Rugged, two-mile-high tropics. He reached remote settlements that were almost inaccessible, where life was cheapest and *machismo* rampant. At first the people thought he was a missionary or a revolutionary. He was robbed twice and came close to being killed. So he hired several personal protectors, including one Luis Hurtado, who was half Indian, half something else, a man huge and mean enough even for Argenti to hide behind.

Argenti became familiar with that part of the country, paid his way into it. He got to key men, made them dependent on his generosity. He noticed that on the perimeter of each of the government-operated mines there was constant grubbing, men hoping to find a scrap of wealth in the tailings. *Canaloñeros* they were called. They created a desperate energy, like a belt of explosives waiting to be set off.

He learned as much as he could about *la materia verde*—the green stuff.

Six-sided crystals concocted in the earth's melting pot. Beryllium aluminum silicate with a trace of iron and a trace of chromium, which made it green. Minus the chromium it is common, comparatively worthless, merely an aquamarine.

Nearly all emeralds have internal imperfections that the trade calls *jardin*, "garden." It is possible to tell whether a stone is from Muzo or Chivor. Muzo stones contain dark flicks of organic matter. Those from Chivor have specks of pyrite crystals in them. Very rarely does one find a flawless stone. Then, however, it is five times more valuable than a diamond of equal size. Even a normal fine emerald, flaws and all, is worth as much or more than a diamond of the same classification. Truth be known, emeralds are scarcer.

They are mined by hand, which, given how unpredictably nature distributed them, is still the best way. Mined on horizontal terraces like giant steps up the faces of slopes, they are found in pockets and veiny clusters, in deposits of shale and sandstone and in matrices of that pale, relatively soft substance called pegmatite.

Most important, for Argenti's purpose, found within a hundred-mile radius—ninety-five percent of all the emeralds in the world.

Unlike diamonds.

The System had to cope with much less predictable circumstances to keep its market under control. Because diamonds kept turning up in substantial quantities not only throughout western and southern Africa but also in India, Brazil, Russia and even in places on the ocean floor.

Argenti, continuing his strategy, spent the next few months helping himself to the upper atmosphere of Bogotá society. He bought a large villa in the fashionable Chico district. Joined the country club, called The Country Club, and took up polo. It was through polo that he became acquainted with General Jorge Botero. Argenti got on the General's good side by allowing the General to sell him three polo ponies for a top price, although the animals were overused, well past their prime. General Botero was Chief of Staff, the top military man in all Colombia.

He was also an entrée to Rufino Vega, the Minister of Defense.

For a start Argenti treated Minister Vega to a week in the Caribbean resorts of Cartagena and Santa Marta. The Minister especially preferred girls with red hair. Any shade of red as long as it was natural. Argenti made a confidential arrangement with a local hair salon. The girls received double fee for the extra trouble. One girl, a very attractive Venezuelan, refused to shave her underarms, claiming that would displease her French lover. So, not just two but all four batches of her hair had to be dyed.

Then, there was Senator Robayo of Boyacá. His habit was gambling. Argenti met him, and not by accident, at the Hipódromo del Techo. Casually, in the course of their conversation, they disagreed on which horse would win the next race. When the race was run, the horse Argenti picked came in first; and being a good sport, he had also bought Senator Robayo a twenty-five-hundred peso (hundred dollar) pari-mutuel ticket. Typical gambler, the Senator was most pleased to have the winner under any circumstances. What he would never know was Argenti had placed equal bets on every horse in that race.

Thereafter, Senator Robayo often accompanied Argenti to the Hipódromo and to bicycle races in the Velódromo. Thanks to Argenti's infallible betting system, the Senator never went home a loser.

Minister of Mines Javier Arias was not so easy to get close to. Arias didn't gamble or lech; he was a stern family man. Extremely conscientious in keeping his public image above reproach. For example, he went to mass at the Divino Salvador every morning.

Argenti believed Arias was overdoing it, trying so hard to appear impeccable only to cover up something dirty.

He dug into Arias' past, bought the memories of certain people, pieced them into a lead, paid well to follow it. All the way to a pharmaceutical firm in Cali. No longer in business. Pacífico Pharmaceutical had in the late 1950s specialized in producing painkillers. Such as cocaine. For medicinal purposes—and otherwise. It had produced much more for otherwise. Arias had been an active partner in that firm only to the extent of getting his cut of the profits. But he had been instrumental in setting up the business. At the time he was an upper-echelon administrator with the Ministry of Agriculture. The growing of coca bushes for commercial purposes was under the control of his office. Such strict control, in fact, that it was a simple thing for Arias to alter the figures of the legal allotment of coca leaves for Pacífico Pharmaceutical: Make *1000 kilos* read *11,000 kilos* and then later change it back to *1000 kilos*. It all appeared neat and legitimate. Pacífico Pharmaceutical went

out of business in 1960, shortly after Arias was appointed
Minister of Mines, and no longer had anything to do with coca.

A sensitive fellow, Javier Arias. The minute he met Argenti
he sensed Argenti knew. Confirmed by the two words Argenti
said to him at the first discreet opportunity: "Pacífico Pharmaceutical."

Thus, Argenti made his enlistments.

He put them to test separately with some minor corruption.
Requested something just illegitimate enough so that each
could easily deliver. He overpaid them promptly.

They each looked forward to doing more business with this
money-minded Italian.

Argenti soon obliged with an invitation to dinner. The General, the Senator and the two Ministers assembled for the first
time. Their guarded respectability in one another's presence
was quickly dispelled by Argenti's candor.

They each stood to make four million plus a year, he said.
Dollars.

Four million plus a year?

As long as they held their positions in the government.

Senator Robayo had three years left in his term, and an
excellent chance of being reelected with that kind of money
behind him.

Both Minister Arias and Minister Vega also had at least
three years and probable reappointment.

General Botero would always be a General.

Four million a year. Plus five percent of the take.

Without ever touching the money. It would be deposited
automatically in separate Swiss accounts that Argenti, as a
show of faith, had already opened for them with an initial
deposit of a million in each.

They didn't even wait to hear the entire proposition before
agreeing.

First move, General Botero, with the cooperation of Minister of Defense Vega, saw to it that weapons and ammunition
from the national reserve arsenal were delivered into the hands
of the men Argenti designated—the *esmeralderos.*

It went even better than Argenti had planned, took only
fourteen months.

Argenti relieved the Colombian government of its losses in
emeralds. On behalf of La Concesión de Gemas, because he
was La Concesión de Gemas. It was he who had signed the

irrevocable lease that gave him exclusive control over all emerald exploration in Colombia.

The System had the corner on diamonds.

Argenti now had the corner on emeralds.

Argenti considered structuring his operation after that of The System. He was familiar with the way that diamond monopoly regulated its market. Each month The System summoned certain diamond dealers to London to attend *sights*—to examine the uncut diamonds The System offered them (a mere formality), and to pick up their packets. The System determined in advance the amount and the quality of stones each dealer's packet contained, more or fewer carats, poorer or better quality, according to what The System knew of the dealer, his business and, often, his personal affairs. A dealer had to accept a packet, pay up on the spot. If he refused, or even quibbled, he was not asked back. Thus, The System maintained absolute world control of the distribution of diamonds.

Argenti would enjoy the same sort of monopolistic advantages. Actually, he had a tighter monopoly than The System. So few emeralds were found outside his territory. Only a scattered five percent of the world supply turned up in Egypt, India and Russia. Those from Egypt came from Cleopatra's ancient mines, were pale, weak-green stones, inferior. India's and especially Russia's yields contained some fairly fine quality every so often, but couldn't be counted on.

Argenti's situation was similar to The System's in many ways. However, The System did not have to hand over a stiff percentage of its take to the government. Nor did it have to slice its profits with four bought partners. Twenty-two percent royalty to the government. Twenty percent due the partners. Nevertheless, Argenti could conduct his business aboveboard and make a healthy profit.

Instead, he decided to convert his handicaps into opportunity.

He wouldn't have dealers come to The Concession in Bogotá for packets. That would make him too accountable. He would deliver the goods to them. To their places of business anywhere in the world, or, if that was too much trouble, wherever he designated. It required a more complex organization, what with the various customs regulations, more bribing and kicking back, but it would be well worth it.

Soon after Argenti's lease was signed, the established mines at Muzo, Chivor and elsewhere were again in production. All did not suddenly go smoothly, however. Argenti saw to that. There were still violent incidents up in mine country, thievery and killing enough to maintain the impression that the government had dealt wisely.

In the lease a stipulation by Argenti was that the government would provide military protection during the takeover period. General Botero was consulted on that point. For the sake of appearance, he argued against it, cooperated grudgingly. Since then, however, the number of troops assigned to guard and police the mines had not been reduced.

Each year for the past six years The Concession had paid the Colombian government its twelve-million rent right on time. How much the government's twenty-two percent royalty came to depended upon how many carats The Concession said it took in.

In 1972, for example, the annual report of The Concession showed a gross yield valued at 42.7 million dollars.

In 1973 it was 56.3 million.

The following year, 48.3 million.

Rather disappointing figures considering the potential, based upon when the mines were formerly producing to capacity.

The Concession's explanation seemed plausible. The mines, as the government well knew, were almost impossible to manage when there was so much violence and underhanded dealing. The *esmeralderos* were even more formidable now, organized under a sort of Mafialike code. For the time being at least, The Concession and the government would have to be satisfied with making what they could.

A separate accounting was known only to Argenti and his four conspirators. It was never recorded, based only on Argenti's word.

The Concession was actually *doing* 200 million a year, give or take 10 or 20 million.

That much skim—about 150 million dollars worth of emeralds, some half million carats—was being taken off the top and out of the country via The Concession's confidential network. Its couriers went out and came back on regular schedules. Air force pilots served The Concession on routine flights. There was so little risk it hardly qualified as smuggling. When someone got caught, whoever did the catching wanted more than anything else to be included in the setup. There *was* risk in that. Often such a person, for instance, an ambitious customs officer, was merely eliminated.

Panama, the island of San Andrés, Acapulco and other resorts along the Mexican Riviera became regular rendezvous for doing business in emeralds. It was not nearly as formal as the way The System conducted its diamond transactions, but it accomplished the same thing. Dealers from Tokyo, Beirut, Paris, New York, all over, had to take deliveries when and where The Concession stipulated. And pay per carat whatever The Concession asked.

Or else do without.

14 ➤➤➤

Wiley's first morning in Bogotá.

Seated on the main terrace at the rear of Argenti's villa. There alone, except for a half dozen white-jacketed male servants who stood ready at their stations, self-conscious about having nothing to do. Wiley's presence held them at attention.

Twenty persons were expected for breakfast. At least, so it seemed. Beneath a blue canopy a long table was set for that many. Beige linen, pure silver, Rosenthal, Baccarat and two abundant arrangements of ranunculus. Another table nearby held silver dishes heated from underneath by burners with blue flames.

Wiley had already eaten.

Rather than sit at the table, which seemed too perfect for him alone to disturb, he had asked to be served on the top step of the wide stone stairway that led down to the grounds. He was now finishing his coffee, had never tasted better. He signaled with his cup. A full one was brought by a servant with almost grateful agreeability.

The shade of a tall cypress had grown over Wiley. He moved across the step to where the ten o'clock sun was hitting. It was a minor comfort, through his trousers, to his buttocks. He used the stub of his fifth cigarette of the day to light his next.

Never. She could never get him to stop smoking.

Look out. Don't look in.

He tried the view for distraction.

Mountains, the Andes, on the clearest kind of day, mauve and gray to black and white-capped, like artwork.

He hadn't mentioned the so-called walking-around money to Lillian, the brand new hundreds she had doled out to him which, according to serial numbers, had been his own.

Foothills with varicose gullies, bad complexions.

She had all of it. Marianna, her secretary, had found the entire twelve thousand for her in the lamp base in Las Hadas.

Not a cloud, plane or anything anywhere in the sky.

Probably she had the pouch of emeralds too.

A mile of lawn from here to there, the denser, taller-bladed kind that showed wherever breeze played on it.

Lillian had lied. Outright.

Like dabs of watercolors, yellow, blue, pink, Argenti's niece and her two friends from school were chasing far out along the edge of the grounds, where there was a line of poplars.

His first inclination had been to put it straight to Lillian. He had her cold. He imagined she would do some quick thinking, invent a simple explanation. Or claim it was merely caprice, a game thing. Or, embarrassed, cornered, might resort to silence, cut herself off and away. From him. What satisfaction in that?

He leaned back on his elbows, gazed overhead at the nothing of sky for a moment. Then, stretching, arching his neck, he saw Argenti's villa inverted.

Three floors, forty-some rooms.

Argenti had purchased three adjacent estates there in the affluent Chico district. He'd torn down the flanking two to provide more grounds for the other, which he had enlarged with north and south wings. The Spanish purity of the house, though architecturally akin to Italian, was not acceptable to him. Argenti constructed a spacious courtyard faced by double loggias with thirty Doric columns. An imposing sixteenth-century bronze wellhead in its center, which he had brought over from a Medici villa in Careggi. It was eight water nymphs, fascinated each with the next in some subtle physical way, and all held high by the graceful force of a wave.

Any structural detail of the villa that could not be convincingly converted was replaced. Cornices, sills, borders, bannisters. Extensive additions were made to the exterior—many of them after the Renaissance artisan Marcello Sparzo as seen in the Palazzo Podesta in Genoa. Numerous arched recesses contained statues and obelisks. Life-size statues with one part or another missing stood at every corner and break of the roofline and along the tops of terrace walls. Gods and goddesses with weatherworn breasts and genitals. (Those not truly antique had been sandblasted to appear so in Naples.)

Despite all these efforts, the Spanish flavor of the house showed through. Why hadn't Argenti demolished it, ordered an Italian villa built from the ground up? Would have been easier. Perhaps once he'd begun remodeling, he didn't want to admit the mistake. Or, more likely, it was a matter of defiance from the start, having to do with his resentment of exile.

His longing for Italy.

It was overstated throughout the interior of the villa, as well. Gold leaf, gesso, intricate plaster work and boiserie. Carrara *fleuri*, that rare, rich blue marble, and *verde antico* and Siena—the most beautiful that could be put underfoot. Some walls were covered with silk, reproductions of antique weaves executed by Scalamandre. Others were done in *trompe l'oeil*: vistas, objects, creatures painted hyperrealistically in perfect perspective.

In the bedroom he occupied Wiley had noticed several classical sketches of female nudes tacked to the wall. The corners of the sketches were curled, edges frayed. Not in keeping with the fineness and order of everything else. He had tried to take a corner of a sketch between his fingers before he realized the illusion. And that morning, when passing through the ground-floor rooms, he had walked smack into a wall that offered an incredibly believable version of wide-open double doors and a terrace. Thus, he was groping before him when he came to the real way out.

Feeling like a fool.

He dragged long on his cigarette, didn't inhale, let the smoke out plosively to put his own cloud in the sky.

Why the fuck should she begrudge him his twelve thousand and the few emeralds he'd gotten shot for? Her with all her money. Did she have to be in such total control? Was that it? Maybe she got some sort of warped feminine amusement from playing lavish Lillian, keeping a man—not just any man, but him—with his hand out. How many others had been in her personal breadline? Or, it could be even more serious. This incident of deceit, uncovered only by circumstance, might be fair warning.

He got up abruptly, as though to erase the possibility.

Common birds were flittering about, anticipating breakfast crumbs.

No matter what, Lillian had disappointed him. Just about enough for him to haul ass out of there. (Three thousand and his new wardrobe would go how far?) Until now Argenti had been the perfect host—away on business. If Wiley left that moment he might have the pleasure of avoiding Argenti. He would also be leaving Lillian to him.

Someone appeared in the double doorway of the house. Out of scale with the doorway, too large a man, extraordinary, tall and thick, like one of those Russian Olympic weightlifters in the superheavyweight class.

Luis Hurtado.

Argenti's man around.

His white suit made him appear all the more gigantic. It must have been tailored for him. No store would stock such a size. Still, the fabric strained across the upper chest and rib cage. He had a big-boned face with ambiguous features and skin color. There was Pasto Indian in him and European and Negro but no telling how much of each because the bloodlines had been crossed and recrossed so many times over the past five centuries. Black hair. He tried to slick it down, but it brushed up, oily.

Hurtado stood in the doorway, arms down in front, hands joined, fingers laced into a relaxed double fist. His eyes fixed on Wiley.

Even at a distance of thirty feet Wiley took a step back.

Argenti came out. With General Botero.

The way they were dressed reminded Wiley of vintage movie directors. Boots and leather leggings, twill jodhpurs, short-sleeved cotton lisle shirts, knotted silk scarves. Dressed identically, for some reason.

Argenti's glance seemed to include Wiley only incidentally. He said good morning as though it were a description, and gestured for Wiley to join them at the table. Argenti mispronounced Wiley's name, said something that sounded like "Wheeler" when he introduced the General. No handshakes.

A servant poured wine.

Another offered a woven-silver basket containing a linen-covered loaf of warm bread.

Argenti tore away a piece, which he dipped into his wine goblet. He brought the bread sopping red to his mouth. The General did the same.

"Worms," Argenti told Wiley. "Wine first thing in the morning prevents worms." He patted his stomach respectfully. "Is that something you already knew?"

"No," Wiley said.

"Then you probably have worms," Argenti said decidedly.
Wiley agreed.

So did the General.

They went on with their wine sopping.

It occurred to Wiley that they were dressed for polo.

"Christ began each day with wine and bread," Argenti commented mostly to himself.

The General touched the sign of the cross on himself and kissed the knuckle of his thumb.

Wiley wondered what extra significance there was in the thumb kiss. He thought about Argenti imitating Christ.

Breakfast was brought: the mounded richness of eggs Benedict and a platter of thin, silvery fish sauted whole to a crisp in butter and olive oil and herbs.

"I was not surprised to hear about Ramsey," Argenti said.

"Exemplary record," the General said.

"The month before last, when I happened to run into him at the Hipódromo, he made me uneasy."

As abruptly as that, Wiley was excluded from the conversation. They were resuming a topic.

Argenti said, "Overambition is something I can sense."

"Really?"

"I have never been wrong, never. Ramsey definitely had it. I knew it merely from his being in my presence those few moments."

"You make it sound like an odor of the body." The General was a trifle facetious. He grinned. Or did he? Upper lip thin, lower lip full, his natural expression was close to a grin or a superior sneer.

"How much do they estimate Ramsey got away with all told?" Argenti asked.

"Conduct Section is preparing its report."

"He was trying to side-deal five thousand carats."

"This time."

"We recovered those."

"Yes."

"Ramsey's arrangement was with one of the new mine supervisors at Muzo, was it not?"

"Since August."

"Four months. Probably they started out smaller, no more than a thousand carats. And increased the amount each month as they became more confident. I would say Ramsey managed to side-deal six thousand carats, perhaps even less."

"Conduct Section will know exactly," the General said.

Argenti speared up some of the tiny fish with his fork. Watching Argenti chew, Wiley thought about what the man was eating. Fish eyes, brains, guts and shit, along with the rest. Without a qualm simply because the fish were tiny. What difference, really, did that make?

Argenti asked the General, "Where do they have Ramsey now?"

"New York. He cannot be brought here for at least a week."

"Oh?"

"He suffered a fall. A peculiar accident. It was as though someone had struck him across both knees with a steel pipe."

Argenti ate more fish.

"There is doubt that Ramsey will ever walk again," the General added.

"Whether he does or not," Argenti told him, "see that he gets to Barbosa."

The General nodded while rinsing wine around the inside of his mouth.

Wiley thought Barbosa was probably either a convalescent home or a hospital. From the mention of such things as carats, mines and side-deals he was beginning to get a different picture of Argenti. Lillian had said vaguely that the man was in finance. It was at Las Hadas, which Argenti owned, that Wiley had had the near-fatal emerald escapade. Wiley went on putting that and this together. What the hell was Conduct Section?

"Have you given any further thought to my proposition, Mr. Wiley?"

"Not really." Argenti got his name right that time, probably could have before.

"Perhaps you did not believe I was serious. As a recall, I was rather offhand."

"That was it," Wiley said.

"Nevertheless, serious."

Wiley had no trouble remembering the offer. Four hundred thousand a year counting bonuses and rip-off allowance. For being a sort of courier, was the way Argenti had put it.

"Anyway, the spot is still open," Argenti said.

No doubt he meant Ramsey's spot.

"Some people prefer bad times," Argenti commented. "An excuse for dependency."

Wiley didn't let the needle get to him. He couldn't imagine working for Argenti under any circumstances. The only reason for the ridiculously generous offer was to enable Argenti to manipulate him, clear the way to Lillian. As though he, Wiley, was actually that much of an obstacle.

"Who would I be working for, I mean what company?" Wiley asked.

General Botero answered, "La Concesión de Gemas."

It was said in such rapid run-together Spanish Wiley didn't get it. He told himself, no matter, he wasn't interested, and that four cups of coffee was the reason he was nervous, clenching his teeth, jiggling his right leg. He looked past Argenti, then aside. Luis Hurtado hadn't moved more than a foot. Wiley studied the huge man, thought of him as a weapon.

Argenti was saying, "If not for the canopy, birds would be shitting all over the table." And then, with hardly a pause, he said, "Tell you what, Mr. Wiley. I am so impressed with you I will better my offer. No salary. Straight commission. Two percent on as much as you handle. And expenses, of course."

"Handle what?"

They were amused that he didn't know.

Wiley was sure he did. He just wanted to hear it.

Argenti told him.

Wiley nodded.

Argenti asked if that was his decision.

Wiley was mentally rerunning a fragment of that emerald escapade on the beach in Las Hadas, the part when bullets had come within inches of his life. He realized now it must have been Argenti Lillian had overheard. Overheard without Argenti knowing it. Argenti who had ordered him killed on that beach called Solitude. However, Wiley had asked for it, played the impostor, meddled. As much as any man could excuse another for his own attempted murder, he had to pardon Argenti. But what about now? Didn't Argenti still want him dead? Evidently not at the moment.

Argenti was offering him that high-paying job.

Wiley shook his head.

He was saved from more on the subject by Argenti's niece, who came to the table with her two school friends. They were breathless from running, groaned melodiously as they collapsed into chairs. The niece's name was Clementina and she was called Clem. No resemblance at all to Argenti. Her very fair hair was irregularly sun-bleached, streaked flaxen in places. Long and straight, it tangled and untangled itself as she moved. She was exceptionally pretty, and although she didn't appear more than sixteen, there wasn't an ounce of adolescent excess on her. Slenderness made her seem sophisticated. She emphasized that. Displayed such confident grace that frequently she appeared to be posing, mimicking a fashion model. Was she really so precocious? Both believing and doubting that of her was a great part of her charm. Often she resorted to uncontrollable gangliness . . . but not for long.

Clem's friends were Astrid and Maret. From Denmark. They were between fourteen and fifteen. Slightly younger versions of Clem, just as pretty. Apparently she had considerable influence over them, and her approval was important.

All three girls were similarly dressed, in sleeveless camisoles and shin-length petticoat skirts of cotton. That was all. Old clothes, actually. Victorian. As though they had raided grandmother's trunk. How easily they belied the intended modesty of those underthings. Camisoles were left with ribbons loosely laced in front to reveal tummy skin and navels, and unlaced entirely from the top to halfway down. Arm holes, much too large, gaping, allowed glimpses and not-so-brief views of breasts. In that regard, Maret, the younger, was slightly more developed, Wiley noticed. The petticoats were sewn with patterns of tiny eyelets for the outlook of their hipskin and thighskin and intersections.

Now, chairs pushed away from the table, they thought nothing, for instance, of raising a leg to place a chin upon a knee, or using the arm of another chair for a high footrest. Were they oblivious to their exposure? Granted innocence by their age?

What they wanted was brought. Fresh red raspberry juice in frosted glasses. It must have required five hundred raspberries to make a single glass. Astrid complained hers contained no vodka. No one laughed and she pouted believably.

"Where do you go to school?" Wiley asked.

"Switzerland," Clem blurted, as though vying to be first with the answer.

"Free for the holidays?"

She disregarded that, told Argenti, "They want to go swimming." Meaning Astrid and Maret.

"So?"

"The pool heater is broken again. The man who came last month didn't really fix it."

"The water is freezing," Astrid said.

Made Wiley recall sharing that inconvenience, among other things, with Lillian. Only three days ago?

Argenti motioned Clem to him, took her onto his lap. She settled, curved up, fit herself there as though it were a familiar place. Her head against his shoulder, his arm around her, holding her, his hand resting heavily on the back of her thigh, close up to her bottom. Argenti cooed to her.

It seemed to Wiley that Clem was too grown up and contemporary for such babying. Especially in front of her friends.

"You can come with me to the club today," Argenti said to the girls, "have a swim there, a nice lunch, and watch us practice. How about that?"

Astrid didn't even consider it. "I'd like to go shopping."

"Again?"

"Me too," Maret said.

"Whatever you want," Argenti said crisply.

The girls brightened. Berry juice stains exaggerated their mouths.

Wiley got up, excused himself in a tone that implied he would soon return. Circumventing Luis Hurtado as much as possible, he went inside. He wandered from room to room as though he had no destination, taking notice of valuable objects and several familiar paintings. In the main salon he came upon a Modigliani that made him wonder again what it was about women that had motivated the artist to portray them with features so out of alignment—squinty, slanted eyes, tight, tiny mouths, lopsided, elongated heads stuck on impossible necks. Maybe Modigliani couldn't do any better, or maybe what he saw most in women was something psychologically askew, deviation, deceit.

Going up the wide marble stairway, Wiley met a housemaid. He asked if she knew whether or not Lillian was awake yet.

"*Sí*, the *señorita* went out."

"Went where out?"

"Visiting. The *señorita* only said to say she had gone visiting."

"Did she mention when she'd return?"

"No, but not today."

Which was the *señorita's* room?

The maid led him to it, showed him in and left him there.

Now he regretted not having found her room last night. The
desire to had certainly pulled at him. But his anger and confusion over the twelve-thousand-dollar lie she'd told had come
between them. He hadn't wanted it to bother him that much.
Now, there he was, and she was gone. Gone visiting someone
without even letting him know. What the hell was he supposed
to do meanwhile, play with Argenti?

On her bedside table were two books. *A New Model of the
Universe* by P. D. Ouspensky and Lawrence Durrell's
Nunquam. According to folded corners, Lillian had read to
page 70 of the first and page 82 of the other. It had also been a
long night for her.

Gone visiting.

Wiley went into the bathroom. Noticed her makeup on the
counter below the mirror. Scattered over the surface. Lipstick
left uncapped, mascara wand out of its holder, a fluffy brush
dropped in the sink bowl. Evidence of her hurry from him.

The least she could have done was leave him a more specific
message. Perhaps she had. He returned to the bedroom to have
a look around, but not really for a note. He opened the top left
dresser drawer. Lingerie and stockings. And there, right on
top, in heavy contrast to those soft lovely things lay the blue-
black steel of two automatic pistols, like the Colt forty-fives
Wiley had fired at Lillian's but considerably smaller. Etched
on the barrel of each was: *Gabilondo y Cid—Elgoibar, Es-
pana—Cal. 9 m/m (380) Llama*. There was also a pair of
silencers and a box of extra ammunition.

His and hers?

Why had she brought those along? Was she planning on
having a little wagering shootout with Argenti? That was probably it. Wiley didn't touch them.

The top right dresser drawer contained scarves and gloves.

Wiley finally found what he was looking for in the bottom
drawer, inserted between the folds of a sweater. Not even in an
envelope. Nine thousand dollars in brand-new hundreds. His
nine thousand, according to the serial numbers.

He riffled through them to make sure, slipped them into his pocket and closed the drawer.

He went to his room.

Sat on the edge of the bed, legs crossed, thinking. For three cigarettes.

He got up to pull aside the heavy brocade drapes, as far as they would go. Through the high double windows the sun struck a large rectangle upon the marble floor.

He took off his clothes.

Chose the appropriate position near the window and began throwing punches and doing footwork. His shadow on the floor shot out from his feet. A dark, lengthened opponent, inescapable, matching him blow for blow.

Jab, hook, cross.

A final flurry of all sorts of lefts and rights won him the decision.

He showered and dressed and returned to Lillian's room.

Exactly as he'd found it, he put back the nine thousand.

15 ≻≻≻

      Air France flight 206 had made its scheduled stop in Caracas and climbed again to thirty-four thousand feet.

Next stop was Lisbon. Then on to Paris.

Wiley was in First Class. No qualms about it this time. Argenti, that is, The Concession, had prepaid $1,893 for the round-trip First-Class fare. Wiley had also drawn an advance of $2,000 against expenses. An excessive amount. He intended to be extravagant but account for every penny.

He had spent most of the afternoon at Número 1 on Calle 1. Argenti had foregone polo practice in order to personally show Wiley around The Concession, see that he was properly indoctrinated. More of an inside look than usual. Probably not what Argenti had in mind at the outset, but he got caught up in the opportunity to nourish his ego off Wiley's plate. He was delighted when Wiley was overwhelmed.

The first twenty floors of Número 1 were the offices of various commercial companies, both local and foreign.

The next seven floors of Argenti's building were leased by the Colombian government—for fifty years at fifty thousand per floor. The federal appropriation for the lease had ridden through on an unrelated bill as though it were written in invisible ink. The bureaus of Transportation and Communication put a few unimportant files and people on floors twenty-two and twenty-three. They rattled around up there.

Twenty-eight was occupied. By Rufino Vega, Minister of Defense. There, at his office away from his official office, Vega often conducted business of one sort or another, usually another. . . redhead.

Senator Robayo enjoyed a spacious place of his own for whatever reason on twenty-nine.

Thirty was the domain of General Botero, luxurious, complete with an electronically equipped fencing room.

Minister of Mines Javier Arias preserved his reputable and

pious image by never going near the place. Unlike the others, he did not believe that being there or anything else for that matter could protect his interests.

From the thirty-first floor on up was The Concession.

Its reception area created the impression of a thriving, active major company. However, beyond the island of green-tinted glass that was the reception desk, beyond the expansive back-drop of paneled walnut, were only a dozen clerks and secre-taries, and even fewer administrative employees. They didn't have much to do—nothing to do directly with the operation. They were there for appearance more than anything else, al-though they didn't know that.

Directly above, on thirty-two, was where The Concession's essential business began. The grading department. Emeralds were sorted and evaluated there. In cubicles all along the north side were benches at which sorters sat with ten-power magnify-ing viewers. Rough stones, one at a time, were held up to special electric-light fixtures that provided a standard brilliant but colorless glow. In that manner the sorters looked past the skin, the natural dull exterior of each stone, to appraise and classify it according to its size, clarity and color.

Color was of first importance. The finest emeralds had what those in the trade called "kelly": the richest, brightest sort of green.

Twice-weekly shipments of rough stones arrived from Muzo, Chivor, Peñas Blancas and the other mines. They came by armored truck with an escort of federal troops.

Thus the sorters were kept busy.

On the average sixty percent of all stones were classified as *commercial goods*, ordinary quality.

Thirty percent were graded *fine*.

Ten percent were graded *very fine*.

At the close of each day the sorted stones and those yet to be sorted were taken upstairs. Only the most trusted supervisors had ever been up there.

The floor above, thirty-three, was home base for Conduct Section. Presented as a hyperefficient personnel department for The Concession, Conduct Section actually saw to it that who-ever got in line stayed in line and whoever got in the way was eliminated. Through its network of informants its computers kept a current dossier on everyone who had anything to do with emeralds. Much of the effectiveness of Conduct Section was a result of the fear it generated merely by existing. Who could know how much it knew? How could anyone be sure who was Section and who wasn't? Only the most desperate or foolhardy man would risk going against The Concession, considering the penalties and those who imposed them. Conduct Section recruited its men from high and low. Many were outcasts from various dark corners of the international intelligence community. Nearly as many were runaways from organized crime, specialists in violence.

The head of Conduct Section was Joachim Kellerman, a tall, middle-aged East German, gaunt as death, with sunken eyes and cheeks and a bony, upturned nose. A touch of jaundice in his normally gray complexion gave him a greenish cast. He never smiled, not even when he was laughing.

Kellerman got his start in the 1950s as a young man in East Berlin. His game was convincing refugees that he could get them over the wall. For a price. He also got a price from the East German police for telling where and when the attempts would be made. He persuaded the police it would be to their benefit if they built his reputation—exaggerated the success of his crossovers and put him at the top of their capture-or-kill list. For a long while he did excellent business there.

Kellerman was a strategist up from the streets. Intuition had always been his best weapon, and his ability to think abstractly kept him a move ahead. However, what made Kellerman most suitable for his job as head of Conduct Section was something he did not have. Not a trace of it, ever. Compassion.

When interviewing a prospect for the Section, right off and right out Kellerman would ask the man if he had ever killed anyone—not had he been indirectly responsible or taken part but had he himself done it, one-on-one or more. The way the man replied was an important factor in Kellerman's eyes. A yes was not a prerequisite, not if a no had enough regret in it.

Kellerman reported only to Argenti. Whose combination town apartment and office was on the next floor above.

It was in his office that afternoon that Argenti repeated his offer and told Wiley he would stand by it, although it was too good an offer and he had been impetuous in making it.

"I know zilch about emeralds," Wiley had said.

"No matter."

"You're really paying for the risk?"

"There is little of that."

"Then what?"

Argenti spoke of the unorthodox way The Concession did business. Clients never came to Bogotá because it was inconvenient, an out-of-the-way place, and dreary, he said. Also, petty annoyances were avoided, such as the red tape of Colombian customs.

"Such as duty charges," Wiley put in with a knowing edge.

"Duty charges," Argenti admitted, as though that were nothing. "Anyway, it is best for everyone that we use carriers."

"You mean couriers," Wiley corrected.

"No, carriers, we call them carriers."

"When you first spoke to me about it, you used the term *couriers*."

"You are mistaken," Argenti said determinedly.

Wiley was sure he was right, disliked letting it go, felt Argenti was using it, rubbing in his earlier remark about not wanting to be anyone's messenger boy. There was certainly a positional difference between being a courier and a carrier.

"Did you know that according to legend the emerald was a symbol of chastity which shattered the moment a woman gave in," Argenti said. "It was also supposed to be good for hemorrhoids."

"I told you I know nothing about emeralds."

"That you did."

Carrier definitely sounded more like a messenger, Wiley thought, or someone with a catchy disease.

"When the *conquistadores* first came to this country, the Indians told them the way to identify an emerald was to hit it with a hammer because a true emerald would not break. Think of the fortune the Spaniards must have smashed away," Argenti said.

There was a crystal compote containing Perugina chocolates on the desk, each piece wrapped in soft silver paper. A far cry from Hershey kisses, Wiley thought as he helped himself to two. The candy taste left in his mouth made him want a cigarette. He lighted up. He recalled, almost twenty years back, saying the greatest sure thing would be to get a corner on a cycle of irresistible cravings. For instance, a cigarette, a soft drink, a candy. Smoking the smoke would make you want to drink the drink would make you want to eat the candy would make you want to smoke the smoke. . .

Argenti got up from his desk, went to stand at the window,

his back to Wiley. His customary view was to the northeast, in the general direction of his homeland. He avoided looking directly below, at all those ugly *barrio* structures held together as though cringing at his feet. He would rather pretend they were not there—nor was he. Often his daydreams transported him to the Piazza San Marco in Venice or to other, more intimate favorite places in Florence and Milan.

Somewhat distantly, and with some envy, he told Wiley, "You can leave this afternoon."

The sooner the better.

Argenti turned abruptly toward him. "Does Lillian know about your going to work?"

"No."

After a long thought: "There is a certain type of woman who seems to enjoy a man bought and paid for, ready to serve her slightest twitch." He smiled and then lost it quickly. "But not Lillian."

"Not her."

"Why do you suppose it is that Lillian and I have such an affinity?"

Wiley just smoked.

Argenti went around behind Wiley's chair, paced back and forth. Wiley remained as he was. He could see Argenti's reflection in the window glass, transparent.

"It is more than money," Argenti said.

Wiley found that by exhaling smoke slowly he could make Argenti seem all the more a ghost.

"She cares for me, of course. Why else would she be so eager to be here in Bogotá? She has told you how much she cares for me?" Argenti left a space for Wiley's answer.

Wiley left it blank.

Argenti went on: "Did you know at one time it was believed that a well-placed emerald would cause an immediate and lasting hard-on?" He paused. "Which leads one to wonder about the other claim, regarding hemorrhoids." He'd obviously said it before, expected a laugh, was irritated when he didn't get one.

Wiley's mind was elsewhere, brought back by Marie Antoinette.

"Marie Antoinette," Argenti said, "made a pledge to reward her lover with an emerald each time she was worked up to an exceptional orgasm. She broke her promise in less than a month. Otherwise the better part of the French crown jewels would have belonged to the Duchesse de Polignac."

"When do I collect my commission?" Wiley asked.

"Not until you've completed the carry, when you return with the receipt."

"Suppose for some reason I don't make delivery?"

"Don't?"

"Can't . . .for some unavoidable reason . . .blizzard, train wreck, whatever."

"In that case, you get nothing."

"Just want to get things straight."

"What else?"

"There ought to be a minimum to how much I carry."

"How much do you suggest?"

It had occurred to Wiley that Argenti might send him out with only a few thousand dollars' worth just to be rid of him.

"Go ahead, set your minimum."

"A million, never less," Wiley said.

"Done."

At that point they went to the floor above, via a small private elevator in which four passengers would be a squeeze. It was the only way up to thirty-five, the top floor. No other elevator, no stairs.

Up there was a large corner room, with floor-to-ceiling windows. The room was done in white, a hard shiny white, lacquered walls and ceiling, a wall-to-wall white wool rug woven so tight it was almost slick. In the exact center was a heavy glass table, waist height, rectangular, five by nine. On it was a telephone, only the instrument, without cords or any type of connection. The top surface of the table was brightly, evenly illuminated by colorless lights that seemed to be embedded in the glass.

The atmosphere made Wiley uncomfortable. It was like an incomplete surgery. And no visible reason for it. The absolute white exaggerated everything: Wiley's usual sense of being out of place, the rapidity of his thoughts, the subtle exertion required to breathe, Argenti's voice babbling on about emeralds again and about himself—Meno Sebastiano Argenti.

Argenti was off to the right, standing before the longest blank wall, facing it squarely as though it offered something to his eyes. He did not touch anything, had nothing in his hands. His gaze alone seemed to cause part of the wall to disappear.

Actually a section of the wall had slid aside swiftly—to reveal a vault about twelve feet square. Same stark white, lighted strongly from above. Along the walls inside the vault were cabinets, wide and white with numerous drawers, shallow drawers, no more than two inches deep.

Argenti reached randomly for a drawer, used only one finger to pull it out.

The drawer contained emeralds.

A layer of emeralds.

Their green better defined against white velour.

They were rough stones, of about five carats each.

Argenti opened another drawer. The stones in that one were slightly larger. Argenti invited Wiley to open a few drawers. He read the question Wiley had in mind. "Fifty to sixty million dollars' worth here," he said casually.

Wiley was so engrossed by the sight of such wealth that for a moment he didn't realize Argenti had left the vault, just left him there with a chance to help himself to a handful. A natural reaction, to feel so tempted. Didn't mean he was a latent thief, Wiley told himself.

Argenti was calling him.

Wiley went out to find another section of the wall was open. Another vault exposed. It appeared nearly twice as large as the first.

Inside was the same sort of cabinet arrangement with shallow drawers. More of them.

Argenti pulled out several drawers to show layer after layer of emeralds. These seemed greener, more vivid, for some reason. Argenti watched closely for Wiley's reaction, the amazement, the anxiety and the envy. Argenti fed on it, prolonged it, allowed Wiley to examine the contents of as many drawers as he wanted, to run his hands over the precious stones.

"A hundred and fifty million here," Argenti said.

Wiley closed the drawers, told himself, hell, they're only stones, only better than pebbles because of scarcity. If someone ever discovered a cliff or a big boulder or even a fifty-foot outcropping that was pure emerald, these here would be worth shit.

He focused his appreciation on the unorthodoxy of Argenti's security system. The ingenuity of situating the vaults on the top floor rather than beneath the building. He complimented Argenti, who took full credit for the idea and therefore was inclined to explain it to some extent.

What about the roof of the building? Couldn't some-one . . . ?

The roof was equipped with radar, a sweeping KU-band type that relayed to a monitoring room continuously manned by Conduct Section down on the thirty-third floor. Not only that, the roof had what Argenti referred to as a listening alarm. Extremely sensitive. Jet planes flying miles overhead had fre-quently set it off. As for a helicopter. . . no way for one to get anywhere close.

The floor below?

The only way up from there was that small elevator. During off hours a steel plate was extended horizontally and locked into place across the elevator shaft, closing it off.

The vaults?

Floors, ceilings, all the sides were of a special cadmium-based metal, four inches thick. A by-product of space research, that metal. No torch was hot enough to cut through it, and according to actual tests Argenti himself had witnessed, it showed hardly a dent when hit by a seventy-millimeter shell fired point-blank. The vaults were impenetrable.

Wiley remarked that he, Argenti, had proved it not so—by opening them.

Argenti raised his chin, aimed it and a smile at Wiley, challenging him to figure that out if he could.

Electronically controlled, Wiley thought. He was certainly no stranger to the workings of things electronic, but there was no way of telling how these vault doors operated. The combi-nation that released them would have to be activated, but Ar-genti hadn't done anything, hadn't gone within six feet of them.

Wiley went to the open vault door, examined the exposed edge of it. No locking device, no visible mechanism, just flush metal. To hell with it.

Meanwhile Argenti had used the phone to summon Keller-man, who came up carrying an Air France flight bag, one of those ordinary plastic satchels with the airline's logo imprinted on it. He and Argenti went into the first vault for several minutes. When they came out they placed the flight bag on the table.

Kellerman was somewhat upset. He'd had only time enough

to run the most cursory check on Wiley, and he still had to make all the other arrangements for this unanticipated trip.

"There is your carry," Argenti said, indicating the flight satchel.

"How much?" Wiley asked.

Argenti told him.

Kellerman said, "Take off your jacket and roll up your right sleeve."

Wiley did as told.

Kellerman removed from his pocket a black leather kit, flat, like a set of drafting instruments. It contained several pens that were battery powered.

Wiley realized he was about to be tattooed. He refused.

"It will not show," Argenti assured him.

Kellerman explained he was using an ink that only made itself apparent under black light, that is, ultraviolet or infrared. It was a requirement.

As Kellerman proceeded to tattoo a letter *C* about a quarter-inch in size on the inside of Wiley's forearm, Wiley couldn't help thinking it stood for *Concession* and that something similar had been a requirement of the Nazi SS.

Now in the better part of the belly of the 707, Wiley was cutting through the night sky over the Atlantic.

His carry was at his feet. He could feel it against the back of his lower legs. He had not, would not for even a moment, lose touch with it.

Five thousand carats of emeralds.

Classified *fine* quality gemstones.

Two and a quarter pounds of them.

Worth a thousand dollars a carat at the dealer level.

Five million dollars altogether.

Two percent commission would be his. One hundred thousand dollars just for taking a quick trip to Paris.

Had to be Argenti was following intuition, trusting Wiley with such a large carry first time out. Argenti was obviously the kind of man who needed to prove himself a good judge of other men. And, thereby, superior to them? That was it, the only reasonable explanation, Wiley thought.

As for Argenti's using this carry as a means of getting Wiley out of the way, that wasn't really a hundred-thousand-dollar motive. Argenti could hardly expect to accomplish much with

Lillian in the short time Wiley would be gone. No, it wasn't a one shot. The tattooing of the *C* on his arm, for example, indicated the intention of doing business long term.

A hundred thousand. Ten carries a year would make him a million. Before taxes. What the hell was he thinking about? There were no taxes there on the shady side. Even if he wanted to pay taxes, he couldn't, and even if he could, he wouldn't— because, for one thing, the U.S. Department of Agriculture might get a nibble of that tax bite. He'd never forgive the Department of Agriculture for fucking up his imported-dirt gimmick.

Strange, though, how crime compounded itself. At once he was also a tax evader. How he'd deal with that depended on how he got paid, by check or in cash. He should have nailed that point down with Argenti. Given a choice, he'd take it in green. A thousand hundreds.

Argenti might not really be such a bad guy, Wiley thought. He questioned his animosity toward Argenti. How much of it was because the man was so successful, powerful? Thirty percent seemed an acceptable figure.

Anyway, as Argenti had promised, he'd had no trouble at El Dorado International Airport in Bogotá. The customs official, as though he'd been on the watch for him, had passed him through without search or question. An invisible *C* on that custom man's forearm?

The flight attendant came offering magazines. Wiley chose *Fortune* and requested another bottle of Lowenbrau. Beer was even better when you could have champagne.

First thing he'd do when he got the first hundred thousand was pay Jennifer and her lawyer off. She was probably having such a shit-fit by now she'd stay out of a sanitarium for half the price. He got a flash of her battling the rats. Why was it more difficult to forget the good things?

He paged through *Fortune*, to an article that featured the forty-four-year-old Chairman of the Board of a widespread fast-food corporation, who had, it said, started at the low-management level of an altogether different kind of business when he was twenty-nine. *Tenacious, amiable, systematic-minded* were some of the adjectives.

Wiley shoved the magazine into the pocket of the seat in front of him, where there was also a vomit bag and ditching instructions.

He got up, took his carry with him to the lavatory.

The moment he slid the door bolt into *Occupé* position the plane started to fight strong headwinds, buffeted sharply. The Fasten Seat Belts sign went on. All right, there was the seat, but where was the belt? The confined space exaggerated the jouncing, made it seem more dangerous. Wiley placed the satchel on the floor, had to take a wide stance. His aim was unsteady but within the stainless-steel target. How many passengers got caught midstream by turbulence and missed? he wondered.

The sink was splash-spotted, had a soapy film. Rather than clean and fill it, he contended with the cold tap. Had to hold the tap down with one hand while he washed the other. He doused his face in the same handicapped manner.

After drying, he took up the satchel, placed it on the counter. Unzipped it and removed his spare shirt, socks and toilet articles. There was the bottom that wasn't really the bottom. It snapped out to reveal a layer of cotton wool. Wiley peeled that aside. The emeralds, 712 of them, were on another layer of cotton wool. So they wouldn't rattle.

Wiley gazed at the five million dollars' worth of emeralds. They didn't look like they were worth five million.

The lavatory light flattered complexions but apparently did nothing for precious gems.

Wiley took out one of the stones. About eight carats. He held it up to the light. When it was cut and polished, it would probably knock eyes out. He started to put it back but recalled Argenti's saying he expected Wiley to steal some. He tucked the emerald into his vest pocket. Not to disappoint.

The flight touched down at Charles de Gaulle Airport at 12:35 P.M., a half hour ahead of schedule.

Wiley was still flying twenty minutes later as he waited in line at customs. At least he didn't feel as though he was on solid ground. Everything and everyone around him seemed either too fast or in slow motion.

Moment of truth that was the moment of lie.

He was next now. There were two customs officials at that pass-through. It was overly optimistic to expect cooperation from both. Perhaps he should have chosen a different line.

They were being thorough with the lady ahead, an innocent-looking middle-aged woman. They had all four pieces of her luggage open, feeling and poking around in them.

Wiley turned, smiled weakly at the older couple behind him. Out of nervousness he noticed extraneous things: the chrome railing, the wrinkles in the seat of a gray flannel skirt on a woman in the next line over, people waiting in the terminal just beyond customs, among them a fat man trying to hang on to four kids, and another man wearing a hairpiece so obvious it might as well have been cut from a black nylon bathmat.

They were done with the middle-aged woman.

It was Wiley's turn. He placed the Air France satchel on the counter.

"*C'est tout, monsieur?*" the taller customs man asked.

"Huh?"

"Is that all?"

"*Oui, c'est tout,*" Wiley replied.

The taller customs man unzipped the satchel, held it open. The shorter one peeked into it rather conscientiously but didn't poke.

The bag was zipped up. It received an approving scrawl with a piece of white chalk.

"*Merci, monsieur.*"

Wiley restrained his smile. "*Merci.*" He walked through and out into the terminal, relieved and buoyed to such an extent that when he passed by the man in the so obvious hairpiece he had the urge to snatch it off and buy him a real convincer.

Heading for the exit, Wiley thought how incredible the reach of The Concession was. Both those customs men were doing double duty. Either that or he'd just experienced the good fortune of French inconsistency. He believed the former.

It was cold outside, flurrying snow. Wiley had come without a coat. He wouldn't need one. While he completed the carry, he'd have the taxi wait, take him right back to the airport.

Place des Vosges.

A square that was once a favorite for illegal dueling and other foolishness. Its all-around identical structures of red brick, white stone and blue slate still displayed much of the majesty, harmony and good nature that Henry IV had ordained more than three hundred years ago.

Victor Hugo had lived at Number 6. Cardinal Richelieu at Number 21. Mme. de Sévigné, Anne de Rohan and Marion

Delorme had resided and done other intriguing things around
the *place*. Many fashionable persons lived there now. The
address Wiley wanted was Number 14, a J. F. Forget, which
was easy to remember although it was pronounced *for-jay*.

The taxi put him there in forty-five minutes. He went into a
foyer. Number 14, like all the apartments, was above street
level, *deuxième étage*. The curved stairway had a lovely seven-
teenth-century iron bannister that Wiley didn't notice. He
pressed the door buzzer and waited. The usual pinpoint
peephole was in the upper door panel. Wiley tried to appear
nonchalant for it. He buzzed again, waited, listened, believed
he heard movement within, but no one came to the door. After
three more insistent buzzes and ten minutes, he gave up.

The taxi driver was irate. He was a Communist, wanted
nothing more to do with this inconsiderate American. He
wanted only his money. He had locked the car doors so Wiley
couldn't get back in. Wiley gave him fifty dollars through a
crack in the window, five times too much, and even then, there
wasn't a *merci* in the man's mumbling as he drove off.

Within seconds Wiley was cold to the marrow, close to
chattering. Spits of snow on his face. The *place* was nearly
deserted, a few cars, no pedestrians along the sidewalk or on
the pathways of its parklike center. The leaden sky had a tint of
red neon in it. And against the sky, the branches of the trees
were like networks of dead black nerves. The time was nearly
two. It would be dark by four, perhaps sooner. Wiley couldn't
just stand there. He remembered Argenti had mentioned that
The Concession kept a suite at the Hôtel Meurice that he could
use. A nice suite overlooking the Tuileries.

Luck! A taxi was letting someone off down the way. Wiley
ran and got it. He gave the driver his destination. Argenti had
said that the suite at the Meurice was the one General von
Cholitz, the Nazi commander, had used as his Paris headquarters. Inasmuch as von Cholitz had been a sort of inverse aes-
thetic hero for not burning and otherwise destroying the city,
probably every suite at the Meurice claimed the same distinction, Wiley thought.

He changed his mind, had the driver take him instead to the
intersection of Rue Royale and Faubourg Saint Honoré. He
walked west on Faubourg Saint Honoré, shopped a few windows but was soon chilled through. He went in at Number 23,
Ted Lapidus. Bought a substantial wool topcoat, dark blue,

silk-lined, double-breasted. For seven hundred dollars. And a pair of picked pigskin gloves for fifty. Protection against pneumonia was certainly a justifiable business expense. He requested a stamped receipt. The sales clerk glanced disapprovingly at the plastic Air France satchel.

Leaving the shop, Wiley turned right, realized it was the wrong direction and turned abruptly, causing a near-collision with a heavy man who had a wine face. Splotchy red and puffy, purplish in the cold. For a moment Wiley and the man were practically nose to nose, and Wiley got a whiff of sour breath. The man seemed startled.

Wiley begged pardon and continued on. He hadn't intended to stay overnight in Paris, didn't want to. The suite at the Meurice sounded like lonely brocade and overstarched sheets. Never mind that he was tired.

He taxied back to 14 Place des Vosges. This time he dismissed the driver with a reasonable tip, went in and up. He buzzed for five minutes, knocked some, pressed an ear to the door, again believed he heard movement inside. But no one answered.

Outside, he paused at the curb. The time was nearly three-thirty. He crossed the street and entered the park, followed the walkway to a bench where he would be facing Number 14. He had a clear view of the front windows of the third-floor apartment, two hundred feet away.

There he sat in his new overcoat. He pulled up the coat collar, scrunched down into it. Wished he'd thought to buy a scarf. No one else in the park. He thought how foolish and lonely he must look hunched there.

Night was coming fast now. It was that brief in-between time when day and night were pausing to bid hello and goodbye.

Lights went on! The tall framed windows of Number 14 were lighted.

Someone there now. Must have just arrived.

Wiley got up and started that way.

He saw the two men enter the park via that same walkway, headed toward him. He was about fifty feet from them when he recognized them. Wine Face, the same he'd bumped into far from there less than an hour ago, and Hairpiece, the one with the cheap rug on his head that he'd noticed at the airport.

Couldn't possibly be coincidence.

Perhaps, Wiley thought, The Concession was looking after him, or anyway, its interests. This being his first carry. Could be.

He took the intersecting walkway off to the left, more briskly.

They followed.

He considered stopping, confronting them. But what if they weren't his guardian angels? His five million carry warned him they weren't. He decided against making a try to reach Number 14. They could easily cut him off.

At a faster pace he left the Place des Vosges for Rue Saint Antoine, a major street, crowded with end-of-workday traffic, people hurrying home, buying their suppers from street vendors and stores along the way.

Wiley glanced back. Perhaps the crowd had discouraged them. No, they were still on him, if anything had gained some.

He continued on, block after block, hoping for any opportunity to lose them. Rue Saint Antoine became Rue de Rivoli. He was in the older part of Paris, the Marais, with many minor side streets that, possibly, in their maze, could offer escape but might as well lead to a dead end.

Rue de Renard. Fox Street. He was the fox. He turned right on to it, quickened his pace to nearly a jog. A short block and then left on Rue de la Verrerie. They couldn't have seen him take that left. Maybe he'd lost them. There was the church of Saint Merri. A large fifteenth-century-style church, architecturally complicated. It might provide sanctuary. In movies men on the run usually took refuge in churches, and, if he remembered correctly, they usually ended up expiring in a pew or on an altar.

Wiley continued on to the Boulevard de Sébastopol, another wide, bustling artery. Hoping to gain distance with daring, he crossed the Boulevard mid-block, against the traffic. Cars didn't swerve to hit nor slow to miss. At times he went up on his toes and stiffened like a matador as they brushed past him, from one direction and then the opposite.

He made it across, paused at the curb to look back.

A red light was holding up traffic now. The Boulevard was practically clear. His pursuers were striding across.

What to do? The city was apathetic. It seemed to offer no safe place. If he tried to hide in a restaurant or shop, he'd be cornering himself. He couldn't go to the police for the very reason he was being chased: the emeralds, the smuggled five million in the satchel. He couldn't even run because that might draw police attention.

A taxi would help. But they were all taken now during the rush. He could get away in a taxi. Better than that, he could quickly return to Place des Vosges, deliver the carry and be done with it.

There was a taxi, right there, waiting for the light that was about to go green.

Wiley opened its door to climb in.

"*Non!*" the driver shouted.

The passenger, a hefty woman, raised her leg immodestly, placed her foot in Wiley's chest and shoved. Sent him sprawling to the gutter. The taxi pulled away.

That sortie cost him. His pursuers were now no more than fifty feet away, dodging with greater hurry through the crowd. They appeared confident, methodical.

Another block over Wiley reached Les Halles. For eight hundred years that section had been the main food market for the fussy palates of Paris. No more. Most of the pavilions had been torn down. Where everything from squid to pork brains had been piled ten feet high, there were now numerous stalls and shops selling *antiquités*. The stalls claimed street space, competed for it. Wiley took advantage of this commercial labyrinth, dodged in, out and around stall after stall, a confusing course. He circled and doubled back and hurried north up Rue Saint Denis, where he ducked into a doorway.

A cautious peek.

He'd lost them.

But he couldn't stay there, nor could he risk the street yet. He turned to the door. Its upper half was a clear glass panel. Inside was a narrow stairway up. Seated on the fourth step for best display under a raw bright light was a woman. A heavy whore. Her complexion was the color of baker's dough, and powdered. Hair an incredible orange, dead and so thin her scalp skin showed. A greasy red mouth that she must have painted purely by guess.

A leftover from former Les Halles nights when farmers brought more than their *artichauts* or *aubergines* to market.

Wiley hadn't noticed her before.

She made lewd eyes at him.

She stuck her thumb into her mouth and worked it in and out.

She pulled aside her coat and blouse to pinch a nipple at him. Her skirt was already hiked up, so all she had to do was part her legs.

Wiley went in.

She was delighted.

He squeezed by her, took the stairs two at a time.

She threw French obscenities at him.

There was only a second floor. A hallway covered with linoleum. The smell of strong disinfectant, cheap cologne and the toilet, with its door open.

Four other closed doors. If there was another way out, a back stairs, it would most likely be the door at the far end.

It was a room. Wiley entered, shut the door behind him. A regular hook and eye was the only lock, screwed into the doorframe by hand. No windows. The room was barely furnished, even for what it was. A bed with a yellow-beige coverlet, above the bed a rectangle of mirror splotched with corrosion where moisture had gotten to it. There was a standing metal lamp with no shade and a blue bulb. A twenty-five-watt bulb in the ceiling fixture. More of that worn linoleum on the floor. Alongside the bed was a bathmat with *Hôtel George V* embossed by its weave.

Wiley sat on the end corner of the bed, on as little of the corner as possible in view of the color of the coverlet. As the minutes passed, he felt more secure. He looked directly up at the tired old looking glass, smiled at himself. He had outsmarted the sons of bitches. They were still searching for him among the antiquités. They would cover some of the bistros and restaurants in the area and then give up.

It was quarter to five. He'd stay there until six. Until seven for good measure.

Sounds down the hallway. Heavy footsteps. More than one person, men. The moment he heard them he realized where he'd made his mistake. The whore. They had asked her by chance. He shouldn't have slighted the whore.

He placed the satchel under the bed to have both hands free. Yanked out the plug of the standing metal lamp. The lamp was light-gauge wrought iron with a tripod base, awkward. He took position to the left of the door. He didn't have a fighting chance, really. They were probably professionals. He would die in an upstairs rear room of one of the cheapest whorehouses in Paris.

The doorknob was tried.

Weight hit the door.

The hook and eye gave.

Wine Face stepped in.

Wiley swung the standing lamp.

Ten inches too low.

The stem of the lamp hit Wine Face across the chest. He absorbed most of the blow with the padlike flesh of his upper arms. It hurt, but it didn't do any serious damage. Wiley swung again, backhand, this time caught Wine Face across the hump of a shoulder.

Hairpiece slipped into the room.

He had a revolver.

Wiley figured they meant to kill him no matter what. He swung the lamp at Hairpiece, who dodged, but didn't fire.

Another swing at Wine Face.

He absorbed it with his arm and grabbed the lamp stem with his other hand. He struggled for possession of the lamp. Wiley released it and, almost simultaneously, stepped forward and let go with a punch, his best right. It glanced off Wine Face's cheekbone.

Being a jabber was nothing in this kind of fight. He should get in close and kick the balls.

Wine Face countered, connected, rotated his fist a little at the last moment to put more force in it.

It dropped Wiley. He went ass down, feet up. His arm was under the bed.

He lay there, stunned and apparently motionless, but his out-of-sight hand felt for the satchel, found it, grabbed its strap tight.

The door was still open.

He'd try for it. When he got his legs back.

Wine Face dragged him by the feet away from the bed, exposing the satchel.

Wiley wouldn't let go of the satchel.

Wine Face tried to pull it from him.

Hairpiece stepped in and brought the heel of his hand down on Wiley's forearm.

Even then, with his arm numb from the elbow down, they had to pry open his grip, finger by finger.

16 ➤➤➤

Wiley had to wait because Marlon Brando was doing the talking.

The Godfather was being shown, a condensed version of it. Argenti had seen the full-length movie at least once each month for three years running. After that he had what he called "the dramatic fat" cut from it. The result was like an hour-long coming-attractions trailer. No dull moments, the way Argenti saw it. His favorite parts were the horse's-head-in-bed and the pinning of the hand to the bar with an ice pick.

They were in the projection room at Argenti's villa, seated facing the motion-picture screen in deep-cushioned armchairs that swiveled. The chairs had high backs, so Wiley couldn't see who was where.

Having arrived midway through, he sat apart, in the back of the room. He had telephoned from the airport wanting to speak to Lillian, but perhaps the message hadn't gotten to her, because the servant had come back on to say Argenti was expecting him.

Wiley had considered forgetting Bogotá and The Concession, going in any other direction, even changing his name. But he realized how guilty that would make him appear. What's more, there was Lillian.

Marlon, jaws stuffed with cotton, did his death scene in the vegetable garden with the orange and the grandchild.

The lights went on.

Argenti swiveled around.

Wiley asked if he could speak privately with Argenti.

Argenti preferred to stay there, said he might want to watch another movie.

Clementina and her friends hurried out rather than chance having to endure *The Godfather* again.

Kellerman had also swiveled around.

Lillian remained as she was, out of sight.

In a way that made it easier for Wiley. He told it all, from his passing through customs in Bogotá and Paris to when he was left on the linoleum with a farewell kick in the groin, the orange-haired whore looking in from the hallway, laughing.

Argenti and Kellerman gave him their absolute attention. They seemed sympathetic, and at times Wiley could see questions in their eyes, but they didn't interrupt.

Silence for a period when Wiley was through.

Finally, Argenti stood, stretched his back, rotated his head to untense his neck. "Monsieur Forget telephoned this morning very aggravated."

"I never got to see Forget," Wiley said.

"An important dealer. Fortunately he cannot take his business elsewhere," Argenti said. Then to Kellerman, "Put another man on that carry."

"Tomorrow, first thing," Kellerman said.

"Someone we know we can trust."

That really wasn't an insinuation, Wiley thought.

Kellerman sat forward, leaned as though aiming his mind at Wiley. "These men you say jumped you. . . "

Say?

". . . what did they look like?"

Wiley described Hairpiece and Wine Face in detail.

Kellerman told him: "Most people recall very little under such circumstances."

Argenti agreed. "When frightened one is usually confused."

"I got a good look at them," Wiley said.

"You were not frightened?"

Wiley thought back to what he'd felt looking up at Hairpiece's gun. "No," he said.

Kellerman knew better.

"The most unusual thing," Argenti said, "is that anyone would even dare such a robbery. Our carriers have never had to worry."

"The holdup in Beirut," Kellerman reminded.

"Five years ago," Argenti reasoned, "and even that, as it turned out, was to our benefit, gave us the opportunity to demonstrate how The Concession would deal with such a thing. We haven't had a problem since."

"Till now."

"Yes, now . . . "

"How could those men know what you were carrying?"

"They knew," Wiley said.

"A leak on this end?"

Kellerman thought that unlikely.

Argenti sighed, ordered a cognac and, an afterthought, asked if anyone else wanted anything.

Wiley could have used a Scotch on the rocks. And even more, cigarettes. He had smoked nearly two packs on the return trip. But he let the offer pass. Lillian . . . was she still there? What were her thoughts through all this? A smile from her would be welcome encouragement.

Argenti told him: "The five-million-dollar loss is painful, naturally. However, what really distresses me is my personal disappointment." Argenti lowered his head.

"You should have taken my advice, waited until I could run a check on him," Kellerman said.

"I have never been more sure of a man," Argenti said, "and he turns out to be incompetent."

"Or dishonest," Kellerman put in.

Wiley had expected to be raked over the coals. But not accused.

"It does not level up, Mr. Wiley," Kellerman said. He was changed now, as though he had drawn a weapon. "First of all, no one knew what you were carrying. . ."

"The guys in customs, here and in Paris. They could have tipped off someone," Wiley offered.

"They never know whether a carry is worthwhile, as in this case, or nothing at all. They wouldn't take the risk for a possible nothing."

Argenti sat back, sniffed at his cognac and swiveled slowly to and fro, letting Kellerman go on with it.

"You claim you went twice to Monsieur Forget's apartment."

"I did."

"He was not there, you say?"

"He wasn't."

"Monsieur Forget swears he was home all that day, awaiting the carry."

"What about him? He knew."

"We know our customers. Monsieur Forget is a French mouse well aware of the traps. Besides, to him five million would be a mere nibble."

Kellerman was closing all the ways out, Wiley realized.

"You would also have us believe the thieves left you semi-conscious."

Wiley wondered if Kellerman had ever been kicked in the balls. Hoped so.

"You got a good look at them. You could identify them. Why did they not kill you?"

"I figured they would," Wiley said.

"I still do."

"Okay, you don't believe me. What do you believe?"

Kellerman hardly hesitated. His words were crisply clipped, his tone unequivocal. "You left Bogotá with five thousand carats of our *fine* quality goods. When you arrived in Paris, you never went near Forget's apartment. You went to a bank, placed the emeralds in a safe-deposit box. After that, you probably did a bit of shopping, had a relaxing meal and probably, as well, an attractive piece of French dessert, if you know what I mean. Then you came back here with your melodrama nicely memorized."

Wiley was exasperated. He appealed silently to Argenti, who asked: "Did you buy anything in Paris?"

"An overcoat and a pair of gloves."

That seemed to decide it for Argenti.

Wiley told him straightforwardly: "Kellerman has it twisted."

"You failed," Argenti said wearily.

"I was robbed."

"You don't expect us just to take the loss, do you?"

A what-else shrug from Wiley.

"You owe The Concession five million."

Ridiculous amount. "Sue me."

"We will think of some way to settle it," Argenti told him.

"When I took the job, there was no mention of having to make up for losses."

"It went without saying."

"All your carriers operate on those terms?"

"Otherwise we might have many situations such as this."

Lillian swiveled halfway around.

Wiley knew, but hadn't realized how much, he needed the sight of her. She was profile to him, didn't look at him, told Argenti, "I'll see that you get your five million."

Argenti dismissed that idea with a backhanded gesture; however, it wasn't a definite veto.

Wiley told Lillian this was his business, his problem, he'd handle it.

She still didn't look at him.

Argenti told Kellerman: "Have Conduct Section keep a close watch on Paris, also the London and Rome markets."

Kellerman would.

Argenti to Wiley: "In all fairness, I suppose we should give you some benefit of the doubt. Perhaps your thieves will validate your story for you by trying to sell off those goods all at once. Even if they try to move five hundred carats at a time, we will know immediately where and who."

There was hope, Wiley thought.

"Meanwhile," Argenti went on, "you are suspended from The Concession. Not fired, merely suspended, and I mean precisely that, suspension."

"I'm supposed to just hang around here?"

"More pleasant solutions come to mind but . . ."

Lillian brought her eyes to Wiley's. The message in them was a warning, not to press. She turned to Argenti with a pleasant, thoughtful look, as though she were about to say something meaningful. "Instead of another movie," she said, "let's play gin."

17 ⟩⟩⟩

"Don't mope about it."

"I'm not, I was sleeping."

"It really didn't sound like moping."

"What time is it?"

"Close to three."

After only five hours' sleep, his first real sleep in three days, Wiley was suddenly wide awake. For her.

She was by the side of the bed, not quite within reach. Wearing a floor-length silk robe of a light-peach shade, 1930s in style. It exactly fit the lines of her and light played softly on it, causing reflections like openings. She had just put on fresh lipstick, brighter red than he'd ever seen on her before, slick.

"If it's any solace," she said, "I blitzed the hell out of him."

"For how much?"

"Sixty thousand."

"He paid up?"

"Didn't have his checkbook and couldn't bother looking for it. Said he'd take care of it first thing tomorrow. What a welcher! In practically the same breath he said that at daybreak he'd be flying to Quibdó, something to do with a platinum mine."

Wiley wondered how it was to do business on the platinum level. "Where's Quibdó?" he asked, hoping it was far away.

"West of here, I think, near the Pacific. If I'd kept count over the years he'd owe me at least a half million. Move over."

Wiley made room for her, lifted the covers.

But she sat on the edge.

"I guess you know now you did a dumb thing." Meaning his trip to Paris.

"Maybe it was almost a smart thing. It happened exactly as I said."

She believed him. "It was dumb."

"I was trying to catch up."

"You can't."

He resented that. Was now the time to bring up her twelve-thousand lie? It seemed less important than ever, but it was still there, between them. "I needed the money," he said.

"Need," she said, mentally assaying the word.

He reached to the nightstand for a cigarette. She intercepted his hand, held it. Such a willing captive.

"What are we doing here in Bogotá?" he asked.

"Just staying."

"Wouldn't you rather be. . . anywhere else?"

"Not at the moment. Besides, you have to stay on now that you've gotten yourself in bondage to The Concession."

"Argenti wasn't serious."

"He'll hold you to it. Five million."

"Can't get blood from a stone."

She winced at the cliché. "You're not a stone."

She was being overapprehensive, he thought. Kellerman and his Conduct Section would track down the thieves and recover the emeralds. Argenti had as much as predicted that. It was a matter of days. That's how it would go. He pushed the main weight of it off his mind, asked Lillian, "Would you really have paid five million for me?"

"Maybe."

"Why?" Obviously fishing.

"If you must know, I was bluffing. I thought it would be better if I owed him, that's all."

"Let's pack and go. Right now."

"No."

"What the hell's the attraction here?"

"You'll see," she said cryptically.

"Is it Argenti?"

"You must be sleepy."

"I'm not."

"You're too tired."

"I look it?"

"You always look a little tired."

No one had ever told him that. He tried to remember the last time he'd seen himself in a mirror.

"Actually, it's sort of fascinating," she said. "Evidence of experience." She thought a moment, unconsciously made a moue. "Did you enjoy your *dessert* in Paris, as Kellerman suggested?"

"All I had was a *saucisson* sandwich in a bistro at the airport."

"You ought to take better care of yourself."

"I'm willing."

"Before you got in up to your ass with The Concession, why didn't you discuss it with me?"

"You were gone visiting."

"And I suppose you couldn't find your way to me the night before."

"I was invited?"

"Expected."

"Is that anything like wanted?"

She hesitated exactly long enough. "Synonymous," she said.

"I love you." It just came out again, over the spillway of his feelings. He was so high with her.

She shrugged resignedly. "You expect me to just forget Route 200?"

"Huh?"

"That first afternoon when you proudly exposed your darker side. Your mistake."

"As I told you before, I was putting you on."

"You were bragging."

"At that moment I felt that being something, anything, was better than nothing, so I pretended. . . . "

One of her eyebrows arched dubiously. "You've never considered the convenience of having a wealthy woman?"

He tried to remember whether or not he had ever lied to her. He wanted to keep his slate clean. In that respect, one big one up on her. Anyway she'd know it was a lie. "It's a common male fantasy."

She smiled, her point made.

He crushed out his cigarette. "Okay, have it your way."

Her expression dropped. "You give up?"

"Might as well."

"Just like that, you give up?"

He nodded conclusively.

"I didn't think you would, not you."

He couldn't really blame her for being skeptical. Even if he hadn't made that *faux pas* at the start, she had good reason to doubt. Probably a lot of men had made tries for her and her money. It said much in her favor that she hadn't been taken. Perhaps she had. Wiley asked her.

"Engaged twice, escaped twice," she said nonchalantly. "Both times at a bargain price."

"Could have been worse."

"Learned all the don'ts from my father, who did them."

"I'd be willing to sign an agreement," Wiley said. "Yours would be yours, mine, mine."

"What would I do, invite you to stay over, tell you not to worry about eating too much beluga? Would you bring your own bottle and jammies?"

She was right, he thought.

"Anyway," she said, "I want to be a one-hundred-percent heart-and-soul believer."

"How about body?"

"You know damn well I'm already convinced."

He thought she would get in with him then, but she rose, took three steps away and hesitated. He noticed she had on delicately scaled sling sandals, high-heeled, bright red. Nothing under the robe, he imagined.

She turned, read his look, outdid it. "How about joining me in a little Holy Bang?"

"Holy?"

"Yeah."

"Sounds rewardingly sacrilegious."

"You have to put it in the hole three times."

"Why three?"

"That's the rule, lover."

"I suppose I could abide."

She told him not to bother putting on anything more than his trousers. On a table near the door she had left two bottles of Latour '61, both opened. Also a pair of leather drawstring pouches. They picked those up on the way out. He padded barefoot after her as she clicked in her heels along the marble hall and down the stairway to the first floor. Through two rooms, to one not quite so large.

She flipped the main switch, turning on the chandelier. A hundred bulbs amidst two thousand pieces of crystal.

"The music room," she said.

There was a grand piano, a Steinway, and a harp. A pair of violins were mounted on one wall, crossed like swords above a small but imposing brass plaque stating they had been made by

Giovanni Paolo Maggini in 1612. They didn't look that old,
Wiley thought. A huge armoire handpainted with various song-
birds contained a complex tape deck, and a cartridge system,
which Lillian snapped on, to get someone hitting and holding a
Puccini high note in *La Bohème*. Lillian yanked out that cartridge, replaced it with a Stevie Wonder. Then went around to
turn on every lamp and lock all the doors.

In the center of the room, directly beneath the chandelier,
was a sixteenth-century Oriental carpet that must have taken a
family in Isfahan two generations to weave. It was about
twelve by eighteen feet, made of pure silk, with 450 knots per
square inch, which came to nearly 65,000 knots per square
foot, which came to over 14 million knots altogether.

"How many?" Wiley asked, incredulous.

"Fourteen million," Lillian told him. She had read up on
carpets.

"How much is it worth?"

"Meno claimed he bought it from a *nouveau*-poor Englishman for two hundred thousand."

"The family who made it probably got paid in goats."

"Maybe not," she said with very little conviction.

They washed the thought away with wine. Hadn't remembered glasses, swigged from the bottle. Wiley had also forgotten to bring cigarettes. He wanted one badly as soon as the
wine taste was dominating his mouth.

She handed him one of the drawstring pouches.

Because it was too dark outside to dig a hole for Holy Bang,
they would play Persian, she explained.

The Isfahan rug had an intricate floral design with a pre-
dominantly blue central medallion well defined on a red field.
The medallion was about five feet in diameter.

That would serve as the ring.

They put in ten marbles each as the ante.

"What are we playing for?" Lillian asked.

"You name it."

"What did we play for last time?"

"Kisses."

"I think by now we ought to up the stakes."

"To what?"

"Winner take all."

"Agreed."

Lillian kneeled and knuckled down tight. Excellent form,

with her shooter resting against the ball of her first finger. She sent it skimming across the silky surface for a direct hit on the bunched-up hoodles. They click-clacked rather painfully against one another, scattered as though in fear. Three went outside the perimeter of the medallion to be scooped up, won by Lillian.

She was about to shoot again when Wiley told her, "No heisting."

Heisting was cheating by raising the shooting hand from the surface.

"Me?" Indignant.

"Just watch it, that's all."

"If you're trying to distract me, forget it," she said. "I've got the concentration of a laser beam." As though to prove that she knuckled down and fired. Her shooter rolled like a bullying marauder, knocking a beautiful striped orange alley, perhaps the prettiest of all, out of the ring.

Lillian paused for a swig of wine.

Wiley had one too.

She went back to shooting and missed. Although she was four marbles ahead, she was disgusted with herself. "I should have cleaned the pot," she said.

Wiley got down to try, took aim, was all set to let his shooter fly when Lillian removed her robe. She tossed it over the arm of a nearby *bergère*.

"That's why I missed," she claimed earnestly. "My arms and everything were restricted."

Wiley saw he'd been wrong. She *was* wearing something beneath the robe. An underthing—a combination pantie and top in one, the sort they had called a teddy back in the twenties and thirties. Bright-red crepe de chine. It fit perfectly loose above, and below, at the leg holes, would be extremely easy to slip in or out of.

Now, the conspiracy of red mouth with red teddy with red sandals.

The illusion of lengthier legs. The lift, tension—a slightly forward thrust, offering of hips and pelvis. Again, but more acutely than ever before, Wiley realized why the last thing a really knowing woman ever took off was her shoes.

Lillian was just standing there. "Your turn," she told him.

If her robe had affected her shooting, lack of it certainly affected his. He didn't even come close.

She got down on her hands and knees again. Head down, back arched, buttocks high.

Wiley gulped wine.

She kept on shooting, intent on it and seemingly guileless about the various positions she assumed. No regard for his point of view, really.

Wiley lost all sense of competition.

She hit the final marble from the ring. "Skunked you!" she said.

"Shall we go again?" he asked.

She didn't reply, went around to turn out all the lights except one weak one. She took the cushions from a sofa, placed them on the rug beneath the piano. Wiley helped. Removed the cushions from every bergère and sofa. What they had created was a sort of plushy bower.

She crawled in. Wiley right after her. They lay on their sides, pressed against one another, not too tightly, so they could feel more. Their preliminary kisses were so delicate their lips barely touched. Wiley wondered if she heard his breath as he did hers, shallow, difficult, like during a climb.

"You won," he said, whispering now.

She undid his trousers.

He wanted very much to make the loser's payment. To satisfy the debt. Oh, to satisfy it. He slipped the tiny straps of the teddy from her shoulders. She arched up so he could peel it down and off. She let him do it, even when the teddy caught on the heel of a sandal.

He kissed the nubs of her ankles, left and right, wide open kisses. Then the same to her kneecaps, and he was that much closer to losing himself in the lover's land.

Whimper of pleasure from her. She took his head in her hands. He resisted but came up so they were again face to face.

They kissed mouths, their touches wandered and he found no reason why she had stopped him.

"I won," she whispered.

She kissed his throat. One spot, various kisses. Then her cheek went down upon his chest, merely pausing, enjoying her influence on his heartbeat.

18 ⊁⊁⊁

By midafternoon that day they were headed out of Bogotá on the Carretera Central del Norte.

Lillian was driving. She had borrowed the jeep. Called General Botero and told him she wanted to go sightseeing, and mainly old statue hunting, up in the high country. He had offered a four-man military escort, which she refused nicely by saying her bargaining power would be handicapped by such an entourage.

The General resisted telling her that with the escort along she would be able to name her own price—little or nothing.

When the jeep was delivered to the garage at the villa, first thing, Lillian painted out all its military identification.

"Otherwise it'll look as though we stole it. Two civilians in an army jeep would surely get stopped."

Almost reasonable enough, Wiley thought. She had made him promise not to slow them down with questions. He was satisfied with the fact that they were going somewhere. However, in his opinion the jeep looked even more stolen now. The khaki-brown paint she'd used was in the right color range but a few shades darker than the original, slightly faded finish. The spots she'd touched up really stood out. Also one coat didn't cover adequately. The white-stenciled army numbers and letters showed through, vaguely, but they could be noticed.

Earlier that morning they had gone to Sears, bought a sleeping bag, other equipment and clothing. Also stopped at a gunsmith's shop, where Lillian ran in for some extra nine-millimeter ammunition, as though she was picking up a last-minute thing for dinner.

Now under way, Lillian swerved to miss the potholes when she could, but she seldom let up on the accelerator.

Wiley asked her what the hurry was.

She wanted to get there, she said.

He had asked where once and gotten only a change of sub-

ject. He assumed she had made arrangements. This trip was
her response to his desire to get away from Bogotá, he thought.
Was her change of heart a result of their good lovemaking?

They hit a hole that jolted to such an extent that for a
moment they were weightless. For that moment she lost control of the jeep.

No, she still didn't want him to drive.

She had on a peaked army cap, her hair up and concealed.
He was reminded of the first time he set eyes on her. She was
more like that now than she'd been at any time since, not only
in appearance but in attitude. She seemed turned up and on,
happy with herself.

He scrunched down, gave attention to the countryside. A
small, poor house alone in a field. Several small, poor houses
together, grouped for courage, he thought. Back from the road
were the large haciendas, only glimpses of their main houses,
situated in the gaps of the slopes. A few of the haciendas had
walls along the road. Whitewashed walls that seemed to go on
for miles, interrupted by a gate. Here and there, handpainted in
red on the wall, was a hammer and sickle and the words *El
gente es el poder* (The people are the power). A little farther
on, workers, obviously some of those *gente*, were repairing
and whitewashing that same wall for pay. In a day or two they
would be covering over the red graffiti. Quite possibly one of
them had inscribed it in the first place. And would again.

They passed through Chocontá and some even smaller
places that barely qualified as places. More chickens than people. They'd been traveling over an hour.

"How far does this highway go?" Wiley asked.

"To Venezuela, the map says. But considering its condition,
it might end any mile now."

"We're not bound for Venezuela."

"Leiva," she said.

"Where's that?"

"About fifteen miles from Tunja."

According to the many road signs he'd seen, Tunja might be
the hub of the world.

"Ever been there?" he asked.

"Tunja?"

"Leiva."

"No. It's only a speck on the map."

"So, what's there?"

Her expression clouded with aggravation. "I hate this gear we bought."

"Why?"

"It's new. Bad for the image. If we'd had time we could have gone to a second-hand store."

"What's the difference?"

"Our boots, for instance . . ."

He put a foot up on the dash.

". . . they don't look as though they've been anywhere," she said.

"Even the most vagrant have to buy new boots someday."

"Not often."

"Especially them."

She didn't agree. "As long as boots have good strong uppers, you can have them resoled and reheeled time and again. One damn good pair is all a person really needs for a lifetime."

Was this his wealthy woman?

"Our backpacks, ponchos, even our long johns are new," she complained. "Imagine the impression we'll make. A couple of naïve gringos."

He realized why she was annoyed. This was the hitchhiker Lillian, the Lillian in the tank top, who slept more peacefully on the floor of a nearly bare room because it was psychologically soothing. That explained the change in her disposition today, her lighter spirit.

"New sleeping bag, too."

"A *double*," he reminded.

Not even that offset her distress.

The town of Villapinzón, then Tunja.

They had to ask directions to Leiva. They got three wrong opinions before a boy told them, for two pesos, to keep going on the street they happened to be on. "Even if it appears impossible, keep going," he said and eyeing the jeep, he asked, "Are you in the army, *señor*?"

The street soon became a dirt road, extremely gullied and rutted but easy compared to the trail it eventually reduced itself to. A trail that would have been impossible for a regular car, it was almost too much for the four-wheel-drive jeep in some places.

Lillian fought it, slapped the gearshift into low-low, avoided the jags of large rocks that loomed right in the middle of the way, kept at least one wheel in contact with the ground at all times. It was a continual but inconsistent climb. The trail properly respected the steepness of some slopes, traversed back and forth to the tops. On others, even steeper, it went directly up at such an angle that the jeep was as close as possible to being vertical, causing the sensation that any moment the jeep would flip over backward. Lillian clung tight to the steering wheel. Wiley hung on to anything with both hands.

There would be seventeen miles of that to Leiva.

With about five to go, they came to a short level stretch. Lillian stopped for a breather.

"Let's have an apple," she said.

He reached back into her pack. Just before leaving she had appropriated a few things from Argenti's larder. Because her pack wasn't quite full was her excuse. Romanoff beluga caviar, Carr's water biscuits, shelled pistachios, supercolossal ripe olives, Oreo cookies and two apples.

Wiley felt for and found one of the apples. It was large, hard, with a green waxy skin. The Granny Smith variety. Had there ever actually been a person named Granny Smith? Probably only a merchandising gimmick. Who could dislike a granny? And Smith was certainly inoffensive. A Granny Weinberg or a Granny Lopez would be another matter, Wiley thought.

He used his sheath knife to cut the apple, handed half to Lillian.

"Do me a favor?" she asked.

"Want me to peel it for you?"

"No. Do me a favor."

"Sure."

"Promise me no matter what happens up here you won't mention that I have money. You can tell them anything else but that."

"Them?"

"It's important."

"Okay, I promise, but . . . "

"Your absolute word."

"You've got it."

"Break it and from then on I'll look right through you."

She meant it. "Mind telling me why?" he asked.

"As far as you know, I'm the same girl who had that house in Bethel, New York. Five years older, but the same girl. Just forget everything else I've let you in on."

"I think you ought to let me in on this."

A young fellow by the name of Miguel Contreras. Lillian had met him in Washington, D.C., during an antiwar demonstration. He was about nineteen at the time. She got to know him over a period of three years.

Miguel was Colombian, born and raised in a small Andean village in the Central Cordillera a hundred miles northwest of Bogotá. However, at the time Lillian met him his home was in Queens, New York. About eighty thousand Colombians lived in Queens—Jackson Heights and Woodside. Many were *indocumentados*—people without papers, always on the alert for "Emilia," which was their name for the United States Immigration Service. "Emilia," one Colombian would whisper to warn another in the subway. The word that Emilia was coming was enough to half empty any theater or restaurant along Eighty-second Street in Queens.

Miguel and his family were *indocumentados*. Family of five, including two younger sisters. His father had served with the Colombian army in Korea.

Miguel had become part of a student leftist group in Bogotá when he was thirteen. While at the Universidad Nacional he was extremely involved. He had cried from tear gas more than anything else in his life. Thus, when he came to the United States, he fit right in with the antiwar movement. He often referred to it as merely "a sort of revolution," as though it lacked much by comparison. He had angered Lillian a number of times with such talk. However, he made up for it with energy and courage. It was always Miguel in the vanguard of a demonstration, stirring it up, taunting the police lines, challenging the hardhats. Miguel could be counted on for any action, the more agitating the better. A bit of a show-off actually.

For instance, once he had walked right into draft-board headquarters on Whitehall Street. With a fresh short haircut, he got past the guards by including himself among government workers who were returning from lunch. Assumed an air of belonging there, exchanged automatic hellos with strangers to enhance the impression, appeared to know where he was going, finally reached it—the heart of, and reason for, the place. The files. Miguel, with yellow pencil between his teeth, yellow pad in hand, appeared intent on work, opening, looking into and closing a file here, another there. In each file, far in the rear, where it was less likely to be discovered and surely would do the most damage, he placed a small incendiary device. Delayed action. Then, with the same unhurried civil-servant attitude, he walked out of the building.

As a result of Miguel's daring that afternoon, some ten thousand young men were saved from the chance of being lost in Vietnam. Miguel also thought of it as doing the Vietcong a favor.

At various times Miguel had reminisced to Lillian about his past life in Bogotá, the revolutionary cause he'd had to abandon. He spoke like a disciple about a man named Santos, Professor Julio Santos.

Then, in the fall of 1972, U.S. Immigration Agents, well supplied with blank warrants, made a random sweep of a block of dwellings in Queens. A hundred and twelve "deportables" were taken into custody. Among them was the Contreras family.

All except Miguel.

Miguel was on the F.B.I.'s wanted list. Gangsters had been replaced; rebels were the public enemies in those days. At post offices the wanted posters, making do with snapshots, looked like pages from high-school yearbooks. If apprehended, Miguel would go to prison. Otherwise he would have turned himself in to Emilia, gladly accepted a free trip home to Colombia. He ran for Canada, stopped off for a night at Lillian's house in Bethel.

That was the last she heard of him. Until six months ago . . .

She had just returned again from a few days here, there. The Hotel du Cap at Antibes and La Réserve at Beaulieu. Seaweed baths in Deauville, oxygenation treatments in Paris. Going on impulse. Just enough Capri, a bit of Sardinia, even a weekend hunt on a grouse moor near the village of St. Boswells, Scotland, followed by Holland because someone mentioned miles of lilies blooming in Voglenzang, and that sounded worth seeing. As it turned out, the fragrance was so intense it gave her a headache.

Where to then? Oh, yes, she'd gone to Newport for the America's Cup trials, then on with a bunch of guests to East Hampton, where she had a summer cottage she'd never seen in summer. Thirty rooms was still a cottage in the Hamptons. She'd wound up in Palm Beach at her father's house, which was practically on the way anyway. She met his latest and tried to want to stay more than three days.

Usually it was a relief for her to be back in Mexico City, to come to a standstill, flop down, reflect on all the inconveniences that she'd endured, no matter how first class they were. And vow never again. But this time the place she had always depended upon as a base seemed just another temporary atmosphere. Really not all that different from a suite at the Carlton in Cannes or a guest wing in Sussex.

Space, just space, with her alone in it.

The mood would pass, she thought, she had merely taken an overdose of the wrong distractions. She did some bare-handed gardening, made an extremely intricate macramé throat band, enameled some chairs, cooked a huge pot of zuki beans, slept all day instead of all night. The feeling persisted. It seemed similar to the aftereffect of a long ride, the sensation of being still on the go. More honestly, it was the urge to go. Not that, she thought, God, no, she didn't want to be doomed like so many of her aimless acquaintances. Direction was what she needed, a cause again. Even if she had to settle for a cause that was something less than she'd known before, it would still have to be something extraordinary.

The suggestion came to her one night soon thereafter, when she was in that pastime room off her bedroom. It was such an obviously good idea that she was peeved at herself for not having thought of it before.

At once she set about to locate Miguel, hired someone in that sort of business who found out that Miguel was in Bogotá. In La Picota Penitenciaría for the disturbances and injuries he'd caused during the last election.

She was rather glad to hear that. Miguel was the same Miguel. He had five months yet to serve on his sentence. She doubted his behavior in there would get him any time off.

She wrote him in prison.

He replied.

They corresponded regularly.

She had seen Miguel for the first time again three days ago. Met with him in a shack deep in the Las Brisas *barrio*, practically in the shadow of Argenti's skyscraper. It hadn't been a happy reunion, couldn't be, because Miguel had just gotten word that several of his comrades had been killed for poaching emeralds in the mountains—among them a girl he loved and the man Julio Santos.

"What mountains?" Wiley wanted to know.

"Near Chiquinquirá, ten miles from here," she said, as though it were a thousand.

The open flesh of the apple had turned brown in Wiley's hand. At least, he thought, her reason for wanting to be in Bogotá wasn't Argenti. Where *did* Argenti fit into all this?

Lillian told him Argenti was coincidental, merely a convenience.

Did Miguel know she was staying at Argenti's?

Yes.

How did she explain that?

Miguel had been amused, believed it might be useful somehow, having someone inside on that level. "I told him that was my reason."

"He bought it?"

"Why not?" She arched. "Looks can get you almost anywhere. You should know that."

A reminder, not a barb, he thought. Nevertheless, it stuck. "I take it we're meeting Miguel."

"We're supposed to be in Leiva by six."

Wiley looked away, across the slopes. Semitropical foliage, weeds and vines, the trees not tall but numerous, vast clumps of bushes, snow on peaks off to the right. The sun was on its way down, a few hours from the horizon but on its way. The air had been still. Now a breeze came, all at once an isolated puff, strong and cold. Wiley tightened. "I don't like it," he said.

"Look, darling, I'm not asking you to conspire in a huge, ugly, complicated lie. All you have to do is leave one thing out, not mention one simple little thing."

Of course that wasn't the reason Wiley had misgivings. More of the picture was fitting into place now. What he was getting into. What she was getting him into. With Lillian, would he always have to be filling things in? He remembered how conveniently she had exonerated her tendency to omit. No excuse for it. Well, he could get out right now, walk down the slope, not even look back at her, retreat, eventually reach Tunja and then someplace else. However . . . even if he could leave Lillian just like that, it would be the wrong move, he thought, considering the possibilities that might lie ahead. Strange, this countryside didn't appear capable of yielding up anything as precious as emeralds.

He sliced away some of the apple's face so it was fresh

again. Took a bite. She had nibbled hers to the core between words. He told her, "Let's hope I remember to call you Penny. It was Penny, wasn't it?"

"Lillian's okay now." She slapped the gearshift into low to get them under way again.

"What about a last name?"

"I'm using my mother's, my middle—Mayo. See? No lie, I'm just omitting Holbrook."

"And who am I supposed to be?"

"My man."

She said it as though anything else wouldn't be the truth.

19 ⤳⤳

They bivouacked on the hillside in a stand of trees, where they wouldn't be spotted from the air.

Miguel had chosen the location. He and his two comrades had cleared the area and made a firepit of loose stones by the time Lillian and Wiley arrived.

Miguel wasn't pleased when he saw the jeep, so obviously a painted-over army vehicle. The first thing he wanted to know was whether it was stolen. Lillian assured him it wasn't, but it still bothered him. He drove it into some thick, tall brush and covered it with branches.

Supper was already on, simmering. *Locro de choclos*, a thick potato soup with whole ears of corn in it, salt and lots of pepper. They ate it as the sun dropped out of sight, and afterwards, when it was surely night, Miguel, Lillian and Wiley went up to the farmhouse.

It was an adobe place, two rooms, a large everything room and a small bedroom. Because it was situated on such a steep hill, the bedroom was on a higher level. The bedroom had been an addition in 1874. There was a wood floor. The owner, Frederico Lucho, was proud there was a wood floor. When he was five he had helped his father put in the floor, handed his father nail after nail. Frederico Lucho was now seventy. He looked ninety but he moved like forty. He had no children. There had been many tries, three wives, one that ran away, two that died, so Lucho believed it was his fault that he had no children. But he never admitted that to anyone.

Wiley found him immediately likable.

They sat around the only table. The light was from two kerosene lamps with round reflectors. There were three votive candles in red-glass containers on the shelf next to a small crucifix. Lucho placed four enameled tin cups on the table and a half-full pint bottle of *aguardiente*. He poured some of the clear liquid into each cup, equal measures, careful not to waste a drop. Wiley read the label. *Aguardiente* meant *ardent water* but translated literally another way it was "to water the teeth."

Lucho grunted for a toast.

They tossed back their drinks.

A gulp that was like a blue-hot coal going down let Wiley know precisely where his stomach was and stopped his breath for a moment. It must have been two-hundred proof. After a while he could taste what he swallowed, anise flavor. He glanced across at Lillian. Her fixed smile was supposed to offset her watering eyes.

Miguel told Lucho, "According to the boundary markers we are camped outside your line."

"Thank you," Lucho said.

"And there will be no weapons on your property, as we promised, not even a machete."

The old man nodded.

"If troops come and there is trouble you are to say we forced you to cooperate."

"How long will you be here?" Lucho asked Miguel.

"Are you nervous?" Miguel asked.

"A little."

"Four days, perhaps five," Miguel told him, "depending upon how it goes."

"I thought a week or two."

Lucho smiled. His front teeth were worn down, upper and lower. Wiley wondered if it was from ardently watering his teeth as the bottle said. Actually it was from gnawing corn.

This was the best chance Wiley had had to study Miguel. He was smaller than the man Wiley had pictured. About five eight, and thin. Not weak thin. Tensile, sinewy, as though capable of springing at any moment. He had the blackest black hair, thick and tight. Full lips and a slightly broad nose. Quick eyes, a dark brown that made the whites appear whiter. His voice was deeper and he spoke more slowly than one would anticipate.

"Let us discuss the split," Miguel said. "How much do you want?"

"I have thought much about that," Lucho said.

"Half?"

Lucho drew his brows together. "No. It would not be good for me. I thought it would be good, but already I am uneasy."

"How much, then?"

"I will take help. One cannot be killed or go to prison for receiving help." Lucho said.

"Explain what you mean."

Lucho gazed upward as though to read the ceiling. "Most growers have children and many grandchildren to help with the picking. I have to hire from the village."

"We are not farmers," Miguel said.

"Anyone can pick a bean," Lucho said. "I will give up my share for five hundred hours' work. You have people, do you not?"

"Yes."

"Ten hours a day, five people for twenty days," Lucho said, "that is what I want."

Miguel lowered his head, shook it slowly.

"I will take four hundred hours," Lucho bargained.

"It is only that I find it incredible," Miguel said. "I tell you what. If everything goes right, we will give you two thousand hours."

That delighted Lucho. He wanted to pour another round of *aguardiente*. He poured into the cups of Miguel and Wiley till the bottle was empty. It was the thing to do. Lucho shrugged at the empty bottle. Wiley pushed his cup to Lucho and said, "I have an ulcer."

Lucho didn't believe him.

Wiley had to drink it. He found this second shot not half so bad.

Lucho turned out one of the lamps.

He and Miguel shook hands to close the deal. Lucho was unsure about shaking hands with the *norteamericanos.* Wiley extended his hand and Lillian offered hers. Lucho, embarrassed but pleased, gave them each a single shake.

They returned to camp and Lillian made some Red Zinger herb tea. They sat near the fire. "Where are you from?" Miguel asked Wiley.

"Originally?"

"Yes."

"Connecticut. How about you?"

"Pensilvania," Miguel said.

Kidding, Wiley thought.

Miguel spelled it for him. "It is a small mountain town about a hundred miles west of here. The people there are mostly Piajos Indians. I am at least three-quarters Piajos."

Evidently it was something to be proud of.

"The Piajos fought the Spaniards for over a hundred years, long after most of the other tribes had given up. They are still known as fighters. It helps to be a Piajos."

"How many Indian tribes are there in Colombia?"

"Close to four hundred."

"That must cause problems."

Lillian reached around and sharply punched the back of Wiley's arm. He assumed that was for getting too close to politics.

"Colombia has had nine civil wars," Miguel said. "Not revolutions—civil wars, the people fighting the people. Meanwhile, Bolivia has had seventy revolutions."

"Seventy? I thought it was more," Wiley said, sounding knowledgeable.

"What this country must have is an incident," Miguel said.

"Like Pearl Harbor."

"In effect. Something that will demonstrate to the people that those who hold the dollar over their heads are not invulnerable."

The dollar over his head, Wiley thought. "Che didn't accomplish much in Bolivia."

"Che Guevera was stupid," Miguel said. "The only thing Che could do at that point was die. He was sold out."

"Tania was a double agent."

"Or a triple," Lillian put in. "Probably she was also working for IT and T."

Miguel laughed, a rather involuntary laugh, sharp and cut short. He was mourning his girl friend and Professor Santos, and although he was functioning well, dejection was just below the surface. "Che didn't fit in any place after the fighting was over in Cuba. He was an embarrassment to the Russians and to the Cubans," Miguel said. "They knew guerrilla warfare in Bolivia was not feasible, but they did not even try to convince Che of that. Actually, they encouraged him. Besides," Miguel added, "Che was not a good guerrilla fighter."

"That's not how the legend goes," Wiley said, not disagreeing.

"For one thing, Che was sick. He had asthma, was constantly in need of drugs. That handicap had to be taken into consideration along with every tactic. Also, Che didn't keep his *foco*, cell, on the move. Maybe he couldn't because he was too old."

"How old?"

"Forty."

Lillian pinched Wiley again, to keep him from making any rash, defensive comment.

Miguel turned his head aside, gazed out into the darkness. "An incident is needed," he said, nodding, agreeing with himself, "a great incident with a hero rising out of it." He got up, kicked dirt onto the fire to put it out and said good night. He was the *jefe* (leader) and they were dismissed.

No matter, Wiley and Lillian were ready for bed. They crawled into their shelter, undressed as fast as possible and were shivering when they got into the sleeping bag.

Against one another, drawing warmth, causing it. They rubbed feet and put their hands between each other's thighs.

After a while her hands went limp and he heard her breathing change, and he knew she had gone to sleep. He closed his eyes, started to drift off. Something hard in his pack was uncomfortable beneath his head. He reached in to rearrange it. The Llama pistol. Lillian had given him one. Kept the other. He shoved the pistol deeper into the pack and covered it with a sweater. Still, when he put his head down, he knew the weapon was there, believed he could feel it.

At dawn everyone was up and about. For breakfast, coffee and crackers. Then they went up to the farmhouse. Lucho was waiting outside for them with the burros. He had a shovel and an ax on his shoulders, and a piece of quarter-inch wire-mesh screen. Miguel offered to carry them, but Lucho wouldn't have it. Miguel's two comrades, Tomas and Jorge, took up other shovels, a pick and some rope.

They climbed. It was about a forty-five-degree slope. Lucho led the way. Wiley was amazed at the old man's agility and energy. Lucho was used to such effort. His property covered four acres and not a foot of it was naturally level. It was notched with many terraces, which were planted with coffee trees, about four hundred trees to the acre.

The uppermost section of Lucho's property was their destination. A number of the coffee trees there had lost all their leaves, appeared dead.

Lucho led them to one tree in particular. He knew exactly

which it was, had spent hours contemplating it. For this tree the burros would not be needed. The tree had been pulled from the ground a week ago but had been set back into place immediately and the ground around it tamped by Lucho, so it appeared as though it had never been disturbed. At the time, Lucho had thought his best day had come. However, as he turned it over in his mind he realized the complications. If word got out, as it usually did, he would lose his land. It had happened to others for the same reason. His land would be taken over. He would have to accept whatever they offered, which would be little. Otherwise, he would eventually face a departmental judge, and the matter would end the same anyway. They would pull up all his trees, his great-grandfather's trees. He owed the trees better than that.

He had been tempted just to forget about it, literally cover it over. But he found he could not. For advice he went to his only living male relative, his cousin Franco in Bogotá. Cousin Franco worked as a janitor. He lived in the Las Brisas *barrio*, where he shared one of his walls with the *foco*. On hearing Lucho's dilemma, Franco took Lucho next door.

Now, there was Lucho at that trouble-making tree. Its death had seemed to be an omen. He would be glad when all the dead trees in that section had been removed, replaced by little young ones. It would take five years for the new trees to bear coffee beans, but that would give Lucho something more to look forward to.

He grabbed hold of the dead tree, pulled. It gave some. Tomas and Jorge helped, and the tree came down and out at the roots.

Miguel squatted, and Lucho was on his knees at the hole. The others gathered close around. Lucho dug away some of the loose earth and brought up a stone. He rubbed it on his sleeve, spat on it and cleaned it more on his sleeve before handing it to Miguel. It was about three quarters of an inch by half an inch, hexagonal, with well-defined planes.

"*La materia verde*," Lucho whispered, rather reverently. The green stuff.

It was an emerald of fairly good quality with some kelly in it. Its skin was dark, nearly black in places, and one end was irregular, attached to a hard white substance, part of its matrix.

The stone was passed around. Wiley took a good long look at it.

Miguel found other stones in the hole and some within the clump of the roots. As though the roots, like fingers, had reached down and brought the emeralds up in a fist.

Perhaps this was a small isolated pocket of emeralds. They pulled down other dead trees with the rope and the burros, shoveled and used the wire mesh to sift the earth along those terraces. They found no emeralds here, found several there, and that was how it went.

They went at it for two hours. Miguel decided it was best that they work only during the very early morning, to lessen the chance of being seen. From where they were they could look across to several hillsides. Anyone over there had an equally clear view.

Back at the campsite, the emeralds were washed and placed on a bandana. Twenty-four stones in all, some smaller but none larger than the first they'd found. Sunlight came through the breaks in the leaves overhead and played on the stones, which played back with hints of glowing green.

Wiley wondered how much they were worth. He guessed from what little he'd gathered about emeralds that what was there totaled about 350 carats. Allowing that they weren't the finest grade of rough, say they were in the $200-a-carat class, that came to . . .$70,000.

Just for scratching around for a couple of hours!

It brought Harry Galanoy to mind. Harry from L.A. who had so envied the guys who discovered Silly Putty and Hula Hoops. Wiley hadn't given Galanoy a thought in years.

In the afternoon Miguel made up another batch of *locro de choclos*. This time he dropped a whole chicken into it. While it simmered, Miguel, Tomas and Jorge napped. Wiley suggested a walk. Lillian just wanted to read and be lazy. She'd brought along a paperback edition of Stendhal's *Le Rouge et Le Noir* and was already into it. Wiley lay with his head in her lap for about a quarter hour. Then he took off on his own.

He made his way down to the dirt road and walked the two and a half miles to Leiva. It was an attractive village with some very old well-kept buildings. Wiley played the sightseer for an hour. There was a church. At its gate, vendors were offering tiny silver replicas of arms and feet, lungs, livers, eyes and especially hearts. To be taken inside and pinned on the skirt of the Virgin as a cure for the appropriate affliction. A woman came from the church carrying holy water home in a Roman

Cola bottle. On that same street, Wiley bought four quarts of Blanco del Valle *aguardiente*, double-checked the label to make sure it was right. As an afterthought he stopped in at a shop that sold religious statues. Plaster of Paris saints in every size and color. He was reminded of the cheap painted-plaster statues of horses and dogs and Hawaiian hula girls that were prizes at carnivals for throwing baseballs or darts. Once he had spent ten dollars of his sidewalk-shoveling, lawn-mowing, leaf-raking money trying to toss a wood hoop over a wrist-watch mounted on a black-velvet-covered stand. The watch gleamed. It looked easy, anyway possible. The stand was the catch, of course. Being black made it appear smaller than it was. It was actually only an eighth of an inch less in circumference than the hoop, a million (or more)-to-one shot. The carnival man had given Wiley a plaster Krazy Kat statue as a consolation prize. Wiley had smashed it on a rock wall on the way home.

The shopkeeper asked which saint.

Wiley had no idea. Saint Ignacio looked pretty good and so did Saint Sebastian. To be on the safe side, Wiley bought Jesus for fifty dollars. The largest Jesus in the place, about four feet tall, Jesus in a shocking-pink robe with a green mantle and red sandals, flesh a Man Tan color. A slightly walleyed Jesus, the way it was painted, wreath of thorns in gold.

Wiley was sorry he hadn't picked the statue up before he paid for it. It weighed about sixty pounds.

What a sight, he thought, as he made his way out of town with four quarts of *ardent water* in one hand and Jesus on his shoulder.

It was three miles to the turnoff onto the even lesser road that went up another half mile to Lucho's land. Wiley was glad to get there. He put the statue and the *aguardiente* out of sight in a clump of bushes not far from camp.

Lillian didn't ask where he'd been. She had gotten through fifty pages of Stendhal, and now Miguel was explaining an automatic rifle to her. She was thoroughly absorbed. This was the first evidence Wiley had seen that Miguel was armed. The rifle had a retractable stock, so it could easily have been concealed in his bedroll. Miguel ran down the specifications in a patient, instructional monotone. It was obviously something he'd done many times before. The rifle was Russian. The 7.62

millimeter PPS-43. Fully automatic, blow-back operated. It could fire 700 rounds per minute.

"What's the muzzle velocity?" Lillian asked.

"Sixteen hundred feet per second."

Lillian tried the feel of it, put the butt of the steel-frame stock to her shoulder and sighted. Miguel showed her how to release and connect the magazine. He only had to show her once.

Wiley thought there she was, his love, sitting high in the mountains in the late light of day, handling a lethal weapon. But really, would he rather she was doing needlepoint?

That night after supper, Lillian and Miguel talked old times. Wiley was a good listener for a while, then got up and went off. He glanced back once, saw he wasn't being missed. Despite the dark he had no difficulty finding the Jesus and the *aguardiente*. He carried them up to the house.

Lucho was glad to have company. It took him a while to accept the fact that the Jesus was a gift for him. He was overwhelmed. Only the finest large homes had such an impressive Jesus. Lucho would build a special shelf for it and get more candles. For now it stood on the table.

Wiley thought perhaps he should have bought a smaller version, for the statue overpowered the modest room. As for the *aguardiente*, Lucho could not accept it.

"You are in my house," he said. "Perhaps when I come to your house you may offer me a drink, but here you are the guest and it is I who should pour for you."

"Have I offended you?"

"No. However, I am ashamed that I do not have a drink to offer you."

"There has been a misunderstanding," Wiley said. "Look, the bottles aren't even open, so how can I offer you a drink? When I go, the bottles will be left behind, because I didn't intend to take them from this house tonight or ever. Sooner or later, perhaps months after I've gone, you will open a bottle, won't you?"

"It would be a long while."

"Then why don't you share with me now that I'm here?"

Lucho appreciated Wiley's having found a way around the situation. It was the sign of a kind man. He broke open one of the bottles and poured double an adequate measure into cups.

When they had drunk to each other, Wiley asked, "How many trees do you have?"

Lucho knew exactly. "One thousand six hundred and thirty-two."

That sounded like a lot to Wiley.

Lucho explained that on the average each tree produced two thousand ripe beans a year.

"How many beans in a pound?" Wiley asked.

"Two thousand beans make one pound."

"So, each tree yields a pound of coffee every year."

"Yes."

Now it seemed very little to Wiley. What could Lucho be getting per pound? A dollar? Probably even less. He recalled that back in the States coffee prices had been extremely high, but he doubted Lucho had benefited from that.

"I could be doing better," Lucho said.

"You will when you get the help Miguel promised."

"Yes, but still my machine is broken. I must pay to use the machine of a neighbor."

Lucho welcomed this opportunity to talk coffee. The *norteamericano* Wiley seemed interested. Lucho explained how the beans came from the tree two to a berry, covered by a tough hull which had to be removed by a machine.

"What kind of machine?"

"Gasoline makes it run. My machine was good but it is through. There is a new machine that can be bought."

"For how much?"

"Five hundred dollars."

"You could have made that much easily from the emeralds."

"That was one of my thoughts. But I also thought, what sense would there be in having the machine if I have no land?"

"No one would know where you got the five hundred."

"I could have gotten the machine and paid for it a little at a time, as I would normally have to do." Lucho was thinking out loud.

"So, tell Miguel you've reconsidered."

"I cannot," Lucho said regretfully.

"Still afraid the emeralds might be traced back to you?"

"It is not that so much now. If I had it to do again, I would ask for the picking help *and* the five hundred. However, I have already put my word on the deal."

"I will speak to Miguel."

"No. It is done," Lucho said.

"There must be some way," Wiley said.

Lucho glanced up at the walleyed Jesus. "I wish it would be shown to me."

They finished off their portions of *aguardiente*, had another. Wiley felt it to the tips of his fingers, a well-being.

"How do you market your beans?" Wiley asked.

Lucho explained how he put them into large jute sacks, a hundred pounds to the sack, took them by burro to Leiva whenever the agent for the coffee exporter was scheduled to be there.

Did Lucho have to sell through the agent?

No.

Maybe he could get a better price by selling more directly.

Probably. But the agent paid on the spot.

"The agent pays according to grade," Lucho said. "The size, weight and shape of the beans."

"At that point what do the beans look like?" Wiley wanted to know.

"They are green, a rich color, like an olive, with a delicate silvery skin."

"I would like to see some."

"I will show you. But my beans are not the best. I have never received the best price."

"Why not?"

"This land is too high to grow the best coffee," he said resignedly.

Wiley wondered if there was any subtle, respectful way he could buy that machine for Lucho. Maybe, to hell with pride, he should come right out with the offer. He was about to when there was a knock on the door. Wiley thought it might be Lillian, come looking for him.

But it was Julietta Magdalena Rosario.

When Lucho introduced her, he ran the names together melodiously as if he were introducing the most sought-after beauty of the area.

She was as old as Lucho and as tall as Wiley. Thin and straight as a rail—to her shoulder blades. From there up, she was hunched, her shoulders nearly to her ears, her head drawn in between. She wore a dark-red, almost black, long cotton skirt and a dark-brown *ruana* with a faded-yellow geometric design woven around its border. A tightly tied black bandana covered her head. Not even a wisp of hair showed, and it occurred to Wiley that she might be bald.

Lucho poured her a drink, a stiff one.

She thanked him with her cup and gulped it down with hardly a change in her expression. Smacked her mouth as though applauding. She appraised the plaster Jesus, patted it rather consolingly.

"Do you live nearby?" Wiley asked, making conversation.

She didn't reply, looked to Lucho.

"He is not from around here," Lucho reassured her, then explained to Wiley, "The belief is she does not need to live in a certain place."

"Why?"

"She is supposed to be a *bruja*, a witch," Lucho said.

"I do not want to disappoint anyone," Julietta said with a grin that greatly altered her face. She had deep lines descending from the corners of her mouth and others just as deep between her eyes and across her forehead. However, when she grinned, her face seemed to become smooth.

"She lives in a shack off the road to Sachica, about five miles from here. Do you believe in witches, Señor Wiley?"

"Yes," Wiley said for the hell of it.

"Julietta has powers sometimes."

"Sometimes," Julietta agreed.

"She can tell your tomorrows."

"Among other things," Julietta said.

"Tell his tomorrows," Lucho suggested.

Julietta studied Wiley intensely for a long moment, then got up and went around behind him. She cupped her hands over the top of his head and then moved her fingers slowly over his skull, feeling firmly from his eyes to his temples, behind his ears to the base of his skull. "Acceptance by others is very important to you," she said when her fingers concentrated on a spot on the back of his head.

What else is new, Wiley thought.

She gave the same attention to an area about two inches above his left ear. "You will be rich," she said.

Lucho chuckled.

Julietta pressed her thumbs to the rear area just above the nub of his spinal column.

"You are a better lover," she pronounced.

"Better than who?"

"Than those who are not so good. You can have any woman you want."

"What about the one I want now?" Wiley asked.

She felt a little more and told him, "She is already yours."

Julietta also told him such things as that he would take a boat trip, live to be eighty-one, have three children, get a new car and fall from a high place but not be hurt.

That was fun, Wiley thought, and realized he was a little drunk.

Lucho was delighted. "I told you she was a *bruja*."

Julietta took two leaves from her pocket, rolled them into a ball that she stuck into her jaw, between her back teeth and cheek. Coca leaves. She offered Lucho and Wiley some leaves.

Lucho accepted.

Wiley thought he should, and did.

Then they were all chewing.

"*Bruja*." Lucho nodded. "Is there anyone you do not like, Señor Wiley? She can cast a spell."

"How far?" Wiley asked.

Juilietta shrugged modestly.

"As far as Bogotá?"

"I have cast as far as Cali and even once to New York," Julietta claimed.

If only she could, Wiley thought.

"What else can you do?"

"I can locate water," Julietta replied.

Wiley acted not very impressed.

"I can also locate the green stuff," she said. Emeralds.

"They came to her," Lucho said.

"Who?"

"From Bogotá."

"The Concession?"

"That is it," Julietta said.

"They had heard of her powers and wanted her to show them where they could find the green stuff," Lucho said.

"Did you do it?" Wiley asked Julietta.

"It would not have been difficult once I put my mind to it, but I did not show them."

"Why not?" Wiley asked.

"If I did it once, they would have had me sniffing around

like a dog for them from morning until night. Not me," she
said. "As it was, they gave me nothing for my bother."

Wiley must have looked skeptical.

"Now do you not believe she has powers?" Lucho asked.

"She is a remarkable woman," Wiley said, drinking to her
and offering her a Camel.

Wiley got switched and mauled by bushes on his way back
to camp. But between the *aguardiente* and the coca leaves he
wasn't feeling any pain.

Dirt had been kicked on the fire hours ago. Not a single
ember remained.

He crawled into the shelter, fought his clothes off and inserted himself into the sleeping bag.

She's asleep, he thought.

"What time is it?" Lillian asked, not the least torpid.

"Around twelve," he said, merely picking a number.

"It was one the last time I looked."

"When was that?"

"Where've you been?"

"I put out the cat," he said and almost laughed. The coca
leaves.

"Did you go to town?"

She was next to him but not in touch with him.

What was it she'd just asked? He tried to reach back for it,
but it was gone.

"I can't remember if I locked the front door," he said.

"It's locked," she said, ambiguously cool.

"Five hundred dollars," he said.

"You're stoned."

"I was up at Lucho's."

"I thought so."

Now she fit herself against him. She put her leg over him,
discovered with it. "What's this?" she said.

What better verification of his fidelity?

He was unaware of his state until she had her hands around
it. Must have been the coca leaves, he thought. Those *brujas*
sure knew how to live.

With the first light of the next day Wiley suffered for his
excesses. He was grateful that Miguel had imposed a two-hour
work limit. Wiley kept up, shoveling and sifting with the oth-

ers, but his head was so blurry he probably overlooked a precious few.

The yield of emeralds that morning from Lucho's upper terraces was thirty-four stones. Worth about a hundred thousand dollars at the dealer level.

It was a little after eight when everyone returned to camp. Wiley's stomach couldn't bear the thought of breakfast. He crawled into the shelter and slept until two that afternoon. He awoke with a terrible taste in his mouth but with a clear head and a grumbling appetite.

Lillian was kind, made him some coffee and served him up a huge portion of *locro de choclos* that had simmered until the chicken was tender down to the marrow of its bones. For dessert a couple of Oreo cookies. There were only six Oreos left in the box. Lillian had been nibbling while reading. She'd deserted Stendhal on page 135 and was now a fifth of the way into Jean-Paul Sartre's *Troubled Sleep*. Wiley wondered if she ever finished a book, or anything else.

He asked her.

"Don't pick on me," she said.

"Just trying to know you better."

"Sounded more like a criticism."

"That's not how it was meant."

"Did you criticize Jennifer?"

Wiley was surprised she remembered the name. "No."

"She was perfect."

"Hardly."

Lillian went back to Sartre.

Miguel was seated nearby with a tree for a back rest. He had been detached, focused on whatever was taking place in the front of his mind.

"You know electronics," he said to Wiley.

"Not as well as I used to."

"Lillian told me that was your profession."

"I try to keep up." True. He subscribed to the journals and understood many of the recent concepts.

"An interesting field," Miguel said. "I wish I knew more about it."

"It's overcomplicated," Wiley said.

"What do you know about missiles?" Miguel asked.

"I'm no expert."

"You built missiles, didn't you?"

"I helped think out and put together certain components. That's about as much as any one person does."

"You know a lot about electronics." Miguel concluded with an inflection that asked Wiley to confirm his opinion.

It was by no means Wiley's favorite topic. To get off it he agreed.

Miguel blinked, his eyes glazed over again as he went back into his thoughts.

Just before dark Wiley told Lillian he was going up to Lucho's for a while. Did she want to come?

She didn't. She needed to catch up on her sleep, hadn't napped that day. "Don't be late and don't be drunk," she told Wiley. He took along the flashlight.

Lucho was waiting for him on the tenth terrace down from the house. He had a shovel and a bottle of *aguardiente* with a couple of swigs gone from it. Julietta was with him. She said she was in high spirits. From the bulge of her right cheek Wiley surmised she had plenty of reason to be. She shifted her euphoric cud to her left jaw, taking a couple of chews on the way. She looked skyward. The night was ideal, she said. There was a seven-eighths moon. A wind way up there was driving clouds swiftly across its face. Gazing at it, Wiley had the sensation that he, not the clouds, was moving.

Julietta showed him what she used to find the green stuff. No forked witch-hazel branch for her. She had some tricycle handle-bars, with red rubber grips on them. Tied to the center of the handlebars was a length of common twine, about two feet of it. A greenish ceramic medallion dangled from the end of the twine, a primitive medallion with a grotesque face in relief on one side and a hexagonal design on the other. Dangling from the medallion was a tiny handmade copper bell.

Instruments for a divining *bruja*?

What more had he expected? Wiley smiled.

To keep from laughing he lighted a cigarette, gave a pack to each of his companions. He couldn't blame Lucho for wanting to believe in Julietta, nor could he fault Julietta for seeking importance. What the hell, he'd play along with them for an hour. He could make up an excuse for not spending more time than that.

Which way to the green stuff?

Julietta was not the least bit uncertain. They would not look

on Lucho's property, she said, because some emeralds had
already been found there and she wanted an indisputable challenge. The adjacent hillside, her instincts told her. She made
for it with long strides, as though she could see in the dark.

Lucho followed after her.

Wiley tagged along, thinking what a good sport he was.

20 ›››

After four more days Miguel decided enough.

They were still finding emeralds on that upper section of Lucho's land, but there was no point in pushing their luck. Each day increased their chance of being seen and reported. They should leave now with what they had.

They had 183 stones, about 2,500 carats. At only $200 a carat, that was half a million dollars' worth. Miguel believed he could get at least $300, perhaps $400 a carat. The stones found during the last three days had been better quality, with more kelly to them.

The most critical phase lay ahead.

Getting the emeralds to Bogotá.

All roads were patrolled by federal troops on the lookout for poachers. Also, at any point along the way they could encounter *esmeralderos*, those emerald-minded gangsters organized by The Concession to maintain fear and violence. Either would be equally bad.

The troops and the *esmeralderos* usually learned of poachers in advance, waited until they were bound for Bogotá, then waylaid them.

Miguel was sure that was what had happened to the *foco's* last poaching expedition, led by Professor Santos. Only ten days ago.

Miguel's original plan was to use Lillian. For her to carry the emeralds to Bogotá. She had the nerve for it, and the enthusiasm, and it was doubtful she'd be stopped. That had been Miguel's reason for asking her along on this expedition.

Now he had changed his mind.

The problem was the jeep. Why hadn't Lillian rented a car, as they had discussed? No matter that she'd thought the jeep would do better up in the rugged terrain. It was suspect on sight. Had probably been noticed on the way up. It offset all her advantages.

Miguel told Lillian that.

She realized and admitted he was right.

Miguel's revised plan was that the emeralds would be carried in equal amounts by Tomas, Jorge and himself. They would depart for Bogotá at different times that day, and each would take a different route to better the chances that at least one would make it.

Lillian was angry at herself, felt she'd failed the cause. She couldn't just leave the jeep there. That would incriminate Lucho. But what she could do was abandon it somewhere else, along the road. With the emeralds concealed on her, she could take a bus to Tunja and rent a car. She'd complain about motor trouble when she talked to General Botero.

She was about to suggest this plan when a simpler, more accommodating solution came to her.

Which route to Bogotá was the worst for traveling by car? she wanted to know.

Why?

Which? she insisted.

There was a road south through the mountains via Sachica and Samacá. In some places, depending on the season, it was impossible by car; at all times it was very questionable.

Sounded ideal to Lillian. "Is that road patrolled?"

It surely would be.

"At night?" Lillian asked, making her point.

Miguel understood what she was proposing. He didn't jump at the idea, but a couple of hours of hazardous driving was certainly better than a whole day of risk by foot and slow bus. He went to check the jeep, to make sure it would start.

For a final meal Lillian broke out the delicacies. Miguel was amused when she told them she'd taken them from Argenti's larder. Miguel scooped up a mound of caviar with a Carr biscuit, and another, and another, popped pistachio after supercolossal olive after pistachio into his mouth.

Come the revolution, Miguel will be looting gourmet shops, Wiley thought.

They packed and were ready to go.

At eight Miguel went up to have a final word with Lucho. Wiley went along.

Lucho showed them the shelf he'd built for the plaster Jesus. Candles flickered at its feet in several ordinary food jars painted red.

Lucho's farewell handshake with Wiley had something extra in it. He also winked like a conspirator.

Then it was dark.

Lillian wanted to drive.

Miguel gave that responsibility to Wiley, leaving Tomas, Jorge and himself free and ready in case of trouble. They sat in the back, Russian automatic rifles covered at their feet. The jeep was carrying the emeralds in a bandana taped to the inside of its spare tire.

The first ten miles weren't easy. The dirt road was unpredictable, with ruts and corrugations. There were some relatively smooth stretches but no straight or level ones. Wiley took it as fast as he could and as slow as he had to, sometimes spurting up to sixty, at other times shifting down and braking almost to a stop. He kept the headlights on high beam.

A fork in the road.

Miguel told him to bear left.

Then they were on even less of a road. By comparison the previous road had been a super highway. This one defined itself in the beam of the headlights as a pair of parallel tracks separated by tufts of dry grass and jutting rocks. Its ruts were vicious and there were sudden drops when Wiley felt not a wheel of the jeep was touching ground. He fought the road turn after turn, kept an eye on the mileage indicator, measuring the effort necessary to cover a mere five miles.

The steering wheel felt small and brittle, as though it might snap in his grip.

Lillian, in the seat beside him, usually had to hang on with both hands, but whenever the road gave her a chance she reached over to encourage Wiley with her touch on his arm, thigh, the back of his neck.

The high night air was cold. It struck the windshield, lashing around and down on Miguel, Tomas and Jorge. They huddled together, hunched down into the necks of their jackets.

On the good side of things: They hadn't seen a house or a light or a sign of anyone since the turnoff. The road and its difficulties partially eclipsed other dangers on their minds.

In the first hour they covered thirty miles. Seventy to go, but only about forty of those would be so rugged. Each mile less to Bogotá increased their confidence.

The road improved a little.

They passed through a small village, its cantina prominent, lighted.

Then the road resumed its challenge.

A sharp curve ahead. Wiley got set for it, expecting it, as most of the others had been, to be banked wrong.

They saw the beam shooting off into the night before they saw the headlights coming from the opposite direction.

Wiley pulled far over, and even then there was barely room. The two vehicles passed with less than a foot of clearance. The passengers caught the merest glimpse of one another.

The other vehicle had been a jeep. Three soldiers in it. A patrol. Perhaps they were anxious to get to that village and cantina. Maybe they weren't equipped with a two-way radio.

Wiley tried for more speed, couldn't really go much faster. The risk of the road was a governor.

Like holes in the darkness behind them. The headlights came into view, were cut off by a curve, reappeared. No doubt it was the jeep. The soldiers had the advantage of knowing the road, their patrol. They were gaining.

Impossible to outrun them or lose them.

Miguel leaned forward, told Wiley, "Around the next curve stop and cut the lights."

Wiley did.

Miguel leaped out with his rifle, took a concealed position just over the shoulder of the road.

The other jeep came around the curve, had to brake fast, skidded to a stop. Two soldiers were quickly out. One stood slightly off, to the left of Wiley's jeep, another to the right. Their automatic rifles at the ready. Then the third soldier got out and walked forward. He had a flashlight in one hand and a service automatic in the other.

He was a Lieutenant.

Lieutenant Costas.

The same who had been in command of the patrol that had killed Professor Santos and the others on the road outside Chinquinqirá. The enlisted men with him now were two of those who had also taken part in that, and the rape.

The Lieutenant shined his flashlight on Wiley's face, then on each of their faces. Evidently he believed that there were only four of them.

Lieutenant Costas asked for papers.

Lillian dug into the pack that was at her feet. She rummaged around quite a bit, acting nervous and tired. Finally she presented her United States passport and Wiley's temporary one. Tomas and Jorge showed identification. The Lieutenant looked them over and handed them back. The United States passports didn't seem to impress him.

He asked Wiley, "What are you doing on this road?"

"We got lost," Wiley said.

"Coming from where?"

"Sightseeing around Leiva."

"Did you see the church in Leiva, the large white adobe church?"

"It was gray and made of stone," Wiley told him, recalling.

"What is your destination?"

"Bogotá."

"You could have taken the road to Tunja and the highway from there."

"I made a wrong turn."

"This is a very bad road."

"That's for sure," Wiley said casually.

"Who are they?" the Lieutenant asked of Tomas and Jorge.

Wiley almost said hitchhikers. "Guides. They were asleep when I took the wrong turn."

Tomas and Jorge confirmed that with guilty nods.

"They tell me this road will eventually get us to Bogotá," Wiley said. "Will it?"

"Perhaps," the Lieutenant said.

He examined the jeep, walked around it slowly, noticed where the army markings had been painted over. He stopped on Lillian's side. "Everyone out," he said.

They didn't move. They couldn't undergo a search. The weapons would be found.

"Out!" the Lieutenant snapped.

Lillian had her Llama pistol hidden beneath her right thigh.

In a single swift motion she brought it up and fired twice. The second bullet went in almost exactly where the first went in. Just above the Lieutenant's breastbone and on through his heart. He clenched his eyes and opened his mouth as he died.

In that same instant, Miguel opened fire. All the while he'd had one of the soldiers surely in his rifle sights. A short burst of bullets killed that one. Only a slight rapid adjustment was needed to aim at the other.

That soldier threw his rifle anywhere and his hands upward. His life fell on the merciful side of Miguel's ambivalence. Miguel frisked him, roughly, ordered him to lie face down on the road. Tomas gathered up the weapons: the automatic rifles of the soldiers and the Lieutenant's pistol. He also found twenty thousand pesos in the Lieutenant's pockets, about eight hundred dollars. Miguel went to the second jeep, saw it was equipped with a two-way radio that was switched on. He smashed the radio. There were some spare magazines containing ammunition on the rear floor. Jorge came and got those. Miguel lifted the hood, used his knife to sever all the connections to the distributor, paralyzing the vehicle.

Tomas wanted to know about the surviving soldier, reminded Miguel, "He knows us."

The soldier cursed his eyes.

"Kill him," Miguel said.

Tomas killed him.

They got under way again.

Wiley wondered if it had seemed as unreal to the others as it had to him. And the steady, unhesitating way Lillian had killed the Lieutenant. Couldn't she have left it to Miguel and his comrades? She was probably feeling the aftereffects now, hollow, sick and shaky about it, fully realizing the deadly seriousness of this adventure.

He couldn't take his eyes off the road and could only spare a hand for a moment, reached over to find hers—still holding the Llama. She took his hand to her mouth, kissed the back of it rather consolingly and returned it to where it was more needed, on the steering wheel. She got the other Llama from his pack, placed it between his legs. Also shoved a couple of spare clips into his jacket pocket. In case there was another encounter. But now that sort of danger seemed behind them.

A sudden downgrade, extremely steep.

Wiley shifted to the lowest gear and rode the brake. The jeep skidded, kept skidding, practically straight down, increasing momentum with its weight. The speedometer registered twenty but they were going twice that, beyond control. If the road curved, Wiley would not be able to match it. No telling how far they would fall. Two hundred feet was equal to twenty stories, Wiley recalled, and a two-hundred-foot drop was probably less than average in these mountains.

The headlights hit upon a milky substance ahead.

It looked like a lake.

They plunged into it.

Fog.

So thick the headlights reflected off it and glared back into Wiley's eyes. All he could do was keep hold of the steering wheel and hope the road was somewhere under them.

Gradually, the grade gave up most of its pitch.

The gears grabbed and growled.

Wiley stopped the jeep.

He needed a breather, took three deep ones, and flexed his fingers, stiff from gripping. There was the taste of sweat on his upper lip.

Miraculous as it seemed, they were still on the road.

Lillian activated the windshield wipers, which helped a little as they continued on, taking it slow. Visibility was less than a dozen feet.

They didn't see the town until they were practically in it.

They didn't see the army truck parked across the road, blocking the way, until they almost hit it.

Lieutenant Costas had used that radio, notified ahead.

Suddenly, yellow searchlights, fog lights, were on them from the left and the right.

Miguel, Tomas and Jorge grabbed their rifles and jumped out into the night.

The first shot from the truck hit the windshield of the jeep slightly left of center, shattering it in an opaque web pattern.

Lillian ducked down.

Wiley slouched as far down as he could.

A barrage of shots pierced or ricocheted off various areas of the jeep. One headlight exploded.

Wiley stomped the gas pedal, pulled the steering wheel hard right, swerved so sharply the right wheel buckled and the jeep nearly overturned. The left fender grazed the lower body of the truck. Wiley caught a glimpse of the soldiers positioned beneath the truck, recoiling, expecting a collision, not getting off a shot.

The searchlight on the right tried to track, but the jeep was too close in. As they passed under the searchlight Lillian shot up at it. Three rapid shots. Her third was a hit.

With the fog, Wiley could only guess how far he had to go to run their flank. The jeep was bucking every which way over the rough terrain. Without letting up he turned full left and a

structure loomed into view. The rear of a building. He thought
he must be running along the fringe of the town, probably
parallel with the road. Given an opening on the left, he would
cut through and get back on it.

Rifle shots came in staccato bursts as the troopers exchanged
fire with Miguel and his comrades. How could they find anything to aim at in this fog?

The jeep kept on bucking over the irregular ground. Wiley
couldn't see, had to take whatever came, several times almost
tipped over one way or the other. There was an abrupt dip into
a gully and up. The jeep hit a hump with a sharp ridge in it, a
long rock like an exposed bone that scraped the jeep underneath, a powerful, damaging sound.

Wiley tried to steer off it.

The jeep was wedged up on the rock, its frame jammed
tight. Wiley slammed the gearshift from low to reverse several
times, trying for momentum, but three of the jeep's wheels
were off the ground, spinning in place. Lillian took over the
driving while Wiley got out to push the jeep with all his loath-
ing for it.

It wouldn't budge.

They abandoned it, ran for cover.

The cluck of disturbed chickens.

A dog barked warning.

The fog that had been their enemy was now an ally that
might be able to hide them. It was so dense it was nearly a fine
spray on their faces, and it fell cold on the backs of their necks.

They reached the rear wall of a house that didn't have a light
on. There were no lights anywhere. The townspeople were
probably lying low inside in the dark. Had been told to.

The rifle fire at the edge of town hadn't let up.

No doubt some of the soldiers had been detailed to pursue
the jeep, them.

Wiley felt he couldn't let anything stop him from getting
away, to Bogotá and away. Not now. But then, a feeling that
was an emotional composite of all the other not-quite's in his
life seemed to counter his determination.

They had to find a car or truck.

But was this town big enough for anyone to have more than
a burro? It probably didn't even qualify as a town, only a
place, a few buildings stuck together for no important reason
on that godforsaken road.

In a half-crouch they went around the corner of the house and along its side. From the front corner, through the fog, they could just make out the front of another structure across the way. That meant Wiley had been right about the road. There it was.

Something rushed at him. He wasn't ready to take it on. It turned out to be a dog, probably *the* dog, a dirty-colored, medium-sized mongrel with a long nose. It sniffed at Wiley's crotch, sniffed even more aggressively at Lillian's and disappeared into the night.

Wiley had the automatic rifle slung over his shoulder, the Llama pistol in hand.

"Cock it," Lillian whispered.

He hadn't yet mastered the Llama, but he knew enough about it to slide the hammer back and get a cartridge into the chamber. She shouldn't have had to remind him. "Stay here," he told her.

"I don't want to lose you," she said.

"I'll come back here."

She wouldn't have it. "Follow me," she said and started off. He stopped her and took over the lead.

They searched along the road, moving stealthily from one structure to the next. Every so often they paused, remained absolutely still while they scanned the fog for a sign of someone.

At one point they couldn't have been more than forty feet from the road-blocking army truck, but lack of visibility made rear assault impossible. All they could see was spits of flame exploding from the rifles of the soldiers, evidence that they would be greatly outnumbered.

Having found no vehicle of any sort along one side of the road, they crossed over to search along the other. They looked between buildings where possibly a car or truck might be pulled in.

They were quietly but swiftly on the move when it appeared. In another four steps, Wiley would have collided with it.

He didn't have time to consider that it was a person. In the fraction of a second that was the difference between living and dying, it was merely a dark hulk of the appropriate dangerous shape. Wiley's well-preserved reflexes saved him, his reaction was as natural as throwing a quick left at a shadow. The Llama did it, really, expended most of the energy. All Wiley did was shove his hand forward and squeeze. The Llama jumped as though trying to leave his hand when it exploded the nine-millimeter bullet down its barrel and out. The bullet was going 720 miles per hour when it struck flesh. Went in at that little notch where the collarbones join. It spread on impact, opened into sections like a four-petaled blossom. Tore through throat, artery, tissue, and smashed into the spinal column. The bullet drove the soldier back. He went down on his ass first, and then the upper part of him flopped over. His final flash of thought was that he and his rifle had killed someone. He'd been that close to pulling the trigger.

Wiley looked incredulously at the gun in his hand, then at Lillian, as if to say, *Do you realize what I just did?*

No time for that.

Survival, as just demonstrated, was a matter of who saw whom first in that fog.

Another hulking shape was barely discernible off to the right.

Lillian, quickly down on one knee, fired twice. She went for the heart, had to guess where it would be. She was right.

Immediately, out of sight, two others began firing, spraying shots wildly.

Lillian and Wiley went as flat as possible. Bullets chunked the dirt around them and disturbed the air just above. They could only grit their teeth and hope against the chance that one of those many pieces of high-speed metal was flying in the direction of their bodies.

Wiley, cheek pressed to earth, looked at Lillian. Her face was turned his way, mouth slightly open as though stopped in the middle of a word, eyes fixed, staring and filmy. Surely, had she been hit she would have cried out.

He was relieved to see her blink. He thought: Some son of a bitch, merely a someone, was trying to take everything from him, them. He felt a change, actually felt it. A sort of inner snap, and suddenly the gun in his hand seemed to fit. He tightened his grip on it.

The firing let up. Perhaps the soldiers were clipping on new, full magazines or were sure that nothing could have lived through their barrage and were advancing.

Wiley and Lillian kept their heads down, used mainly their elbows and knees to crawl like infants. They reached the front porch of the nearest house, crawled along the side of it, did not get up until they were around back.

More alert now, more stealthily, they continued their search for any sort of transportation. A dilapidated thirty-year-old truck would do. For that matter, a horse. Anything that would get them away. Wiley was considering going back to the jeep to give it another try. Either that or head out into the fog on foot. Maybe they wouldn't walk off a cliff.

They came to a house that was not much more than a shack. The most unlikely so far. It was the last house on the road. They went around the side of the place.

It was the fog playing a trick.

It had to be an illusion.

It was white like most illusions.

Wiley didn't believe it until he put a hand on it, ran his hands over it.

A white Cadillac El Dorado convertible. That year's.

Steal it? Hell, yes, make it up to whomever later.

But all its windows were up and the doors locked. That meant probably the keys weren't in it. They'd have to slash the top. Wiley would jump the wires to start the car.

Lillian thought it would be easier, perhaps even faster to get to the owner.

They went around to the front of the house, rapped on the door. No one came. Again. No one . . .Wiley tried and found the door was open. They entered.

It was a one-room place that smelled of garlic, licorice and woman. The licorice odor Wiley recognized was *aguardiente*. An oil lamp was burning low on a table off to the side. At the back of the room was a bed, very mussed up. There was a woman on it, sitting on the edge. She was also mussed. An extremely fat woman with large breasts down to the folds of her stomach. It wasn't particularly warm in the room but she was perspiring.

Off to the right a man was dressing. He already had his shoes on. They were shiny even in that low light. Patent leather or plastic or a very high buff. He stepped into his trousers, tucked in and zipped up.

He was forty-some. A Colombian, mixed Spanish and Indian. Under five six, and thin, couldn't have weighed over one-thirty.

Wiley apologized for the intrusion. He felt as though he'd come into a wrong hotel room.

The apology went unaccepted. "What do you want?" the man asked. A strong voice for his size.

"Whose car is that out there?" Wiley asked.

"I have the keys," the man told him.

Probably, Wiley thought, the car belonged to whomever the man worked for and he'd used it to come here to this woman.

"Could you take us to Bogotá?" Wiley asked.

"I could," the man said.

"For a thousand dollars," Wiley said.

The woman uttered something religious at the sum. No reaction from the man. He was having trouble with his shirt cuffs, getting the links into the holes.

"Two thousand," Lillian said.

The man smiled agreeably. "Let me finish dressing," he said, reaching for his vest.

"Hurry," Wiley told him, and went to the front window to keep watch with Lillian.

The fog seemed thicker than ever.

No more rifle fire coming from the other end of town. It must have just stopped. Not because anyone had given up, Wiley imagined.

He put his arm around Lillian.

"It's going to be all right now," he whispered to the situation. "We'll soon be safe in Bogotá."

There was no mistaking then what Wiley felt pressed behind his ear. Or what Lillian felt against the back of her neck. The small cold metallic circles that were the muzzles of guns.

The slight man owned the Cadillac.

He was Rico Morales—*esmeraldero*.

21 ➤➤➤

The cell.

Narrow like a stall with a high ceiling and a window just out of reach. The window was too small for anyone to escape through, but it was barred nevertheless. The floor of concrete had an open drain hole about eight inches in diameter that a prisoner could use for his wastes. No furniture, not a stick.

Wiley squatted on his haunches, away from the wall because it was cold and damp, as was the floor. He had thought his bare feet would eventually get used to the cold, but they got worse. Now all fifty-two bones in his feet were aching, and his soles felt like they'd turned to gelatin.

When the Captain had told him to strip, he'd presumed it was only to facilitate their search. That they hadn't given back his clothes was uncalled for. What satisfaction for them to have him shivering? If they'd been gaping and getting their sadistic kicks, at least that would have been a reason, but no one had even looked in on him.

He had been separated from Lillian as soon as they had arrived at this place. Brought under heavy guard in the back of an army truck. It was only about an hour's ride from where they'd been captured. The *esmeraldero* Rico Morales had been glad to turn them in. On the way, one of the soldiers had smirked and said they were going to Barbosa, as though that should be meaningful.

Barbosa.

Wiley remembered it was the place Argenti had mentioned about a week ago during that breakfast on the terrace with General Botero. In Wiley's presence they had discussed the underhanded side-dealings of one of The Concession's carriers. What was the man's name? Ramsey. Yes, that was it. Coincidentally it seemed, this fellow Ramsey had had an accident in New York City in which he'd smashed both his knees. Argenti had told the General to be sure Ramsey got to Barbosa.

Thus, Wiley had assumed it was either a convalescent center or a hospital.

This was Barbosa.

Where did they have Lillian?

Not in any of the several other cells nearby, because Wiley had called out for her over and over, loud enough. He seemed to be the only prisoner. However he was on the second floor, and probably there were other cells on the first, and that was where they had her.

In the passageway a short ways down from Wiley's cell, a soldier stood guard. Actually, he sat—on an ordinary wood chair, tipped back, his rifle leaning against the wall within easy reach.

Wiley called to the guard, said he wanted to speak to him.

The guard ignored Wiley.

Wiley said please.

The guard picked up his rifle and came to Wiley's cell, kept well back away from it.

"Where is the woman?" Wiley asked.

The guard grinned and lowered his head to one side, as though embarrassed.

Strange reaction, Wiley thought. "Is she downstairs?"

"No."

"Is she all right? I mean, is she comfortable?"

The guard had to look aside.

"It's not as bad as this for her, is it?" Wiley indicated his cell.

"No."

Wiley hoped that was the truth.

The cell stunk.

The whole place had a peculiar heavy stench. Wiley had noticed it on the way in. A sort of shitty farm odor.

A smoke would help camouflage it.

He'd give anything for a smoke.

No harm asking.

"How about getting my cigarettes for me?"

The guard took one of his own from his pocket, lighted up. He looked as though he was about to offer one to Wiley.

"Smoke your cock," the guard said and returned to the chair.

Wiley's hands became fists. He called out to Lillian. Again and again, till he was yelling without allowing time between for her to answer. The soldier didn't appear bothered. Evidently it made no difference how loud or long Wiley yelled, because no one came to complain.

Wiley gave up on it.

He sat and suffered the cold on his ass cheeks while he tried to rub some warmth into his feet. Improvising, he sat on his hands. On the palms for a while, then the backs for a while. Palms down was the most tolerable.

He had to bite down a little on his teeth to keep them from chattering.

Probably, he thought, it would be warmer in the daytime. What time was it now? He reviewed the night and tried to estimate how much time had elapsed in each sequence. He had no idea how long they were in that town in the fog. It could have been only thirty minutes, it had seemed like hours, still seemed so.

Between two and three in the morning now was his guess.

Lillian. He couldn't get her out of his thoughts. She was in the front of his mind, like a transparent image through which he was required to view everything.

Remember, he told himself, you're the man who married Jennifer.

That was enough to make him think.

His life had been in radical change when Lillian came into it. Was that why she'd made such an impact? Perhaps, cutting through the bullshit, he really didn't love her all that much. Perhaps he only needed to believe he did.

Besides, what was there about her to love? She was rather spoiled, captious, definitely lethal, had a will like a wall, was neurotic in a way or two, seemed there was more than a pinch of suicidal compulsion in her. She was devious too (the twelve-thousand lie), too independent, with every intention of remaining independent. Noncommittal. Not once had she said she loved him. A few times, at certain peaks, it seemed the words had been right there in her throat, and he had done everything that should have brought them out, but they hadn't come. It was goddamn frustrating. How many times had he told her he loved her and not gotten a response? Twenty times at least, aloud. A thousand times without saying. What a smartass she was, really. A user. A rich, one-way chick looking for temporary satisfactions. Him a temporary. It was time he came to his senses.

He hated her.

An insignificant, random thing came to mind: her disciplining her hair back from her face the way she did, with her fingers like a comb.

He loved her.

As for having gotten into this terrible spot, really, he had only himself to blame. At any time down the line he could have put his foot down harder, she would have acquiesced, but, instead, he had gone along with her. His choice. No tag-along puppy, him, no matter how it seemed.

He had killed that soldier.

No one ever did anything they didn't want to do, he'd always told himself.

Up to the moment when he killed that soldier his existence had been on a course to that moment. Plane from Kennedy International, car to Las Hadas, jeep to Leiva, and so on. It had been unavoidable. Just as it was never meant for him to walk away from Lillian.

Life was a ride down a slippery slide of time.

Lillian had killed two, counting the Lieutenant.

What would the army do?

There would be a trial.

How do you plead?

On his hands and knees.

What hurt as much as anything was that again, oh, again, he'd come a hair away from getting everything he had ever wanted.

So close this time.

His thoughts were interrupted by a noise from outside. An animal sound, a kind of snort.

Then on the ceiling a rhomboidal shape appeared as an outside light was turned on.

More snorting, louder.

Wiley got up.

He heard men outside.

What was going on out there?

He stood beneath the window. It was about ten inches above his reach. Normally, not much of a jump, but from the cold, he felt brittle, as though any jar or sharp movement could break him.

Those snorts were increasing.

He wanted to see.

He flexed his shoulders, arms and fingers and did a couple of deep knee bends before taking the leap. He grabbed one of the bars, got hold of another and pulled himself up.

What he saw out there was a large penlike area surrounded by a tall chain-link fence. The near section of it was brightly flood-lighted. The rest was in the dark, but apparently it included considerable ground.

Three soldiers were at the fence with several buckets of garbage, which they emptied over into the pen.

Hogs. About a dozen huge lard-type hogs snorted and crowded to get the garbage. That was the reason for the stench: the hog pen. It was almost directly below Wiley's cell window.

Why the hell were they slopping hogs at this hour?

Wiley was about to give it no more attention when another soldier came into view. Pushing a wheelchair. In the wheelchair was a naked man, whose legs extended straight out because there were plaster casts on both knees.

Wiley knew that had to be Ramsey, the wayward emerald carrier.

Ramsey was strapped to the chair around his chest and arms.

There were more hogs now, close to fifty. And more coming on the run out of the darker part of the pen. They were real heavyweights of four hundred, five hundred pounds, some even larger. It was surprising how fast they could move on their stubby legs. Their snorting and grunting had become a din, as they competed for those few pails of garbage, which couldn't possibly satisfy them.

They seemed frantic with hunger, as though they hadn't been fed in a week. Some threw their heads up and opened their mouths in anticipation. Wiley saw their pink raw-looking snouts, their tusks and rows of teeth.

Ramsey's mouth was taped.

One of the soldiers tore the tape away.

Ramsey's mouth immediately opened, but his scream was lost in the cacophony of the hogs.

The soldiers used hammers on Ramsey's casts. Only some of the plaster broke away. Evidently it was plaster bandage. One soldier went and got a pair of heavy-gauge wire clippers, and those were used roughly to cut the casts off.

Ramsey never stopped screaming.

They cut his bindings away.

The chain-link fence bulged under the pressure of the hogs. The fenceposts had to be buried deep in cement to withstand that much weight. Still, the soldiers seemed somewhat circum-spect.

Ramsey writhed and flailed. With the casts off, his useless legs bent painfully out at the knees.

Three of the soldiers lifted Ramsey, who twisted and bucked and hit out at them. Meanwhile, the other soldier shoved a two-foot-high platform into place next to the fence. They climbed up on it with Ramsey, hoisted him above their heads and threw him as far out as possible into the pen.

Ramsey landed front up, arched over the hairy back of a hog.

They got to his legs first.

Their snorts and grunts were suddenly louder. They climbed all over one another and fought one another to get a piece of him.

The soldiers watched.

Wiley dropped to the floor of his cell.

He was sweating.

The coldness of the floor didn't matter now. He slouched down, and clenched his eyes as though he could shut out what he'd already witnessed. He crawled to the open drain and retched. Nothing came up. His insides were too constricted with shock to let anything up.

He rolled over and lay there, fixed on the window.

So that was how The Concession dealt with anyone who got out of line. An example of the dread it imposed on its world of emeralds.

That was what was in store for him, Wiley thought. Maybe this was feeding night and he was the next course. They could be coming for him now.

He stood quickly and went to the window, jumped and pulled himself up again.

The soldiers were pushing the wheelchair away.

The hogs were scattered now, rooting around with their snouts and scratching with their hoofs at the spot where Ramsey had been.

No sign of the man, not a tooth, bone or hair.

That's how ravenous the hogs were.

Non corpus delicti.

No body, no crime.

Wiley thought probably this had been Kellerman's idea. It

smacked of Belsen and Dachau. And Argenti had most certainly approved.

Wiley dropped to the floor.

The outside lights remained on.

Several times Wiley gave in to the urge to look out the window at the hog pen. Like a man on death row, if allowed, would probably not be able to resist visiting the electric chair while waiting for it to take his life.

Dawn was like a reprieve.

About ten o'clock that morning, two soldiers came for Wiley.

Perhaps, he thought, night or day didn't make a difference. It surely wouldn't matter to the hogs.

He expected the soldiers would bind his hands. If they bound his hands, they'd have to drag him, he decided, but since they didn't bind him, he walked between them.

Down the stairs and, naked, out into the sunshine.

The first thing Wiley noticed was the jeep. No mistaking it, it was the one—its identification was painted over. Its spare tire was missing.

Then Wiley saw the black limousine, a stretched Lincoln, with the army insignia and four gold stars on its door.

Someone threw an army blanket around Wiley.

He was led to the limousine.

Lillian was in the back seat, huddled down.

Wiley got in.

Lillian had on only a man's coat. She looked small.

Wiley asked if she was all right.

Without looking at Wiley she told him, "Hold me."

He brought her into the cave of his arm.

The built-in bar was open. Silver tumblers of cognac had been poured. Wiley took one and put it to Lillian's mouth. She sipped like a child. She put her arms around him and hugged tight, holding on for dear life.

There were cigarettes on the bar tray, Wiley noticed. He didn't want one.

General Botero came out of the headquarters building with the Captain. They stood near the limousine and talked. Wiley lowered the window a crack and found he was within hearing range.

"They were with the *rebeldes*," the Captain said.

"Did it occur to you that they might be hostages?"

"They had weapons."

"Weapons that were abandoned by the *rebeldes*."

"Possibly," the Captain said.

"You acted rashly," the General told him.

"They killed two of my men."

Three, Wiley mentally corrected.

"Your men had orders to kill them," the General said.

"Yes, but . . ."

"Then it could have been in self-defense that they killed the two."

"There is the jeep . . ."

"I myself loaned the jeep to the lady."

The Captain called attention to the painted-out army markings.

General Botero credited that also to the *rebeldes*. "How many emeralds did you say were found in the spare tire?"

"Eighty-three," the Captain replied.

A hundred and eighty-three, Wiley mentally corrected.

"I am sure they were poaching," the Captain said.

"The woman is a *rica*, very wealthy. She has no need to claw around for a few emeralds. Let me tell you, Captain, it is fortunate for you that I came as soon as I received word. You might have added to your mistake. What happened to their clothing?"

"The men took the clothing as usual."

"Get it back."

"By now," the Captain said, "anyone might be wearing it. But here are their passports." He handed them to the General.

Wiley mentally added, how about my cash, nearly three thousand?

"You *searched* the woman I suppose," the General said.

The Captain was reluctant to answer.

General Botero pressed him.

"Yes," the Captain admitted.

"How many searched her?"

"Two."

"How many?"

"Four."

"*You* searched her before the others."

"No."

General Botero looked aside to avoid the lie in the Captain's eyes. "Are you certain, absolutely certain, that they saw nothing—you know what I mean—during the night?"

"It was impossible for the woman."

"That I believe. What of the man?"

"He saw nothing."

General Botero ripped the bars of rank from the Captain's jacket, tossed them away. The Captain just took it, without a flinch or a word.

General Botero huffed once and got into the limousine, the front seat. He ordered the driver to get under way with a wave of his glove.

22 ➤➤➤

They arrived at Argenti's villa around two.

General Botero hadn't spoken a word to them during the trip, or even looked back, and from that Wiley assumed a colder reception awaited them. He half-expected Argenti to be pacing the courtyard. However, Argenti was nowhere about.

They went straight up to their suites. Wiley showered and shaved quickly, dressed and went to Lillian.

She was taking a bath, submerged except for her head. The tub was made of chrome, like a deep mirror, and the opposing sides of it presented infinite Lillians.

Wiley put the lid down on the commode and sat. "Are you all right?" he asked.

The water in the tub was already steaming, but she used her toes on the tap to have more hot.

Wiley asked again.

"I will be," she said.

She ducked under. Her breath bubbled to the surface. She stayed under for what seemed an impossible time to Wiley. He was about to save her when she came up, red-faced and gasping. She took some deep breaths and the water in the tub became calm again.

"Poor Miguel," she said.

To hell with Miguel, Wiley thought. To hell with everyone else. They'd leave Bogotá as soon as they could. Now she'd want to. If not tonight then tomorrow they'd pack up and go. Her Gulfstream was on standby at the airport. He'd call and make sure it was ready to fly.

She got out of the tub and into a long white terry robe.

Was she hungry?

She didn't think so.

He ordered up some cheeses and fruit.

They sat in soft chairs before tall open windows looking out over the grounds. A sunny day. Far out Astrid and Maret were trying to get a kite up, but there wasn't enough wind. It would only stay up as long as they were running. The laughter of the two girls matched the afternoon, but it was incongruous with the emotional atmosphere in Lillian's presence.

She wasn't melancholy and neither did she seem bitter. She was more pensive than anything, as though her thoughts kept ricocheting off everything, every sight and sound.

Wiley knew what was on her mind, let her know that by not speaking about it.

She nibbled on a plum.

Wiley leaned over and kissed the corner of her eye, so tenderly she didn't even blink.

She turned and looked at him as though judging him.

For a long moment.

Then she got up and went to the bathroom.

Wiley heard her drawing another bath.

That night Argenti didn't once mention their mountain escapade or Barbosa. It was as though they'd never been away. He did remind Wiley that there was still a deficit of five million over his head, said Kellerman hadn't come up with anything to substantiate Wiley's story.

Other than that, all through dinner Argenti was in an excellent mood. He told some dated ethnic jokes that niece Clementina, Astrid and Maret gave polite ratings of three: ha ha ha. Lillian gave the jokes at least ten, and it sounded to Wiley like she was genuinely entertained. She was also interested in Argenti's account of the polo match in which he'd played that afternoon. He had scored the winning goal late in the third chukker, he claimed.

Lillian listened attentively, filled every opening Argenti offered with at least a sound of admiration.

Such a change from the way she'd been that afternoon. Her eyes were bright and quick, and her voice had a happy ring to it. More animated than Wiley had ever seen her. Also, she had taken much care to appear casual and at the same time seductive—in silk crepe de chine by Saint Laurent, a dress with a deep, loose neckline, ample sleeves that trailed her gestures. Her hair was ever so slightly in disarray, achieving the intended suggestion.

It seemed to Wiley that she flashed her teeth quite often and only a few times allowed her eyes to catch his. It got so that

Wiley was juggling his leg under the table and tensing his toes in his shoes to let out some of his irritation. He also studied the way Argenti ate, pushing food into that hole in his beard. One of the courses was char-broiled dove. Argenti crunched his, bones and all. Wiley found himself hoping Argenti would mistake one of his fingers for a wing.

Still at the table, over Amaretto and espresso, Lillian provided the amusement by calculating Argenti's biorhythms. For this purpose she had a small plastic device made of interlocking wheels and inscribed with exact-looking numbers and a red graph line that peaked and plunged like a Dow Jones average. Each wheel represented a different biorhythmic aspect: emotional, intellectual and physical.

She set the wheel according to Argenti's birth year. "What's today?" she asked.

"December eighteenth," Clementina said.

Lillian adjusted the device and told Argenti, "You've just gone through a terrible emotional low, but starting tomorrow you're on the climb again."

Argenti accepted that.

"Intellectually, you are now on a high. Really sharp."

Argenti nodded.

"Physically . . "

Argenti leaned back in his chair, confident.

". . . at the moment just so-so. . . "

He sat forward.

". . . and it seems as though you have a nasty drop coming later this month and early next."

"I'm going to fall down?" he asked.

"That's not what it means literally, but could be. Anyway, Meno, you won't be feeling marvelous."

He shrugged. "What about financially?"

"You're worried about that?"

"Hardly," he said, bobbing his head like Giancarlo Giannini.

"Tell me mine," Clementina asked.

Lillian disregarded her, told Argenti, "I've never seen anyone with such extreme biorhythms." From her inflections she might as well have been complimenting his sexual endowments.

He rather took it that way, tugged at his beard and smiled.

"Do me," Clementina insisted.

"Do yourself," Lillian said ambiguously, as she tossed the device across to her.

Wiley thought it was all nonsense, and even if there was anything to it, who the hell wanted to know tonight that tomorrow was going to be a lousy day.

It was announced that the movie of the night was *The Valachi Papers*, another of Argenti's cinematic condensations.

Lillian said she would prefer some gin.

Argenti had seen the film a dozen times but not in six months. He was more in the mood for it than Lillian's systematic, unfathomable, quick-knocking gin rummy play. Besides, she might bring up the eighty thousand he'd lost and forgotten to pay the last time. Nevertheless, he went with her to the game room.

She didn't mention the eighty thousand.

They played with high-stake intensity for nearly three hours.

Wiley wandered around looking at paintings. Every so often he returned to the game room to silently kibitz.

Luis Hurtado stood off to one side in case Argenti's body should require more active guarding. Hurtado also kept an eye on Wiley to see that he didn't give Lillian any advantages.

Wiley had a hard time remaining still and deadpan. Several times Lillian held gin and didn't declare it, and once, when Argenti knocked, she was caught with a gin hand and had to make the excuse that she had mistaken a heart for a diamond.

Argenti enjoyed every second of it. What a fantastic streak of good cards. He knocked, boxed, blitzed and scored, while she acted an exasperated victim of horrible luck. When they totaled up, she was a sixty-five-thousand loser. She had a check ready, borrowed Argenti's pen and made it for that amount. He folded the check once and slipped it into his shirt pocket in a blasé manner.

The welching, one-way son of a bitch, was Wiley's silent opinion. He'd tell Lillian to stop payment.

There would be no creeping the halls that night. Wiley went with Lillian to her rooms and stayed. They got to bed at one-thirty.

"Why'd you do that?" Wiley asked.

"What?"

"Let him win."

"Just casting a little bread, hon," she said.

Wiley questioned further and suggested she stop payment, but she didn't answer. She could have been asleep.

Wiley went with her.

At nine that morning he was still dozing. He sensed her absence, shifted from his side of the bed, reached with his legs and didn't come in touch with anything. That brought him abruptly up on his elbows, wide awake.

Lillian was across the room having coffee and croissants from a silver tray. She was dressed.

"Going somewhere?" Wiley asked.

"Been," she said.

She had gotten up at six and driven to town. "Tomas and Jorge were killed," she said.

"Miguel?"

"He used the fog, went cross-country and made it. Got back last night."

"Good for him," Wiley said in a conclusive tone.

"Two Cubans are there now."

"Where?"

"At the *foco* with Miguel."

Lillian poured Wiley some coffee and buttered a croissant for him.

"What were the Cubans like?"

"Quiet, black and anti-American," she said.

Wiley disliked the thought of her roaming around in the *barrio* alone, no matter how well she believed she could take care of herself.

"Miguel was going on and on again about the need for an incident," she said. "The Cubans were all for it."

"For what?"

"Miguel's incident."

"What does he have in mind?"

"I asked Miguel, but he wouldn't say. The Cubans seemed to know all about it, though."

Wiley lighted a cigarette. The smoke he exhaled rolled in the sunlight. "Anyway, it's none of our business," he said.

"Apparently, the emeralds that were in the spare were supposed to help finance the incident."

Wiley couldn't have cared less.

"Now," she went on, "Miguel has to do something else."

"The Cubans will think of something," Wiley said, holding his croissant out for her to glop it with fresh raspberry jam.

"Miguel already has," she said and waited for Wiley to ask what. He didn't but she went on as though he had. "We're going to hold up the armored truck when it brings the weekly emerald shipment to The Concession."

"We?" Wiley asked calmly.

"I think it's a good idea, not great, but good."

Wiley told himself that if he kept his temper everything would be all right. "We just got back from nearly getting killed maybe twenty times and you . . . "

"Miguel needs the money."

"Give it to him."

"I can't."

"How much does he need?"

"From what I gather, a lot. Anyway, too much for me to come up with without revealing all."

"Miguel wouldn't give a damn where it came from."

"I'd hate being tagged as a rich lefty dabbler, really hate it. Better I just fuck off, ride the world like most people I know."

"I still think . . ."

"Miguel has it all planned. He knows precisely when the armored truck gets there, how many soldiers in the escort, the best way to escape through the *barrio* and everything. The Cubans are going to help."

Wiley got up for the bathroom. He walked so hard he hurt his heels. He wondered if she'd be so eager if she knew about the hogs, but then, she'd probably think he was inventing it to dissuade her. Back in the bedroom, he put on his trousers, and for some reason, felt less vulnerable.

"Haven't you had enough?" he asked.

"Not yet," she said and added thoughtfully, "especially not now."

He understood, sympathized but wasn't swayed. "You won't be satisfied until you've got a tag around your toe, having died from holes like a good rebel."

"Not true."

"I suppose it's a slightly more constructive way to go than sticking your head in an oven."

That hit home.

He wished he could take it back.

"Anyway," he told her, "not me, I'm out."

"You're quitting me?"

"Self-preservation."

"I didn't think you would."

That approach wouldn't work this time, he told her.

"You've quit a lot of things in your life, haven't you?" she said.

That also hit home. "I started more than average," he said.

"You're strange."

Jennifer had said that numerous times, Wiley remembered. Particularly when they disagreed.

"It's one of the things about you that I like," Lillian told him. "You go against the grain."

He wanted to kiss her for that. Instead, tried an appeal to her logic. "Look, Lillian, you've got to realize what a loony thing this is and how bad the consequences could be. Those soldiers will be goddamn sharpshooters, and this time there won't be any fog to fuck up their aim. I don't care if Miguel has fifty Cubans and a hundred *rebeldes*, it'll be a slaughter."

"Not necessarily."

"Believe me."

"We'll take them by surprise."

"Never. It's exactly the sort of thing they expect. They know it's tempting, their making that delivery right there in the *barrio*. It's their most alert moment. Every soldier in that escort will have his finger on a trigger. Hell, you'd stand a better chance going for the top of that building and the whole goddamn load."

His last sentence hung in the air.

For a moment he thought he'd convinced her.

She tossed a hunk of croissant into the air. "Now, *that* is a great idea," she said.

What had he said? The top of the building, all those emeralds? She was indeed a nut.

"I need money," he said.

"Bottom drawer." She indicated the dresser.

He took it all. His nine thousand. Picked up the rest of his clothes and walked out.

To hell with shadowboxing. He packed and called a taxi, which took him to El Dorado International Airport. The next possible flight was at three o'clock: Avianca nonstop to Miami. Fine. He'd drive down from Miami to see the folks in Key West. He'd only been down there once, hadn't called them in several weeks. They'd be good for him. After that, he'd see what came.

He bought his ticket. Economy class again.

Had a two-hour wait, decided against a drink and spent the time in the regular passengers' lounge, munching unfamiliar candy bars and smoking between bites while reading a week-old *Wall Street Journal*.

With a half hour to go he was just sitting there, as though immobilized by the space he was in.

The three o'clock flight was announced for boarding.

At ten after three Wiley got up and headed for the exit.

At the curb, in a yellow Ferrari 365GT Berlinetta Boxer, was Lillian.

Wiley tossed his carry-on satchel into the back and got in. "Missed my flight," he said.

"When's the next?"

"Who the hell knows." He tried not to look at her. "Am I this predictable?"

"No," she said. "I was this hopeful."

It was, he thought, the nicest thing she'd ever said to him.

"My luggage is going to Miami. I don't have anything to wear again."

"Don't worry. We'll get it back . . ."

"Yeah," he said dubiously.

" . . . or else we'll go on another shopping spree."

They kissed. Three times. She didn't give a damn who saw where she had her hand.

"I love you," he said.

"You kissed the legs right out from under me, Mr. Wiley."

He could remember the time when such a confession was practically a commitment. Which showed how old he was. Besides, she seemed to have excellent coordination and strength in her legs as she worked the clutch and accelerator to get the Ferrari into traffic.

"I talked it over with Miguel," she said.

"And?"

"He agrees with you."

"No armored car, then."

"Nope. We go for the big batch instead. I told Miguel it was *our* idea. You don't mind my stealing some of your thunder, do you?"

"Help yourself." He still had an erection.

She glanced over at it and up to his expression. They didn't seem to correspond.

"What's the matter?" she asked.

"Nothing."

"Something"

"I've got one foot in reality and all my weight is on the other."

"I know what you mean."

Maybe she did, Wiley thought. But he doubted it. She'd pick daisies in a mine field.

"By the way," she said, "I'm having dinner out tonight with Meno."

"Call him Argenti."

"Okay, Argenti. Anyway, I want to try to spy around a bit. Don't you think it's a good idea?"

"Good," he said flatly.

"You've been up there already, haven't you?"

He assumed she meant the top of The Concession building, where the vaults were. "Once," he replied.

"What was it like?"

What was the most discouraging description he could come up with? He settled for one word: "Impenetrable."

"But it's not," she said. "No place is one hundred percent burglarproof. A guy I knew in New York back in the sixties told me there's always a way in if you put your mind to it. He was an expert. Name it, he'd steal it. We called him Jack the Ripper."

"Small time."

"Hell he was. Once during the noon shopping rush, all by himself, he ripped off an eight-foot sofa and two armchairs from Bloomingdale's. The armchairs didn't match, so he went back the next day and ripped off two that did. He was ingenious, one of the most resourceful guys I've ever known."

"Where's old Jack now?"

"Well, I don't know, but I'd say if he hasn't lost both hands he's in jail somewhere."

Laughing with her was wonderful, Wiley thought. That's what the self-improvers ought to get into, how to laugh together.

He took out a cigarette, used the car's lighter. She immediately opened her wind wing all the way and asked him with a please to do the same. He had expected one of her usual antinicotine remarks, such as how coated with gook his lungs had to be. This time, however, nothing. Perhaps she was temporarily conceding for the sake of his nerve.

In that case . . . without even one more drag he flipped the cigarette out.

"I want to know what to expect up there," she said.

Back on that again: the top of The Concession.

Maybe if she knew what they'd be up against she'd back off, he thought. No need to overelaborate. The truth was bad enough.

He told her what he'd been shown and told by Argenti that afternoon at The Concession when he'd become a carrier.

A cadmium-steel plate, one solid piece, locked horizontally into position, blocking the elevator shaft at the next-to-the-top floor. Stairways also ended at that level.

So, there was no way up to it.

Radar and listening devices on the roof prevented a helicopter from getting anywhere near it without being detected.

So, no way down to it.

The vaults were not ordinary modern vaults with twelve-inch-thick impervious doors and intricate multiple combinations and time locks.

Worse.

The vaults were behind walls of cadmium steel, absolutely plain walls without a dial, knob, wheel or anything.

No way of knowing how they opened.

"But weren't you there when Argenti opened the vaults?" she asked.

"Right there."

"He must have pushed a button or something."

"He was standing about six feet from the wall and even farther away from anything else."

"With his foot."

"Nothing there but floor."

"Then he must have had a remote control thing. Probably something as simple as a television channel switcher."

"I looked. He didn't have anything."

"Well, the vault didn't just open itself."

"That's how it seemed."

"You missed something, must have."

"Possibly. At the time it wasn't all that important."

By then they were on Avenida 58, El Saletre Park on the

right. Kids were playing football, Wiley saw, dribbling with the sides of their feet and with their toes and heels. No hands allowed. Couples and family shapes punctuated the grass. It was a large park. Wiley noticed particularly one man alone, lying front up with his legs spread and arms out as though he'd fallen back dead. He could be dead, and when night came everyone would go off and just leave him there, Wiley thought. The man had a paper bag over his face.

"God, we've got a lot to do," Lillian thought aloud.

Wiley agreed with a grunt. Preoccupied with the man in the park, he must have forgotten to filter out the pessimism.

"You still think we can't do it?"

It came to him at that moment. "The radar," he said, matter of fact.

"What about the radar?"

"It's up there strictly for looks."

"You mean it's not real?"

"Oh, it's real enough probably, but it can't do the job it's supposed to. It's a type that's called KU-band. Which has a frequency of about fourteen thousand megahertz. Used for tracking air-to-air missiles, guided missiles, things that require distant coverage."

"So?"

"The roof of that building, what can it measure? Three hundred feet by two hundred. That's about it, I'd say. Argenti's radar couldn't define anything that close, and even if it did pick something up, one sweep and the blip of it would be gone, not like a plane or missile that's in the air for a longer while."

She was impressed, had *my man* written all over her face. "Then we don't have to worry about the radar."

"But," he reminded her, "the listening alarm up there is a different matter."

23 ⋗⋗⋗

       That night Lillian gave Wiley a promissory peck on the mouth and asked for a compliment on the way she looked.

He told her lovely.

Her little insincere thank-you smile said she'd expected something stronger.

Fuckable, he thought as she snapped her evening bag shut and went out. A few moments later he heard her voice and Argenti's in the drive below. She was into that same buoyant role as the night before. Wiley resisted going to the window. Two car-door slams and she was gone.

Wiley tightened his stomach muscles as jealousy delivered a body blow.

La materia verde, he thought, jealousy, the green stuff.

He had planned to stay in. But when the first ten minutes seemed like an hour, he freshened up, went down to the garage and borrowed one of Argenti's cars: the yellow Ferrari Berlinetta Boxer 365, because it was the one most conveniently parked.

The last thing he'd steered was that jinxed jeep, a far cry from this twelve-cylinder, 380-horsepower beauty. He turned left out of the drive, went north on Carrera 7, which soon became a *carretera*, highway. The speed indicator on the Ferrari's dash offered 250 kilometers per hour, which in miles is about 155. First straight stretch, Wiley took 100 miles of it, found it enjoyable and helped himself to 20 more. He had the urge to take it all, defy a road sign that warned of a curve ahead with a safe speed of 40, floor it and see where to hell he got.

His life time divided into fast fractions.

At the last split second he shifted down and barely managed to match the curve with a curve.

He'd played footsie with death, teased it with his toe. Only for a moment, but now, as a result, came an intense sense of vitality. The blood in all his parts seemed to be hurrying to the hollow of his chest, bringing tribute. Some laughter came up out of him like silver bubbles along with some swear words. His palms weren't even moist.

He turned the Boxer around and drove at a modest, contented speed back to the city. Along Carrera 7 and the main way, Avenida Caracas. He cruised the central area, following his whim, left or right or straight ahead.

He might just happen to see Lillian. Where was she at the moment? Somewhere decorating Argenti's ego. Wiley pictured Argenti slipping his hands around, stealing touches here and there, and Lillian having to cooperate.

To prevent his imagination from getting to him, Wiley gave himself a different problem.

The vaults.

He hadn't been completely honest when he'd told Lillian there was no way of knowing how the vaults opened. From a professional point of view, and certainly electronics were involved, there could only be so many possibilities. Not many at that.

First it was unlikely Argenti had preset the vaults to open at the exact moment they did. Under those circumstances, Argenti would surely have glanced at his watch a few times. He hadn't, that Wiley recalled. No, it had been spontaneous. Rule out a preset timer.

How about a heat-sensitive setup? Not unless Argenti's body temperature differed from the average. Rule that out.

Also, it was improbable that it had been anything as obvious as a pressure device at a certain spot on the floor.

Same went for an automatic remote-control unit concealed somewhere on Argenti's person. Even if it worked on frequencies like a touch-tone telephone, any expert could analyze its circuitry and unscramble it. Argenti would have considered that.

Wiley thought it down to two possibilities. Purely speculation, of course, but he was quite sure Argenti's installation, the mysterious little open-sesame trick Argenti believed so dumbfounding, involved either one system or the other.

If he'd taken a closer look at those vault doors, the surfaces of the panels, he'd know now whether he was right.

What difference did it make? There was no way of getting *to* the vaults. There was satisfaction, though, in outwitting Argenti, even if only mentally.

So much for that. He'd walk some.

He parked the car in a lot near the Plaza Bolívar.

On a side street he came upon an open barber shop, a small two-chair place with no customers at the moment. Wiley could use a trim.

As the barber covered him, he visualized ending up with a white-necked electric clip à la Bogart in *The Treasure of the Sierra Madre*. Barbers seldom hear the requests of their victims. However, this one was a whiz, clicked his scissors with admirable precision, trimmed away little by little and asked for Wiley's approval as he proceeded. It was enough to make Wiley feel maybe his luck had changed.

A man came in for a shave, occupied the other chair. He read *El Tiempo* for a few minutes and then struck up a conversation with Wiley. His name, he said, was Raphael Bermudez. He was about Wiley's age, evidently meticulous about his appearance. This was his second shave of the day. He had on a pale-lavender shirt and a navy tie. A pinky ring set with a single fair-sized pale emerald, not kelly.

"Call me Ralpho," he said in English, which seemed to be the only English he knew. He had never been to the United States because, he said, from all that he'd read and heard it was a cruel country. He was surprised when Wiley agreed. "Most *norteamericanos*, tell them that, they want to break your face," he said, "which is a very unreasonable attitude. If someone tells me Colombia is a cruel country, I am a Colombian and I agree, because it is true. Anyway, you are a very unusual *norteamericano*.

Wiley paid and overtipped. As he left the shop Ralpho was having the hairs in his nostrils clipped.

Out on the street, Wiley took a few steps and a small boy ran smack into him, bounced hard off Wiley's legs and went down onto the sidewalk. A boy of about eight, a skinny little waif in tattered clothes, his skin caked with city grime. He lay there writhing, whimpering. A nasty spill, he had to be hurt, Wiley thought. He kneeled beside the boy, and as he did, about ten other boys came at him. They brushed, jostled and grabbed at Wiley.

Ralpho came quickly out of the barber shop. He shouted, shoved the boys away, kicked one in the seat of the pants, sent them scurrying. The one who had taken the fall made a miraculous recovery, jumped up and gestured obscenely at Wiley as he ran off.

They were *bagos*, Ralpho explained, boys of the street, homeless. They were called *bagos* because they usually slept anywhere in paper of burlap bags. They were the best pickpockets in the world. Had they gotten anything from Wiley?

He checked. His watch was gone. Without his feeling it, they had slipped it off his wrist. But he still had his money, his passport and the emerald, that one emerald he'd taken as a souvenir from his carry to Paris. If it hadn't been for Ralpho those little piranhas probably would have stripped him down to his socks. Wiley thanked Ralpho and offered to buy him a drink.

Ralpho accepted, knew just the place.

Club Carrencol on Calle 25.

Nothing fancy from the outside, a two-story place. Inside, an atmosphere like a whorehouse, bare walls and floors, so much smoke in the air that every breath was like taking a puff. There were twenty rooms containing plastic-topped tables and substantial chairs—and men.

This was Friday night, by machismo tradition the weekly night out. Man's time to overindulge in whatever he chose: drink, boasts, self-pity—usually phases of each, as the night passed.

The men had on their best black suits, their hair slicked. Guitarists went from room to room, nearly sobbing songs about loves lost or impossible for some reason. Many of the lyrics touched upon infidelity, as though it were inevitable. Always it was the woman who strayed, often inadvertently and not because of lack of attraction. Forgiveness never exceeded the explanation that she could not help herself, nor was she ever reaccepted.

Wiley and Ralpho stood at the bar. They drank straight *aguardiente* and sucked on sour orange slices for a chaser.

"How long will you be in Bogotá?" Ralpho asked.

"I'll be leaving anytime now," Wiley told him. He noticed a man at a table nearby, sitting straight and still with tears streaming down his cheeks.

"Tomorrow he will be happy," Ralpho said, "because he leaves all his sorrow here tonight."

Wiley looked around. Many of the men seemed on the verge of tears. The music accompanied their emotions.

"They are having a marvelous time," Ralpho said.

"In America we call it the blues," Wiley said.

Ralpho nodded. "Blue is a beautiful color."

Wiley had to turn from the room as another welled-up man let go. It could be contagious. He asked Ralpho, "What do you do?"

"I have a store."

"What kind?"

Ralpho thought a moment, exonerated himself with a shrug and confessed, "Actually, here is my store." He patted his jacket pocket. "I sell emeralds along Calle 14."

The coincidence amused Wiley. "How's business?"

"There is much competition. But I have been honest most of the time, so I do well. I do not think I have cheated more than eight, maybe ten customers this year."

"*Norteamericanos*?"

"Yes. Would you be interested in an emerald or two?"

"No."

"I would not cheat you."

"I believe you, but no thanks."

"You are an unusual *norteamericano*. I would like you to be treated fairly. I would sell you a good stone for whatever it cost me. No profit for me."

If he only knew, Wiley thought. He had his hand in his pocket, rolling his souvenir emerald between his fingers. It was about ten carats. He took it out and showed it to Ralpho.

Ralpho was unreadable as he looked at the stone.

Impressed, Wiley thought.

Ralpho took out a loupe to examine the stone under magnification. "How much did you pay for this?"

"Someone gave it to me," Wiley said.

"In that case, you lost nothing."

"What do you mean?"

"It is not an emerald. It is only emerald quartz." He handed the stone back to Wiley.

"You must be mistaken."

"I am a third generation street dealer."

. . . Who is trying to take me, Wiley thought. "How much is the stone worth?"

"Next to nothing."

"Would you give me fifty dollars for it?"

"As much as I like you, no."

Wiley tried again. "It's yours for fifty." He placed the stone on the bar in front of Ralpho.

"You need money?" Ralpho asked.

"No."

"Then let us have another drink."

Wiley was stunned. He picked up the stone. "Emerald quartz?"

"You do not believe me, ask that fellow over there." He indicated an older man at a table. "He is also a dealer."

Wiley had to know for certain. He went over to the older man, who verified Ralpho's contention. The stone was worth no more than an ordinary pretty pebble.

Wiley returned to the bar. He apologized to Ralpho and ordered a double, downed it quickly.

That five-million-dollars' worth of *fine* quality goods he'd carried to Paris had been worthless?

God, what a job they'd done on him.

It had been a charade from the start. Wine Face and Hairpiece had been Concessionmen, hirelings of Conduct Section. Probably there was no one named Forget. Anyway, whoever lived in that Place des Vosges apartment had been in on it, had been home all that afternoon.

Such an elaborate scheme, but it had been relatively easy for The Concession with its facilities.

But why?

The obvious reason. Argenti wanted Wiley down. Not just down; he wanted his knee on Wiley's neck. If it hadn't been for Lillian, no doubt Argenti would have eliminated Wiley. Then again, if it hadn't been for Lillian, Wiley wouldn't have been implicated at all.

Wiley recalled Kellerman's interrogation in the projection room in Lillian's presence. No wonder Argenti wouldn't see Wiley in private. And Argenti's expressed disappointment in Wiley, and his insistence that Wiley was into The Concession for five million. Only the night before last at dinner, Argenti had mentioned it again.

Other parts of it came back to Wiley now: his sweating it out through customs, his freezing his ass on the bench in Paris, the wear on his nerves, the fears and the guilt he'd endured. Not to mention the kick in the balls from Wine Face.

All the while Argenti had been looking down his throat.
Argenti had made him feel small.
Made him look bad.
Rubbed his nose in it.
That devious, welching son of a bitch, Argenti.
Now it was Wiley's turn.
Argenti owed.
Would pay, Wiley vowed.
No effect from the five *aguardientes* he'd had. He walked straight and fast to where he'd left the Ferrari, drove it south on Carrera 10, went left on Calle 1 for three blocks and stopped. From there he had a good view of Número 1, The Concession's building. He was only slightly surprised to see Argenti's limousine parked in front. The chauffeur slouched in it, probably expecting an all-night wait. With the *barrio* all around, he'd better have the limo's doors locked, Wiley thought.
The steel-and-glass tower was black against the night sky, defined only by the reflections of the city that played upon it. A section of the thirty-third floor was lighted. Conduct Section, Wiley recalled, was on thirty-three, and of course that was where the controls would be located, with someone on duty round the clock. The only other lights were on thirty-four, next to the top, Argenti's private floor.
Wiley reminded himself that he wasn't there to be jealous.
The building.
If he could, he'd blow it to bits, reduce it to rubble, bring it down to the level of the *barrio* that it stood in. But, hell, that would only inconvenience Argenti for a while. He'd just put up another building.
No. The ultimate satisfaction, Wiley thought, would come from the idea Lillian had latched onto: taking the frosting right off the top of Argenti's piece of cake.
If possible.
Wiley sat there for over an hour, nearly two, and couldn't come up with a way to do it. He considered every angle, every logical approach, and when he started offering himself ways he'd already rejected, he decided he was stumped. It was impossible to reach that top floor and the vaults. Argenti had made it impossible. As much as Wiley hated to admit it, Argenti had him outsmarted.
He gave up on it, drove back to the villa. It was shortly after

midnight. He went up to Lillian's suite, used her toothbrush and got into her bed.

She came in at five to four.

He pretended he was asleep with the light on.

She didn't believe him. As she undressed, letting her clothes drop anywhere, she told him, "It was exactly as you said."

"Huh?"

"He just stood there, and part of the wall slid open."

Wiley lighted a cigarette.

She speared him with a look. "Please don't smoke in here. I'll wake up with a headache."

He'd never seen her with such a bad disposition.

No ashtray. He got up, went to the bathroom door, took a final double drag and flipped the cigarette in the direction of the commode. The bathroom was dark, but he knew he'd hit target when he heard the extinguishing *phht*. He returned to the bed. She was on it, at the foot, sitting with legs crossed. She gathered her hair and tied it back with a ribbon.

"Nothing in his hands?" he asked.

"Nope. Both his hands were in sight and they were empty."

"Good."

"What the hell's good about it?"

"You didn't happen to take a close look at those walls, did you?"

"Not real, real close. Why?"

"How did all those emeralds grab you?"

"I thought how much better they'd look not there."

"Argenti must have given you a bad time."

"His hands weren't always empty, if that's what you mean."

"Anything for the cause, I guess."

"Relax your imagination. Argenti didn't get lurid. Actually, he was in a serious romantic mood."

"I got a haircut."

"We had dinner at his club."

"I almost got my pockets picked."

"All through dinner he kept saying how well suited we are."

Wiley decided it was better she didn't know about the emerald quartz, what a mark he'd been. Someday he'd tell her.

"He caught me off balance with a ring," she said. "An enormous diamond from Cartier. He opened the box and put it on the table in front of me. I was sure he'd insist on slipping it on, but he didn't, never touched the ring. It was strange. He asked me to marry him."

Wiley felt as though he'd jumped slightly out of his skin. "What did you say?"

"Maybe."

"But you didn't really mean maybe."

"He didn't like maybe, not at all, and he wanted to know why maybe and I told him because I doubted he could afford me in the long run. After all, I had noticed he couldn't even pay his gambling losses."

"Good girl."

"With an absolutely straight face he said he paid his gambling losses annually, said he wasn't about to submit a financial statement to me, but of course he was very well off, and I said so it appeared. For some proof he took me to his building, where, after opening some champagne, he also opened King Solomon's high-rise mines."

"Then what?"

"He popped the question again."

"You told him to fuck off."

"Not even in so many words. I told him I'd think about it."

"Why?"

"There was no advantage in dashing his hopes. Anyway, tonight I didn't learn a damn thing."

Make some points, Wiley told himself. He waited a beat and said casually: "I figured out how the vaults work."

"You didn't really."

"I did."

"You're just saying that because you love me and want to make me feel better."

He shook his head, definitely not.

She was so delighted she dove on him.

"How?" she wanted to know.

"That's what the Indian said to the mermaid."

"Wiley, this is no time to sound your age. Can we get the vaults open, can we?"

"I'm almost sure of it."

"How much is almost?"

"About eighty-twenty."

"We're eighty."

"There's still the problem of getting up there."

She was on her elbows, the upper part of her supported. Her

face above his, her breasts grazing his chest. The rest of her body lay lightly on his, stomach to stomach, legs to legs.

"Don't worry, we'll solve that somehow," she said. "You're remarkable. In and out of bed." She kissed him.

He was scoring and loving it. He told her, "I already know a way to get up there."

Since he'd arrived home, to keep his mind off Lillian and Argenti, he'd focused it on the building. Besides, it was like him to want to go an extra round. In his earlier bout with the problem, logic had gotten him nowhere, so he'd chucked that, told himself: Pretend you're Jack the Ripper, the most resourceful man she's ever known.

Top him.

Wiley had let his imagination fly, let it zoom and zap and woosh all over, up and down and around the place like an animated cartoon. All sorts of crazy ideas had come to him. He tempered them with reality, not logic, just reality.

The ideas had dissolved when reality was applied.

All but one.

One wild, desperate chance.

"Tell me," Lillian demanded.

"First, you tell me."

"Anything, what?"

He decided it wasn't something he should bargain for. He substituted: "You want me."

"Often at the most inopportune times, darling. Feel." She guided his hand.

He doubted that could be from Argenti's pawing. "I'll tell you all about it tomorrow," he promised.

"No, now."

"I'm tired of thinking." True.

She was relentless.

He had to tell her or he wouldn't get to sleep or anything. He made it as brief as possible.

Even during the most technical part she didn't ask questions or interrupt. Afterward, however, she jumped off him and ran into the bathroom. When she came out, she explained she'd gotten so excited she'd had to go. She paced the room, recalling things Argenti had said and done that night that seemed to validate Wiley's theory regarding the vaults. As for getting to the top of the building, Wiley's idea, she said, was positively outrageous. A rating above sensational.

Wiley still thought it was ninety percent insane and ten percent slim, but he didn't say so.

At dawn Lillian was still scribbling notes, diagramming, elaborating, expanding on Wiley's ideas. Although Wiley wasn't up to mental par, he contributed and kept her within reasonable check. By eight o'clock they had worked out many of the details and a timetable.

"I have to call Marianna," Lillian said. Marianna, her personal secretary in Mexico City.

"That can wait."

"I know exactly where to reach her at this hour. She'll be over the garage with Bryan."

"Her boyfriend?"

"My driver, her service man." She direct-dialed the number, and spoke to Marianna for about three quarters of an hour, had her repeat every instruction.

Wiley imagined a sexually sated and soporific Marianna, so when Lillian hung up, he asked, "Do you think she got it all straight?"

"She's extremely bright, and dependable as a hawk."

Wiley believed that from past experience.

"Are you still sleepy?" Lillian asked.

He wasn't. He'd passed through that barrier, felt wide awake.

She got a pair of jeans from the closet, put them on. They were a perfect snug fit and, Wiley noticed, her stomach was so flat and tight she didn't even have to suck in when she zipped up the fly. Thinking aloud, she said, "I can't wait to tell Miguel."

24 ➤➤➤

The next three were tense, busy days for them.

The meeting with Miguel went well. Although he wasn't enthusiastic, as Lillian had expected, he believed it was a better idea than a direct assault on an escorted armored truck. How would they finance such an operation?

Lillian was quick to say that according to her estimate, if they watched their pennies, it wouldn't cost all that much, and that Wiley had just sold a family farm in Ohio and was glad to chip in.

Miguel put in that it would be easier if he saw to some of the arrangements because he knew the country and had underground connections of just about every sort. Never mind that he was being sought by F-2, army intelligence, as well as agents of the D.A.S., the Departamento Administrativo de Seguridad. He wasn't about to hole up, preferred being on the offensive. Did Wiley know that D.A.S. personnel were trained in torture techniques at Langley, Virginia? he asked offhandedly. Anyway, he would do his part. They could count on it.

Two black Cubans sat in on the meeting. They had been sent from Havana as advisors; however, they made no suggestions or comments.

It was Lillian's opinion that someone should be in charge of the operation, and, all things considered, it should be Wiley. She thought that would get a rise from the Cubans. They merely nodded. Miguel gave it a moment's consideration and agreed.

Wiley didn't want the job but didn't refuse it. On second thought, if he was going to die, better he should die under his own direction. He also realized that if Lillian remained true to character, she would surely be assuming much of the responsibility. That might have been her reason for nominating him.

First thing that afternoon they rented a house. A modest five-room unfurnished place, situated in a development among hundreds of similar others. In the western part of Bogotá, an outlying section called Ciudad Kennedy—Kennedy City. The house was about twenty blocks from the racetrack, which was perhaps its only distinction. It would serve as their safe house.

The Cubans moved right in.

Miguel remained in the *barrio*, for the time being.

By midafternoon Wiley and Lillian were at the gunsmith's, the same small shop where she had bought those cartridges for the poaching expedition. The proprietor was Alberto Cordero, a man in his sixties. He had the mild, patient manner of a craftsman.

Lillian told him she wanted to buy two Llama nine-millimeter pistols with silencers. (Their previous pair had been confiscated along with their clothes in Barbosa.)

Cordero had only one such Llama in stock but could have another by tomorrow.

Fine, she'd also need four extra clips and two cartons of center-fire ammunition. And by chance did Cordero have a forty-five caliber Colt automatic for sale?

Yes. He showed it to her.

She'd take it . . .

Cordero's eyes were like adding machines.

. . . along with some hollow-point ammunition.

Cordero was sorry to say he had no hollow points, by law was not allowed to sell them.

Lillian appeared disappointed enough to cancel the entire order. She told him unequivocally she wanted a large, heavy, slower-moving slug, a hollow point. She took out a thousand dollars, held it in her hand, ten hundreds.

Cordero tried to not look at the money. He also tried the excuse that he didn't have the mold necessary for making hollow-point forty-fives. When he saw that fail, he asked how many rounds she would need.

Enough for two clips.

Only eighteen? Why hadn't she said so. He really did not have the mold, but he could bore the points of eighteen.

She placed the thousand on the counter and asked when she could have them.

He placed the Colt forty-five on the money like a paperweight and promised they would be ready in three days.

From the gunsmith's they went to a camera store. Bought a motorized Nikon that could take as many as five exposures per second, along with a two-hundred-millimeter lens. They also bought a Sony TC-56 tape recorder that was a little smaller than the average paperback book. It had a built-in electric condenser microphone that would pick up easily within a twenty-foot range, and a frequency response of ninety to ten thousand for excellent fidelity. It took a standard ninety-minute cassette.

That night Lillian dedicated the early hours to keeping Argenti optimistic. She let him win at gin rummy again and also consented to try on the engagement ring. She extended the proper finger, expecting Argenti to oblige. He gestured that she should help herself. It was as though he had a phobic aversion or allergy to diamonds, she thought.

She retired early and agreed with Wiley that sometimes being tired made lovemaking exceptionally pleasant.

The following day, more shopping. Procuring, Lillian called it, reminding Wiley when he arched that the word did not apply exclusively to pimping.

They had passport photos taken, with grim expressions.

A bedding shop agreed to deliver five twin-size mattresses that day to the Kennedy City house.

At a military surplus store in the El Ejido district, Lillian found the crash helmets, goggles and boots they needed. High-top combat boots. Also nylon duffel bags. Three regulation size and two smaller. Coveralls. Did they come in black? Only in white and khaki. Lillian decided on white, three pairs—one large, two medium. A square yard of half-inch-thick foam rubber was their final purchase of the day.

They dropped everything off at the Kennedy City house and returned to the villa. It was not yet three o'clock.

Lillian had suggested to Argenti that they have a late lunch at home, alone on the terrace, so they could talk.

She put some extra effort into her appearance, wore a Marc Bohan flirting dress in a blue-printed mousseline, completely off the shoulder and pouffy skirted.

Argenti said he adored the way she looked.

Throughout the long leisurely lunch she had no difficulty getting Argenti to talk about himself. Where was he born? Had he spent much time in Marbella? Why didn't he ever go to the United States or Europe? Of course it was because he enjoyed Mexico and South America so much. What was his middle initial? She wanted to have something engraved for him, just a token from Bulgari. Oh? What did the *S* stand for?

Meno Sebastiano Argenti.

What a beautiful name. A lovely sound to it, especially the way he said it. So mellifluous.

Meno Sebastiano Argenti.

Meanwhile Wiley was wandering around the grounds photographing the far-off mountains, architectural features of the villa, various flowers.

Argenti inquired when he caught a glimpse of Wiley, who was about a hundred feet away, not intruding actually.

Lillian explained that Wiley was an avid amateur photographer who focused his interest primarily on nature subjects. She had bought Wiley the camera to keep him occupied.

Argenti understood with a superior smile and paid no further attention to Wiley.

Wiley exposed two rolls of Plus-X film and took them into town to a photo finishing laboratory. He could have the film developed and contact prints made by the following noon. For a special rush order price. Double. Enlargements normally took three days, however . . .He slipped the laboratory clerk a personal twenty dollars and was assured same-day service. Lillian, he thought, was rubbing off on him.

When he got back to the villa she was in her bathroom applying vitamin E cream to her upper thigh. There were red welts, irritations, where adhesive tape had held the tape recorder.

She ouched for sympathy.

"Looks like the afterglow of a little S and M," Wiley said. "Have you ever been into that?"

"A girl once wanted me to spank her with her father's bedroom slipper."

"Did you?"

"You must have ripped the adhesive tape off," he said. "Should have used alcohol. Or is it acetone?"

"Kiss it well."

He was sitting on the edge of the bidet. She put herself in range. He didn't have to pull her even an inch toward him.

"Vitamin E is good for your lips," she said.

He kissed around.

"Did you?" she asked.

"Hmmmm?"

"Spank her."

"No. Anyway, only a little."

"They say pain is the sister of passion."

"Who says."

"I believe it was sky-written over Malibu Beach one Saturday afternoon."

He got a little of the skin of her hip between his teeth, as little as possible, nipped her.

The sound she made wasn't entirely complaint and she didn't flinch.

He'd do anything to please her, he thought, anything. How selfish of him that was, really.

She picked up the tape recorder, rewinding it as she went into the bedroom. When the cassette was completely rewound, she pressed the play button. Argenti's voice boomed out so loud it made a crystal wall sconce tinkle before she could lower the volume. If Argenti was anywhere near, he must surely have heard. Wiley opened the door to the corridor and peeked out. No one. He also took a look out the window. There was Argenti. But far out on the lawn, walking with his niece, Clementina.

The tape contained about forty-five minutes of Lillian and Argenti's luncheon conversation. Lillian remarked that she sounded dreadful and silly. At a few places on the tape the voices became momentarily muffled.

"That's where I forgot to keep my legs apart," Lillian explained.

Several times they rewound and played what they believed was the critical part. They went into the bathroom, closed the door and windows and played it at normal speaking volume. The fidelity was excellent. As though Meno Sebastiano Argenti was there in person.

The following day they went to the *barrio* to check in with Miguel.

He too had made progress. Most important, he had arranged for a training site at a place in the mountains near the town of Pacora, which was close to where he'd been raised. He thought it would serve their purpose well. It was isolated, had a small house for their living quarters and a patch of open field with not too much of a slope.

Another thing. Miguel had "obtained" a car. He hadn't seen

it yet, but it was being driven up that day from Cali. Actually it was a panel truck, as he'd specified, an older model, beat up, incapable of much speed and certainly inconspicuous.

Would Wiley and Lillian need weapons? Miguel asked. He could easily supply them with sidearms and automatic rifles.

They already had weapons, Lillian told him. He should see to his own.

Miguel needed money.

How much?

Two thousand dollars.

Lillian looked to Wiley.

Wiley gave Miguel two thousand in hundreds. He had noticed Miguel's lips purse to say one, change to say two.

Miguel told them how good he felt about this operation. He complimented Wiley, said it proved how valuable an education in electronics could be.

And a family farm in Ohio, Wiley put in.

Miguel said that if this operation was successful he would be able to go ahead with the major incident he had spoken to them about. As though he hadn't always been cryptic about it.

Again, Lillian asked what it was he had in mind.

For now they had enough to concern themselves with, Miguel said. Not to worry, they'd be in on it when the time came. Wiley would be especially useful. Anyway, he expected enough money from this operation to finance the incident and launch the national uprising that was certain to follow. Argenti and all his kind would fall and never get up again.

Great, Wiley thought, but come the revolution, he'd be long gone to some peaceful place—Lillian or no Lillian.

Before leaving the *barrio*, they took a look at their objective. Seeing the building now, in daylight, using the windows for a measure, Wiley realized he'd been off quite a bit on his estimate. The building was no more than 120 feet long, judging by its proportions, 100 feet wide.

From the *barrio* they dropped in at the Kennedy City house. The mattresses had arrived. The Cubans had unpacked theirs but left the others in the cardboard containers. The Cubans weren't around. Lillian remarked that they were probably off to the races. Wiley noticed the wide ring they'd left on the only bathtub, along with several curly hairs that were probably pubic. He reminded Lillian to get some Ajax.

At least, she said, they were taking baths.

On the way back to the villa, Wiley and Lillian went to the photo laboratory to look over the contact prints.

"These are right on the button," Lillian said, indicating a series of exposures.

They were of Astrid and Maret sunning nude at the pool, unaware they were being photographed. Thus the angles and details were of Wiley's choosing, even more revealing of him than of his subjects. With the two-hundred-millimeter lens he'd gotten a number of shots so close they were anatomical puzzles. Others of that sort were quite recognizable.

"I got bored shooting gargoyles and trees," he explained.

"What's so entertaining about an armpit?" She pointed out a certain photo.

"That's not an armpit."

"It looks like a European armpit."

"Armpits are concave."

Out of the two rolls of film, seventy-two exposures altogether, Wiley had managed to get about half in focus. All the vital ones, however, were sharp, would enlarge well.

That evening, Lillian gave Argenti another dose of encouragement. Told him she needed time, but only a little, to think about his proposal. Also, his presence was certainly not fair to her. She didn't want to be swayed, had to be objective, thought she could reach a decision sooner if she went home to Mexico City. Which way was she leaning? Well, he shouldn't yet order the engraving but he might doodle an invitation list.

Later that evening, aside, Argenti told Wiley he understood Wiley had almost run out on him three days ago. That would have been unwise, he said. Kellerman had been upset about it, wanted to take some sort of action. Wiley should stay put, considering the five million still outstanding on his ledger with The Concession.

Wiley nodded compliantly.

He told Lillian about it when they got to bed. How could he go to Mexico City with her when he was Argenti's prisoner of debt?

She'd finagle Argenti into letting him go along.

Wouldn't Argenti be jealous?

Some people just weren't, ever, Lillian said. Didn't Wiley think Argenti knew what had been going on in his own house?

That was true, Wiley thought, and odd.

Next day, as scheduled, Lillian's secretary and driver arrived in Bogotá.

Wiley and Lillian met with them in a suite at the Hilton.

This was the first time Wiley had seen Marianna. An intelligent blonde of about thirty. Attractively understated. She knew which side her toast was caviared on. Not for an instant did she compete with Lillian, while giving her the limit of her competence.

As for Bryan, he was merely along for the ride, would do whatever he was told. He made double the pay of most drivers for working half as much, and Marianna was a fringe benefit more attractive than Blue Cross.

Wiley noticed right off that the jeans Bryan had on were a pair from his own original Las Hadas wardrobe. If there is one thing a man knows, it is his jeans, and these were definitely the straight-legged, slightly vibrant blue pair he'd bought last spring on East Sixtieth at the French Jean Store.

Now was not the time to make an issue of it, Wiley decided. No doubt his entire original wardrobe was over the garage in Bryan's closet. His most recent one was sitting in baggage claim in Miami.

Lillian had Marianna order up some breakfast. No ham, bacon, or sausage for Wiley, she stipulated. He had developed an aversion to pork in any form since Barbosa.

They got down to business.

Marianna had brought the equipment Lillian had requested. It hadn't been available in Mexico City. She'd flown to New York for it.

Wiley squatted for a closer look at the three identical black packs that were side by side along the wall.

While in New York, Marianna had also arranged for the four passports. She had already fixed up two of them.

Lillian brought out her and Wiley's passport photos. Marianna glued them in proper position on the third pages of the other two passports. Wiley and Lillian signed them. Then Marianna used a pressure stamp on the faces of the photos to emboss an official State Department seal.

Cash. Marianna handed a manilla envelope to Lillian, who, without a look inside, passed it on to Wiley. He found it contained five bound bundles, a hundred hundreds to each bundle. He riffled through a bundle twice just for the feel of it.

Breakfast came.

Wiley ate too fast and finished first. He went out on the balcony to have a smoke. Twenty-five stories below was the Circo de Santamaría, Bogotá's bull ring. At the moment it was concentric circles of empty seats. There were two figures against the pale ground of its center. Flashes of bright pink and blood red, billows of those colors. Wiley watched the two matadors practice with their capes, whirling in place time and time again. Smart of them, he thought, to get acquainted with where they would face death. Cutting down assumptions.

One of the matadors spun, lost balance, and went down covered by the red of his cape.

At that moment Marianna came out to give Wiley another envelope, something else from New York.

What was in it told him Lillian had made a point of remembering the name of his divorce lawyer. She'd paid the Jennifer tab. That part of his life was right there in his hand, signed and settled.

It was more than a favor.

Wiley did the final errands.

He took along the three black packs. Picked up the photo enlargements and the guns and ammunition. Dropped everything off at the Kennedy City house.

The two Cubans were in the backyard playing catch with a baseball. Wiley observed, unnoticed, from a rear window. The Cubans were catching barehanded. They wound up and burned the ball as hard as they could to each other. Stinging smacks when it hit their palms but only one drop in ten throws.

It was enough to make Johnny Bench wince.

Lillian was dressed for travel. Tan slacks, blue sweater, blue-and-beige figured scarf and silver-framed aviator-style dark glasses. Wiley wore what he'd had on for the last four days: navy blazer, gray slacks.

The limousine was loaded.

Argenti offered to take the ride, see them to the airport.

Lillian told him not to bother.

Argenti insisted, mildly.

Lillian told him she would prefer not to remember him in such an unsuitable plebian atmosphere as the air terminal.

He was dissuaded.

Lillian gave him three farewell cheek kisses that were actually more lip sound than contact.

Argenti touched the outside corner of one of his eyes with the tip of a little finger, supposedly to prevent a tear.

Wiley nodded once for good-bye.

Even before the limousine pulled away from the steps, Argenti had gone into the villa.

In a half hour Wiley and Lillian were at the airport. Her Gulfstream was checked out, warmed up and waiting. Her luggage was put directly aboard, carted through customs as though it were invisible. She and Wiley went to a terminal newsstand to buy several magazines. On the way to the international departures area Lillian went into the ladies' room. Wiley went into the adjacent men's room.

A few moments later, Marianna came out of the ladies' room wearing tan slacks, blue sweater, blue-and-beige scarf and silver-rimmed aviator-style dark glasses. Bryan came out of the men's room in a dark-blue blazer and gray slacks. They walked at a leisurely pace to the international departures area and on to customs, where they produced their passports.

Marianna's photo, Lillian's name.

Bryan's photo, Wiley's name.

Everything in order. The customs clerk inked his stamp well and used it like punctuation to his *"Buen viaje."*

25 ➤➤➤

That same night Maret and Astrid were booked on the ten o'clock flight to London, with a connection from there to Copenhagen.

They didn't have much packing to do. Because they'd been doing it throughout their two-month stay. They had each arrived with one cheap cardboard-type suitcase. As they shopped and accumulated things they stashed them away in Charles Jourdan luggage pieces which they kept out of sight in the deepest part of their closets. So as not to appear obviously greedy and, as well, to lessen the chance of having anything taken back should Argenti suddenly become displeased.

Now servants came for their luggage. Brown belonged to Astrid, black to Maret. Twenty-eight pieces, requiring a second limousine.

Clementina came to tell them Argenti wanted to say goodbye. They remembered to kick off their shoes before going to his most private study on the second floor.

Clementina stood inside by the closed door.

Maret sat on Argenti's lap. He kissed her an open kiss while his hand went inside her blouse, so carelessly it ripped off a button. She made little animal sounds and squirmed appropriately. Then he had her stand before him while he felt for proof that she was genuinely aroused.

Astrid was put through a similar test.

Argenti said they were good little girls because they were such bad little girls.

They giggled for him.

He held up identical Piaget wristwatches.

They ran with the proper excitement to get their going-away presents.

They tried to kiss him their thanks.

Instead he had them kiss one another.

They positioned their heads so that he could see their

tongues. And without being told, they did a few other things as though they could not help themselves. Just a little to remember them by.

They left the room. Clementina stayed. She told him Maret had recommended her younger sister. Just thirteen, only touched by herself and that only recently.

Argenti's interest was stirred.

Clementina would accompany the girls to Denmark. From there she would go home to Stuttgart for a week with her mother. Her mother was saving nearly every penny Clementina made. Clementina was a twenty-year-old who looked sixteen. Posing as Argenti's niece, she had been arranging these matters for him for the past three years. She had a backlog of candidates agreeable to a South American holiday. Most were from large poor families. Throughout Europe, especially in the north, many of the poor seemed to have a practical attitude toward their daughters. Whatever happened was bound to happen to them soon enough anyway, a father usually reasoned, and took the money.

This time Argenti gave Clementina two thousand above her salary for having done so well with Maret and Astrid. And ten thousand more she was to use as needed in her recruiting. He expected her to return within ten days with at least two new friends.

He remained in his study.

Opened a bottle of Le Montrachet Grivelet '66. He appreciated its color and bouquet before taking a sip.

If things went the way they were headed, he'd have what he wanted.

Lillian was instrumental, the key.

He had invested a great deal of time and patience in her. No doubt, she would marry him. With their interests fused to that extent, it would be in line to have Corey approach Brandon to approach Sir William on his behalf.

Sir William was head of The Consolidated Selling System, the London-based diamond cartel Argenti had once been associated with as a privileged dealer. The System that he had side-dealed on, and been found out by. The System that had spared his life at the last second and imposed exile instead. Their terms had been explicit: restriction to South and Central America and Mexico. If he ever set foot on any other territory he would be killed. The same penalty would be imposed if he ever touched another diamond.

The System.

Brandon was on The System's board of directors. Recently elected because of the extensive diamond discoveries made and controlled by one of his companies in Western Australia. With the South African and West African situations tenuous and slipping, those Australian finds became all the more important to The System, and Brandon was a man to be heard.

Corey was Brandon's friend on both a business and a personal level. Corey was chairman of the conglomerate that was the financial web spun out of the Mayo holdings—Lillian's source of wealth. Several of Brandon's important companies were dependent upon agreements with Mayo firms. A normal one-hand-washing-the-other relationship; however, Corey had the soap.

Thus, Argenti believed marriage to Lillian was the solution. His influence on her would start the chain reaction. Lillian to Corey to Brandon to Sir William. His exoneration would come, probably in person, politely, from Sir William himself.

Then Argenti would be free to go when and wherever he pleased. For example: the Biffi alla Scala next door to the opera house in Milan. There, most certainly, he would order *risotto milanese con tartufi*—rice seasoned and yellow with saffron, rich sauce ladled over it, and that topped with white truffles from the Valle D'Aosta. The truffles sliced into delicious slivers, before his eyes, with a special silver instrument with razorlike blades.

Many times over the years of exile he'd ached himself sick for such places: La Nosetta, that intimate *taverna* on Lake Como.

Where Karen had gone with him.

The best ever for him, then and still, sweet Karen.

With his usual constant antennae for such things he had noticed Karen at the railway station in Lecco. Just arrived and on her way to Erba to visit her mother's sister. She took his ride instead of the bus, and he drove slowly to prolong it. She was from Feldkirch in Austria, only five miles from the Rhine. Her eyes sung as she talked, he thought. Such fine features, a slight, very becoming overbite. She noticed when he passed the turnoff to Erba, but she wasn't alarmed, chose that moment to say she was not expected at her aunt's until the next day. There had been a mix-up on dates and her aunt did not have a telephone, so she had just come ahead. She was much too choice, he'd decided, for anything usual, such as merely hands, along some back road in the car. He took her to La Nosetta for a late lunch outside, right over the lake. She was awed by the dessert cart. He could tell from her shoes that they were her best only other pair. He excused himself, went into the *taverna* and registered for a room, just in case. No one doubted she was his daughter. He knew that if she was still there when he returned to the table, she would stay. It was an adventure for her that, minute by minute, she allowed to happen. Special Karen. Her hands so clean, the nails pared so the tops of her fingers showed. There had been an apricot tree outside their room, its blossoms pressed against the window screen—he would always remember. She had removed her clothes carefully, folded and hung them with respect. White cotton underpants, as he had hoped. She did not try to conceal anything but her shyness. Her heavy, healthy hair, straw blond, seemed longer down over her bare shoulders. The longest of it tried to hide her breasts. She said she was fourteen. She was thirteen, just turned. She had never felt anything, only wondered. Perhaps that day was her first possible day, that hour or even that minute might have been the first time she was capable. Almost as soon as he touched her she was frightened by sensation. Within moments she thought she was dying. She came into the pleasure he gave her that fresh, that easy. Lipping wet around one of her nipples for a minute was enough to cause her to achieve. She had given him the virginity of her body and her mind, he had always thought.

Sweet exception, Karen.

He never saw her again. She went lightly down the road to her aunt's house and into his life forever as a fixed impression.

He had never been able to recapture her with anyone else. Either they couldn't yet or had already, one way or another.

He thought, when his exile was over, soon now, he would go back over some of those roads. It had been more satisfying for him when he'd done his own hunting, and he would again. Perhaps in the railway station at Lecco or Como, Lugano or Varese, he would find another Karen.

One thing was certain: He would never be sexually up to Lillian, no matter what she resorted to. As a matter of fact, the more complex she made it, the more adult, so to speak, the worse it would be. He planned to go through the motions, be perplexed by his failure, act distressed. The question would be, why should such a thing happen to him at that time? She would realize she was the difference in his life, and, therefore, blame herself. He would have her sympathy, and against that emotional background, it would be a small thing for her to speak to Corey on his behalf. Everything would work in his favor.

Didn't he find Lillian desirable?

Only cerebrally so. She was a beautiful woman by womanly standards, but spoiled. Many times over. Spoiled by experience. Practiced and physically demanding. He had long ago given up trying and failing with her sort. (It made him despondent to think that somewhere Karen was now a thirty-year-old issuing children and sexual directions.)

He no longer had any uncertainty about his libidinal preference, or any misgivings. Over the years, that which pleased him most had determined him. No use fighting it and no shame. But he would never tell Lillian. Somehow he would keep it from her, be more careful, extremely discreet. Until the exile was lifted, until her body ran out of patience.

That was where this Mr. Wiley fit in. That was the reason for having gone through the complications of setting up Mr. Wiley so that he was five million on the down side. That was the only reason Mr. Wiley was not dead by simple elimination. Argenti could have had it done at any time by the point of his finger.

Mr. Wiley would serve.

Evidently, from what he'd gathered, Lillian found Mr. Wiley a fairly good bedfellow. All the better. Argenti wouldn't begrudge her that. People in their class were always sweeping things under the rug. Well, he, Lillian and Wiley would sweep everything under the rug and all get under there with it.

The telephone. His direct line to Conduct Section was ringing.

Kellerman was on to tell him, "The report is she landed in Mexico City an hour ago and went immediately to her house in the Pedregal section."

"Wiley was with her?"

"Of course."

"Good. If he runs out on her, kill him. Did you by chance have that talk with Robayo?"

"The Senator wants a retirement fund," Kellerman said.

"Wants?"

"Demands."

"That was not in the original terms."

"So I reminded him."

"Doesn't he realize the new Senator from Boyacá will assume his responsibilities and, as well, his rewards? *Merda*, if he kept only a third of what went to Switzerland for him these past seven years, he is a wealthy man."

"He gambled."

"That much of a loser?"

"He seemed to enjoy not winning."

"Well, we can't stuff his mouth with money," Argenti said.

"Unless you're prepared to keep stuffing."

"Wait until he is out of office. Meanwhile, go along with whatever he wants."

"Exactly."

After the phone call Argenti remained at his desk. He poured more of the Montrachet and moved a paperweight that was one pound of pure platinum, polished and engraved with his three initials in Spencerian script. He took up a letter from the man in Amsterdam, an associate in the international minority organization called The Golden Triangle. Members traded material and local advice. Many prominent men. This man in Amsterdam had some exceptional color snapshots. A sample was enclosed: the girl in a most delightful, gawky stance, hand shielding her eyes from the sun, crotch barely glossed—*the golden triangle*. Not a hint of guile, unless it was her underpants around and under one foot, toes peeking out.

Argenti tried to think what in his collection he might offer in exchange. Something of quality that had used up his interest.

He opened the desk drawer.

There was the red Cartier box.

He placed it on the desk and pressed the lid up.

The ring Lillian would accept.

The diamond, a few points over twelve carats, flared at him, even in that low light.

He got up, bolted the only door. Drew the drapes over all the windows and returned to his chair behind the desk.

Even then he was uneasy, glanced around.

Slowly, he brought the first finger of his right hand to the ring.

Even the slightest change in his point of view caused the diamond to differ in its refractions. It was a round cut, what those in the trade called a brilliant.

The tip of his finger was only a half inch from it.

It would be the first time since.

He dared. Touched the diamond and quickly withdrew his hand, as though to avoid being burned.

He glanced around the room again.

Shook his head as though to shake away a spell.

He had been ridiculous.

He took the diamond from the box, looked into its table, that largest facet on its top, gazed into its cold, clear substance. He rubbed the diamond on the back of his hand and on his wrist where his life was represented by his pulse.

He put it in his mouth, moved it about in there with his tongue.

The System?

He spat the diamond out with such force it landed halfway across the room.

26 ⇥⇥

Lillian hummed a few bars of an old Beatles song and went on nonstop into some of another and another.

Content. There were mattresses on the floor, candles stuck around in their own melt, incense and a nice edge of apprehension in the air.

She picked up the long wooden spoon and stirred the black liquid in the pot. The Kennedy City house came with a gas stove, but the stove had only two burners. So, she had been at it practically all day. That morning she had cooked up a pot of zuki beans and a pot of brown rice. She was glad she hadn't lost her touch with rice. It came out neither stuck together nor stuck to the bottom.

Now what she had cooking on the back burner was a pair of coveralls. Dying them black. The pot could only hold one pair at a time, so with three pairs to do, it would take a while.

On the front burner was a small cast-iron pot containing lead. The lead was just now beginning to melt. She was ready for it.

Wiley offered to help.

She told him he could put out his cigarette and watch.

She placed four bullets on the counter next to the stove. Set them upright. They were four of the hollow-point forty-fives the gunsmith Cordero had made for her. The lead nose of each bullet had a hole bored in it, about three eighths of an inch deep, one eighth in diameter.

Wiley wanted to know what she intended to do with them.

"Don't ask so many questions," she told him. "I have to concentrate."

Using a regular glass eye-dropper, she filled the nose hole of each bullet with ordinary water. Then, she took up another dropper, similar but made of stainless steel.

The lead was melted by now.

She sucked some of it up into the length of the stainless-steel dropper, careful not to get too much, because the lead was hot enough to burn through the dropper's rubber vacuum bulb.

She held the dropper less than an inch above a bullet, making sure it was exactly over the nose hole. She squeezed the dropper bulb, gently. A bead of the molten lead grew until it fell by its own weight exactly on the hole. Immediately it cooled and hardened.

The object, she explained, was to seal the water in the hollow of the bullet. Perhaps it looked easy to do, but if the lead wasn't dropped precisely, if it was off even slightly and left a little opening, the water steamed and escaped.

She examined the bullet she'd just done. "A perfect seal," she said.

He assumed it was something she'd done before, wondered for what reason, asked her.

"I've only heard about it," she said. "They call these hydraulic bullets."

"What good are they?"

She didn't say, went back to it. She had difficulty sealing the second bullet, didn't get it sealed until her fourth try. Several others also gave her trouble, but after about an hour and a half of intense effort, she was through sealing all eighteen. She used a fingernail file to remove any excess lead from the bullets, making their gray noses smooth. She inserted the bullets into two clips, nine to each. Shoved a clip into the stock of the Colt forty-five automatic.

Wiley went out with her to the backyard.

"You're not going to shoot it here?" he said.

"Sure."

"What about the neighbors?"

"They'll think it's a backfire. Besides, noise doesn't bother people much until they get to be middle-class."

There was a plank, a piece of one-by-ten about three feet long. She propped it up against the cement-block foundation of the house. She stood off about fifteen feet, cocked a bullet into position, raised the pistol and fired at the plank.

A regular forty-five-caliber bullet would have made a regular forty-five-caliber hole in the plank, nearly the size of a dime. A regular hollow-nose, or dumdum bullet, as they are called, would have made a hole the size of a dime going in and a hole as big around as a silver dollar going through and out the back.

The hydraulic bullet blasted the plank apart.

Lillian explained why, as much as she knew about it.

Upon impact, the lead bullet slug compressed. However, water was one of the few substances known that could not be compressed.

Wiley knew that from high-school physics. A cubic foot of water remains a cubic foot of water no matter how much pressure is exerted upon it from all sides.

Thus, when the slug hit, its compression, its give, so to speak, met with the absolute stubbornness of the water inside it. Force against counterforce caused explosion.

Wiley picked up what was left of the plank. He imagined what a bullet like that could do to a person. "What are you going to use it for?" he asked.

"You'll see," she said.

They went into the house.

She put the gun away and finished dying the coveralls. Wiley strung a line for them to dry on. They sprayed the crash helmets black, and Lillian cut soles from the foam rubber, which she glued to the bottoms of the combat boots.

Off and on all day Wiley had fussed with his socks, pulling them up. The reason was, he had four of Lillian's ten-thousand-dollar bundles stashed in them. Lillian had the other ten-thousand bundle tucked into the front of her bikini panties, which, of course, exaggerated her *mons veneris*. There weren't any good money-hiding places in the unfurnished house, and the Cubans gave the impression they would cut throats for a lot less. That afternoon, when the Cubans were playing masochistic catch, several wild throws had put baseball dents in the car Wiley had rented from Hertz. Lillian believed they'd done it on purpose.

Early the next morning, Miguel showed up. He, Lillian and Wiley packed the car and left for the training site.

It was ten days to Christmas.

27 ➤➤➤

Fires were not uncommon in the *barrio*.

The average was about one a night. More than that during the Christmas season, with all the candles, fireworks and *aguardiente*.

On this Christmas Eve four fires broke out there.

Someone finally notified the fire department.

The firetrucks passed through red lights with their usual priority but, otherwise, they only sounded as though they were hurrying. It was a *barrio* alarm.

Thus the fires got a big blazing start.

Barrio inhabitants crowded around and got in the way of the hoses.

Firemen accepted swigs. Kids tossed firecrackers at the firemen's boots. It was festive, more like a celebration than an emergency.

None of the officials on the scene gave any thought to the coincidence that all four fires had started at precisely ten o'clock, or that their locations corresponded to the four corners of Argenti's building.

At that same hour that night, a Cessna 172 Skyhawk skirted the mountains southwest of the city. The sky could not have been clearer. It was as though the Savior had ordered all the stars and a full moon out. No wind; heaven seemed to be holding its breath.

From an altitude of two thousand feet the pilot of the plane identified the straight, brighter-lighted city artery below as Avenida 13. He used it for a heading.

Wiley was next to the pilot, in a tight squat position on the floor, facing aft. Lillian and Miguel had the passenger seats. They were all cramped in by equipment, had been for over an hour. Their spines and legs were complaining.

The door of the plane had been removed on Wiley's side. Raw air blew in. Still there was the smell of marijuana. Droppings of the stuff filled every crack, crease and angle of the plane's interior, and whenever the plane was in flight a fine marijuana dust was stirred up. Wiley was willing to bet a good going-over with an Electrolux would have yielded at least a pound. Little doubt what the plane had previously been used for.

The pilot was one of Miguel's part-time comrades. Carlos Johnson by name. His father was an American merchant seaman who had jumped ship at Buenaventura in 1950 and never worked another honest day. Carlos had learned English from his father. One adjective described everything, whether it deserved it or not. Such as now, when he poked Wiley and shouted over the noise of the propeller: "About three fucking minutes."

Wiley felt not entirely in register with reality. And as though he was under a slight general anesthesia. The metal floor of the plane was hard on his ass bones, but that was inconsequential. He was looking directly at Lillian. Her face seemed small inside the helmet, a little-girl game player. They had tried to talk during the early minutes of the flight but had to shout and couldn't keep that up. That wasn't the reason they were silent now. Wiley was thinking that he wasn't going out that door. They weren't ready, he wasn't. Ten days of training wasn't enough.

Only ten days ago had been the first time. At twenty-five hundred feet over a plateau near Pacora. Carlos was to instruct them. He'd learned from a guy who'd learned from a guy who'd learned in the army. A lot had been left out along the line.

Ordinarily, such training included extensive preliminaries on the ground, theoretically what and what not to do, how and how not to do it. Carlos' method was like teaching someone to swim by throwing him overboard in the middle of the Atlantic.

He had them put on their chutes.

He took them a half mile up.

One at a time they stood in the open doorway.

"People have to fucking bail out all the time," Carlos said. "Don't worry."

They didn't jump.

He shoved them out with his right foot.

Suddenly they were in a tumble of earth over sky over earth, not knowing which way was up, grabbing at the nothing of the air while the fear of falling stopped their breaths and spurted their adrenaline. They had to fight through freeze to pull the ripcord ring.

"Unless you pull the ring, you won't feel a fucking thing," Carlos had said.

Their parachutes flowed up and filled out and saved them. They floated down wherever the wind happened to take them, landed at least a thousand feet from the patch of open field that had been their target.

"Not so fucking bad," Carlos later said while showing them how to pack their chutes.

Marianna had brought good chutes. Thirty-two-foot Para-commanders of black nylon, the kind with slots in the rear of the canopy that gave the jumper a certain amount of maneuverability. The Paracommander came with a reserve chute attached to the harness across the front at waist level.

One thing Carlos constantly reminded them was to be careful with the reserve chute any time they were up in the plane. They should keep their left hands over the ripcord handle of the reserve chute to protect it from being pulled accidentally. He never told them why.

Lillian found out.

One afternoon the plane dropped sharply into a large air pocket.

Lillian grabbed.

The reserve chute sprang out.

She tried to contain it with her arms, but it billowed and caught the wind stream on the open side of the plane. Then the entire chute was out and inflating behind the plane while she was still in the cabin. It would snap her against the fuselage with force enough to break her. There was only one thing to do, and she had about two seconds to do it. She dove out, just missed by inches losing her head on the plane's tail fin.

Another time Wiley's main chute malfunctioned because he hadn't packed it right. When the chute opened, two suspension lines weren't straight down from the canopy as they should have been but looped over the top of it and down the wrong side. What experienced chutists call "a line over." It caused Wiley to go into a spiral, a downward spiral, of course. Completely out of control. Carlos hadn't said what to do in such an event, but Wiley wanted to live enough to pull the reserve chute.

Then there was the jump when Miguel's ripcord handle stuck, and he struggled with it longer than he should have. From twenty-five hundred feet to the ground is about an eighteen-second fall. Miguel misjudged the time and the ground, had used up fifteen seconds before he went to his reserve chute. It popped open loudly and grabbed just enough air so he could land without serious injury. His left knee knocked him unconscious.

How many jumps had they made in those ten days?

Wiley knew exactly.

Thirty-two each.

He also happened to know it took a falling person, such as one whose parachute failed, only twelve seconds to be falling at a rate of 176 feet per second—120 miles per hour—which is terminal velocity. He was disturbed by the term *terminal*, the death connotation to it.

It brought to mind Endicott, the man who had flashed by Wiley's office window on his way down from the top.

Anyway, over the past ten days, since that first do-or-die jump, they had all covered a lot of air. Carlos' crude, accelerated course was terrifying and frequently painful, but within a week they got so they could maneuver their chutes and come down in that small open patch three out of five times.

That had been out in the country in the daytime.

Not over a city.

At night.

Wiley was sure he wasn't ready. But then, he doubted he'd ever be.

They were coming up on target now.

Four fires to starboard.

No difficulty finding Argenti's building. It stuck up from the *barrio* like a misplaced monolith.

Carlos made a trial pass, went almost to the mountains and banked back.

The plane would blip on Argenti's radar screen, Wiley thought, but nothing to alarm the Conduct Section men on duty at the control console on the thirty-third floor. Just another private plane going by, not a helicopter and not really near.

On the next run Wiley was up and at the exit. He would be first. Lillian and Miguel were ready, would follow in that order.

Carlos adjusted the altitude to two thousand feet. At that

height, with no wind factor, they would descend on a diagonal line and land seven hundred feet from the spot over which they jumped. That was the normal jumping formula. It would take about two minutes from opening to landing.

The Hospital de San Juan de Dios was about seven hundred feet from target and a large enough structure to serve as their opening point.

It was coming up below.

Carlos cut the engine.

Wiley blanked his mind and leaped.

He said his full name aloud four times and pulled the ripcord handle. After half a second of uncertainty he felt the harness snug up around him as the chute blossomed open above.

He looked up to see if he had a line over. He couldn't tell with the black chute against the night sky. He wasn't spiraling, so he assumed all suspension lines were in order.

But where were the fires?

He was supposed to use the four fires as quadrants, draw an imaginary line from fire to fire and aim for the center of that square.

He was falling about fifteen feet per second.

There they were, the fires, off to the right.

He had to adjust. He pulled down on the wooden handle that was on the back side of the right riser, just above him. Pulling that toggle, as it is called, distorted the shape of the canopy and allowed air to spill out of its rear right slot.

The harness with Wiley in it rotated slowly to the right.

He immediately released the toggle and, according to the four fires, was now descending on the correct line. His rate of forward glide was a normal ten feet a second, still going down at fifteen a second.

What if he undershot and landed in the middle of some busy intersection? He wouldn't have to be far off to end up in the Plaza Bolívar in the midst of people on their way to Christmas Eve mass. He could see his picture in the newspapers and the expression on Argenti's face.

In keeping with his training average he had only slightly better than a fifty-fifty chance of being on target.

At a thousand feet now, he estimated.

It appeared he was going to be long.

Way long.

He braked, pulled down on both left and right toggles. Of

course, it wasn't like braking a car; there was no stopping or slowing him. What it did was reduce his forward glide by opening both slots in the canopy. At the same time it altered the angle of his fall to almost vertical.

After a moment he released the toggles, glided a ways. He braked and glided alternately several times; it was like going down a flight of steps.

At six hundred feet he realized he was off to the left. At that point he was only two hundred feet above the roof, had only a few seconds to make the corrections. He yanked down on the left toggle, the canopy responded at once.

He came down on the roof about ten feet off dead center. A soft, stand-up landing, like an old pro. He found it incredible that he'd actually done it. The roof, though unfriendly territory, felt solidly comfortable and welcome beneath his feet. With the layer of foam rubber Lillian had glued to the soles of his boots, he'd landed with barely a sound. He recalled that when the *bruja* Julietta had told his tomorrows, she'd said he would fall from a great height but not be hurt. What a coincidence.

His chute lay relaxed on the surface of the roof. He slipped out of the harness as he gazed skyward.

Lillian was about a hundred feet up.

She was going to overshoot.

Wiley kept himself from shouting to her to brake, so as not to set off the listening alarm. But what the hell did it, or anything, matter if she wasn't going to make it?

She missed the roof by six feet.

A section of her canopy brushed the edge, overlapped the roof.

Wiley dove, made a stretching reach and got a crease of it with his fingers. The canopy was nylon and slick. It slipped away, but not before he grabbed out with his other hand and got a better hold. In that prone position it took all his strength to stop the momentum of her fall.

She dangled along the side of the building. Her legs extended below the thirty-third floor, outside the window of Conduct Section's control room. The men on duty needed only to glance in that direction. She could do nothing to avoid hitting against the window. The toes of her boots barely missed bumping it, as she swung back and forth.

Wiley fought the expanse of the canopy and finally grasped

the suspension lines. Slowly, hand over hand, he hoisted her up onto the roof.

She thanked him with her eyes.

"I love you" wanted to come out of him again, but there could be no talking because of the listening alarm.

Miguel came down directly in front of the rotating radar beacon.

That caused a momentary blank-out on the screen in the control room below. The radar man on duty noticed and was alert for any further sign, but the sweep on the screen was immediately clear all the way around and remained so. He attributed the lapse to a minor discrepancy somewhere in the circuitry.

Wiley had been right about the radar. It was designed for longer range, couldn't pick up and define anything as close as the roof. To prevent its waves from constantly bouncing off other high buildings and the mountains to the east, the radar's rotating beacon had been set at an upward angle, missing the roof and anyone on it.

Also as Wiley had thought, the listening alarm was an honest and formidable device. A series of miniature transmitters, supersensitive no doubt, were built into a low raised ledge that bordered the roof all around. Thousands of transmitters, so not an inch of the roof was unprotected. Apparently it was a custom installation. Anyway, Wiley had never seen or heard of anything like it. He had the urge but not the suicidal compulsion to yell right into it, rupture a couple of eardrums down on thirty-three.

He put his finger to his lips, reminding Lillian and Miguel to maintain silence.

They packed the chutes.

Wiley went to the window-washing apparatus.

It was actually a cumbersome vehicle, with thick rubber wheels that fit into a pair of six-inch-deep tracks. The tracks ran parallel around the perimeter of the roof. The electric motor that powered the apparatus was housed in a large metal box fixed to the vehicle's weighty steel frame. As part of the frame, two structural beams, left and right, ran up and out, armlike. From them a permanent scaffold was suspended by steel cables. An arrangement similar to the way lifeboats are suspended from overhanging davits so they can be swung out and lowered down the side of a ship. The platform itself was made of steel. It was about fifteen feet long, four feet wide, enclosed by waist-high mesh, like a cage, on the outer side and at both ends. The ignition and directional control switches aboard the platform were wired to the motor.

Wiley wondered how much noise the motor would make. Could be whenever the building was having its windows washed Conduct Section was notified and cut the listening alarm.

He flipped the ignition switch.

The motor didn't go on.

Did the building turn off the power up there at night?

He flipped the switch on and off several times. Nothing.

Maybe there was a disconnect at the housing. He kneeled beside the box that contained the motor, saw the wires were intact. The housing was solid, sealed.

Well, that was it. Stopped, right off.

Wiley slouched futilely against the housing. He realized then that he was feeling a vibration. Very slight. He put his ear to the side of the housing and heard it, an ever-so-faint hum. The motor. It was running. Why the hell hadn't he tried the scaffold controls instead of assuming the worst. Evidently the inside of the housing was extra-insulated to prevent the motor's noise from interfering with the listening alarm. Probably Kellerman had ordered that so surveillance would not be interrupted. Thank you, Kellerman.

Lillian and Miguel placed the packs and other equipment on the scaffold and climbed aboard.

Wiley would operate the directional controls, which were as simple as could be: one switch for up or down or neutral, another for left or right or neutral.

He flipped the switch to down.

The scaffold moved out over the edge of the building to the end of the davits. In motion, the scaffold seemed much less secure. It swung a bit more than Wiley and the others had expected. They braced themselves. Wiley flipped the switch to neutral for a moment.

Now there was nothing between them and a thirty-five-story drop except the floor of the scaffold. The floor also was constructed of steel mesh, which made them feel as though they were sort of standing on air.

They glanced down to the street.

The fires were still blazing, and there was still the confusion of the trucks and hoses, halfhearted fire fighters and the crowds from the *barrio*. The pops and the booms of fireworks exploding. Some seemingly childish grown-ups were using slingshots to send fireworks high into the air, timing them so they exploded at their peak. Some reached nearly halfway up the building. It was like an assault.

Directly below, at the base of the building, a cordon of armed troops had taken position. Evidently, someone, most probably Kellerman or Argenti, had been informed of the crowds and fires, and as a precaution, this contingent of troops had been ordered to the scene.

Wiley estimated there were about fifty men. It was something neither he, Lillian nor Miguel had anticipated. If even one of these soldiers happened to look up and believe he saw something silhouetted against the sky. . . . The fire trucks were equipped with searchlights. The soldiers with their rifles would be able to pick them off easily.

Best not to think of it now.

Wiley flipped the down switch again.

The scaffold descended by its cables slowly, steadily. Wiley stopped it when it was level with the top floor.

They were on the west side of the building, the side they wanted; however, the vault area was at the southwest corner.

Wiley flipped the appropriate switch. The scaffold moved to the right. It took about twenty seconds for it to reach a window of the vault room.

Conduct Section's control center was on the second floor down. They could see its lights spilling out.

The window to the vault room measured about twelve feet wide, ten feet high. Heavy plate glass, at least a half-inch thick, from the sound when Wiley rapped it with his knuckles.

Lillian positioned herself opposite the midway point of the window. She estimated exact center. Taking a solid stance, she aimed the Colt forty-five automatic and squeezed off a single round.

The bullet with water in its nose hit the window glass.

They might be wounded by pieces of glass flying outward. A greater danger would be the reaction of the soldiers when glass fell to the sidewalk.

The hydraulic bullet shattered the window all the way to its four frames. The tremendous spreading force of the bullet caused the glass to implode. Huge shards and smaller pieces flew into the room. Hardly a splinter fell outward, and the frame was bare, as though the window had been removed by a glazier.

The shot set off the listening alarm on the roof just above.

In the control room on thirty-three, the Conduct Section man on duty saw the decibel needle jump to the limit. He waited to see if it stayed at limit or jumped again, but it settled back to normal level on the gauge. He cut the alarm, reset it and made a notation in the log. He had phoned Kellerman three times since ten o'clock, whenever the alarm had gone off. It was the fireworks. Otherwise, the decibel needle would have stayed up there more than a second, Kellerman had told him. Kellerman had sounded miffed, short with him during the last call. So, he wouldn't call Kellerman this time. Good thing he hadn't had the earphones on just then. He liked his job but not enough to go deaf for it. Goddamn fireworks, and Kellerman for that matter.

He told the other man on duty to watch after things for a moment. Got up and went into the adjacent room. The armory, they called it. A dozen automatic rifles were in place on a rack. He reached down behind the rack and brought up a fifth of Smirnoff hundred proof. He drank from the bottle. It was against regulations, of course, drinking while on duty, but with vodka his breath wouldn't give him away, and this was Christmas Eve, and turning out to be a hell of a night.

Two floors above, Wiley, Lillian and Miguel were in the vault room. Glass crunched under their steps. First thing, Wiley examined the wall closely, played his flashlight on it. He didn't find what he was looking for right off, because they were so tiny, unnoticeable.

Holes not large enough to stick a pin into.

Hundreds of such holes within a six-inch-square area on the surface of the wall. About five feet up from the floor.

That the holes were there was encouraging, Wiley thought. He had never been a hundred percent sure they would be. Eighty-twenty, he'd told Lillian, sixty-forty had been more the truth.

He tried to recall exactly where Argenti had stood that day. He decided on a spot about seven feet out from the wall. Lillian also remembered and agreed that was about it. She got the tape recorder from her pack. It was cued up, all she had to do was stand on the spot and turn it on.

Argenti's voice.

Ominous at that moment in that place.

Wiley resented that it caused him a shiver.

"Meno Sebastiano Argenti," the tape said with Italian flavor.

Wiley had surmised that the vault would open in response to Argenti's voice, specifically those words. That the perforations on the wall concealed an electronic receiver which would transmit the voice to a computer. The computer would be programmed for the exact inflections, pitch and resonance of Argenti's speech. Those sounds would be translated by the computer into vibrations on a scale, much like the notes in a score of music. The vibrations of Argenti's exclusive vocal configuration processed by the computer would give the vault doors' internal mechanism permission to unlock.

However, it didn't happen. Nothing happened.

"I think I had it too loud," Lillian said. She rewound the tape, turned the volume down a bit and played it again.

That made no difference.

Possibly they had selected the wrong key words. They had settled on his name because it was the only thing they both remembered him saying those separate times when the vault doors had opened. It seemed to stand out, but they could have been wrong.

"Play the whole tape," Wiley told Lillian.

She did. Nothing on the tape had any effect.

That left only one possibility.

Lillian got the photographs from her pack. They were eleven-by-fourteen-inch black-and-white enlargements of Argenti. Front view head shots, life-size, ten and a half inches from chin to top of head. Argenti's beard and full crop of hair had made it difficult to determine exactly where his chin and top were. Using the motorized Nikon camera, with its ability to take five exposures per second, Wiley had been able to get a series of Argenti saying his full name.

Lillian stood on that same spot facing the wall and held up one of the photographs.

Wiley and Miguel shined their flashlights on it.

Wiley had also speculated that the perforations on the wall might serve as an electronic unit, much like an ordinary television camera. Argenti's image would be received and relayed into a computer. The computer would be programmed exclusively for Argenti's features. His various shadings and shapes would be scanned. The total resolution of Argenti's face would be the only thing acceptable to the computer, which, when satisfied, would activate the vault to unlock.

It didn't.

Lillian tried another photograph. Then each of the photographs in the series.

The wall remained intact.

Maybe the photographs should have been in color. Or could be what was missing was a mere wink from Argenti.

Wiley had been wrong.

Argenti still had him outsmarted.

"What now?" Lillian asked.

Wiley hated to say it. "Unless you or Miguel have any bright ideas, we try to go home." He was disgusted with himself. Realized now how sure he'd been. Otherwise, he wouldn't have gone this far, jumped out of a plane at night over Bogotá. Shit. All Argenti had suffered was a broken window.

He lighted a cigarette. The first in over two hours. His nicotine craving had been nullified by anxiety. Now the cigarette didn't taste good, or maybe it was the bad taste of failure.

Anyway, how *did* that goddamn vault unlock?

He berated himself with a closed-mouth scoff.

Okay, electronic smartass, if not acoustically *or* visually, how?

It was probably something simple, but he couldn't come up with it. He could hardly think beyond his acoustical and visual theories. His mind had become too set on acoustical or visual . . .

. . . or.

"Let's try one more thing," he said.

Lillian resumed her position seven feet from the wall. She held up one of the photographs.

At the same time Wiley played the tape.

Acoustical and visual combined.

That didn't work either.

But Wiley had the feeling he was onto something.

There were five photographs, taken in a series when Argenti was saying his name. Wiley and Lillian hadn't thought to number or in any way note their sequence. They tried to determine that now. The only thing they had to go on was Argenti's mouth, which was hidden completely by his beard in one photograph and only barely visible in two.

When they believed they had the photographs in correct order, Lillian stood on that spot facing the wall.

She held up four of the photographs, her fingers separating them. She couldn't handle five, so Wiley held up one photograph, the first in the sequence.

Miguel kept his flashlight shining on them.

The tape recorder was adjusted to allow some lead time. They had to wait for it to say "Meno Sebastiano Argenti."

Simultaneously, Wiley pulled away the photograph he was holding, revealing the next held by Lillian, who released and showed the photographs one after another in sequence.

The object was to synchronize the motion with the words. The photographs were printed on heavy enough paper so they dropped away swiftly when Lillian's fingers let them go. Also, their slick finishes helped if they happened to touch.

The problem was being able to do it smoothly within two seconds.

Wiley frequently missed his cue.

Lillian was either too slow or too quick or she fumbled.

It seemed they would never be able to do it.

They tried again and again until their arms were tired and their backs ached from retrieving the photographs from the floor.

They took a break.

"Do you think this will work?" Lillian asked.

"No," Wiley said.

Nevertheless, they went back to it.

The interruption must have been beneficial. Now it was easier. Lillian seemed recharged with dexterity. There was a flow to the way the photographs fell away, a rhythm that matched the cadence of Argenti's voice. A perfect timing with the emphasis Argenti placed on certain syllables.

"Me-no . . ."

". . . Se-bas-tian-o . . ."

". . . Ar-gen-ti . . ."

The part of the wall that was the vault door slid open so quickly it seemed to dissolve.

They were stunned, didn't react immediately to the bright lights that had gone on inside the vault when it opened. Six inset spots. The lights reflected off the white interior of the vault and out into the main room.

If anyone down on the street, especially a Conduct Section man, should look up and notice the vault room lighted . . .

Lillian took care of the lights in the most expedient way. With the silencer on, her Llama automatic seemed to spit the lights out.

Inside the vault, Wiley pulled open one of the many shallow drawers of a cabinet. He played his flashlight on its contents.

Uncut emeralds, a crowded layer of them. They glowed green.

Fifty to sixty million dollars' worth in this vault, Argenti had said. Wiley also remembered the urge he'd had the last time he was there to help himself to a handful of wealth.

Now he could.

But first they should open the other vault, while they were in form.

It took them only three tries with the photographs and the tape before the wall of the second vault slid aside.

Lillian again shot out the lights.

It occurred to Wiley that in an oblique way Argenti had opened the vaults for them. At least he had been a big help.

Lillian got the black nylon duffel bags from her pack.

They went to work. Miguel in the first vault, Lillian and Wiley in the second. The second, larger vault contained more cabinets, more shallow white velour-lined drawers, more emeralds. A hundred and fifty million dollars' worth, according to Argenti. The emeralds in the first vault had glowed, these blazed. They were better quality. They clicked stone against stone as they were loaded into the duffel bags.

Wiley and Lillian got the loading down to a method.

Not to overlook a drawer, they worked on a cabinet from the bottom up.

A drawer was pulled open. Using the heels of their hands they swept the emeralds into a pile at the front of the drawer. Then they scooped the emeralds up in double handfuls and dropped them into the duffel bag.

It took nearly an hour and a half to empty every drawer in both vaults.

They had about two hundred thousand carats.

Eighty-some pounds of emeralds.

Worth about two hundred million dollars.

They sat on the floor for a rest, their backs against the wall opposite the vaults.

Wiley lighted a cigarette.

It tasted great.

How do you like your tricky vaults now, Meno Sebastiano Argenti? Your *empty* tricky vaults.

Wiley had a laugh in his gut. He let a little of it out. Stop snickering, he told himself, you're not out of this yet.

Lillian offered him a carrot stick. She had brought some in her sack. Also some celery and unroasted cashews.

Miguel had brought along some whiskey in a small canteen.

Wiley took a swig, chased it with the cigarette and then munched on the carrot so his mouth was fresh for the next drag.

Across the way in the dim light the two open vaults were darker rectangles. They took up only two thirds of the wall, Wiley noticed.

Merely curious, he got up and went over to where the wall was intact. He beamed his flashlight on it, searched close up.

There they were.

The same sort of minuscule perforations.

What were these for?

Would whatever device that was behind them respond to the photographs-and-tape routine?

Miguel was for leaving well enough alone. They had the emeralds, why risk messing with this? It might set off an alarm.

Lillian, however, was as curious as Wiley.

They played the tape and exposed the photographs to the perforations on the wall.

That section of the wall slid aside.

It was another vault.

Smaller than the second but containing the same type of white metal cabinets.

Wiley pulled open the top drawer of the nearest cabinet.

Like a layer of green-hot coals.

Emeralds.

Not rough. These were cut, faceted, polished. There must have been five hundred stones in this one drawer. They were cut in the traditional emerald fashion: an oblong table facet (face) with a crown (upper edges) of eight sections, two or three steps to each section. They were of various sizes, from about two to twelve carats.

There were more cut emeralds in the next drawer, and the next.

Wiley was awestruck.

If Van Cleef, Tiffany, Cartier, Winston and Bulgari pooled, they wouldn't come even close.

Other cabinets contained stones not yet cut. Wiley immediately recognized the difference in this rough. It was better quality, the finest grade, practically pure kelly.

Tucked in the front corner of one top drawer was a square of fluffy cotton. With something protected in it, Wiley discovered. Two somethings. Cut emeralds of approximately twenty carats each. They were brilliant cut, that is, round in shape. Emeralds were rarely cut in this fashion. Partly because their hexagonal formation facilitated the square cut, but also because emeralds, by nature, were not hard enough, too flawed, to withstand the stress. A normal first-quality emerald of any important size would more than likely crumble in the cutter's fingers if he tried to cleave and grind and polish so intricately.

But here was the exception.

A matched pair of exceptions.

With fifty-eight facets to catch and throw light they were obviously more scintillating, livelier, these two.

Wiley thought they were too special to drop into the duffel bag with the rest. He slipped them into his shirt pocket.

They emptied all the drawers in that unexpected vault.

It was quarter after two.

Down below on the street the fires had been put out and the trucks and firemen were gone. No crowds now. Only a few celebrating stragglers.

However, the soldiers were still there with rifles slung, standing in a well-spaced file around the base of the building. Had they been ordered to remain all night?

If so, Wiley, Lillian and Miguel were stuck up there, their getaway blocked. They sat on the floor as before, opposite the vaults. Every so often Miguel went over and looked down to the street. The situation remained unchanged. Lillian broke the silence by crunching on raw cashews. She said she was tired. She slumped against the wall and Wiley.

He thought about the vaults, wondered, why three?

What little he knew about La Concesión de Gemas was superficial. He had no idea how it really worked for Argenti.

The first vault was for The Concession's official inventory. As far as the government was involved, it was the only vault and the entire inventory. The government took its percentage according to The Concession's neat accounting of the emeralds that flowed in and out of vault number one.

The second vault was for the skim. It accommodated the greater portion of the yield from all the mines. The profits from the stones kept in vault number two were shared equally by General Botero, Minister of Defense Vega, Minister of Mines Arias, Senator Robayo and, of course, Argenti. The only other person who knew this vault existed was Kellerman. His cut was two fifths of a percentage point from each of the five men. Not bad, considering the take was a hundred million a year.

The third vault was for Argenti's skim of the skim. Those emeralds he held out on the others. He saw first and put away for himself the choice of all the stones that came in. It was Argenti's secret, well kept. Kellerman was nosy enough to have detected vault number three but wise enough not to let on.

Three vaults.

That was why Argenti had gone through the bother and expense of such a complex system. There could be no exterior evidence of three, no dials, knobs or handles. And so, Argenti could rest easy; only he had the combination.

Wiley suspected the third vault was special. Not just because it had contained a higher grade of stones. He sensed it was somehow personally significant to Argenti. All the more reason to be glad it hadn't been slighted.

Nearly four o'clock now.

If the soldiers didn't leave soon they would have to change the plan. Come daylight the window-washing scaffold would surely be noticed out of place. The only alternative would be to take the scaffold to the roof before then and remain up there until the next night. It would mean at least seventeen hours of pressure, their lives hung on the chance that no one would look in on the vault room that entire day.

Already the eastern horizon was beginning to hint dawn.

Might as well get to it.

Miguel said: "They're moving out."

Below, three canvas-topped army trucks were at the curb. The soldiers broke rank, climbed aboard. The trucks pulled away.

Had all the soldiers gone? A sentry or two might have been

left on duty. Wiley scanned the street. A couple of dogs sniffing around, otherwise it seemed deserted. Possibly sentries were posted on the other side of the building. No way of telling without going up on the roof, and not enough time for that.

They put the packs and duffel bags onto the scaffold. Wiley made a final check of the vaults and the vault room to make sure they hadn't left anything incriminating. A couple of carrot sticks weren't important. They wouldn't give Kellerman much to chew on. Lillian had retrieved all her spent cartridges.

She and Miguel were waiting on the scaffold. Wiley got on. He flipped the control switch to down.

They kept their eyes on the ground.

It seemed a long trip.

There was the illusion that the ground was coming up to them.

They were ready to act as soon as they reached it.

Wiley flipped the control switch to neutral.

Lillian jumped out and stood watch with Llama ready.

Miguel tossed the parachute packs and duffel bags over the side. The parachutes weighed forty pounds each. Miguel gathered them by their harnesses and slung them over his back.

Wiley shouldered left and right the eighty pounds of emeralds in the two large duffel bags and also took up one of the smaller duffels containing twenty pounds' worth.

Lillian reached back into the scaffold to flip the control switch to up. She lugged her equipment pack and the other smaller duffel. Heavy for her, but it saved risking a second trip.

They ran for the *barrio*, didn't stop until they were well within that labyrinth. They looked back at Argenti's building. It loomed large, appeared foreboding and impregnable as ever, but they knew it was beaten. In the day's beginning light they could make out the scaffold on its climb, nearing the top. It reached the davits and, like some huge creature, nestled in above the edge of the roof.

The *barrio* was sleeping, silent except for snores, fragments of babies' cries, a radio that had been left on. Miguel led the way through the maze of shanties and soon they came out on Calle 1-S, a minor side street.

No traffic at that hour. The only moving thing was them. The beat-up panel truck Miguel had had stolen was parked where it was supposed to be. They opened the rear doors, threw in the parachutes and duffel bags.

Still one important thing to do.

They transferred some emeralds into common brown-paper shopping bags, one bag for each, and hurried back into the *barrio*. They went separate ways to cover as much of the area as possible.

They scattered emeralds along the confusing narrow paths and alleys. On the run they flung emeralds into the air by the fistfuls. The precious stones fell upon the makeshift *barrio* roofs like hail. They tossed emeralds into doorless houses, softly pelted sleeping families.

It wasn't merely a matter of distributing the wealth or repayment for such favors as fires and fireworks.

Lillian especially got carried away. She came upon an old man asleep outside with his Christmas bottle empty and one shoe on. She filled the empty shoe. Three tiny bare children, the earliest up, were allowed to help themselves from her bag as though dipping in for candy. She sowed emeralds like seeds along the cardboard sides of houses, tamped them into the dirt with her feet. She shoved them into surprise places, such as the pocket of an only pair of trousers, washed and put to dry over a window ledge.

The *barrio* was starting to stir by the time Lillian's paper bag was empty. She had no trouble finding her way back to the panel truck.

Miguel was edgily racing the engine.

Wiley was on his third cigarette.

Lillian acted out of breath and said she'd gotten lost.

28 ➤➤➤

First thing that Christmas morning Argenti phoned Lillian in Mexico City.

He had tried several calls to her over the past ten days and been told each time by her secretary that she'd given a strict do-not-disturb instruction. Ms. Holbrook was alone, mulling over a vital decision, her secretary said in a tone that insinuated reassurance.

It wasn't, of course, that Argenti was aching to speak to Lillian. Enough that he gave that impression.

He was certain, however, that she would come to the phone this morning, perhaps to give him her yes answer for Christmas. He had barraged her with gifts: a matinée-length necklace of ten-millimeter Burmese pearls from Van Cleef, a Russian lynx bedthrow, a thousand-dollar hamper of delicacies from Fortnum and Mason and another from Fauchon. A case of La Tache '61 at a hundred and fifty dollars a bottle. (Her cellar could use it, judging from the comparative *ordinaire* he'd been served the last time he was there.) A little sentimental something: one huge cabbage rose of silk for her hair, attached to the steering wheel of a fifty-thousand-dollar Lancia Stratos.

However, this morning Argenti got her secretary again and second-hand gratitude: he was so generous, the gifts were so tasteful and persuasive and, rest assured, he would be hearing from Ms. Holbrook soon.

Argenti asked to speak to Mr. Wiley.

Who?

Was Mr. Wiley there?

Silence.

Argenti said he knew Mr. Wiley was there. No need to hide the fact.

Her secretary said she believed Wiley was somewhere around. Last seen, he was brooding out at the tennis court, smashing balls at himself on the bangboard.

Argenti clicked off. He was impatient and not quite satisfied. He placed another call to Mexico City. A Conduct Section agent confirmed that neither Lillian nor Wiley had left the house since their arrival ten days previous. Twenty-four-hour surveillance had been and was still being maintained.

Argenti thought he might fly up to Mexico City tomorrow or the day after and help her make up her mind. Probably all she needed was a little romantic nudge.

He was sure of that when he found a gift from her beside his breakfast plate.

A solid-gold shoehorn from Bulgari with his first, middle and last names engraved on it. The accompanying card in her handwriting said *More and more inclined, L.*

Argenti heard the birds that had been singing all the while.

He had a light breakfast, would have a rich, filling lunch with Emanuel Diaz. Who was favored to succeed Robayo as Senator from the district of Boyacá. Robayo was stepping aside because of ill health. The Boyacá district was where the most important mines were located. A scrupulous Senator could be troublesome. Better it should be someone more typical, like Diaz: hungry and corruptible. The election was less than a month away. Argenti was quite certain he had Diaz in his pocket. Today he'd show Diaz what would be put into his.

The lunch was set for two o'clock in Argenti's office at The Concession.

Argenti arrived there an hour early.

General Botero dropped by. He kidded Argenti about their last polo match. Argenti had missed an easy beneath-the-neck shot, but his pony had kicked the ball in for the winning goal. The General said he believed Argenti had trained the pony to do it. Argenti countered by making a gift of the pony to the General, because, he said, the General hadn't scored a goal in the last nine chukkers and the pony might save him from further disgrace. The General reminded Argenti they had a match at four and left him in good humor.

Argenti called down to Conduct Section, the control room. The man on duty answered on the first ring. At Argenti's request he bypassed the timer, pushed a button on the console to electronically withdraw the steel plate that blocked the elevator shaft. He told Argenti the way was now clear.

Argenti went up.

When he stepped out of the small elevator he first noticed

the broken glass on the floor. His thought was that a flaw in the glass had caused it. He would raise hell with the . . .

Then he saw the vaults open. All three.

He rushed into the third vault, yanked open a drawer, and another drawer, and another. He ran from vault to vault, frantically pulling out drawers.

Impossible.

He clenched his eyes because they had to be lying to him.

But every drawer had been stolen clean. Not even a single stone had been dropped on the floor.

Argenti felt as though his stomach and bowels were exchanging places. He was going to either throw up or shit. Voltage was crackling back and forth between his frontal lobes.

Taking a wider stance to remain upright, he bellowed for Kellerman.

29 ➤➤➤

Kellerman got the blame.

Argenti hung it on him and Conduct Section.

Incompetent, stupid and blind, overconfident about minding the store. Argenti even suggested Conduct Section might have pulled off the robbery, but he did not go so far as to imply that Kellerman was directly involved. He had to depend on Kellerman's expertise and cunning, now more than ever.

No need to impress Kellerman with what a catastrophe this was. The Concession could not absorb such a huge loss. Most of those emeralds in inventory had already been scheduled for delivery within the next eight weeks. Even if all the mines worked triple shift round the clock for the next six months, it was doubtful the yield would be sufficient to cover those outstanding orders.

Of course, Argenti could stall the clients. They would have no recourse but to wait, inasmuch as The Concession had its monopoly. However, they would be resentful and suspicious. The Concession had already driven its per-carat price to the limit. Clients would believe the squeeze was being put on them again. It would strain relations. But The Concession could endure it.

More critical were the payoffs that were due all the way down the line. Not only those to General Botero, Ministers Vega and Arias and Senator Robayo but the lesser ones to key people on other levels, customs officials and the like. And especially the *esmeralderos* with their have-or-have-not mentalities. There would be no explaining or putting them off. It would take The Concession months to recover, to regain the confidence of the *esmeralderos*, if ever. Many of them were barely cooperative as it was, on the verge of rampage. This could snap the tie. The *esmeralderos* alone were capable of turning The Concession's operation into chaos—in a week.

Altogether those payoffs amounted to a formidable sum. To

maintain them for six months would put The Concession so deep in the red it was likely to go under.

What if the three hundred thousand carats that had been stolen were to find their way onto the market? The price per carat would dive. Clients, with little love for and no loyalty to The Concession, would jump at the opportunity to buy short. The Arabs for sure. The Middle East was one of the strongest markets for colored stones. Those Saudi and Kuwaiti oil princes could buy the lot at a bargain price and use them as party favors, inducements for arms deals, intimate and otherwise. No matter which way it went, three hundred thousand carats flooding the market would ruin it for a long time to come. On the other hand, if the thieves dribbled them out over a year or so, that might be even more harmful, certainly more painful.

The bottom line was that as a result of the robbery, The Concession, the house of sticks built on a base of corruption, had no better than a fifty-fifty chance for survival.

Kellerman assured Argenti that recovery of the inventory was imminent. Argenti believed Kellerman. Because Kellerman stood to lose over two million himself, his percentage on the emeralds that had been in the second vault. It was impossible now to keep the existence of the third vault from Kellerman. There would be no way of explaining the hundred million surplus when the emeralds were recovered. Everything would have to be put back in the same order as before the robbery. Kellerman's cooperation would be necessary.

Kellerman remained death-mask passive when told of the third vault.

Argenti didn't have to explain what purpose it served. He offered Kellerman one percent—one million—of vault number three if and when. As extra incentive, was the way Argenti put it.

Kellerman held up two fingers and, that quickly, doubled his take.

First thing, Kellerman took care of some of Argenti's dirty work. He met with General Botero, Minister Vega, Minister Arias and Senator Robayo. They were stunned at the bad news. And disgruntled. They were not used to losses.

It was agreed in that meeting the local police would not be called in, nor would the press. The robbery was to be kept as confidential as possible, and by no means was the true extent of the loss to be revealed. Conduct Section with its international network of informants, agents and people of various specialties on the shady side was best geared to handle the problem. The confidential help of the army and army intelligence, F-2, would be appreciated, naturally.

General Botero pledged it.

Likewise any assistance from the D.A.S., the Departamento Administrativo de Seguridad.

Minister of Defense Arias would see to that.

It was decided a reward would be set, word would be leaked out and around. For information leading to apprehension of the thieves (find them, find the emeralds), the offer would be $250,000. Certainly adequate in the likeliest circles, where men often valued others' lives at $249,000 less—if that much. Still, the extent of the robbery would not be revealed. Only that there had been a robbery of sorts and that an object lesson was due those who had defied The Concession.

Botero, Vega, Arias and Robayo left the meeting still downcast, grumbling, but also indignant now and eager to do their part to bring about justice. Getting them on that side of the crisis was the true purpose of the meeting. A holding action. Maybe it would hold long enough.

Kellerman set about to determine the methods of the robbery. He realized, of course, that the *barrio* fires and the ensuing disorder had not been coincidental. He reviewed the entries in the log books, interrogated the men who had been on duty. They related exactly what they had witnessed on the radar screen and the decibel indicator of the listening alarm. It was more or less understood that they shouldn't mention having called Kellerman those times when the listening alarm was set off, and, in turn, he wouldn't admonish them.

Kellerman went to the roof.

There were tracks in the gritty dust. Flat-soled shoes. From the different sizes he knew three persons had taken part. One set of tracks was considerably smaller than the others. Those of a boy or, possibly, a woman.

Other impressions indicated something expansive, like a fabric, had lain upon the roof, swept across the roof in places. From those he deduced how the thieves had gotten up there— or down, to be more exact.

It was a lead. At least a sniff. They had to be either very experienced amateurs or former paratroopers.

The window-washing apparatus. Its motor was still on. He

rode the scaffold down and stopped at the glassless window of the vault room. He guessed a low-gauge shotgun had been used to blow the pane out.

Conduct Section specialists had already dusted for fingerprints throughout the vault room and vaults one and two. The only prints that came up were Argenti's. Vault number three was closed. Argenti had had the presence of mind to close it right after the initial shock.

Kellerman examined the pinpoint openings in the wall where Argenti had kept his private skim. He'd noticed them before, but they were worth two million now. The robbery could be his good fortune.

He found no clues in the vaults or the vault room, no signs of the vaults being forced. How the thieves had managed the latter, Kellerman couldn't even speculate. That was one of the few things Argenti had been able to keep from him—the combination.

He rode the elevator down to Argenti's floor, took the other one down to his own office on thirty-three. He phoned Argenti, who sounded surprisingly calm. To keep Argenti out of the way, Kellerman said he already had a significant lead and he promised to have much more within forty-eight hours. Insinuated by that time the emeralds would be recovered and everything would be business as usual. Argenti pressed for details, but Kellerman got away with leaving it vague.

He set his organization in full motion. Personally placed calls to the key positions in his network. When he was through, no one could make a move with those emeralds anywhere in the world without his knowing it inside of ten minutes.

This was going to be too easy, he thought.

By nine o'clock the following day, Kellerman had ten arrests. Six of those arrested were sidewalk dealers along Calle 14 who had three times more stones than normal in their possession. The others arrested were poor, frightened *hombres* looking to sell a few stones of fine quality for whatever they could get. After brief, intense questioning, it was obvious they knew about as much about where the emeralds had come from as they did their value.

By noon a hundred and fifty people had been picked up and brought in. By late afternoon over three hundred.

Some were sidewalk dealers.

The rest had one puzzling thing in common. They were *campesinos* who lived in the *barrio*.

The interrogation of Geraldo Morales was typical.

"How old are you?"

"They say seventy-one."

"Where did you get these emeralds?"

"I did not steal them."

"Where did you get them, old man?"

"I found them."

"Where?"

"I was sleeping."

"You found them in your sleep?"

"No. I found them in my shoe."

"How do you think they got there?"

"I ask myself the same question."

"Who put them there?"

"I believe God."

That first day nearly ten thousand carats were recovered. Certainly they were emeralds from the robbery, but it was frustrating to have so many suspects who were so obviously unqualified. Not for a minute did Kellerman believe any of those people capable of engineering such an intricate theft, and he doubted they knew any more than they were telling. He didn't even bother to hold them.

Reflecting on that first day's efforts, Kellerman came to the conclusion that the thieves had salted the market, somehow put a sizeable amount of stones into circulation as a distraction, to cover up their own activity. It was damn clever. He was sure now he was dealing with hard, extremely experienced professionals.

The following day, from the earliest hour, Calle 14 was a scurry of buying and selling. The sidewalk dealers were so numerous and eager to get in on the good thing they overran the sidewalks and the street. It got so that the section between Carrera 5 and Carrera 7 had to be blocked off by the traffic police. The price per carat for all classifications of emeralds, from ordinary to fine, had dropped to half and would probably go lower. Ten thousand carats changed hands between ten o'clock and noon.

By day's end five hundred arrests had been made. Kellerman had decided not to bother with the sidewalk dealers. Otherwise trading would go underground and the chance of turning up a lead would be that much hindered.

Conduct Section didn't let up on their interrogations. It was a laborious task, trying to get anything out of *los pobres*, the poor. There was still that common factor. The *barrio*.

At quarter to four one of the interrogators was presented with an incongruity.

"Where did you get these emeralds?"

"I found them."

"Where?"

"In the *barrio*."

To that point nothing.

"How long have you been in Colombia?"

"Three weeks."

"Your passport, please."

The black face in the photograph matched the black face across the desk.

"Did you serve in the military in Cuba?"

"Is that a pertinent question?"

"It is a question."

"I served in the military."

"Perhaps you are still in the military?"

"Perhaps." The Cuban bristled and then tried to smile his way out of it.

"Have you ever used a parachute?"

"No."

"You realize, of course, we know how it was done. Before long we will have those involved."

The interrogator read the Cuban's eyes carefully.

"The first we bring in will be the lucky one," the interrogator said.

"Why lucky?"

"He will be able to give testimony in exchange for exoneration. And then there is also the reward, a quarter of a million."

"I am not interested in money."

The interrogator called Kellerman.

The Cuban was taken to a different room.

Relief showed on Kellerman's face the moment he saw the Cuban. He would take over the questioning, do something to earn his keep.

It was as though Kellerman had an anatomical chart in his head. The nervous system. He seemed to know precisely where the ganglions crowded. The zones for pleasure, of course, corresponded with the zones for pain. Usually he took more time, made use of the victim's anticipation, fear that eventually he would get to the genitals. Good painmaking was much like good lovemaking in that respect.

The Cuban did not break easily. An average man would have lasted an hour at most. The Cuban broke at half past seven that night, after nearly three hours.

But then he told it all.

Kellerman did not let on that he knew any of those the Cuban named and described. When he learned Wiley and Lillian were involved, he was momentarily surprised. That told him even more than what he was getting from the Cuban. Kellerman was not interested in motives, although he wondered how Argenti would react when he learned he'd been so neatly used. It was the worst sort of insult.

The Cuban revealed the address of the Kennedy City house where the others, and the emeralds, had been since the robbery.

He asked for a drink of water and also wanted to know about the reward.

Kellerman told one of his men to see that the Cuban got his reward. In Barbosa.

Twenty minutes later twelve Conduct Section agents and twenty-five army troops were in Kennedy City. Carrera 74 and the other streets in the vicinity of the house were blocked off by the troops. The agents, armed with automatic rifles, took up surrounding positions.

There were lights on; however, the windows of the house had been sprayed with black paint, so there was no way to see in. There was the smell of something cooking. Whoever was inside could not possibly escape.

The agents moved in, cautiously.

On signal they broke simultaneously through the front and back doors and every window.

They found three parachutes and some other equipment, several photographs of Argenti. And a huge pot of zuki beans and rice close to scorching on the stove.

30 ⋙

 At that moment Wiley and Lillian were in the fifth
car from the engine on a train. Headed north for Cartagena, the
old Colombian port on the Caribbean.
 They were in second class. In first or third they would have
been too obvious. Also, they had taken seats apart from one
another. From where Wiley sat he could see only the back top
of Lillian's head. She was reading a paperback edition of
Confessions by Jean Jacques Rousseau. Every so often, in a
natural, passive manner, she glanced around and caught on
Wiley's eyes, just the briefest sort of snags, but he believed it
said a lot. Wiley wondered on what page she would desert
Rousseau. He bet himself the forty-some thousand dollars he
had in his socks that it would be within ten, one way or the
other, from page 178. It was one of those things about her that
he would have to learn to live with.
 At least, he thought, Bogotá was behind them. They were on
the way, *their* way, at last, he felt. He wouldn't worry that they
hadn't settled on an eventual destination. There hadn't been
time to discuss that. It was just good to be going with her.
 The day before yesterday, after the robbery, they had gone
to the Kennedy City house. A sheet was spread on the floor and
the emeralds were dumped on it.
 A pile about two feet high.
 They were all tired but too wound up to sleep. Besides it was
impossible to be indifferent to $300 million dollars. The
Cubans, although not in as much of a state of euphoria, joined
in the high of it. One of them plopped himself down right on
the precious heap and beamed as he sank into it. Miguel put a
comradely arm around Wiley's shoulder and they exchanged
congratulations. Lillian sat by the edge and chose some emeralds, about twenty, that she intended to have made into marbles. She might as well have been picking through pebbles on a
beach. Wiley kneeled beside the pile and cupped up a handful,

let them drop through his fingers. He imagined a raving Argenti, furious to the foaming point, literally epileptic, throwing a fit, with Kellerman grabbing his tongue to prevent him from choking to death. Let go, Kellerman.

Finally, the flush of success subsided enough for Wiley and Lillian to catch up on their sleep.

The next day Miguel let them in on what he had planned, what the money from the sale of the emeralds would make possible.

The *incident* he had frequently mentioned.

It involved Panama.

The entire territory of Panama had once belonged to Colombia.

That fact, Wiley recalled, had been an underplayed sidelight in the news during the recent controversial treaty negotiations between the United States and Panama.

Miguel elaborated, knew his side of the story by heart: Through a deal with the Colombian government, a French company began digging a canal in Panama in 1881. The company failed, went bankrupt. The United States snatched up the French equipment and other assets at a good price and made its own treaty for a canal with Colombia. Before the ink on that treaty was barely dry, the United States started stirring up a revolution among the Panamanians. It gave encouragement, guns and money. Colombia sent troops to Panama. The United States countered with sympathy, a cruiser and a force of marines. Colombia had to back off. No contest.

Thus, the United States had a due bill from the new Republic of Panama.

Right away it got what it was after: the Canal Zone, a ten-mile-wide strip from Atlantic to Pacific that cut Panama in two. Ten million cash and a quarter million a year went to Panama. The United States got control of the Canal Zone forever. Not for just a hundred or even five hundred years but *in perpetuity*, as the agreement said. Colombia got a twenty-five-million token payment and a spit in the eye for its loss. The Colombian government didn't formally recognize Panama or the deal till twenty years later, which was sort of like being indignant after being sodomized. Anyway, the left side of Colombian politics never swallowed it, and it was still the surest way to whip up anti-American enthusiasm.

That was why Panama was perfect for an incident, Miguel said.

The Panama Canal is forty-two miles long. In most places it is five hundred feet wide.

It takes about eight to nine hours for a ship to pass through. The average rate of traffic is thirty-five ships a day, mostly in the twenty- to forty-thousand-ton class. It cannot handle a ship exceeding sixty thousand tons.

Usually, there is a back-up of ships waiting to go through the Canal. They tie up or anchor at Colón on the Atlantic end. And at Panama City on the Pacific end. The ships in holding positions enter the Canal according to the order assigned them in advance by the chief pilot of the Canal Zone Company.

Altogether the Canal has twelve locks. Six going east, six going west. There are three sets of locks at Gatun, one set at Pedro Miguel and two sets at Miraflores.

Miguel intended to sabotage them.

All twelve locks.

In effect, wipe out the entire Canal.

And Wiley would help.

Wiley, with his knowledge of electronics, would play a vital part. They had already been through much together; they would go on to share this greater glory, Miguel said.

The Canal was vulnerable.

Despite the fifteen thousand troops that guarded it.

SOUTHCOM, the U.S. Armed Forces Southern Command, had fourteen bases in the Zone. Army, navy, air force. There were underground tunnels, gun and missile emplacements, landing fields and the most sophisticated security and attack warning devices. The CIA also had a large and very active base in the Canal Zone.

No matter. The Canal was vulnerable.

It would be relatively easy to buy information from someone in the Chief Pilot's Office. Especially when the information would seem innocuous. All that would have to be known in advance was what ships in what order were scheduled to pass through the Canal on a given day.

From that, Miguel said, they would be able to work out a timetable. There was a required rate of speed at which ships traveled from one set of locks to another, and routinely, it took a ship thirty-eight minutes to make its way through a lock. Thus, they would be able to determine ahead of time precisely which ships would be in which locks at a certain moment. Twelve ships in the twelve locks. Six headed for the Pacific, six bound for the Atlantic.

Before those particular ships entered the Canal, while they were still in holding position, they would be armed. Packs of C-6 plastic explosives, at least twenty pounds to the pack, would be attached magnetically to their hulls—on each side of their bows, and starboard and port of their sterns. Below the waterline. That would be accomplished at night by an underwater team. Not a tough task, really. The divers would only have to swim around the ships and plunk the explosives in place. Two men would be able to arm a ship in a matter of minutes.

Each of the explosive packs would contain a detonator. Remote controlled.

The bursting charge and the heaving force of that much C-6 would be extremely powerful. For example, the explosive force of a single pack would be enough to blow a railway locomotive twenty feet in the air and probably to pieces.

The master remote control would be situated at some high vantage point, such as on a mountainside overlooking the Canal near the town of Nuevo Emperador.

At the moment when all twelve ships were in the locks, the remote-control button would be pressed. (Perhaps Wiley would have the honor.)

All forty-eight packs of C-6 would explode.

Some of the ships would have their bows close to the gates of locks that were about to open for them. Others would have their sterns just beyond gates they had passed. The gates, although five feet thick, would be blasted apart. They were old, had been in use for nearly seventy years. They would be torn from their hinges as though they were ordinary doors.

Possibly the dam at Gatun Lake could also be blown. A single well-placed pack of C-6 would do it. That would flood the lower locks. Millions of tons of water would crush all the United States installations. The 163-square-mile lake would drain, leaving ships high and dry. The channel of the Canal would have hardly enough water left in it for a rowboat.

The Canal would be rendered useless. Perhaps it would never be restored.

A retributive day for imperialism.

A shining one for Colombia.

Appropriate that emeralds from Colombia's own ground should make it possible.

It was evident Miguel had done his homework on Panama.

Wiley's first question concerned the crews on the explosive-bearing ships, their welfare.

Miguel said three thousand had been killed in Pearl Harbor. He wanted a positive reaction, approval from Wiley and Lillian. Didn't Wiley believe they could pull it off?

Wiley had to say yes.

What about the electronic requirements? Were they feasible?

No problem, Wiley thought it best to admit. He made up for his lack of enthusiasm by nodding thoughtfully and appearing intensely intrigued.

Lillian tried to seem genuinely fascinated.

Miguel left early the next morning for Barranquilla, where he would meet a representative of someone who might purchase as many as a hundred thousand carats. The buyer was from Japan. Miguel would make the price irresistible. He took along an honest sample of stones.

Wiley and Lillian got up at ten. Neither had slept well. Both had avoided discussing Miguel's proposed incident.

Lillian finally brought it up, asked offhandedly if it really, honestly, no shit, could be done.

Wiley told her, no shit, it could.

She said it seemed farfetched.

He said he wished it was, but that anyone who wanted to do it and had the financial wherewithal could damn well do it.

She looked off and said Miguel meant well.

Then why didn't he do something sane, like send out two or three hundred letter bombs, Wiley said.

He just might.

Wiley was for their leaving that moment.

Lillian didn't think that would solve anything.

With the emeralds, Wiley added.

No comment from Lillian.

Was she playing with the idea of going ahead with Miguel and his scheme? Did she have that much of a hate-on for the United States?

It wasn't that and had never been that, she said.

What to hell, then, was it?

She was no deserter. She remembered when everyone had

run out on her, left her holding the cause. The dreadful disillu-sionment, how awfully alone she had felt.

This was different.

It was, wasn't it?

Wiley reassured her it was only about ten percent similar.

She was concerned about what would happen to Miguel.

More to the point, what would happen to all those men and families in the Canal Zone.

She knew, of course, and admitted, that Wiley was right. To stop Miguel they really would have to take the emeralds, wouldn't they?

Yes.

She remarked knowingly how inconvenient and convenient that was.

Wiley told her it was the only way, that they had done it and now would have to undo it.

They went out to the same military-surplus store as before. Bought two metal footlockers, four hefty padlocks and fifty bath towels. Returned to the house to pack.

The Cubans were off somewhere, hadn't been around all day.

Lillian spread a towel in the bottom of one of the footlockers. Wiley layered it with emeralds, which another towel covered for another layer of emeralds.

They got them all padlocked in, the three hundred million dollars' worth.

And because of the towels there was hardly a rattle.

They loaded the footlockers into the rented car, drove to find a public phone and a directory for the city of Cartagena.

The third call Wiley made to Cartagena was to a novelty shop on Calle de Quero. A woman answered and, when Wiley inquired, said she was the owner, Señora Silva.

Wiley told Señora Silva his name was Bryan Beckley. He represented a company in the United States that offered some very novel items. He was planning to be in Cartagena soon, perhaps by the end of the week. He would like to visit the señora's shop and show her his line.

He pulled out all stops, called on his full reserve of charm. Had to be sure, with so much at stake.

The señora got it. Her voice fluttered, had a little more lilt to it when she said she would be glad to see what Señora Beckley had to offer.

Wiley asked if by chance Señor Silva would be there?

Only if by chance he could rise from the grave, the señora said lightly.

Wiley told her that in that case he had some very entertaining items that might interest her. The sort of things available only in places such as Denmark.

Could he not be there before the end of the week? she wanted to know.

He was afraid not. But might he ask a favor? He would like to send his trunks on ahead. Two of them. Perhaps she would keep them for him until he arrived.

She'd be glad to.

Hasta luego.

Wiley and Lillian went straight to the *estación de ferrocarriles* (literally, the station of iron rails). They shipped the two lockers by freight. The next train to Cartagena was about to leave on track seven.

They just made it.

Now they had been on it for almost four hours. It was eight o'clock, getting to be night outside.

The train passed over the Magdalena River and stopped in the town of El Dorado.

Wiley couldn't see even the top of Lillian's head at that moment. She was scrunched down, perhaps napping. He recalled the trivial premise that the constant motion and erratic vibrations of trains, motorcycles and such made women feel sexually aroused. Maybe, but if so, it was another of their libidinal advantages, he thought. All it was doing for him was making his coccyx sore.

Some vendors came aboard at El Dorado.

Lillian sat up and bought two cheese tamales, a Roman Cola and a banana.

When the vendor got to Wiley, he bought a meat pie, a sticky chocolate-filled *pastelito* and a lemon drink. Everything except the drink tasted better than he expected, probably because all he'd had that day was a cup of yesterday's coffee and half a bowl of the perpetual zuki beans and rice.

From another vendor he bought a tiny cross, which he held to his eye to see the image of the Virgin through a peephole. Anything to pass the time.

He gazed out. The train was now following the course of the Magdalena, a wide river with some flecks of orange on its far side where it was catching the last of the sun.

He wished it was a nice normal trip and they were the *norteamericano* tourists they were pretending to be. Instead, they were on the run. All of Miguel's lefties would be after them now. And also, The Concession, although it probably didn't know yet who to look for and might not ever. Kellerman would have his Conduct Section men on the move. And then there was General Botero and the entire Colombian army. For the moment, Miguel and his comrades were the worry. They could be anywhere and they knew who to look for.

It was enough to make Wiley slouch, turn toward the window, put all his weight on the right side of his rump and tuck his head down behind his shoulder.

Shortly before midnight the train reached Puerto Berrío. As it pulled in Wiley noticed a group of soldiers outside the station. A search party? Maybe he was being paranoid. Anyway, the army wouldn't be searching for them. Maybe they were looking for deserters or poachers or . . .

Wiley got up and went down the aisle. On the way he poked Lillian's shoulder emphatically.

She joined him forward between cars.

The soldiers were starting their search back a ways, about three cars.

Wiley opened the train door on the side away from the station. He jumped down to the roadbed, turned to help Lillian, but she was already in midair, landed beside him. He reached back up and shut the door. It was dark on that side. They paused there to decide which was the best direction to run. The soldiers were going through every car. Wiley and Lillian heard them on the platform talking to one of the conductors, asking about two *norteamericanos*, a man and woman. The conductor said there were several *norteamericanos* aboard but not a man and woman together.

No doubt now who they were looking for, Wiley thought. The army? That meant General Botero, and that meant Kellerman and Argenti and everyone else was on their ass for the robbery. How had they found out? He must have overlooked something.

They hurried across two sets of tracks to a wire fence and

along the fence until they came to an opening. Then they were on a side street of the town.

All the streets of Puerto Berrío were like side streets. Unlighted except for a couple of cantinas.

Wiley and Lillian heard the train pull out. Perhaps the soldiers had questioned other second-class passengers who knew two *norteamericanos* had been aboard. The soldiers might search the town.

Wiley and Lillian made their way through the town and then cut back across the railroad tracks to the Magdalena. There was a bridge. Making sure the way was clear, they went across.

On the other side of the river was Puerto Olaya, a different town of the same sort. From the bridge they had noticed barges tied up along the bank. They went around and down to the riverside.

Besides the barges there were three tuglike boats. One of the boats had a light on. Wiley and Lillian went aboard. The cabin door was open. In the cabin in a bunk was a boy of about sixteen. He was reading by the light of an oil lamp. Actually he was looking at pictures in an overhandled eight-year-old copy of *Playboy*.

They had caught him at a secret moment, and he was embarrassed.

Wiley asked for the captain, owner or whatever.

The boy said he was all those.

Wiley had no immediate choice but to believe him, asked, was he going down river to the Caribbean?

In the morning.

Would he take them as passengers?

It was not a usual request, especially from *norteamericanos*.

Lillian explained they had stepped off the train for a moment at Puerto Berrío and it had left them stranded. They would pay for their passage, of course.

The boy liked the look of Lillian, and he didn't try to hide it. How much would they pay?

Wiley answered fifty dollars at the same time Lillian said a hundred.

The boy accepted Lillian's offer by introducing himself: Javier Bravo.

31 ➤➤➤

The Magdalena was wide but difficult to navigate. Many shallows and sandbars, and the water entertained itself often with devilish little whirlpools. White herons in the jungle trees along the shore were flushed and remained unsettled till the boat went by. There were sudden, rather teasing rainstorms, a great deal of intense lightning but, strangely, no thunder.

Any doubts Wiley had about Javier Bravo's qualifications as captain were put to rest the first morning. The sixteen-year-old took the river as though it were a boy's everyday path. Anticipated the way it ran, accepted its hazards and noted its changes. He stood at the wheel wearing only a pair of khaki-colored cotton trousers and a visored cap that had once been white. The cap was too large for him, but he'd put paper inside the inner band to make it fit. It appeared as though it was always about to fall over his eyes.

Javier had never been to school. The river and the boat were all he was supposed to learn. His father had fallen overboard a year ago on a trip upstream. The water took his father, but Javier held no bad feelings for the river. Nor did he completely believe when the priest told him it was God's will. If anything, it was his father's. Javier went to church only if he happened to be in a port on Sunday and also if on that Sunday it wasn't raining or too hot or he didn't sleep late.

On this trip Javier's boat was pulling eight barges. Four loaded with rice, two with iron ore, two with coffee. Rather unconsciously Javier would glance back to see that all was well with the barges. They were linked together closely, and it was possible to climb from the boat to the first barge and then from barge to barge.

The first night they moored in La Gloria.

Javier gave up his bunk to his passengers.

Wiley and Lillian felt safe and slept well.

On the third night they reached Barranquilla, where the river contributed to the Caribbean. They tied up at one of the minor docks. Wiley gave Javier an extra hundred in his handshake for being such a good captain. Lillian gave him a hug and a kiss between the eyes. They went ashore, asked the first man they saw in a car if he'd drive them to Cartagena. It was about seventy miles west on the coast. They told the man they'd pay five dollars a mile. He told them he would drive to Chicago at that rate.

They arrived in Cartagena at eleven that night. There were many large luxurious hotels, such as the Caribe. They were tempted, could use a little first class for a change. But they couldn't risk it. They settled for a front room on the second floor of a private house that took in tourists. It was on Calle Bonda, practically in the heart of the old walled city.

Across the street from the tourist house was a combination *taverna-lonchería* called El Globo—The Balloon. While Lillian prepared for bed (a wash basin in the corner but the toilet down the hall) Wiley went across the street to El Globo for two fried-egg sandwiches and four bottles of beer, a local beer called Poker.

When he returned to the room, Lillian was on the floor, the bedspread under her, her feet propped on the bed. She sat up for the food. Wiley undressed. Last off were his socks. He took the banded wads of hundreds from them. The money had made an impression on his lower legs. And it was a relief to have that matched pair of brilliant-cut twenty-carat emeralds out from between his big and second toes. He placed the money and the two emeralds on the night stand and sat on the spread opposite Lillian.

A paragraphic moment. His point of view toward her shifted. He was able to see her more as a person than as his love object. He contemplated her—her, intent on the sandwich and the beer. It was strange that she should need to eat and drink. He wondered what her hunger and thirst felt like. There was a childishness to her face, scrubbed honest, an innocence to her arms and shoulders and the recesses of her collarbones. In their time how many different ways would he see her?

Her breasts brought him back to his usual perspective. He leaned forward and kissed one of them and promised, without saying, that after his sandwich and beer he wouldn't slight the other.

Early the next day they went shopping for a boat.

The two brokers they went to offered boats that were too small for their needs or too large and attention-getting.

They took off on their own, walked along the waterfront of the bay, the Bahia de las Animas. Tied up there were boats of all sizes and sorts. The first likely looking one they came to, Lillian went right aboard. Wiley waited for her to get chucked off. When she didn't, he went after her.

A stocky, gray-haired man in floral-patterned bathing trunks was hosing down the deck.

"Your boat?" Lillian asked.

"Yes." His inflection said why.

"Want to sell her?"

"Not really." The owner was English. He had the type of fair English complexion that couldn't take much sun, and yet he apparently enjoyed few things more than the feel of the sun on him. He was more red than tanned. The bridge and tip of his nose were peeling.

"For seventy thousand?" Lillian asked.

"May I offer you some tea, a gin and tonic or something?"

"Tea will do nicely," Lillian said.

They followed the owner below. He had the tea kettle on. He talked about how fond he was of the boat and how much he would regret ever having to part with her.

Wiley saw through all that, thought they'd probably have to fight their way off if they withdrew the offer.

He was right. The Englishman was three payments behind and had no outlook for a charter. Seventy thousand was about fifteen to twenty more than the boat was worth.

The Englishman showed them around.

It was a custom-built forty-five footer. A cross between a trawler and a sportfisherman. It had the lines of a trawler and sat in the water like a trawler, but it was equipped for deep-sea fishing. Among other things, it had a live-bait hold in the rear deck.

"When would you want to take her over?" the Englishman asked.

"Immediately."

The Englishman got out the papers.

Wiley and Lillian went, one after the other, into the head and came out with the money.

The Englishman became short of breath when he realized they intended to pay cash.

Fifty-five thousand now. The balance tomorrow.

The Englishman said that gave him time to get his gear together and have a farewell night with the vessel he loved.

When they were ashore Lillian told Wiley, "See? Intuition."

Wiley let her take the credit. But he wondered if they'd ever not have to overpay for things. It was a way of life, he supposed, but it had its psychological drawbacks.

They used a public phone near the Cartagena branch of First National City Bank. Lillian put in a call to Marianna in Mexico City.

Marianna answered: "Ms. Holbrook's residence."

Lillian hung up. That wasn't how Marianna normally answered the phone. In fact, she'd told Marianna that was precisely how she didn't want her to answer. It had to be Marianna's way of warning her that someone was there, listening. Conduct Section agents, no doubt.

Fortunately, Lillian hadn't said a word. No way they could know it had been her.

She phoned Benjamin Corey in New York, the chairman of her board. He would cable $25,000 at once to First National City Bank in Cartagena, Colombia, payable upon demand to Marianna McLean (the name on Lillian's passport). The money would be there by tomorrow noon at the latest, Corey promised.

Almost as easy as ordering a pizza, Wiley thought.

He was up first the next morning.

Dressed and went across the street to El Globo for a coffee and roll.

He sat at a table near the door, his back to the street. The place was crowded. He got only a glimpse of the man in a booth at the rear of the room. And the man got only a glimpse of him before other customers blocked the view. But Wiley thought surely he'd been recognized by Carlos Johnson.

The pilot, parachute instructor, part-time comrade of Miguel.

Wiley got up, hurried out and across the street and into the tourist house. He peeked back, and after five minutes, when Carlos didn't come out, he decided that perhaps Carlos hadn't recognized him after all.

But it was too close for comfort.

Carlos recognized Wiley right off.

He stood up on the booth seat to see Wiley rush out, across the way and into the tourist house.

The man having coffee with Carlos was a comrade named Luis Hoyos. A full-time lefty recently arrived from Guatemala. His notoriety as an agitator had preceded him. He had already been welcomed into the periphery of the Colombian left wing, and it was only a matter of time before the inner circle accepted him.

Carlos told Hoyos, "I just saw the fucking guy."

"Who?"

"The one who ran with the emeralds. The *norteamericano*. He is in the house across the street."

"Are you sure?"

Carlos went into the bar side of the place. There was a telephone. He called Miguel.

Miguel was staying in a safe house in an outlying poor section of Cartagena. His priority now was to get back the emeralds and punish the two traitors. He had made the deal to sell a hundred thousand carats in two equal lots. The transaction would have taken place there in Cartagena. He figured Wiley and Lillian would try to get out of the country from one of the Caribbean ports. He had comrades on the lookout also in Barranquilla, Santa Marta and even the smaller coastal towns. Every commercial hotel was covered and, of course, every airport.

Carlos told him where and when.

Miguel was on the way.

Carlos joined comrade Luis Hoyos at the bar.

They had a whiskey with their coffee.

Hoyos said he had to phone a girl.

He went to the phone in the back and called F-2. Army intelligence.

Hoyos was an infiltrator.

Ten minutes later a gray sedan came down Calle Bonda and pulled up in front of the tourist house.

Miguel and three comrades, including the remaining Cuban.

They were out on the walk, about to enter the tourist house, when two other cars pulled up.

Four F-2 agents and five from Conduct Section.

They spotted Miguel immediately. His was the face they knew and had been looking for.

Miguel was so intent on his own purpose that he wasn't as alert as usual.

Three bullets hit him almost simultaneously. Two in the chest, one in the head. He was spun around and slammed down dead on the veranda of the tourist house.

The Cuban threw up his hands.

Which made it that much easier for a Conduct Section agent to kill him.

The other two comrades had no more of a chance. Were caught in the open. They managed to get off only a couple of shots.

The F-2 and Conduct Section agents jumped over the bodies and rushed into the house.

In the upper front room they found an empty bed and a full ashtray.

Wiley and Lillian had found a back way out.

They separated.

Lillian went to the bank.

Wiley went to the novelty shop.

The Señora Silva imagined by Wiley from their phone conversation was a hundred-and-fifty-pound forty-five-year-old with a pigeon breast, a wartish mole or two someplace around her mouth and too much black overpunished hair. Otherwise she wouldn't have been so evidently receptive, he reasoned.

The Señora Silva he found at the novelty shop on Calle de Quero was a slender twenty-five-year-old, an extremely attractive, neatly cut blonde with large brown assertive eyes.

From the way she looked at Wiley, he was also more than she had expected. She offered coffee, led him to the back room.

He saw his two footlockers standing on end in one corner. When asked, he told Señora Silva (call her Elena) that he was staying at the Caribe. She told him he should have come there directly, intimated she would have suggested a place more accommodating.

The store was not small, at least not a hole in the wall, but like most novelty shops, it was overstocked. Wiley thought Elena probably got to meet a great many salesmen. Wasn't a novelty something new and different?

Browsers entered the store, required attention. Wiley told Elena he had appointments, would take his samples and return shortly. She said she would close early, gave Wiley's hand a squeeze. She had a very communicative, purely feminine touch.

Wiley carried the footlockers out to the street. A taxi took them and him to the waterfront, to the boat. The Englishman had just departed. Everything was in order, the transfer-of-ownership papers signed and witnessed. Lillian was on the bridge at the wheel. She had the engines running.

"What kept you?" she asked, meaning, who?

"I got waylaid."

"I thought as much." She revved the engine so as not to hear anything else he had to say.

He unhitched the bow and stern lines, had to jump aboard because Lillian backed the boat so quickly from its slip. Maneuvered it well out into the Bahía de las Animas and then, despite the urgency, at a safe, inconspicuous speed down the bay and out through the mouth of the breakwater.

In ten minutes the northern coast of South America was only a far-off gray strip between the sea and the sky. It wouldn't be a short trip. They would have to make stops for fuel and supplies.

The two footlockers were sitting on deck. Wiley could store them below just as they were, but he had thought of a better safe place to hide the emeralds for the time being.

The live-bait well was situated on the afterdeck. It extended about a foot and a half above deck level and was recessed about four feet below. It measured about four by five, which made it considerably larger than usual. Deep-sea fishermen kept small fish alive in such wells, to be used as bait. But this one was large enough to bring home fresh a fair-size catch of red snappers or blues.

Wiley removed the cover from the live-bait well. It was clean inside, enameled high-gloss white. Nearly two thirds filled with seawater, as it should have been.

He unlocked the footlockers and, layer by layer, dropped the emeralds into the well. They reflected and gave the water an ideal green hue. That was it. The water seemed green, not the stones in the bottom. Same premise as turquoise-looking water in a turquoise-painted swimming pool. Unless someone looked closely, the stones, except for their texture, might go unnoticed.

Wiley replaced the well cover and stored the footlockers below. He was glad he'd decided to put the emeralds in the well, felt easier for it.

Lillian had the boat on a course due north, cruising at ten knots. First stop would be Haiti. Then they would island-hop to the Bahamas and on to Fort Lauderdale.

Wiley took over so Lillian could go down to the galley to fix something to eat. "Keep her steady as she goes," Lillian told him.

He kissed her instead of saying aye-aye.

He acquainted himself with the instruments. The electronic compass, depth sounder and speedometer. And the switches, all clearly labeled, that controlled the various automatic systems throughout the boat. The fuel indicator said *full*. The sea ahead was vacant, its surface not unruly but neat and repetitive, dabbed with small waves like a pointillist painting. One scanty streak of cloud in the sky, nothing in front of the sun.

Lovely day.

They'd gotten away—away with it.

Some people he knew were miserable, but he was feeling fine enough to sing, full out, the oldie:

> *Just a gigolo,*
> *Everywhere I go,*
> *People know the part I'm playing.*
> *Paid for every dance,*
> *Selling each romance,*
> *Every night some heart betraying . . .*

Keeping only a finger on the wheel, he leaned out and sang louder, down to the galley.

A sharp but distant *boomph* was what he heard first.

Then a sibilant sound of air being cut.

An explosion geysered the sea about two hundred feet ahead, a few degrees to port.

Wiley grabbed up a pair of binoculars, sighted the ship. About two miles off the starboard beam, bearing directly at them. It was war gray, had the huge, condensed numeral *18* on each side of its bow. Wiley could make out the horizontal yellow, blue and red of the Colombian flag and the sailors in white manning its forward 3.50-inch gun.

Another sharp report like a command.

This time the shell exploded so close it drenched the boat with spray.

Wiley put the engine in neutral.

Lillian hurried to the bridge. "We're past the ten-mile limit. They can't do anything."

Wiley took off his shoes and socks and removed the matched pair of emeralds. If he was searched there would be no acceptable explanation for having forty carats between his toes. He handed the emeralds to Lillian and told her to get rid of them.

The Colombian warship was closing in now, less than a half mile off and coming full speed. Wiley could see its bow splitting the water. It was a frigate. About three hundred feet long, not quite as fast or heavily armed as a destroyer. It continued to bear down, looked as though it intended to ram. But when it was about two hundred feet off it bore hard to port, reduced its engines, reversed them and held parallel with the trawler.

The power launch was lowered over the side of the frigate. Six crewmen and an officer in it. The launch came alongside the trawler. The officer and five of the men came aboard. The men had automatic rifles, the officer a sidearm.

Immediately two of the crewmen patted Wiley and Lillian's bodies for weapons. They were quick and efficient about it.

The officer didn't introduce himself. He was a two-striper. He demanded their passports.

Lillian got them, handed them over.

The officer put on a pair of glasses, was a little self-conscious about needing them. He studied first one passport and then the other, held them up to compare the photographs with the faces of Wiley and Lillian, whose expressions were now equally grim. He slid the passports into his jacket pocket.

He dropped his chin, shifted his glasses down his nose to look over them at Wiley. He looked hard at Wiley, a sort of diagnostic stare, and then at Lillian in the same manner. He stepped closer, shoved his glasses up into usable position and was face to face with Wiley. So close Wiley could feel the officer's breath.

The officer cocked his head, seemed to be examining Wiley's nostrils. He grunted rather approvingly and made the same close inspection of Lillian.

He asked to see the boat's papers, ownership and registry. When he had looked those over he said, "You purchased this boat today."

"This morning," Wiley said.

The officer didn't ask why. It seemed he knew. With a nearly imperceptible nod he ordered the boat searched.

The crewmen went to it. Below decks first.

Wiley scratched at his underarm, which was wet. He imagined himself and Lillian naked, being lifted over that chain-link fence in Barbosa, being thrown, landing stomach down over the back of one of the hogs, the first sensation of the bristly hairs like needles. Flailing, falling between hogs to the ground, cloven hoofs slipping around, cutting into them. The five-hundred-pounders snorting, crushing, competing to get at them, over them, pinning them with their weight, their snouts wet and hot, and the first bite, like some part of his body being caught in the teeth of gears. The chewing into him, the crunching all the way to his bones. He would not feel it when they ate his heart, but the last thing he'd hear would be Lillian's scream.

"Okay if I smoke?" he asked.

The officer gestured permission.

Wiley's pores were spraying. Even his legs were wet. He felt trickles down the middle of his back. He reached for the pack of Camels on the ledge above the instrument panel. Fumbled the pack, dropped it on the deck. Cigarettes spilled out. Wiley hoped he appeared naturally clumsy, nervous.

Nothing to look forward to now but Barbosa. This time Argenti would have his pounds of flesh . . .

. . . but that was all he'd get.

As Wiley was picking up the cigarettes he located the switch with his eyes. It was in straight-out neutral position, a chrome flip-type switch labeled L. B. Well.

Should he flip it up or down? He braced himself with his right hand on the panel as he got up. In the same motion, hand over the switch, he flipped it down.

There was a click that sounded loud to Wiley, but the officer didn't seem to hear it.

A short while later the crewmen returned to the bridge. They reported having found nothing except three pistols. The two Llamas and the Colt forty-five.

Had they searched thoroughly?

Stem to stern.

No secret compartments? No fake bottoms? Were they sure? How about in the engine area?

Nothing, the crewmen said.

The officer hated to hear it.

Wiley knew what would come next. The frigate would escort the boat back to Cartagena. The boat would be ripped apart, searched down to the bare hull.

The officer's expression changed. He made an indifferent mouth, took off his glasses and put them away. He placed the passports and other papers on the chart table. Without another word he and the crew boarded the launch and returned to the frigate.

Wiley quickly flipped the L. B. Well switch to neutral.

"They were looking for dope," Lillian said. "Probably had a tip or something on that Englishman. A lot of coke comes out of Cartagena."

Wiley was already off the bridge and rushing aft. He pulled away the cover to the live-bait well.

The switch Wiley had flipped in his spite controlled a pump attached to a two-inch pipe that ran from the well to just below the waterline at the stern. It served to draw fresh seawater into the well or expel what was in there.

The water and the emeralds had been sucked out.

The emeralds had fallen like underwater rain, a torrent of drops that tumbled and swirled as they sank, shot out glints and final verdant flashes until they were out of the sun's reach.

Three hundred million dollars down the drain.

32 ➤➤➤

Kellerman watched Argenti's hands.

He expected them to fist, but the fingers remained relaxed and the wrists didn't go rigid. The hands lay lightly on the thigh of the crossed-over leg.

Argenti's face revealed only little more reaction. The two vertical creases between the brows deepened and the lips pursed, as though tasting something bitter. The eyes remained steady, unreadable. Kellerman couldn't see anything in them, and he was an expert at eyes, could detect and define an inner feeling from no more than a blink.

"Why would she want to do such a thing?" Argenti asked almost casually.

"Out of boredom, I'd say."

Kellerman knew better. For two years he'd been compiling a dossier on Lillian. He'd known all along she was a dabbling activist but had kept it to himself. When she'd gone poaching for the left and ended up in Barbosa, it was Kellerman who'd got her out of it. Without Argenti's knowing, Kellerman had invented the excuses and convinced General Botero not to mention it. He'd made it seem he was doing the General a favor, since, as he said, the army had blundered and abused.

Kellerman couldn't have cared less for Lillian really. And he wasn't looking out for Argenti. He was protecting his own ambitions.

The way he saw it, Lillian was essential to getting Argenti's exile lifted. Once Argenti was free to go, he'd go so gladly he'd rarely ever return to Bogotá. For a while Argenti might try to continue to run The Concession at an enjoyable distance. He'd find it difficult, soon impossible. The Concession was too complex. It required someone in charge on the spot. Kellerman was the obvious choice. From then on Kellerman would make changes, reposition loyalties, distribute his own patronage and, eventually, edge Argenti out. At the least, Kellerman would have the chance to skim as he wanted.

Thus it had been important to Kellerman that Lillian's slate be kept clean. Now, however, to admit he'd withheld such information would be putting himself in the line of fire. He told Argenti: "Perhaps she's one of those who can't enjoy anything unless there's risk in it."

Argenti grunted.

"Often it gets to be a sexual thing, you know, a mix of stimulations."

"That the best you can offer?"

"It seems to fit."

"You're wrong, Kellerman. Way off, except in one respect."

"Her boredom."

"Her crotch. He's had her by the crotch all along."

"You're overestimating him."

"No, that's her *shortcoming*." Argenti waited for Kellerman to appreciate his off-color play on words. "Wiley worked her up to it. Dangled the carrot, so to speak, in front of her nose."

Kellerman smirked, nodded thoughtfully, although he didn't agree. "Why would she go to such an extent for him?" His inflection said *of all people*.

"Common behavior for her type, the more common the better, as a matter of fact. I'm sure it's a form of temporary insanity, lowering herself, using love as the excuse."

"Anyway, he's our man."

"Balls for brains."

"We'll get him."

It amazed Kellerman that Argenti could discuss Lillian and Wiley with such relative objectivity. Almost as though Lillian and Wiley were merely problem acquaintances, and there was nothing important at stake. Where, Kellerman wondered, was the indignation, the humiliation, the fury that should have erupted from having been manipulated like that? Incredible that Argenti had that much composure. Perhaps he hadn't seen into the man as clearly as he'd thought.

Two weeks since the robbery.

Less than twenty thousand carats had been recovered, despite a severe crackdown on street dealing. A federal law was pushed through, prohibiting emerald transactions without an official certificate. The proper government form might someday be printed.

The Concession needed every emerald it could get, but this legal measure accomplished little. A couple of thousand carats was all. The street dealers had seen it coming. They deserted Calle 14, hid themselves and their goods elsewhere. The more enterprising conducted business during late-night hours in the *barrio*, buying up the stones that had been thrown there.

Five Conduct Section operatives were sent into the *barrio* during the first week, five more the second. They posed as street dealers or *campesinos*, poor fellows from the country.

Not one of the ten came out.

Sending the men in had been Argenti's idea. He loathed the thought of those grimy *bastardos* of the *barrio* gaining from his loss. They sang while he suffered. He wanted every pocket and asshole turned inside out.

Tactfully, Kellerman made him realize how futile such efforts were.

For the most part during those days, Argenti tended to business with sober efficiency. He spent long regular hours in his offices at The Concession, meeting each crisis as it came.

The clients were putting the pressure on. What about orders? When could delivery be expected? Demand would soon be felt, backing up from the retail level.

Argenti took every call, even those from clients whose yearly handle was comparatively minimal. He smoothed them down, bought time with the excuse that The Concession was undergoing an audit, voluntary naturally, requested by its board of directors just to make double sure where it stood. Seemed business was too good to be believed, he said lightly.

On top of all that, he told clients, there had been a tremendous find about fifty miles northeast of Muzo. Stones such as the world had never seen. The finest quality ever to come out of Colombia. Practically every stone had kelly in it. Why, at that very moment before him on his desk was an emerald as big as his fist, and he swore he could see clearly halfway into it, there were that few flaws. The new find was so extensive it was certain to affect price. Supply would balance out with demand, of course, everyone would benefit, but especially those on the first level of distribution. Understandably, The Concession needed a while to get its breath, to integrate these new holdings. No one wanted to ruin the market, now, did they?

There was a tone of confidentiality in the way Argenti told it. Implying future favoritism, while all he asked for was patience. Argenti knew the common ground was greed, and he worked it.

He was sorry now that when he had structured The Concession he hadn't allowed for a bad time such as this. He could just as well have stipulated that a percentage be taken off the top and set aside. Instead it had always been only a matter of running the funds through—operational costs and profits. Not counting his private skim, of course.

He put it to his cohorts, Vega, Arias, Robayo and Botero. They would have to chip in to help keep The Concession going. Expenses ran a million a week. The largest chunk of that went to Conduct Section's world-wide network and all the people bought by the week down the line along the various lines.

Senator Robayo said he wished he didn't have his own financial problems.

General Botero said his investments were so complicated it would be impossible for him to put his hands on enough cash soon enough to be of help.

Ministers Arias and Vega thought it unfair that they should each have to bear a third rather than a fifth of the brunt.

Argenti walked out while they were still arguing that. It was evident that if there was to be any shoring up he would have to do it.

A million a week.

More than that.

Twelve million was due the government on its lease. The Concession also currently owed the government twenty million in royalties. So as not to jeopardize its lopsided agreement, The Concession had never been late in its payments to the government.

Argenti went it alone. Withdrew from his Swiss accounts. Fifty million.

That would hold things for a while.

Practically every day Argenti went up to the vaults. The window had been replaced, the broken glass cleaned up. Everything appeared normal. Except the cabinets, all the empty drawers.

It hurt to look at them, but soon they'd be full again.

In the meantime orders were for the mines to put on extra shifts round the clock. Floodlight the hillside terraces so they could be worked at night. Triple the yield, if possible. Couldn't offset the losses, but it was better to have something coming in.

Then, there were the *esmeralderos*.

All at once they wanted double compensation. Were they deliberately taking advantage of the situation?

Exactly.

The *esmeralderos* did not know what was wrong at The Concession, but they knew it was something serious. There was a rumor line almost as fast and often more reliable than the telephone that ran between the mountain villages and the *barrio*.

Representatives of the *esmeralderos* showed up unexpectedly one morning at The Concession's offices. Ten altogether, one on behalf of each of the most powerful families. They had on their black city-and-church suits and very pointed black shoes. Their suits were so tight their guns were obvious.

Argenti received them.

He was very cordial.

They were polite and reticent. They wouldn't sit and had to be urged into accepting cigars.

They finally got around to telling Argenti what was wanted—double pay.

He asked for a reason.

They knew his asking was only a formality.

They gave him several reasons that he knew were lies.

Double pay would amount to five to six million more a year.

Argenti agreed to it as though he had a choice.

It wasn't enough.

No money would be enough.

The *esmeralderos* wanted their old ways back. They were weary of having to be violent according to instructions, of killing not when they wanted but in keeping with some set quota. Order, alliance had taken too much from them. There were too few chances to express their *machismo*. That was their biggest gripe, the thing that The Concession had deprived

them of. Authentic opportunities for a man to prove and re-
prove he was a man.

On the third night after Argenti agreed to pay double to the
esmeralderos, the headquarters of the mine at Coscuez was
raided. Fifteen guards were killed. Only the superintendent
knew the combination to the safe, so he must have opened it.
The yield of ten days, about two thousand carats, was removed
from the safe. Left in its place were the superintendent's genitals.

Two days later an armored truck and its army troop escort of
twenty men was set upon only a few miles from the main mine
at Muzo. The truck was carrying all the emeralds that had been
found in that most productive area over the past two weeks. It
was a brief, intense battle. The troops were outnumbered and
outgunned. The last of them knew there was no hope in sur-
render, tried to make a run for it. Grenades were lobbed,
landed ahead of them, so they ran themselves to death.

Over two hundred killings occurred in mine territory that
week. Twenty of those were *esmeralderos*. The families were
already at one another. The old codes were being re-
established.

Bad news for The Concession.

And not one carat.

Each day before leaving the office Argenti met with Kellerman for a progress report. Kellerman's dossier on Lillian,
which he was still keeping to himself, was valuable now. She
could hide anywhere—for a short while. However, those
places where she was likely to be for any length of time were
numbered, known. It was only a waiting game now. Lillian
would emerge, with Wiley clinging to her skirts.

The emeralds, the three hundred million dollars' worth?

Kellerman doubted Wiley and Lillian would move to market
the emeralds. They certainly hadn't. There wasn't as much as a
trickle of extra stones anywhere in the world.

Argenti said that if Wiley was smart he'd salt away the
emeralds, leech off Lillian until the time was right. Although
that would require endurance. He laughed.

The two men spent at least an hour or more recapping each
day and discussing the next day's tactics. The situation was
becoming more and more critical, but Argenti remained in
control. Kellerman had to admire Argenti under stress, not a

chink in him. He didn't even have dark circles beneath his eyes, looked as though he was getting good sleep.

Truth was, however, while Argenti gave his days to business, he kept his nights.

From the moment he arrived home, shut the door behind him, he let out his anger. He bellowed like a wounded, raging grizzly, tore off his clothes and prowled from room to room.

He was alone in the villa. The servants had fled in fear.

He detested everything, especially whatever was beautiful, fragile, irreplaceable.

"*Quella vecchia troia!*" came out of him, guttural, as though he were bringing up phlegm. Those words looped in his head. He viewed everything through them. They required more expression. He printed them in red ink on the creamy-colored silk of a lampshade next to his bed.

He couldn't stay still.

He turned on every light in the villa.

He rampaged downstairs, up and down again, and around. In the caretaker's supply room he found several pressurized cans of enamel.

QUELLA VECCHIA TROIA

he sprayed in foot-high red letters along a beige damask-covered wall and diagonally up another wall to ruin a most believable scenic *trompe l'oeil*. The enamel ran from the bases of the letters. He enjoyed the effect.

Other surfaces asked for it. He scrawled, condensed, extended it, made it small or as large as possible. Around the belly of a grand piano, across the back of a needlepoint *bergère*, over the face of an Aubusson tapestry. Did it a letter to a square on the parquet Carrara floor and on the bottom of his blue-gray St. Anne marble bathtub.

He ran out of enamel long before he ran out of surfaces or the incentive. He dropped the last spray can into the bathroom wastebasket, and stood facing the floor-to-ceiling mirror, a kind mirror tinted slightly pink.

Looked at him looking at him.

The dark hair on his forearms glistened red from the mist of enamel that had settled on them. And the hair of his chest and the tighter hair of his groin, beaded with it, seemed to be bleeding. His nostrils were red where he had inhaled his hate.

A sob moved up into his throat like a bubble. His facial muscles made his eyes smaller and his mouth larger, and the sob came out as a strained whimper around the words "*No, dolce madre, no*" (no, sweet mother).

He pressed against the mirror to embrace, comfort himself. Left his red imprint.

Exterior cries intruded.

The window was open. They were the love cries of all the little creatures that ran wild and brave in the night grass.

He hurried to an adjacent room, where he removed his favorite shotgun from its fitted leather case. A Beretta SO2 over-under twelve-gauge. He also chose a pistol, a SIG 210 automatic, twenty-two caliber. And took along several cartons of shells.

On the second-floor landing at the top of the wide stairs he stopped to load the shotgun. He held it at his side in ready position.

Pull!

As though skeet shooting, he brought the gun up swiftly to the snug of his shoulder, swung it to target and fired both barrels.

The enormous settecento-style Venetian glass chandelier that hung over the reception hall shattered.

Two more shots and it was bare, like an inverted tree that had lost all its delicate crystal leaves.

Argenti went down to the main salon.

He sat on a velour-covered taboret in the center of the large room.

Across the room on a side table was a pigmented terra-cotta figure of a woman by Giovacchino Fortini, done in the 1690s.

Argenti blew it in half with the pistol.

To the right of that a glass case. Containing figurines of jade, pink and mutton fat and spinach green. Also a blue-and-white Ming bowl that had gone for $220,000 at Sotheby's. And a pair of *famille-rose* vases with imperial-pink ground of the K'ang Hsi period.

One twelve-gauge shot destroyed them.

A *purpurine* and *sang-de-boeuf* porcelain cat by Fabergé.

A bronze of a young girl by Bugatti.

Another done in the sixteenth century by Alessandro Vittoria.

Blasted to bits.

His sights came upon a pair of rare Ming Buddhist lions of
streaked brown and green and blue glazes. He found momentary fascination in their protruding eyes, the way they were
reared back defiantly, their oversize ears alert and their whis-
kers proudly exaggerated. He mentally snarled at them a moment before he pulverized them.

For variation he splintered off the slender front legs of an
eighteenth-century Florentine table, so the crystal-and-ormolu
candelabra and the Lalique covered candy dish that rested upon
it crashed to the floor. He thought of it as the price of dependency.

Paintings.

A Titian portrait of a lady done four hundred sixty-seven
years ago.

Without hesitation Argenti shot the lady's face away.

He peppered a Giacometti until the canvas hung in tatters,
and he tortured a Modigliani, a portrait of the artist's wife. He
used the twenty-two pistol on the Modigliani, shot precise
holes in the slitty eyes, forced open the prim mouth and created
a pattern up the elongated neck. He put her out of her misery
with the Beretta, both barrels. What shreds that were left of the
canvas slid down the wall along with its frame.

"*Quella vecchia troia,*" he uttered.

That fucking old cunt.

Emphasis on *old*.

Lillian, of course.

33 ⪢

East Hampton, Long Island.

Third town from the tip.

That was where they would lie and wait. Not hide. They had considered trying to hide but realized they couldn't. The Concession's reach was too long and relentless, and they honestly doubted they'd be able to put up with the drawbacks of total obscurity. Fading into the ways of some small town suited the predicament but not them.

So they'd decided on off-season East Hampton. Somewhere more crowded might seem safer but actually wouldn't be, they reasoned. In a crowd how could they tell who wasn't after them? It would wreck their nerves.

Isolation also offered another advantage, albeit slight. They might, when the time came, be able to notice whoever was after them a moment or two in advance.

Lillian's East Hampton place was situated on the dunes of Georgica Beach. A two-story house, stretched out to make the most of its vantage. Forty of its windows presented the Atlantic, and a wide veranda ran its entire length. It was typical of the summer houses that were built along Georgica by monied people seventy-or-so years ago. Brown shake shingle siding with white trim.

The next, nearest house to it, similar in stance and profile, was five hundred feet down the beach. Between the two were mutual hedges so tall a ladder was needed to shear them.

On the inland side, four acres buffered the house from its town street, Lily Pond Lane. The grounds were not formally kept, or even too neat. There were a few oaks, real heavyweights. Wild flowers were allowed, black-eyed Susans and asters.

A private drive was surfaced with a crunchy, gray gravel. It didn't run straight in, deviated enough so that only the peaks and chimneys of the house could be seen from the street. In summer, one section of the drive was like a tunnel, the way branches of tall lilacs meshed above it. White lilacs that dipped, bowed to bid sweet welcome, brushed against windshields.

But not now, in January, for Wiley and Lillian.

Now shrubs and trees were skeletal, dark. No way of telling what might be dead. Brambles were more apparent bare. They seemed to be everywhere: thorny wild roses and blackberries, formidable as barbed wire. Miraculous the way sparrows and finches flew so casually into such tangles without being wounded. Or perhaps they were.

Wiley and Lillian arrived from Haiti on the seventh day of the new year. A Saturday afternoon. Over all, the sky was low and leaden. The temperature in the twenties. They had called ahead, been assured the house would be made ready. The caretaker was part-time, a man from the town. The key wasn't on the door ledge where he was supposed to have left it.

Wiley told Lillian to wait in the car while he searched for a way in. All the windows were shuttered. He went completely around, tried every door. When he returned to the main entrance, he found Lillian had used a frozen flower pot to smash a pane from the door and get to the bolt. She stood in the entrance hall, hugging herself, her head hunched down into her coat collar. She had on a wool cap, over her ears and brows. Only her nose and eyes were visible, watery.

It seemed colder inside. A dankness permeated the place and everything in it. There was that moldy odor the sea inflicts on such enclosed coastal places, actually the smell of deterioration. To counteract the sea, the interior of the house—floors, walls, ceilings—was varnished wood, years and years of coats. White sheets covered the furniture and were gathered and tied around lighting fixtures.

"I guess I should try to start some heat," Wiley said halfheartedly.

"This wasn't really such a good idea," Lillian said.

"Well, we're here now."

"Palm Springs would have been better."

"You have a place in Palm Springs?"

"I don't think so."

"Where's the furnace?"

She didn't know.

Wiley went looking for it, a door down to the cellar where

the furnace would be. All he found were a lot of closets. Perhaps this was purely a summer house, and the caretaker hadn't turned on the heat because there wasn't any. However, that didn't explain the absence of electricity, the dead phone and the lack of water from the faucets.

Wiley thought they should get to a motel and consider another place to make their stand. Lillian was sure to agree.

But Lillian wasn't where he'd left her in the entrance hall.

He called out. Her answer was from somewhere upstairs, muffled. He went up to a long center hall, found her in one of the bedrooms.

Her clothes were thrown over a chair. She was in the bed beneath several blankets and two eiderdown comforters. All Wiley could see was her breath, a funnel of white. It looked as though the bed was smouldering. He suggested the motel.

"We're here now," she said.

"There doesn't seem to be a furnace."

"How about food?"

He had looked. The only thing in the pantry cupboards was a dried-up bottle of ant poison. Not even a can of peaches or tomatoes. Houses like this always had a lonely, left-behind can of peaches or tomatoes. "How hungry are you?" he asked.

"Hungry."

He minded a little, but he was dressed and she wasn't, and it was only a mile to town. "Will you be all right while I'm gone?"

She stuck her right hand out from the covers, holding the Llama automatic.

"What shall I get you?"

"Tea and anything," she said.

He drove down Lily Pond Lane to Ocean Avenue. It was dusk and nearly all the nice white family houses had some lights on. Cold and complex as they appeared, Wiley thought they were probably warm within. And uncomplicated. At least compared to what his life had come down to.

What would he settle for now—besides not ever having heard of Argenti and The Concession?

How about Lillian? If the condition was never having known her in exchange for more hopeful circumstances, would he go for that?

Never.

After a short ways Ocean Avenue became Main Street.

Stores on both sides. A wide street and very clean. Nothing rundown that Wiley could see. The stores were confidently understated along there and along the only other business street, Newtown Lane.

He parked and went into a supermarket, pushed a cart down the aisle, like a family man.

When he returned to the house, he called out as soon as he had closed the door behind him. To let her know it was him. With the windows shuttered, the house was pitch black. Wiley had to feel his way with his feet, shuffled up the stairs and down the hall.

He had bought four fat candles, which he lighted to place a pair on each side of the bed. They created the impression of warmth.

Lillian sat up for her tea, holding a comforter around her. Tea kept hot in a styrofoam cup. Wiley removed the lid for her.

"Strip and get in," she said.

"You have everything off?"

"Except my cap and socks. What did you get to eat?" She dug into the bag while he undressed. "Why did you get all this junk?" she asked.

"The rib roasts were too fatty."

"I mean, you must have been reading my mind."

She tore the tough cellophane wrapper from a package of cookies. Oreos, of course. She dunked one into her tea. Before she could get the cookie to her mouth the saturated half of it fell into the cup. She tried to get it with her tongue, then her fingers. The tea was too hot. She let it float. Undaunted, she dunked another with more success.

Wiley had also bought Devil Dogs and Twinkies, a Sara Lee cake, Wise potato chips, Cheese Doodles, Fig Newtons, marshmallows, Milky Ways, Almond Joys, Butterfingers, french-fried onion rings and a half dozen jelly doughnuts.

Black coffee for himself.

He got under the covers, chilled and chattering.

"They say if two people snuggle they can't freeze to death," Lillian said. "Wonder why. I mean, it's not like rubbing two sticks together."

Their legs were entwined, thighs to crotches. After a while they were warm enough to move.

They ate themselves to the verge of nausea and moaned

about it. Wiley swore that if he ever saw another Twinkie or Devil Dog he'd stomp it. Lillian said she'd felt the same about Oreos at least a thousand times.

Wiley lighted a cigarette.

Lillian read a paperback.

When he exhaled he couldn't tell what was smoke and what was merely breath, and that subtracted from his enjoyment.

Even with all four candles on her side Lillian couldn't see well enough. She missed words and skipped entire sentences.

He put out his cigarette in one of the coffee cups.

She folded the corner of page 120 and dropped a Muriel Spark to the floor.

They lay there with their separate thoughts.

The surf was beating time.

She couldn't see the true color of Wiley's eyes, but remembered.

She wondered if he blamed her.

She wondered if he really loved her as much as she believed he did.

Among other things, she wondered about the way he'd reacted after he flushed the emeralds down the Caribbean. Why hadn't he bitched and been bitter? All he'd done was go around with a long face for less than a day. He hadn't mentioned emeralds since, not once. That blasé about it. Strange . .

Wiley came up out of sleep as though he had on six overcoats in a sauna. He was perspiring all over, and Lillian was sticking to him. He fought the blankets off, sat up on the edge of the bed.

The room that had been freezing the night before was stifling now. Wiley felt as though his brain was being baked. He got up, raised the nearest window, unlatched and pushed open the shutters.

Lillian moaned, irritated, hadn't yet opened her eyes. She shoved and slapped at the heavy covers, as though trying to fend off an assailant.

Wiley left the window open six inches. He put on his trousers and went to investigate. Heat was coming from a metal louvered transom in the floor. He went down the upper hall and the stairs. The entire house was heated. The kitchen sink faucets gave water. There was electricity, and a dial tone on the phone. A bag of groceries and the Sunday *Times* on the kitchen counter.

Evidently the caretaker had come and gone. The man must have made some noise. It demonstrated how easily they could be caught off guard in this place, Wiley thought.

His watch said ten-thirty. They had stayed awake talking until three. Telling true stories about long agos, avoiding any mention of tomorrows.

One of Lillian's recollections had been her first pair of grownup gloves, when she was four. White kid antelope, the same as her mother's, with a tiny bluebird stitched in the palm. For her, a bird in hand. Wiley had recalled climbing hickory trees as a boy, when the sectional skins of the nuts were bitten open by frost. How he'd scraped his legs and arms on the scales of the bark, climbed as high as possible and shook to make the nuts fall. More hard shell than meat, those nuts, not worth the effort and, yet, each year how irresistible they had been.

He found a pot and made coffee.

Cup of steaming black in hand, he wondered how he could have overlooked the furnace, was about to go try to find it when Lillian came down. Hardly bending her knees as she walked, making no quick movements. There were impressions on her forehead from the wool knit cap. She had on panties and socks, was unaware that she had stepped on a Milky Way wrapper and it had stuck to her left foot.

She came right to Wiley as though he was her destination, put herself against him, her arms folded up in front of her, close to herself so she could be more completely held.

Wiley avoided touching her bare skin with his hot coffee cup. He thought even in her little-girlness she was a desirable woman. She whined a little for sympathy, said she'd had bad dreams. Probably stirred up by the past times she'd talked about. Wiley shaped his hand to fit her forehead and gently, but with reassuring firmness, stroked over her hairline.

She came out of it abruptly, arched back from him and beamed. As though she had taken whatever and all she needed. Asked him to get the luggage from the car.

She made breakfast while Wiley watched and browsed the Sunday paper. It was the first time he'd ever seen her eat bacon. Knowing her health-conscious attitude toward meat, especially fatty kinds, he took this change in her behavior as a sign of her lack of faith in the future. Could eating bacon be existential? Most certainly. It was, he understood now, for the same reason that he'd bought the Twinkies and all that other junk. He didn't mention it.

She asked for part of the paper, like a wife, he thought.

Out of old habit he looked through the classified section, focused upon those ads under the heading *Business Opportunities*.

"Hey, listen to this," Lillian said. An item she'd happened across, a sort of filler on page 18 in the main news section. She read aloud. Dateline Bogotá. It said Colombian federal authorities were cracking down on left-wing activists in Bogotá, Cali and other cities. The push came in the wake of the recent confrontation between government troops and leftists in Cartagena, during which one of the country's leading radicals, Miguel Contreras, had been killed.

Wiley asked to see it.

Lillian handed it across.

They felt sad about it and somehow, to some extent, responsible.

After breakfast they went outside to learn the lay of the land.

Originally, a hundred feet of lawn had separated the house from the dunes. The way down to the beach had been an easy, sandy incline. Until two years ago there had been a normal amount of erosion. Then the ocean had a sudden turn in temper. All winter long it slashed and beat that section of coastline harder and higher than ever. As though taking out old grudges. Ate away about fifty feet of the dunes and transformed their gradual slope into a sharp thirty-foot bluff.

At that rate, in another year or two, Lillian's house and most of the others along Georgica would be undermined or toppled over.

Access to the beach now was a sort of bridge built on pilings driven deep into the sand. It extended out beyond the drop-off for about sixty feet—a series of steps and landings with a final flight of twelve steps at the end. Those steps, like a ladder, could be lowered to the beach by a pulley. When it was raised, the only direct way to get from the beach to the house was to shinny up one of the pilings. Wiley doubted anyone would come that way.

He and Lillian investigated the terrain around the house. Went over it thoroughly and made it their territory. They would have at least that slight edge. All in all, the house was fairly well placed for their purposes. On one side was the tight, very high hedge, practically as good as a wall. On the opposite side was an impenetrable thicket of brush, most of it over-grown forsythia that ran all the way to the crumbly edge of the bluff. And there were extensive patches of brambles on the inland ground.

They stood out on Lily Pond Lane and looked toward the house. What approaches were offered to their adversaries? Despite all the natural barriers, there was the drive. Like a long welcome mat. Short of planting mines, there was nothing they could do about that.

They could, however, help their cause to some extent inside the house.

The kitchen was on the extreme east end. One of the rooms adjoining it was a sort of relaxing room. On the second floor, directly above the kitchen, was a bedroom and a spacious sun porch. A solarium actually, comprised entirely of small panes on all three sides and overhead. It was furnished in bent-bamboo lounges, sofas and tables. Thick reed matting on the floor.

Wiley and Lillian would limit themselves to those four rooms, go up and down by way of a flight of narrow back stairs intended for servants. They shut all doors that connected to the rest of the house. Unfortunately, the doors had ordinary old keyholes that almost any old key in the world would fit and anyone with a minimum of patience and dexterity could open about as fast as they could pick their teeth.

They spent most of the rest of that day getting settled in. Not that they expected to be there long, but they might as well be comfortable for the while. Lillian put the kitchen in order. Wiley vacuumed and straightened the relaxing room. It had a fireplace. Wiley opened the flue and started a newspaper fire. In less than a minute smoke had backed up and puffed out into the room. Backdraft, Wiley thought. But when the air was smoky enough to cause tears, he knew it was more than that. Determined to have a fire, he went up to the second floor and, at the far end of the center hall, found a trap door. He used a chair to get to it, pushed the trap door away and hoisted him-self up into the crawl space beneath the roof. A hatch opened onto the roof. He went out, walked along the peak, avoiding icy areas. A heavy metal cover was on the chimney, to prevent birds or wasps from nesting. Wiley lifted it from one side and shoved it off. It fell to the pitch of the roof, slid over the edge to the ground.

Wiley went down and built a fire he was proud of.

There was a built-in vertical tape deck, which he got working. Found some reels, including some Sinatras. Played Frank while he gave his attention to the television, which had an incorrigible vertical hold. Just when Wiley believed he had it, and stepped back, the picture would begin flopping over. He glowered at the set, mentally threatened to take it apart. Rather than be operated on, it behaved, held its picture steady. But the moment he turned away, it flopped contemptuously.

Furnace, fireplace, television—he was having to try for everything. Omens?

He insisted on helping with the upstairs rooms. They made the bed together. Lillian snapped the sheets and made them billow. Wiley was reminded of their parachutes. He enjoyed her efficiency, the way she held the pillow by her teeth while she slipped the case over it. As though she did it every day. Anyway, could.

A slant board was improvised for her. From a pair of dining-table leaves Wiley found in a downstairs closet. She got on it and Wiley sat close by, observing her.

She lay there inverted, eyes closed, perfectly still.

He doubted her thoughts were as tranquil as she appeared. Probably inside she felt the way he did. He pushed a chair and table aside to have a clear wall. Removed a shade from a standing lamp, positioned the lamp. Took off his clothes and switched on the hundred-fifty-watt bulb.

He didn't limber up. Hesitated a long moment to appraise his shadow, his dark ephemeral creation. It seemed darker than ever. He swayed left and then right and half expected it not to match him. He shifted his stance, distributed his weight properly, bobbed once and threw a left cross—not a flick, but a fast, full-power left.

The following day was a Monday and the stores in town were open.

Wiley bought heavy-duty Segal vertical bolts, which he installed on all the interior doors that led to their four rooms. That left the side door off the kitchen the only quick, direct

way in and out of the house. It was already equipped with an
adequate lock. Wiley installed another.

They sat at the kitchen table, cleaned and oiled their pistols.
The two Llamas and the Colt forty-five, which still had six of
those hydraulic bullets in its clip. It was while they were
cleaning the pistols that they realized how aware they were of
practically every noise the house made. A creak or thump or
any idiosyncratic sound caused them to pause and listen. Being
realistic about it, they felt it was probably a bit too soon to
expect anyone.

That night they went to bed early and for the first couple of
hours did not sleep well. Around midnight a storm struck, a
squall that drove with such ferocity that the house groaned and
trembled. There were all sorts of noises—but, at least, a natural reason for them. No one would come in such weather.
From that hour on they slept deeply.

The next was the first clear day since they'd been there. An
immaculate winter sky, not even a wisp of cloud—but a lot of
wind, gusts, like invisible things dancing.

The beach was deceptive. Looking out at it, it appeared
bright and baking as in summer. The sparse grass along the
edge of the dunes seemed seared by the sun.

Midmorning, Wiley and Lillian went for a walk. The tide
was out, the sand of the beach darker and firmer where the
water had receded. She held his hand in his pocket. Every so
often, the surf surprised them, ran farther in, as though reaching for them. They had to scurry to keep their feet dry. Wiley
played show-off some, competed with the sea, went far out
when it waned and made it chase him in. It was relieving to
laugh.

Two figures came into sight far down the beach. Wiley's
hand went in under his jacket to find the Llama. He kept his
grip on it until they were close enough to see the two were
women with a dog, an Irish setter in a sleek winter coat that
came to get petted.

They walked as far as the golf and beach club called the
Maidstone. It looked more off season than any place else. On
the way back, they followed their footprints, step for step on
one another's impressions. Many had already been washed
away.

When they were nearly home, Lillian broke away, ran

ahead. About thirty paces from him she stopped, in profile, squinted out to sea as though searching it.

Wiley stopped in Lillian's tracks, far enough from her not to intrude.

She turned to him. The wind furled her trousers and jacket, defining her body, and her hair streamed behind her, so her face was entirely clear.

She smiled.

And said: "I love you."

Her words were lost to the wind.

Wiley shouted: "What?"

"I love you."

Again the wind blew her words away.

Wiley had read her lips but did not trust his interpretation. He went to her.

She placed the words surely in his ear.

They pulled the mattress from the bed out to the floor of the enclosed sun porch.

The porch was heated, the air warm there, although the many hundreds of window frames were coated with frost. The crystals on the glass refined the sun into the most benevolent sort of light, no shadows, only honest contours.

"I love you," Lillian said whenever her mouth was not otherwise occupied—and, as well, when it was. Seemed she had an immense backlog of that declaration. It poured from her upon him. She wanted every part of him to know.

Also, now, there was a desperation to their lovemaking. A sense of doom drove them like an erotic whip.

Between times, still in touch, never relinquishing touch, they lay there uncovered, side to side.

Quietly, she said, "I'm so happy."

"Me too."

"Inside happy, honest to God happy. I love you and I'm able to let you love me. It's incredible."

"I know."

She thought back. "How did you ever put up with me?"

He almost said it hadn't been easy.

"I was such a conniver," she said. "You have no idea what a conniver I was."

"I know."

She didn't miss the ambiguity in his tone. "I almost blew it, didn't I?"

"You did your best."

"I was afraid, afraid to need you and at the same time afraid to lose you."

That, Wiley thought, was the truth of the twelve-thousand lie—when she'd held back his Las Hadas money. Her reason for wanting him dependent hadn't been to belittle him but just to make that much surer that he went along—with her and everything. Couldn't blame her for that. Would he have gone along otherwise? Of course. It was easy now to believe he would have.

"I love you, Wiley." It just came out of her the way it had been coming out of him.

"What's that?" Asking for more.

She said it ten times, ten different ways.

He didn't doubt a one.

She brought his hand to her mouth. His relaxed, after-a-love-making hand. Kissed the nub of his wrist and traced her lips over the back of it so lightly the hairs tickled her.

"You're definitely not a distraction," she said somewhat to herself.

He said he hoped not.

"And I'll never get the crazies. You'll see."

The future tense. They'd been avoiding it.

Her eyes clouded. "I'm sorry."

"So am I."

"It's my fault, this mess we're in."

"Lillian, I didn't do anything I didn't want to do."

She smiled gratefully.

"What do you think our chances are?" she asked.

"Somewhere between slim and slight."

"You're an optimist."

He agreed with a shrug.

She kneeled straight up beside him, her knees and thighs perfectly together, her hands folded in her lap. Neatness to underline her sincerity. "I want you to know something."

He saw she was close to crying.

"Say this awful trouble didn't exist. Or, if by some blessing we could manage to get through it okay, I want you to know . . .I'd try. I wouldn't just leave it up to hope, I'd hang in and really try to try, if you know what I mean."

He knew. He said: "I'd help."

The sun went.

They remained on the mattress on the sun porch. Fell asleep, after another loving, and another around eleven o'clock. Fortunately The Concession didn't come that night. Neither of them was in any condition to put up much of a defense.

Next morning, Wiley smoked two cigarettes before breakfast. For the past week he'd puffed about a pack more than usual per day. Lillian had stopped nagging him to stop. He had a carton in reserve. He got it from the shelf in the kitchen, put it inside his windbreaker and, without saying anything to Lillian, went down to the beach.

She watched from an upstairs window.

At the water's edge he flung the carton of cigarettes as far out as he could.

Also, that morning they went into town again.

Wiley bought a new pair of shoes. Natural-colored leather loafers by Ralph Lauren. Not cheap.

Lillian bought a hanging plant, a huge, flourishing Swedish ivy. She listened intently while the florist gave her watering instructions.

People who have no belief in tomorrows don't buy another pair of shoes to walk on or plants to care for.

Anytime now, they expected whoever was coming to come.

They were never without their pistols, not even inside the house. Wore them in shoulder holsters. Each had two spare loaded clips. Wiley carried another ten rounds loose in his pocket.

It was comforting to keep a fire going constantly in the fireplace. They sat by it and diverted their minds to some extent with discussions. On topics such as the possibility of parthenogenesis in humans, or whether or not the world would have been better off if it had continued believing in a matriarchal deity. Lillian found an edition of *Fleur de Neige* and other fairy tales by the Brothers Grimm. In French. She read aloud. Wiley understood enough but was really entertained by the sight of her going through *Le Vaillant Petit Tailleur* while unconsciously fussing with her pistol harness and holster.

That night, Wednesday night, passed without event.

Thursday night the same.

The constant foreboding, though often temporarily alleviated by lovemaking, frayed their nerves. They stayed up later each night, and each night Lillian preceded Wiley upstairs to bed while he saw to the bolts and whatever.

Saturday morning Lillian sensed Wiley's absence, opened her eyes quickly and sat up. It wasn't like him to be up earlier. Usually, they embraced some before letting the day take hold.

She got up quickly, put on his shirt of yesterday and padded down the back stairs.

He was sitting on a kitchen counter, legs dangling. Telephone receiver pressed between shoulder and ear. He appeared caught in the act and momentarily undecided about whether or not to discontinue the call.

Lillian surmised where he was calling, let him know with a gesture that she too felt it was better to have it done with than be kept on such an excruciating edge.

Wiley had dialed Bogotá direct.

The person who answered, evidently one of the servants, said Señor Argenti was not at home.

When was he expected?

The servant did not know.

Could the Señor be reached somewhere?

The Señor was out of town.

It was extremely important, an emergency, when did he leave?

Señor Argenti left with Señor Kellerman one Saturday ago.

Wiley said he would call back.

Lillian poured him a coffee and thought he certainly looked as though he could use a cigarette.

That night she claimed intuition. Insisted they sleep with only their shoes off. No lovemaking. They would need their legs.

34 ⟫

At ten minutes to midnight a blue Buick sedan came down Lily Pond Lane and, as though on familiar ground, turned sharply into the drive. It went in beyond the bend and stopped where it couldn't be seen from the street.

There were five men in the car.

Three Conduct Section specialists.

Argenti's personal huge man, Luis Hurtado.

And Kellerman.

Kellerman had a radio receiver-transmitter, a powerful solid-state type, fixed to a certain frequency. It fit easily into his jacket pocket. He took it out now and said into it, "We are here."

The voice that came from it was Argenti's: "Remember, keep me informed."

That was the third time Argenti had reminded Kellerman. Argenti had wanted to come ashore and observe the action first-hand; perhaps, if necessary, he'd said, take part in it. However, still hanging over his head was The System's stipulation that he should not set foot on any land outside of Mexico and Central and South America. He doubted that The System, as literal and severe as it was about such things, would be anywhere around this remote place. (He had defied one of their other edicts, hadn't he—touched diamonds?) Nevertheless, he had decided not to chance it, remained aboard his yacht, *Oscuro*, in every way more comfortable.

Kellerman had been efficient in locating Lillian and Wiley. Conduct Section operatives were assigned to watch all Lillian's places. Within an hour after she and Wiley had arrived at the house on Georgica Beach word had reached The Concession. Within another two hours the *Oscuro* had sailed from Cartagena with Argenti and Kellerman aboard.

Kellerman had suggested that, instead, he fly alone to New York, rendezvous with his men and go on to East Hampton to

attend to the matter in two days, three at most. Argenti knew
how much of a strain that would be on his disposition. He was
tempted to use an assumed name and passport and fly along.
He compromised by making the trip the longer but more pru-
dent way. Placated his anger by promising that it was headed
full speed toward satisfaction. The *Oscuro* had sighted Mon-
tauk Point that afternoon, continued around to Block Island
Sound, then Gardiners Bay, and taken the channel into Three
Mile Harbor. She was granted permission to anchor because at
the moment there were no slips available to accommodate a
two-hundred-fifty-footer. Three Mile Harbor was only about
three miles from East Hampton.

Argenti's instructions to Kellerman had been explicit:

Get back the emeralds.

Do away with Lillian and Wiley.

If, without inconvenience, Lillian and Wiley could be taken
alive, they were to be brought aboard so he (Argenti) could
participate in dealing with them.

If it came to a choice of killing one or the other, make it
Wiley.

Kellerman wondered about that last consideration. Possibly
it meant Argenti still had hopes of using Lillian as planned to
get out of exile. In that case Kellerman's own ambitions were
not yet entirely out of the question.

The men checked their guns.

Kellerman carried two in a double shoulder holster arrangement, left and right. He made sure the radio was on transmis-
sion before slipping it into his coat pocket, so Argenti would
be hearing everything as it happened. They all had on dark
overcoats and wool-lined leather gloves. No hats. They didn't
expect to be outside long enough to feel the need for hats.
However, after they were out of the car only a few seconds the
cold bit at their ears. The temperature must have been in the
low twenties and the ocean dampness made it more penetrat-
ing. The night was clear except for a high, thin mist that
somewhat diminished the full moon, softened its edges and put
a ring around it.

The gravel of the drive crunched under the footsteps of the
men. Seemed loud. The only other sound was the surf. When
they were nearer the house they avoided the gravel, walked
upon the frozen ground along the side of the drive. Some of the
most reaching brambles snagged at them ineffectively.

The Conduct Section man who had kept watch on the house had diagrammed the exterior layout for them, so they knew it now, expected it to be shuttered. They went around to the ocean front and across the strip of lawn to the east end of the house.

Light showed through the cracks around the shutters of one of the downstairs rooms. Kellerman signaled the others to remain back while he cautiously approached that window. He tried to see in from one side and then the other, but the light was coming at an indirect angle. The openings allowed him nothing of the room. There were, however, voices:

"You're making that up."

"I'm not. I read about it last fall on a plane from London. Someone left a scientific journal on the next seat."

"Rabbits actually became pregnant without the usual help?"

"They used electrical stimulation."

"Bet some old randy male cottontail hopped in and out so fast no one noticed."

"It was all done under strict laboratory conditions. And not just once but many times. The scary thing was all the rabbits born that way were females. How about that?"

"A lot of research scientists these days are lying for attention . . ."

Kellerman recognized the voices. Unmistakably, Wiley and Lillian. And from the tone of them, off guard.

Kellerman led the men to the west end of the house, as far as possible from the room occupied by Wiley and Lillian. They would enter without being heard.

One of the Conduct Section specialists went to work on the shutters. Used a sharp chisel to gouge away the wood where the shutters joined at the center and, then, when space allowed, inserted a pair of diamond-edged cutters that sliced through the inside metal crossbar as though it were paper. Altogether it had taken less than two minutes.

The shutters opened and presented a pair of regular sash-type windows with a simple clamshell lock. The specialist brought out what appeared to be a short length of three-quarter-inch pipe. With the deliberate wrist motion of a dart thrower he punched the pipe at the lower middle pane of the upper window. It was done so swiftly it caused hardly any noise and left a neat hole in the glass. He simply reached in with a finger and swiveled the lock. The window was warped some, swollen tight in place, but Luis Hurtado raised it with one hand.

They climbed in.

So far, nothing that could have alarmed Wiley and Lillian.

The four men, spaced well apart, made their way toward the other end of the house. They proceeded slowly, placing each step softly on the varnished wood floor, avoiding the white humps of covered furniture. They did not draw their pistols till they were standing outside the room the voices were coming from. A line of light shone out across the bottom of the door.

Very carefully, Kellerman placed his ear against the door panel. Heard them, Lillian, saying:

"Fifteen hundred women responded. They culled it down to fifty absolutely sure ones, who couldn't possibly have gotten pregnant from men."

"How couldn't?"

"Hadn't even been near any."

"You realize of course you're talking about immaculate conceptions being quite commonplace."

"Parthenogenesis."

"You believe it?"

"Certainly. Don't you?"

"No."

"You don't want to."

"Those fifty women . . . were they knocked-up electrically?"

"I presume."

"Christ. Con Ed will be asking for another raise in rates."

Laughter.

Kellerman thought, how easy. He was catching them completely unaware. They wouldn't have a chance to resist.

He considered trying the doorknob, decided they wouldn't be that careless. Anyway, it wasn't much of a door, an interior door. It couldn't have much of a lock. Locked or not, Luis Hurtado would smash it off its hinges with one lunge.

Kellerman gestured to Hurtado, who backed off a few steps and went at the door.

His shoulder broke through the upper panel and the upper hinge tore away, but the Segal bolt Wiley had installed held and Hurtado had to smash himself against the door twice more before the other hinge gave.

The Conduct Section specialists rushed in with pistols at the ready.

Followed by Hurtado and Kellerman.

It took a few moments for them to comprehend there was no one in the room.

The voices they'd heard were still coming from the tape deck speakers.

An early warning arrangement. Perhaps, Kellerman thought, even a diversion to allow escape. He sent the men to make a room-to-room sweep of the house, first floor first, then, if they encountered no one, on up to the second.

The moment Hurtado hit that downstairs door, Wiley and Lillian were snapped up out of sleep. At once their minds were clear and their bodies quick.

They put on their nylon windbreakers, zipped them up partway and tucked their shoes inside them. They cocked their pistols, checked to make sure the silencers were screwed on tight.

The Colt forty-five containing the hydraulic bullets. Wiley shoved that into his windbreaker pocket. And also took along a regular three-cell flashlight. He retracted the bolt on the bedroom door and they went out into the upper hall. It was pitch black because all the windows were shuttered. They slid their stockinged feet along the varnished floor, moving with hardly a sound, could detect any slight noise caused by the men below going from room to room.

When they reached the well of the main stairway, they heard whispers from below. Listened carefully but could not make out what was being said. Merely sibilant fragments. But that close. They would not try going down that way, continued on along the completely dark hall. To the end of it, where a week ago Wiley had left the chair. The chair he'd used to climb up into the shallow space beneath the roof.

They would go up there.

But hold on, Wiley thought, what the hell. Were they trying to escape, or what? Hadn't they decided not to run or hide? The reason for being there was to make a stand, wasn't it? They'd reacted automatically, gone on the defense. Better they should use the advantage while they had it.

They went into the nearest room, which was just another bedroom. Wiley felt the floor with his feet, located the old-fashioned metal louvered transom of the heating system. He kneeled beside it. The louvers were shut. There was a lever that worked them. The tip of the lever barely protruded above the surface, not enough to trip over but just enough so a thumb could work it back or forth. To open or close the louvers and regulate the flow of heat. Often such old metal devices became stuck. Chances were this one was rusted tight from the ocean.

In total darkness, by feel alone, Wiley put his thumb to the lever and applied pressure.

The lever didn't budge.

Greater pressure.

It still didn't budge.

Lillian, kneeling in the darkness beside him, had only a notion of what he was trying to do.

Instead of pressing the lever, he tried pulling it.

It gave. Easily, in fact. The louvers rotated in unison until they were in wide open position.

The transom was paired exactly with another in the ceiling of the area below. The louvers of that ceiling transom were already open, so Wiley and Lillian were able to see down through. A very limited view and dim. A faint light provided from the relaxing room more than half the length of the house away. Neither Wiley nor Lillian saw anyone down there; however, they heard a creaking of a floorboard and another, suggesting the weight of someone's steps.

They waited.

No one came into sight.

Still, they felt quite sure someone was down there.

Wiley took a loose bullet from his pocket. He dropped it clear through the transom. It struck the bare hardwood floor below and made a sound of exactly what it was: something small but relatively heavy dropped—accidentally, anyone would think, under these circumstances.

Within the minute, a figure moved stealthily to investigate. Drawn to the spot. He was crouched with gun in hand. His head was no more than three feet below.

Wiley, still kneeling, straddled the transom. He inserted the silencer-tipped muzzle of his Llama pistol between the metal louvers, careful not to hit or scrape against them. Aimed the pistol straight down. Thought how unfair it was but thought, what a damn fool thought. Squeezed up the slack of the trigger and, when he knew he had it all, continued squeezing.

The nine-millimeter bullet went point-blank into the top of the man's skull. His shoulders hunched, ass stuck out, legs folded. As though he'd been struck on the head by a sledge-hammer. He didn't cry out because the bullet didn't stop in his brain, traveled down through that soft substance and tore into his windpipe.

He was one of the Conduct Section specialists. Anyway, had been.

Wiley waited a moment for someone else to come into view and, thus, into range. Wasn't anyone concerned, even curious, about the man's condition? Evidently the others had heard the silenced spit of the shot and already figured out where it had come from.

No reason to be so quiet now. Wiley and Lillian hurried out into the hall. Wiley used the chair to climb up through the trap door to the crawlspace beneath the roof. Lillian moved the chair to just inside the nearest bedroom so it wouldn't give them away. Wiley extended his hand down to her.

She was reaching up for it, trying to find it in the dark, when she heard something—someone. Down the long hall, moving slowly toward her. Unless Wiley pulled her up, she was cornered there at the dead end of the hall. Where was his hand? She had to be just missing it. He was whispering useless directions.

She stopped trying for it, concentrated on her oncoming adversary. The pitch blackness was her protection and a handicap. She strained to make out any variation in it, a shape of any sort. Should she fire a shot blindly? Might he? The hallway was about seven feet wide. If he was coming straight on, the odds were about four to one against her making a hit. If he was moving in profile, offering as slim a target as possible, her chance of a hit would be maybe only one in eight. Out of habit she raised the Llama to eye level, as though she could see to aim. Her sense of direction was all she had to go by, and the longer she hesitated the more indecisive she became about that. Possibly she was aiming at nothing but wall.

She'd have only one chance. As soon as she fired she'd be giving her location away, inviting precise retaliation.

Wiley was calling to her in a more desperate whisper now.

She took up the slack in the trigger.

She altered her aim a little to the left, then down to the right a bit. Guessing.

Then she saw it.

The elongated triangle.

Glowing. Not brightly, but discernible. About two thirds of the way down the hall.

Him. He must have been moving in a crouch and had just straightened up. That was his second mistake. His first was wearing a new white shirt. A cheap one. Its fabric had been treated with a chemical whitener that made it phosphorescent. The triangle was wider at the top, formed by his neckline and the lapels of his coat. Where the lapels met would be about the center of his chest, Lillian estimated.

Still she couldn't see to aim. But at least now she had something to shoot for.

She went for the heart, judging where it would be according to the low point of the phosphorescent triangle.

She didn't hear the bullet smack in.

The man let out a short painful grunt and stumbled back, brushed against the wall and fell, dead weight, to the floor.

The others would be cautious, but coming.

Lillian looked up.

Wiley flicked his flashlight on for a fraction of a second for a bearing. She reached up, stood tiptoe. He found her hand, got a sure grip on her wrist and hoisted her up.

They fitted the trap door back into place.

Wiley switched on the flashlight.

For the moment they were safe, had a sort of advantage. Anyone who tried to come up through the trap door would be an easy target. And there was no other way up.

Wiley glanced at Lillian. Recognized something in her expression that he hadn't seen before. At least, she'd never shown it.

Fear.

She smiled, but he could tell she was merely pulling the corners of her mouth up. She bumped her head on a rafter because there wasn't enough space to stand. A hard bump, but she didn't even grimace. Anesthetized by danger. What difference, between now and when they'd fought the soldiers that foggy night in the Andes?

The stakes had changed.

Same stakes, but changed.

They put on their shoes.

They heard some rumbling and slamming about below. The

place was being searched, and not only for them. Wiley knew what else they were looking for. What he'd lost to the Caribbean. From the sounds, he tried to estimate how many men there were. He thought four, conveyed it to Lillian by holding that many fingers up. She held up her opinion: three.

Wiley considered: Should they remain there in the crawlspace? Wouldn't it be only a matter of time before the trap door was discovered and their pursuers realized where they were? Better to make use of that time. No use cowering. Stay on the offensive. But how?

He moved in a crouch, stepped from raw beam to beam. Lillian followed. Across to the hatch Wiley had used to get out onto the roof a week ago.

He pushed it open.

They climbed up and out. Closed the hatch behind them.

Then they were on the peak of the roof. It wasn't a sharpangled peak. Wiley had been able to walk along it with hardly any concern about balance when he'd uncapped the chimney.

The idea now was to find a way to the ground. The pitch of the roof was not all that steep. They could inch down it and lower themselves to the roof of the veranda; from there would be an easy drop.

They took several steps along the peak, were committed to it before they realized how slick it was. The sea and the night had moistened the entire surface of the roof, and the cold had frozen it slick.

The foot Wiley had his weight on slipped from under him. Lillian grabbed to help. They both fell hard.

There was nothing to get hold of. They tried to dig in with their heels but couldn't even slow their slide. Down the pitch of the roof, helpless, the rough shingles scraping their backs, backsides and legs.

They shot off the edge.

It was a two-story drop and they expected the impact of the frozen ground.

Instead, they were caught, as though by a net, by the thick growth of rose and berry brambles along the edge of the house. The bushes, dense as they were, gave, sprung, held—and took a price. Thorns stabbed through clothes and got to skin.

Lillian couldn't keep from crying out.

It was as though they'd fallen into a basket of angry cats. Claws by the hundreds went at them as they tried to check their awkward sprawls. Each movement brought more pain, and it was no better to move gingerly.

They managed to stand. Waded swiftly through the tangle, tore through it while it ripped at them, inflicting pain to the very last snag.

Wiley had thought being outside would give them the advantage of surprise and a better chance to pick off another of the men—or more. But their descent had been anything but sneaky, and Wiley reminded himself that they were up against professionals.

They made for the bridge that spanned the eroded dunes. Crossed over it and, when they reached the end, jumped the ten feet down to the beach.

Not unnoticed.

Two men came from the house, and then a third, headed for the bridge.

From the size of one, Wiley gathered it was Luis Hurtado. Wiley recalled Hurtado's hands, twice the size of average hands, capable of breaking someone's forearm like a stick of kindling.

They ran down the beach.

The tide was flowing, so they had to keep close to the dunes to avoid the wash of the breakers. Wiley looked for someplace on the way that might be good for a stand. Anything that might give them an edge. There weren't even any rocks along there, only large, closed-up houses above the sheer dunes, not easily accessible.

They kept going.

The sameness of the beach, the water, the dunes lessened their sense of reality. The night seemed to be holding itself over them, over everything, like an apathetic spectator, and the light from the misted moon appeared artificial.

They came to a fence. Ordinary wooden slats connected by wire. Meant to impede the drift, the eating-away of the dunes. And a short ways farther on were some gray-green painted structures. They were one-room places, little more than shacks, about twenty of them in an evenly spaced line facing the sea. Each had the same eaves, door, windows. Identical in every way, even to the size and placement of the white-enameled wooden nameplates fixed above each door. The plainest sort of black lettering, professionally done, said so-and-so Vanderbilt, so-and-so Whitney, so-and-so Hutton.

Members of the Maidstone Club used these shacks to change in at the beach. In summer they were places for wet suits and plastic floats, mats, folding canvas recliners and gallons of Bain de Soleil. But now, on the opposite side of the year, the shacks were empty, the doors left unlocked.

To Wiley and Lillian the shacks offered welcome cover. They ducked in between two, peeked back up the beach. Their pursuers were barely perceptible: three upright, dark shapes moving against the sand and dunes. About four hundred feet, at the most, a minute away.

Was this a good place to make the fight? Wiley wondered. How could it best be used? How would a professional use it? Wouldn't their adversaries approach these shacks with the utmost caution, anticipating a move? No way, therefore, of pulling off much of a surprise. Most surprising would be not to be there. Also, it would take their adversaries time to check out the shacks, give them precious moments to set themselves up elsewhere, Wiley decided.

He and Lillian went on.

Just beyond the last shack in the row was the Maidstone Club proper. A wide cement deck up off the beach. Steel poles, permanently embedded in the deck, formed a framework that would be for awnings. A short distance in from the beach was the swimming pool, empty now. The cement deck ran around it. Just back from the pool's edge, along each side, were more of those same gray-green shacks.

Directly ahead, presiding over it all on the crest of the dunes, was the main clubhouse. An extensive building of turn-of-the-century design. Leading up to it were two identical flights of steps on the left and right, and a black-topped drive that served a beach-level parking area behind the shacks, not visible from the pool.

Sand blown from the beach occupied every crack and corner. There was as much as five feet of sand in the far end, the deep end of the pool. Surfaces were smooth and had a slight powdery coating, rather like talcum, from being sandblasted almost perpetually.

How about here? Wiley and Lillian considered. What would be the least expected, most advantageous positions they could take here?

Worst place would be down in the empty pool. The pool was an obvious trap. A four-way dead end.

Best place would be any of the shacks.

They decided on a little of each.

Wiley jumped down into the pool. The shallow end. It was too shallow for him to crouch. He had to kneel to get entirely out of sight. That end of the pool was nearest the entranceway, the way the men would most likely come.

Every few seconds Wiley took a one-eyed peek. Kept his head horizontal and raised it so one eye was just above the level of the pool's edge.

It seemed they were a long time coming.

Now that he was no longer on the move, the cold got all the way into Wiley. He felt himself thickening inside, becoming brittle. His knees were ball-like aches and his hands burned so it didn't seem he had hold of the pistol. He gripped it tighter to make sure it was there. Surely he wouldn't have feeling enough to be able to squeeze off a shot. He put his trigger finger into his mouth. The entire finger. Soon it was thawed enough, flexible, ready, but he had to keep it in. Once he removed it, wet with saliva, it would begin to freeze. He also unzipped his fly, shoved his left hand in down between his legs to warm it.

Although he kept alert for any sign of them, he took the time to think.

About really losing.

All the other times when he'd come close, when what he'd believed he wanted had zigzagged by just out of reach, all those times altogether didn't amount to anything, compared to this. Nothing had ever been so important to him, he knew. He viewed his death not so much as the loss of him as a loss by him. The loss of her, his ability to love her. An awful thought: never again to experience her, not even with his eyes.

An offsetting thought followed, one that by no means completely consoled him but which helped nonetheless and caused him to smile inside. Pleased with himself that he'd been able to love her that intensely. Her or anyone, for that matter. It was an accomplishment, be it the last or not.

Apparently, it would be the last.

No matter if these three failed, Argenti would merely send another set of killers. At least it was a better way to go than Barbosa, Wiley thought.

He took another horizontal peek.

There was something. Something off to the side that broke the line of the entranceway.

Definitely one of them.

Wiley kept his eye on him.

The man advanced a few quick, light steps at a time. He was about sixty feet away. Wiley watched the man's footwork, the way he shifted to the left and right, always forward but never straight on, scooting along smoothly in a crouch.

The other two men appeared, spaced well apart. Apparently the first was scouting the way, about twenty feet ahead.

Wiley's eyes were watering from the cold and the strain of intense focus. He clenched them and a couple of tears dropped.

How long should he wait? How close should he let the man get?

The man was now only about thirty feet away, standing out in the open on the concrete deck but ready for action from any direction.

Wiley became aware of a clanging.

It was the tall metal flagpole up by the clubhouse. The flag-raising lanyards were whipping in the breeze, striking their metal clips against the pole. Like a knell.

The man was less than twenty feet away now.

Wiley didn't just rise up suddenly. He had thought he would, but he was cramped with cold and he didn't trust his free hand aim that much.

Careful not to make any abrupt move, as though the man were a bird who would fly at any sudden motion, Wiley brought his right hand, with the pistol, up to the edge of the pool, rested his wrist on the edge.

The man didn't notice it.

He did, however, notice the upper half of Wiley's head when it came up to aim. But by the time his brain had conveyed that information to his gun hand, Wiley's first bullet had hit him. Hit him three inches to center of the top left button on his double-breasted overcoat. Straightened him up and drove him back. Wiley's second bullet was unnecessary. Went in just above the right hip as the man's body twisted on the way down.

Hurtado and Kellerman dropped flat to the concrete deck.

Wiley made for the deep end of the pool. He was supposed to have gotten out by way of the steps at the shallow end, but

his knees had been a problem, rigid, the fluid in them viscous
from the cold. He couldn't run, hobbled down the incline of
the bottom, which was steeper than it had appeared. The sound
of his steps reverberated loudly, and he got an objective mental
flash of himself—trapped in a depressed rectangular box.

The deep end of the pool was in shadow. By the time Wiley
reached it, Hurtado and Kellerman were firing at him. They
were kneeling, one knee down on the deck near the shallow
end.

Wiley expected any second to feel the splat of a bullet into
his back. He kept low, tucked over, dodged. The slugs that just
missed him chipped sharply off the hard interior of the pool
and ricocheted around until spent.

Wiley got to the right-hand corner of the far end, where
there was a permanent pool ladder. A tubular-metal ladder with
fat chrome rails and wide, substantial steps. He put his pistol
away and jumped for it. The five feet of sand in that end of the
pool helped. Otherwise the ladder would have been way out of
reach. He grasped the bottom of one of the rails where it was
fixed to the side of the pool. Pulled himself up. The metal was
so cold his bare hands almost stuck to it.

He didn't try to climb out of the pool. He couldn't, without
offering them too easy a target.

He used only the bottom step, brought his right foot up on it
and pivoted around. He clung to the side of the ladder, used it for
cover. Put it between himself and them. Better than nothing.

All the while Hurtado and Kellerman had been firing at him.
Only the quickness and unpredictability of his movements and
the deep shadows had kept him from getting hit. Twice, three
times, he thought he felt bullets brush the fabric of his windbreaker, and perhaps one had creased his neck just below his
right ear but he wasn't sure. There wasn't any pain. Too cold
for such pain.

They didn't waste bullets on him now. They had him, hung
up on the side of that ladder. All they had to do was improve
their angle.

His hands were too cold to reach in for his pistol to fight
back.

Kellerman darted in between the third and fourth shacks on
the left side.

Hurtado advanced along the concrete deck on the left side of
the pool. After he'd gone about a third of the pool's length,

Hurtado had a clear chance at Wiley. But didn't take it. Each step brought him closer, gave him an easier, surer shot. When he was directly opposite where Wiley clung, only the width of the pool away, Hurtado stopped, raised his pistol and took aim.

Lillian shot Hurtado in the back.

From the position she had taken up between the ninth and tenth shacks on that side.

Hurtado didn't go down. The impact of the bullet only caused the huge man's body to jerk slightly. He turned around to face the shacks, as though irritated at the interruption.

Lillian shot him in the chest.

Hurtado took three steps in her direction. It was as though she were firing blanks.

She shot him again.

He absorbed that bullet also.

But it stopped him.

Her next shot started him going the other way, against his will, bent like a man fighting a strong wind.

She had four rounds left in that clip. She squeezed them off quickly but accurately.

As though they were individual shoves, they drove Hurtado back. Over the edge. He dropped dead into the pool.

Wiley took advantage of the diversion to climb the ladder to the concrete deck and roll swiftly across it to the space between shacks twelve and thirteen.

He joined Lillian behind the shacks. They hurried across the parking area.

Kellerman tried a shot from the rear corner of shack four.

They sprinted up the drive.

Kellerman after them.

They impulsively bypassed the clubhouse, followed the drive around to the inland side. There was the golf course. That part of it an entirely open gentle slope.

Kellerman was only about a hundred feet behind them.

Lillian ejected her empty clip. On the run she tried to fit in a fresh one and, giving her attention partly to that, stumbled and fell. It took her a moment to recover.

Kellerman went down at practically the same time. He reached beneath his coat for his other gun. It had a longer barrel. He extended both his arms. In a prone position, he used the ground to support his aim. Did not hurry this shot, knew he was well within range and had a good enough view of his target.

Lillian continued on for a dozen more strides or so before her legs gave out. She collapsed on the frozen grass at the edge of a sand bunker, fell forward into it in a contorted position, a leg and an arm pinned under her, the weight of her limp head stretching her neck. Her eyes were fixed in a stare and her mouth was open as though in amazement.

Wiley glanced back, stopped when he saw Lillian down in the bunker. He rushed to her, kneeled, straightened her body, hating the lifelessness of her arms and legs, the way her neck didn't have the life to support her head, allowed it to loll to one side so her cheek was pressing the cold damp sand.

Somehow he had always thought he'd be the first to get it, not her. Oh, God, not her.

He heard a voice, low but loud enough for him to recognize it as Kellerman's. Talking to someone.

Wiley looked over the shoulder of the bunker, not cautiously, saw a single figure about a hundred feet away. That could only mean Kellerman had a radio. What was he saying? The cold air carried his words, but Wiley couldn't make them out. No doubt, however, who Kellerman was in contact with.

Wiley took out the Colt forty-five. His hands were so cold he had to force his fingers to bend. He snapped the bolt back, and the pistol inserted a bullet into the firing chamber.

One of those hydraulic bullets she'd made.

She owed Kellerman one.

Wiley would see that Kellerman got it.

If it was the last thing he did.

Kellerman had put the radio away now. He checked his pistol and headed straight for the bunker. He didn't know the bunker or Wiley was there. It had appeared to him that Lillian had fallen over a small rise and that Wiley had gone on.

Wiley waited, watched through the fringes of dead grass, waited until Kellerman was only a few paces away.

Wiley loomed up, fired at the middle of the man with the death-mask face.

Wiley had jerked the shot but it still hit. Below Kellerman's right collarbone. The bullet with the water in its nose exploded as it was supposed to when it met the resistance of Kellerman's flesh. It blew away Kellerman's entire shoulder. His right arm

landed thirty feet behind him off to the right. The rest of his
body pumped the life out of him in seconds.

Wiley removed the radio from Kellerman's coat pocket.

He pressed the receiver switch.

"Kellerman! What's happening, Kellerman?"

"Fuck you, Argenti."

"Wiley? Wiley?"

"I'm the only one left."

"The emeralds, Wiley, where are the emeralds?"

"Up your ass."

"I'll make a deal with you . . ."

Wiley threw the radio as far away as he could.

He returned to the bunker, to Lillian. Hope made him feel
for her pulse. Nothing registered through his numb fingers. He
placed his ear to her breast, couldn't hear a heartbeat. Her open
mouth. It seemed he should be able to pour life into her. If only
he could. If he could, he would give her all his breath.

He held her to him for a moment, rocked back and forth,
unconsciously trying to animate her.

He picked her up, took her dead weight on his shoulders and
carried her up the slope and down through the club area to the
beach. The tide was at its highest now. There was no dry place
to walk, but when the icy water ran up, soaked, and should
have shocked his feet and legs, he wasn't fazed. He was feeling so much he couldn't feel anything.

He carried her up and across the bridge to the house.

He placed her gently on the sofa in the relaxing room,
arranged her arms and legs, put a pillow under her head. No
reason she should look uncomfortable.

He sat on the edge of the couch.

Just sat there.

After a few minutes he noticed her cheek twitch, just once.

A left-over impulse, he thought.

In less than another minute her mouth closed.

Wiley tried for her pulse.

Now his fingers were warm.

He found it, felt it, the vital surge in her, extremely weak
and slow. Nevertheless *there*!

She was wounded, not dead yet, wounded. How badly?
Where?

Her eyelids fluttered slightly.

He removed her windbreaker and the rest of her clothes.
There were numerous scratches on the front of her, red raw,
the deeper ones accentuated by dried blood.

From the brambles.

But nothing serious.

He turned her over, expecting to see the hole Kellerman's
bullet had made.

There were only more scratches.

And on the left side of the small of her back a tiny puncture
from which considerable blood had flowed. It looked as though
she'd been jabbed there with a needle.

He made her comfortable again, covered her with a blanket.

Watched with amazement and gratitude as she blinked, tried
to focus her eyes. On him. Was coming out of it, whatever it
was. She couldn't speak yet, tried to wet her lips and take
deeper breaths. He went to get water.

It was then he noticed the dart on the floor near where he'd
dropped her windbreaker. He must have pulled it out when
he'd undressed her. He picked it up, examined it, saw that its
business end was actually a hypodermic needle about a half
inch long, connected to a miniature capsule that, no doubt,
injected its contents on impact.

He imagined it had contained a tranquilizer, a concentrated
dose, instantly immobilizing.

The emeralds, he thought. Kellerman needed to know where
the emeralds were.

What other possible reason could Kellerman have had for
not wanting Lillian dead?

35 ⟩⟩⟩

Out in Three Mile Harbor.

Aboard the yacht *Oscuro*.

Argenti would wear the shin-length genuine-camel-hair top-coat that had been made for him by one of his regular tailors in Milan. Over a black cashmere turtleneck sweater with a white silk scarf tied loosely. For that much of an underworld air. *Capo di tutti capi* (boss of bosses), he thought to the mirror. However, a wide-brim cream-colored Capone-ish felt hat, he decided, was a bit much.

From one of the drawers of his wardrobe he chose one from a half-dozen pairs of black gloves. Kid that was butter-soft, stretchable so they'd be skin tight. He worked his fingers and hands into them, smacked fists against palms left and right and approved of the extreme shine of his black wing-tipped shoes.

No gun. There was a nickel-plated thirty-eight automatic on the wardrobe top. But he wouldn't need it.

He left his cabin, went up to the lounge, where he poured an ample, last-minute brandy. Took a mouthful and let its fumes burn up into the passages to his nose. He tossed down the rest. A larger gulp than usual. For the cold, not nerve, he told himself.

He'd thought out how he'd handle Wiley. He couldn't leave it to anyone else. Even Kellerman had proved incompetent. The situation required his, Argenti's finesse and insight. He was sure he'd read Wiley correctly, right from the start. Such obvious, futile ambitions. He'd play on them now. Go face to face with Wiley. Take him to the top of power mountain and show him the view. Wiley was a fool, but smart enough to realize he couldn't possibly safely market all those emeralds. Better, he'd reason with Wiley, make a deal for them. A choice: Come in as, say, a quarter partner in The Concession or settle now for fifty million. He'd feed Wiley the numbered-Swiss-account bullshit, even name the bank in Geneva.

No matter which Wiley chose, he'd end up in Barbosa.

Argenti went out on deck.

He paused, surveyed the shore.

It was, he realized, the United States, one of the many forbidden lands. But the time was three-thirty, reassuring, and this place was so remote, and the lights that were on were scattered all-night lights, unthreatening public lights, none moving.

Such as those that illuminated the landing about a hundred yards away, allowing him to see the three men there, waiting, shuffling their feet in place, trying to keep warm. The three Conduct Section men he had summoned to go along as his escort. How much alike they looked, Argenti thought. All Conduct Section men looked alike. Where had Kellerman recruited them?

The power launch was ready, gurgling the water as it idled alongside. Argenti went down the boarding steps and climbed aboard. At once it pulled away.

The harbor was practically waveless.

The launch headed for shore.

Argenti kept his eyes on the three men.

He gestured to them, a leader's sort of acknowledgement, as the launch pulled in.

It would be a steady, easy transfer from the launch to the landing.

Argenti placed one foot up on the slip-proof rubber-matted area of the gunwale. Brought his weight up onto that foot. His next step would be on the landing.

In that moment, during that motion, he glanced at the three men. Their faces, stances.

And knew who they really were.

Not his men, or Kellerman's.

They were there for The System.

The System—which had with reluctant lenience reduced his death sentence to exile and warned him precisely what would be the consequence if he ever, even once, violated those terms.

Argenti tried to recall his step, but his weight had already shifted.

The moment his foot touched the landing he was shot dead.

36 ⤷⤷⤷

Three days later.

"I've got it," Lillian said, digging into her pocket.

They were in an exact-change lane, had it clear, but Wiley steered to the next lane over, where several cars were ahead of them.

Lillian cocked her head at him quizzically.

He pretended not to notice.

She shrugged, put her exact change back into her pocket.

He took a five dollar bill from his, handed it out to the black woman toll-taker in the booth and thanked her by the name etched on the plastic plate over her breast pocket. The toll-taker didn't say anything, not even with her eyes, but Wiley didn't blame her, thought he sure as hell wouldn't want to be saying thanks ten thousand times a day.

He drove down the grade and into the Queens-Midtown Tunnel, got into the left, the faster lane.

"Where are we going?" Lillian asked.

"I told you, I have some business to take care of."

"What sort of business?"

Wiley shoved in the ashtray to have the cigarette stubs out of sight.

Lillian noticed that many of the ceramic tiles in the ceiling of the tunnel were missing. She closed her eyes and tried to think of anything other than a whole river above her. She peeked through her lashes a couple of times, but didn't really open her eyes until they had come out of the tunnel and turned up onto Thirty-seventh Street.

Wiley headed the car crosstown.

"My scratches itch," Lillian said, and used her fingernails on her left thigh.

Wiley's mind flashed back to their fall into the brambles. No more of that, he told himself. No more Argenti. With Argenti and Kellerman gone, so was The Concession, its purpose and the way it had been organized. They were in the clear. Wiley still found it difficult to accept.

Sunday morning last he'd thought surely another five or six Conduct Section men would arrive any minute. He'd bolted all the locks and nailed boards across the door Hurtado had broken through. Sat in the relaxing room with groggy Lillian, resigned to it all starting again, knowing they weren't in any condition to go another round.

By dawn Lillian was less woozy. And Wiley felt better, because they probably wouldn't come in the daytime. Lillian did some breath-control exercises and got on her makeshift slant board for half an hour to get rid of her tranquilizer hangover. Wiley tried to sleep, was too adrenergic.

They first learned of Argenti's death on the radio. Between a David Bowie and a Jefferson Starship. They thought they were hearing things.

They saw it on the television news.

The three bodies had been found at the Maidstone Club, were as yet unidentified.

Police were trying to piece it together.

Especially Kellerman, Wiley had thought to himself.

There was believed to be a connection between the three dead men at the Maidstone and the killing of Meno Sebastiano Argenti.

An underworld massacre was the slant of it.

The television reporter repeatedly used the full name—Meno Sebastiano Argenti—as though he enjoyed the sound of it.

That night, Sunday night, Wiley had removed the other two bodies from the house, loaded them into the gray Buick and left it parked in East Hampton, alongside the fence of the West End Burying Ground.

Now, with all that behind them, Wiley and Lillian were pulled up at a light at Forty-second and Seventh Avenue.

A manhole was spouting steam into the cold air a few feet ahead. Thick, extremely white steam, clean-looking. Off to the right, a place called itself The Dirty Bookstore.

"We deserve a vacation," Lillian said.

A sort of affirmative grunt from Wiley.

"Why don't we go someplace different, like Fiji or Ireland? I'd really love to go to Northern Ireland. I understand there are some nice, not-too-grand but large-enough houses for sale there now. And the help are so friendly."

And there's also that rebellion, Wiley thought, remembering her mother's name had been Mayo.

"Another area I haven't seen enough of is the Eastern Mediterranean, especially Cyprus."

And it occurred to Wiley that it just so happened that the Greeks and Turks were boiling at one another over Cyprus.

She abandoned that tack abruptly, because just then they were entering the Holland Tunnel. She closed her eyes again and hummed the tunnel time away with some random notes. When they were out on the New Jersey side she said, "Marry me."

"Nope."

"Please marry me?"

"Not yet."

"When?"

"After I make my first million."

"I love you."

"I know."

"How soon after?"

"Right after."

"Is that before or after taxes, the million?"

"Take-home," he told her.

She thought there had to be ways she could make him that rich without his knowing she was involved. She'd talk to Corey, her chairman, about it. But hell, why did Wiley have to make it so complicated?

"I'm going to knuckle down," he said.

Which reminded her. She reached into her purse, took out a small, drawstring chamois pouch, the kind she carried marbles in. There were two emeralds in it. Twenty carats each, brilliant cut. The matched pair Wiley had concealed between his toes. Instead of throwing them away, she'd concealed them. Since then she'd been waiting for the right moment. Anyway, that was what she'd told herself. Holding out on him again? Only sort of. The matched pair were worth a half million each, at least. That could be his million, if he skipped taxes. She was about to open the pouch when . . .

"I mean it, Lillian," he continued. "I've been spinning too

long on the wrong tracks, and the promised land was never just around the bend anyway. I realize that now."

"Good for you," she said just to say something.

He told her, "What I have to do is put my nose and ass to the grind like any regular, normally privileged American. When they play the song, salute. Know what I mean?"

She nodded, thought, He *has* been under a lot of strain.

"I'm ready to settle," he said decidedly, "for a split-level out somewhere on the outskirts of somewhere. A refrigerator with a door that spits out ice, cubed or crushed, and plays music. A microwave oven that can bake a medium-size potato during a commercial break. An FHA loan. For once in my life I want to go into any bank, have someone give me a financial proctoscopy and qualify."

He's serious, she thought. "Instead of business, wouldn't you rather just get into me?"

He didn't say no, but that didn't mean yes.

"Okay, then, what sort of business do you have in mind?" No matter what it was, he'd be a practically overnight, huge, at least two-million-dollar success. She'd call Corey first chance, from the next pay phone if she could.

"Who knows?" Wiley said. "Like today, it's a little import-export deal. For starters."

By then they were in Hoboken.

Wiley turned left and left again and pulled into the parking area outside United States customs shed number thirty-eight.

Lillian waited in the car.

Nearly a half hour later Wiley came out wheeling a hand dolly. Loaded with two burlap sacks, hundred-pounders.

He put the sacks in the back seat, returned the dolly, got in and drove away. Deadpan.

The sacks were stenciled: COFFEE FROM COLOMBIA.

"Coffee?" Lillian asked.

"It's like gold these days," Wiley said.

He must have arranged for it sometime while they were in Colombia, she thought. At least he deserved a good mark for foresight.

He pulled up and parked on the next side street, a warehouse kind of street, everything closed at the moment. He cut the motor. Without a word, got out and got into the back seat.

She kneeled up on the front seat, noticed stenciled further

down on the sacks in smaller letters: GROWER: FREDERICO
LUCHO.

Thank the plaster Christ . . . the likeable old man now had a
new coffee-hulling machine, would never again have to pay to
use his neighbor's. And Julietta Magdalena Rosario, who had
told Wiley's tomorrows, had more than she'd ever need to
sustain her image. Only a *bruja* was so well provided for by
mysterious sources.

The late-night expeditions with those two were still fresh in
Wiley's memory. The coca-chewing *bruja* with her absurd
divining rod. What a laugh. Lucho traipsing along after her,
tending the bottle of *aguardiente*. Wiley patronizingly following over and up the slopes. How ridiculous.

Wiley used a penknife to slit both sacks down the middle.

The coffee beans poured out onto the floor of the car.

They were hulled but otherwise not processed. Almost as
they'd been picked from Lucho's trees.

Green with a smattering of red.

And mixed in here and there were much greener greens.

Emeralds.

La materia verde, the green stuff.

Five pounds of it.

Twenty-two thousand seven hundred and twenty carats. A
lot of it kelly.

Worth, roughly, in the respectable neighborhood of eleven
million.

More Bestsellers from Berkley
The books you've been hearing about and want to read

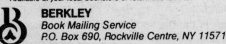